Published by New Generation Publishing in 2025

Copyright © Jae Malone 2025

First Edition

ISBN 978-1-83563-611-4

www.newgeneration-publishing.com

New Generation Publishing

IN TOO DEEP

By Jae Malone

Cover Design by Cathy Helms of

ALSO BY JAE MALONE

The Winterne Series

Silver Linings
Queen of Diamonds
Fool's Gold
Avaroc Returns
When Wolves Cry

Historical Prequel: From Knight to Knave

Short Stories

Sanctuary
One Hour Story – Leaving
One Hour Story - The Bus Station
A Stain in Time
Kathy and Charlie
To the Devil, a Doctor
Freedom (Finalist in the King Lear Prizes Real Story
Competition 2021)

Animal Stories for Younger Children

Lorna and the Loch Ness Monster
The Raven and the Thief
Blue Teaches A Lesson
Mrs Pringles Needs A Nurse
Tib and Tab Make A Friend
Sammy, The Squirrel Who Missed Christmas
Maisie – a Rescue Dog (coming 2025)
Ace Malone, Boy Detective: The Case of the Missing Cat (coming
soon)

This book is dedicated with love and thanks to my husband, David. His love, support and encouragement have allowed me to do what I love doing, writing and encouraging others to find their own joy in writing.

Acknowledgements

There are a number of countries David and I have visited and enjoyed, but two of the most memorable, for all good reasons, are Gozo, and Spain's La Gomera and Tenerife.

We first visited Gozo on the first week of our honeymoon in 1992. This honey-coloured Mediterranean jewel is the most wonderful location, relaxed, sunshine, sea, beautiful scenery, historically important, with lovely, friendly people. At that time, it was as though we had gone back in time by around fifty years. Things are a little more up to date now, but it still retains that relaxed charm.

In 2022, we returned to Gozo and the same hotel we had stayed in thirty years before; The Cornucopia in Xaghra, and it had barely changed. As a tribute to this enchanting hotel, and its first rate staff, led by Mr Brian Caruana, I have my main character, Luke Rutherford, staying there for a month, and I do not apologise for using the hotel as a main location for one or two chapters.

Next, I must thank our son, Greg, for the four years he spent living in the coastal village of Alcala on the island of Tenerife. If he had not gone there to work, we may have taken the occasional holiday there, but we would probably not have had the opportunity to see as much of the island as we did, and to develop a great affection for it. It also gave us an interest in taking a look at another island we could see, across the channel: La Gomera.

La Gomera is a lovely quiet, peaceful, island, more mountainous than Tenerife, and the view across the island, from the ferry harbour at San Sebastian to the Valle Gran Rey area is breathtaking.

It is out of fondness for these islands, that I have set this story, and most of the locations mentioned are real … the criminals mentioned are not.

I also need to thank Greg for producing my promotional material, filming my readings of 'Blue Teaches A Lesson', and 'Lorna, and the

Loch Ness Monster' and posting them on You Tube, and for live streaming my last two book launches, for 'From Knight to Knave' and 'When Wolves Cry'.

My thanks to friend, Mark Ellis, who lives in Tenerife. With the diving background and knowledge that he and Greg have, I was able – I hope – to give some accurate technical information on scuba diving. Mark also gave me a novel way to kill someone underwater which would make it look like an accident. Ingenious and thanks, Mark.

I have been incredibly lucky during my years of writing to make some amazing friends. Helen Hollick, a remarkable lady and a gifted author of historical novels, and more. If you enjoy stories of King Arthur, then her Pendragon's Banner trilogy is a tremendous read. You won't want to book the book down. Helen's Jesamiah Acorne, 17th century pirate series is spellbinding and her Jan Christopher cosy crime series, set in the seventies, is really good fun.

There are some very dear friends who constantly give me support, and I take this opportunity to show my appreciation. They are Sally Holmes, Shona Rowan, Amanda Boden, Darren Cook, Jeremy Lewis, David Wayman, Ellaine Monk, Jane Brown, Adrian and Sue Woods, Sharlean Plummer, Lesley Rhodes, Patricia Daniels, Sharon and John Butterworth, Mark and Cristo Ellis, Danny Ellis, Jenny Tossell, Pam Pracy, Lisa, Matthew and Ann Slaughter, Becky Evans, Donna Quarless-McGee, Anne Crosbie, Sandra and Peter Barnes, Moira Hodgkinson, a modern day witch and writer, and YA Sci-Fi writer, Ian Douglas, and lastly, but absolutely not the least, is radio and local television presenter, Mark Dennison. Thank you so much everyone. Your belief in me keeps me writing.

And, as always, when looking for a new cover, I go to the hugely talented Cathy Helms of Avalon Graphics, who created the fabulous covers for my Winterne Series. Cathy, intuitively, always generates the perfect designs.

Lastly, I want to thank Daniel Cooke, the Managing Director of New Generation Publishing. Daniel, together with the forbearing, David Walshaw and the Production Team are a joy to work with, and I know it's not always plain sailing.

Reviews

Reviews for 'The Winterne Series'

Silver Linings :

Intriguing read. This book would work on the big screen.

Alan Clifford – BBC Radio

Trilogy's stirring start.

Dawn Bond, Newark Advertiser

An imaginative adventure with a dark streak.

Jeremy Lewis, Nottingham Post

Queen of Diamonds :

Jae gets better with every book and could easily give J K Rowling a good run for her money.'

Newark Advertiser

A loving and wholesome read.

Jeremy Lewis, Nottingham Post

Jae Malone's imagination is on the same wave length as legendary J R R Tolkien. She writes with vividness, intensity and sophistication.

Amazon Reader

Fool's Gold:

Jae has a fluid, easily accessible writing style, while the stories feature richly layered plots where high fantasy, school-year tribulations and dark nefarious deeds interweave.

Steve Bowkett. Writer, storyteller, educational consultant, Member of Society of Authors & National Association of Writers in Education (NAWE)

'The author is a fine storyteller who seems effortlessly to combine the natural and the supernatural worlds.'

Editor: Nottinghamshire Today

'Wow. I can't wait to read this new book. I have so enjoyed reading the three previous books.'

Facebook Reader

Lorna and the Loch Ness Monster:

What a delightfully charming little story! Nicely written, beautifully illustrated and a pleasure to read. Absolutely ideal for any family with young children who are intending to visit Scotland for a holiday - but just as suitable for any family anywhere!

Helen Hollick, Best-selling and highly acclaimed author of historical fiction

Amazon Reviews for 'From Knight to Knave'

5.0 out of 5 stars Page turner

Reviewed in the United Kingdom on 20 February 2023

I should start by saying that this book says it is for readers 10-18: I am considerably outside this age range and I honestly felt that the book was aimed at readers like me. This, I feel, is testament to the skill of the author at her craft. Unlike many books the key character of From Knight to Knave is Winterne Manor as it changes hands through the centuries. I quickly got caught up in the histories as Jae brought her characters to life with her storytelling. The historical research that must go into her books is incredible. I couldn't put the book down; at every opportunity I was found book in hand. I've since bought the rest of the Winterne books to read.

5.0 out of 5 stars Historical adventure recommended for teenagers

Reviewed in the United Kingdom on 26 July 2023

These are colourful prequels to the author's accomplished Winterne series, with a strong sense of location (rural Somerset) through the ages. The action, with its supernatural strand, is anchored in painstaking historical research as we follow the fortunes of the Maitlands of Winterne Manor from the 14th Century to the present day. The sort of book you'd like your teenage children to be reading.

5.0 out of 5 stars Incredible!
Reviewed in the United Kingdom on 16 May 2023
I can't get over the detail within this book. Jae must go to phenomenal lengths with her research! From the intricate characters to the gripping storyline, you won't put this book down. Don't let the age range put you off, I'm 40 and had the best time reading and glimpsing into her incredible mind and writing. Ten out of ten!

5.0 out of 5 stars **What a great read.**
Reviewed in the United Kingdom on 3 May 2023
Rarely get the time to sit down and read, but received this recommendation from a friend and after reading a couple of chapters from her copy, I purchased..... loved it. Great storytelling, really takes you into the story and immerses you deep into the world and characters. Brilliant work. Have ordered a copy for my 13 year old daughter now.

5.0 out of 5 stars **More than a story**
Reviewed in the United Kingdom on 1 March 2023
What I loved about Knight to Knave was the detail in the historical parts of the book. It really transported me into a past world and made me think about what life was like for people in those times. It is also a fine story unfolding as you progress through the book and meet the characters. The main characters are lovely and you'd want to meet them today but they exist in a more brutal world than the one we experience. My top tip would be to take your time reading Knight to Knave, let your imagine go a little bit and think what it was like for our ancestors, and the hardships they endured to build the life we have today. Knight to Knave is the story of one family. I couldn't help feeling, as I read the book, that I had visited many of the places in the story, and perhaps even stayed in Winterne Manor, or at least somewhere close by, which made me feel like a little part of the

story. I've not really felt involved in a book as much as I did in this one.

5.0 out of 5 stars page turner

Reviewed in the United Kingdom on 9 March 2023

After reading the first three Winterne books some time ago I was intrigued about reading the prequel. Love the telling of the story of the house from different stages in its history. Also explained some of the events which had happened. Looking forward to re-reading the first three Winterne books before starting on Avaroc Returns. Would love to see these stories on the big screen, but in the meantime I will have to settle for them in book form. Excellent read and I can't recommend highly enough. I would compare this to Harry Potter in that it appeals to all ages. However, this is a much better read.

5.0 out of 5 stars From Knight to Knave

Reviewed in the United Kingdom on 16 April 2022

I have read all of the Winterne series of books and I was so looking forward to this prequel to the series. I sat down to begin the adventure and was drawn in immediately into an absolutely wonderful story. From the moment I met young Will Hallett I was totally hooked by his story. The haunting story of the hardships of The Hundred Years War were brought home to me, and I read for several hours following his story. We move on through the ages and follow his ancestors to 1510 and the time of Henry VIII. I was fascinated and so enjoying the lives of the Knight, The Monk, and The Knave as they passed through the ages. I would thoroughly recommend this book and the whole of The Winterne series.

5.0 out of 5 stars An excellent book

Reviewed in the United Kingdom on 1 September 2021

Jae Malone has written a superb collection of imaginative short stories in her usual spellbinding way. This is another book that captures interest and is impossible to put down, combining history and adventure. I thoroughly recommend this book. It is truly a book of indulgence and escapism and I loved it! I would also recommend all the books in Jae's earlier Winterne Series - 'Silver Linings' 'Queen of Diamonds' 'Fool's Gold' and 'Avaroc Returns'. All brilliantly written and a jolly good read – Thank you Jae, please keep them coming!

5.0 out of 5 stars Wonderful series
Reviewed in the United Kingdom on 27 September 2021
Would strongly recommend reading The Winterne Series. The amount of historical research she must have undertaken for from Knight to Knave is outstanding. Jae cleverly links time periods to enhance the readers understanding of not just this masterpiece but her earlier books. An outstanding and hard to put down series of magical stories. Just waiting for the film now.

Preface

La Gomera Island. On this Seventeenth day of October, in this year of Our Lord, Seventeen Hundred and Twenty Two. Dawn is breaking as I write.

This is not a confession, it is more an admission to myself that my sins have caused me to come to this point, to this condition of misery. By whatever name you think to call it, it will be my final communication with the world.

I am Don Alphonso Ruis de Casals, youngest son of the Duque and Duquesa de Leon, Ramon and Marguerita Ruis de Casals of Madrid, Cadiz, and La Gomera. My father is cousin to His Royal Highness, King Felipe IV of Spain of the Habsburg Royal Line. My mother is distantly related to Her Royal Highness, Queen Mariana of Austria, to whom she has become a valued companion. At present, in consideration of their duties, my parents, older brother, Tomas and sister Anabella, reside in our home close to the Zarzuela Palace in Madrid.

I, however, due to my family's shame in me and my obsession with wagering on dice and cards for money, have been exiled to La Gomera. I have made many attempts to curtail, or stop giving in to my compulsion, but the vice always draws me back to the table. And it is thus that I find myself in this unalterable situation, and I have lost everything...but, I must explain.

My mother and her brother, Alphonso de la Mendoza, after whom I was named, are the children of Luis de Mendoza, His Eminence, Governor de Canarias. My uncle, although outwardly charming and amiable, is far too ambitious, which makes him ruthless, and not to be trusted.

But I have wandered away from my account to some extent, and must return to the relevant detail.

As I live here permanently, when my uncle visits, I am always in residence. On his last visit, a few months ago, he greeted me well, dined with me, and it was pleasant to have his company. Having been newly appointed as a Cardinal, he amused me with tales of the Vatican, the Pope, and other cardinals for a while, but then after a few days, his wine-fuelled conversation turned to more chilling issues, revealing an unpleasant side of his personality that I had not previously been aware of. I discovered he was not particularly religious, although he had always professed to be, and had certainly played the part of someone devout. He simply saw it as a way of gaining power and wealth. However, he needed more wealth than he currently had to enable his rise through the ranks.

In bed that night, his words went round and round in my head, and dawn was breaking when I finally slept. Thankfully he was not an early riser, and it was not until late morning when we sat breaking our fast on the terrace overlooking the channel between La Gomera and Tenerife. During my night time deliberations, a thought occurred to me that might be of benefit to us both, and I waited until my uncle had filled his cup with Rioja for the fourth time, and was clearly feeling mellow, before I revealed my thoughts. I suggested that as there were many treasure ships sailing between the Americas and Spain, it was a pity that we could not take advantage of the wealth across the Atlantic Ocean to help further our own causes.

For a moment he said nothing. He just continued looking out over the channel, watching the gulls gliding on the warm air while searching below for fish. He turned to me with a frown, that became a smirk, and said that he knew two unscrupulous privateers who might be agreeable to sail to Cartagena, taking men loyal to him, who would employ their own methods to appropriate enough treasure to satisfy our needs. Of course, they would require payment, as would the privateer and his crew. They would have to undertake the voyage in secrecy avoiding harbour officials or dealing with the risk of being stopped by ships of the naval fleet. Whichever ship was chosen would have to be fast, fast enough to outrun any pursuers, and he knew of such a one, the *Katerina-Thereza*. She was small, well built, moored in a bay near to Cadiz but away from close observation, and she was swift. In addition, not only did the captain owe him a favour, but he was always happy to line his own coffers, and enjoyed taking risks.

He then asked me what I would want to gain from the venture. I explained my desire to be free of debt, free to travel where I wanted and, most of all to be able to approach Don José Alvarez of Cadiz to ask for his daughter, Arraté's, hand in marriage. She had been my secret sweetheart for almost a year, but in my current situation I was unable to propose. Soon her father would arrange a marriage with someone he considered a suitable match for her, therefore my time was running out.

My uncle said nothing more at that time, and avoided my company for the rest of the daylight hours, I even sat alone during the evening meal. Although he had seemed amenable, even enthusiastic, about my suggestion, his elusiveness said otherwise, and I began to wish I had not said anything.

Later, as I sat alone on the terrace with a carafe of Rioja, watching the stars twinkle in and out, and the thin clouds streaking the moon, my uncle joined me, silently poured himself a goblet of wine, made himself comfortable in a chair, and

3

asked me how much it would mean to me if we took the course of action I had suggested.

I replied that my life on La Gomera was not worth living. The island was beautiful and I had good people serving me and that some had become friends, but I had no future, nothing to look forward to, and I might as well be dead. My uncle nodded, sagely. Then he informed me that he was prepared to go ahead with our plans, but wanted to know if I had any funding to invest as my part of the bargain.

I did. Or rather my father did. There were gold coins hidden in the cellar that belonged entirely to my father. Unfortunately, without his knowledge, I had already used some of my father's gold and silver Reals to repay previous gambling debts. I struggled with my conscience over investing more of my father's funds in this plan, but my uncle convinced me that all would be well, and in my eagerness to try for this new life, and to have the chance to marry my love, I allowed myself to be swept along by his obvious passion and, as he kept reminding me, it was my idea.

However, I now sit, imbibing my third glass of brandy without feeling the least bit intoxicated, writing this missive by candlelight, and having lost everything. Last night we had one of the worst storms I have ever seen. It formed without warning.

My friend, Miguel Flores, a servant since my childhood, pointed out a ship in the channel that was being blown onto the reef at the bottom of the cliff below this villa. He, and some of our men, descended the cliff, at risk of their own lives, but were only able to rescue two men who they brought here, and one died of his injuries during the night.

We had hoped and prayed that our ship would evade pirates, our own navy or the fleets of our enemies. We understood the risk of storms, but I believe neither my uncle or I considered our vessel would be so near to safety, or how devastating the storm God would send against us.

The lone survivor who, with the grace of God is likely to recover from his injuries, gave me the news I did not want to hear. The ship was indeed the *Katerina-Thereza*, and we had watched her hit the reef, break up and slowly sink into the channel. There was nothing we could have done to help. The survivor, one Carlos Cherro, had been the first mate on the ship and confirmed that, she had been carrying gold and jewels worth hundreds of thousands of Reals, and that they were heading for San Sebastian when the storm come upon them unexpectedly. The treasures were now at the bottom of the sea together with fifteen members of the crew including the captain. With them went my hope of a happy future life, and my dream of marrying Arraté.

The realisation that I can never repay my father, and the disgrace are hard to bear, but I fear Miguel, his mother, wife and their twin children will also suffer punishment for my deeds. My father, who trusted Miguel to watch over me, to keep me from my own stupidity, will vent his anger upon them. I have, therefore instructed Miguel to take his family, and the sailor, Carlos, away from here. Miguel is to take the horses and both carts, plus all their possessions, and go to the other side of the island where they have relatives, and hide in the caves. Their family there will protect them, conceal them, and help them look after Carlos until he is able to make his own choices.

To provide for them, I have given Miguel a belt concealing several gold coins, and two bags of silver. Carlos has already received a pouch of silver coins. I anticipate that in time he will take a ship from San Sebastian back to Cadiz, but I will never know that. Miguel, protested loudly that he did not want to abandon me, but was finally persuaded by Rosa, his wife, and his mother Anna, to leave for the sake of his children, and they departed a little over two hours ago,. By the time of the setting of the sun, they will be on the other side of the mountain, and safe from the wrath of my father...with the grace of God.

I pray to God that my uncle never rises to any position of great importance. Power in his hands would be the most terrible thing to behold.

By my left hand is a loaded pistol. Strangely, it feels comforting. I did not expect that. To my right is a small, but strong wooden box into which this communication, together with the miniature image of my love, Arraté, will be concealed, forever mayhap. To those who know my beloved, her image would be easily recognisable, and her father would punish her if her image was found to have been in my possession. That I cannot allow.

I kiss the small portrait of my love and place it gently on the scarlet velvet lining. I could never have been good enough for Arraté, and I know that in time I would have disillusioned her. I cannot bear the thought of seeing her brought down by my failings. It is my fervent hope that God will guide and protect her, and allow her a happier life than I could have given her.

Beside this precious image is my favourite crucifix, gold with diamonds and a large single emerald at the centre point. It belonged to my grandmother and is precious to me. There is no-one other than Arraté to whom I would have given it, but now that cannot be.

On the table by the window is a bowl containing beeswax, two thin wooden boards, a roll of linen and length of leather. They will protect the parchment on which I have been writing, and the box. But first, there is something I must do.

From our wine cellar, I collected four bottles of Brandy de Jerez, our finest brandy, and sprayed the brandy on the table, chairs, bed and the curtains in my bedroom. The next room is our library. I had to smile as I look around the room. There are so many prized books in this room. If my mother knew what I was about to do, she would swoon. I do not know which will affect her more, my death or the destruction of her books. I have poured the brandy onto the curtains, the beautifully upholstered chairs, and the remainder of the room. I then turned my attention to the kitchen and dining room. There is so much wood within this house which will burn easily when doused with brandy. The last room is the study where two candles still burn. I thought I would be frightened, that my strength would fail me, but it is not so. I feel unusually calm as I take the last bottle of brandy, the box, leather, linen, wooden boards, my quill, bowl of beeswax, and my loaded pistol out to the terrace, where I place them on the table. Then I return to my room and pour drops of the brandy around the room and hold my breath. It is time.

I have just tossed one of the lit candles onto the floor and watched the flames grow and spread across my bed, the sparks flew to the garderobe. It was strangely satisfying to watch them burn.

I look back at the house. Flames are now licking around the curtains and I can see the inner door is ablaze. It will only be a matter of minutes before the flames spread to the other rooms. The brandy will ensure the fire spreads.

I smear the linen fully with beeswax, some of it clings to my fingers as I reach for the leather. But no matter. The linen surrounding the box I cover tightly with the leather, and tie it with a leather thong. The edges of leather I smear with beeswax again, and then use the last piece of linen to preserve and protect the box from earth and damp.

I fold the parchment and press it between the two wooden boards, tear a long strip of linen from the roll, wrap it around the boards, place it inside the box and close the lid. Then I take more of the linen and wrap it tightly around the box.

'To protect the box containing the items I wish to preserve, I will smear the linen fully with beeswax, then wrap it tightly with leather and bind it with a leather thong. The edges of leather I will coat with beeswax again, and then use the last piece of linen to preserve and protect the box from earth and damp. This parchment will be placed within the two wooden boards, and wrapped in linen. Once all is laid inside the box, and the lid closed for the last time, the box shall be covered by more linen and leather. I can think of nothing more I can do to protect these evidences of my life, and testify that I once existed.

When all is done, I will take my precious bundle to a place by the dividing wall between the terrace and the formal garden, where I have already prepared a safe place in which to bury it. It is under the overhanging branches of a leafy bush by the wall where it is unlikely anyone will notice disturbed ground. After the heavy rain, the ground is soft and the digging was not difficult. I created a hole deep enough to cover the box with a good amount of earth above, which will not be loosened by another downpour. When interred, I will disguise it a little with a few stones to make it appear completely untouched.

As I stand here on the terrace I look up to Heaven as the breeze gently wafts the few white clouds across the sky, and the billowing smoke rises upwards and across the channel towards Tenerife, and Mount Teide. I can feel the intense heat from the flames, and there is a pungent smell from burning furnishings. Nonetheless, it is a beautiful morning, which surprises me after the force of the storm just a few hours ago. I am gratified to have such a glorious day on which to die.

I think of Miguel and his family and wonder how far away they are. Will they see the fire? The crackling sound of flames grows closer to the front of the villa, but there is no hurry, not for me.

If, in the years to come, someone does discover this box, I would ask that my valuables within could be passed to the descendants of my steadfast friend, Miguel Flores, in memory of his service and loyalty to me. I hope that one day someone will read my last words, and that they may understand and even, perhaps, pray for my soul, which I find I cannot do, but may God forgive me for what I do.

And so, before I commit my final statement to the ground, I sign my name. May God have mercy on my soul.

Alphonso

-o0o-

'Papa! Look!' Louisa pointed back the way they had come.

'Miguel! The villa is on fire!' said Rosa, Miguel's wife. They turned to stare at the curling smoke that could only have come from the villa, which had been their home for so many years.

'Alphonso! I must go back!' said Miguel, lowering little Stefan from his shoulders. 'He will need me.' A gunshot echoed around the valley,

9

flocks of startled birds took to the air. Anna, Miguel's mother, took his arm and gently pulled him away. 'Come, my son. There is nothing you can do for him now. No tears, my son. He is at peace.'

Chapter One

Birmingham - Redundancy

Steve Bates, Human Resources Manager, walked into the office carrying two black zipped briefcases, and paused in the doorway. His brows set in a frown, his lips pressed thinly together, he surveyed the team of seven loyal and enthusiastic employees, whose contracts he was about to terminate, and he was angry.

Occupied with what they were doing, it took a few moments before anyone noticed Steve's presence, while everything continued as usual. Conversations went on, phones rang. Everything appeared perfectly normal. But the trouble was it wasn't perfectly normal. This was the most abysmal day Steve could ever recall in all his twenty-one years with Rochford Credit and Banking.

Luke Rutherford stood in the doorway of the small kitchen area, leaning against the wooden frame, observing Steve. From the resigned expression on his face Luke understood exactly why Steve was there, and what was about to happen.

'Oh!' Sandra nudged her colleague, Myra, and nodded towards where Steve stood waiting. Within seconds, others noticed him and the lively buzz of conversation tailed off. One by one, heads turned towards him, pens were put down, keyboards stopped clacking, and the entire office waited for Steve to speak. The room was quieter than Steve had ever known. Thirty minutes before, he had paced his office rehearsing what he hoped would be the right words to bring some kind of comfort to those who were about to lose their jobs. This decision was no fault of theirs, and he was furious that the situation had come to this. He wrote notes about what he was going to say, tore them up or rolled them into a ball and chucked them in the waste bin, and tried again. No matter how he started, nothing sounded remotely comforting. None of it made any sense. And, although there had been no official consultation, everyone knew what was coming; the office grapevine had been active for weeks.

Luke walked over to stand beside Steve and looked down at the briefcases that contained all their futures. Steve was grateful to have Luke stand beside him.

Steve coughed, looked down at the floor, and inhaled deeply before raising his head and looking around at all the troubled faces in front of him.

'You all know why I'm here,' said Steve, looking down at the briefcase. 'I can't begin to tell you how sorry I am that it's come to this.'

'Not half as sorry as we are,' said Donal. 'At least you'll still have a job and an income.'

Steve looked around at Luke, then back to the other members of the team.

'Well, I tried, I really tried everything I could, but ... oh, what the hell! Look, I'm not going to lie to you. You know as well as I do mistakes were made on high, and I couldn't do a bloody thing to help you keep your jobs. With the contracts we had having been cancelled because of the cockups, there were no options left to save either team. And, Donal, this won't change anything for any of you, but I was so angry and frustrated at what had happened, that this is my last day here as well.'

There were surprised gasps and one or two expletives from the team. Luke looked shocked. 'But why, Steve. You only have what is it ... another six years before you can retire with a decent pension?'

Steve nodded. 'Yes, but I can't work for a twat like Ted any more. Not after this. If things carry on the way they are and, Sir Peter doesn't get rid of the little shit, the entire company will collapse. Ted jumps at any new idea without thinking things through. Brain like a butterfly flitting from one bloody stupid notion to the next, and then whines when things go wrong blaming everyone else. He has some good people around him but thinks he knows better, and has too much ego to listen to anyone who tries to give him good advice. God only knows why Sir Peter keeps him on.'

'Ted's his son-in-Law,' Luke gave a wry smile.

'Well, if Sir Peter wants his daughter to be kept in the manner to which she has become accustomed, he's going to have to foot the bill for that himself, because Ted's not going to be able to do it much longer. Sometime soon, this company will fold and then ... perhaps ... Sir Peter will open his eyes. I guarantee it won't be long after that that sweet little Rosalind will be heading to the divorce lawyers. She's too smart, and too used to the good life to stay with Ted. The embarrassment of his failure will put an end to that marriage. Unfortunately that won't be of any comfort for you.' Steve looked around, aware that although some people turned away quickly as he glanced in their direction, most of the team were fully fixated on what he was saying.

'Sorry everyone. Just venting. As you will realise, this whole business has pissed me off as much as it has you.'

'So do you think us and Maggie's team are just the first tranche? I hadn't realised it could be that bad,' said Luke.

'I'm convinced it will be. I cleared my desk half an hour ago.' He turned to the team who were still following the conversation between him and Luke. 'I'm not serving my notice. I'm out of here today, and if anyone would like to join me for a glass of something fizzy at The Lion after work, I'll be there from five o'clock, and the first round is on me.'

'What did Kate say when you told her you were leaving?' Luke asked.

'Oh, she's heard enough of my whinging over the last year, since Ted joined the firm. When I told her last night how I felt and wanted to quit, she told me I should. Said I'd given enough time to the firm and that, with our savings and her salary, we could manage at worst for a year or so, but that she thought I'd get another job before that with all the contacts we both have. She's coming to the pub, so you'll see her this evening.'

Steve handed one of the briefcases to Luke. 'You know what's in here.' He looked down at the briefcase. 'All the envelopes are sealed and addressed to each member of your team. It's the standard type of redundancy letter for a company letting under twenty people go. The terms aren't bad, everything done under government rules, I've made sure of that.' He looked up at Steve and reached out to shake his hand. 'Now I have to do this again for Maggie's team.' He looked down at his feet and sighed. 'Right, I'd better get this done. You have my personal mobile number to keep in touch Luke, and see you at The Lion later.'

Luke shook Steve's hand. They had always got on well together, if not exactly friends, and Luke knew what it must have taken for Steve to have turned his back on the firm. He had been a conscientious and caring manager, and had always been honest and straightforward with employees. While the firm continued, Luke knew Steve would be missed. On his way out of the office Steve called out; 'Bye all, see you later.' And the door closed behind him.

Luke looked at his redundancy offer letter and smiled. That amount would boost his bank account by a little over thirty grand. He put the letter down on the desk, leaned back in his chair, clasped his hands behind his head and raised his legs to let his feet rest on the desk that he would not be sitting at for much longer.

He and Ellie had worked so hard, for so many years, and this money, when added to what they had in the bank, would give them some time off to travel before thinking about getting another job. It was something they had often talked about, and now they would be free to do what they wanted.

He Googled a map of Europe. Where would they go first? Expanding the image his eyes were drawn to Malta. Lowering his feet to the floor again, he sat forward, enlarged the image again and then concentrated on Gozo. His brother, Jake had been there for four years and they hadn't seen each other in all that time even though he and Ellie had talked about taking a holiday there. Jake had invited them every year, but Ellie could never get away from her job at the same time as Luke, so it had never happened. They only managed short breaks together. By all accounts Jake loved the island and the people. Gozo would be a good start to a long holiday and it would be great to see Jake again. They had always been close growing up, and he realised just how much he had missed his brother.

Now the money would be there within the week, once he signed to accept the offer of course. He just needed to persuade Ellie to jack in her job. She would get another one easily with her qualifications, project management experience and contacts, and a couple of months off would do her good. He could afford to keep the flat on while they were away so they would have a home to come back to.

He decided to surprise Ellie by taking her out to dinner that night to her favourite Greek restaurant in the centre of the city, put her in a good mood, tell her what he wanted to do. They both worked so hard and were drifting apart. They lived together but hardly saw each other. It had been so good at first, and he wanted to get back to what they once had. Only time together, to relax and enjoy each other's company again, would let them do that.

Luke looked around the open-plan office at his team who had all received their redundancy offers. Mollie and Pete looked worried. Sandra looked over just at that moment, nodded at him and smiled. He was relieved to see that she looked perfectly satisfied with her offer. They had worked together for years, been involved in several projects together. In fact it had been Sandra who had trained him when he joined the firm. Everyone loved patient, kindly Sandra Bennett, in and out of the workplace, but he and Sandra had a special friendship. He knew all her family well, and had been to many of their private celebrations. He thought back to the day Jim, Sandra's husband, had a dizzy spell and had fallen, fracturing his wrist and the bones in his forearm. Luke had driven them to the hospital for the results of tests taken at the time of the fall, and was outside waiting when they returned to the car after receiving the news that Jim had Multiple Sclerosis. That was ten years ago and recently the disease showed signs of progressing more quickly. Now Sandra could retire to be with Jim. Luke was happy for her. That money would make life easier for them both.

Kuldip, Raj, Donal, all seemed content with their offers as well, and Luke wasn't worried about Mollie and Pete. They were both excellent at their jobs, and were well qualified, but at this moment, with their futures unknown, and especially in the case of Mollie who lacked confidence in her abilities, he understood their concerns. He would talk to them both later to see what he could do to help. He was sure they would find another local employer very soon and would make sure Ted gave them good references.

Redundancy could seem terrifying for many, but some saw it as an advantage, as it gave them the opportunity to do something new; maybe start up their own business, travel, learn a new skill. For some it was a release from their working years as it allowed them to retire early without having to wait until their pensions started. It wasn't always the end of the world.

When he had first been told that his team, and one other, were being laid off due to lost contracts, Luke was furious. He knew Ted's management style would cause problems for the company. Ted had been parachuted in from the parent firm, exalted as the wiz-kid who was going to be the be-all and end-all, but had proved to be nothing more than a Yes-man to Sir Peter Green, the Chief Executive, and had no idea how to run a credit-referencing and banking business, but the problem was, he thought he did. Arrogant and prepared to sacrifice anyone to climb to the top, he refused to take responsibility for the loss of the contracts. Now fourteen people had lost their jobs.

But for Luke, it gave him the freedom to see other places, find the sunshine, see mountains, the sea, the sky, breathe fresh air, take long train journeys across countries he had never seen other than in movies, maybe even go skiing. For the last few years, he had seen the office, had online meetings with international clients online at all hours depending on their timelines. He often went to work in the dark and went home in the dark. He had had enough.

Luke wandered off to the kitchen for a coffee. One of the girls had hung a mirror on the wall and he looked at his reflection. 'Thirty-three in a few weeks but you look fifty-three. You've got bags under your eyes, your skin's pasty and there's grey hairs in what a little while ago used to be brown.' He pushed strands of hair to one side. 'And you need a haircut, mate.' He stroked his chin. 'It looks like you've put on a little weight as...'

'Talking to yourself, Luke?' Sandra stood in the doorway. 'Don't worry, boss. You're still handsome in my eyes.' She walked over to the coffee machine to make herself a cappuccino.

'Have you decided what you're going to do?' she asked.

Luke smiled 'I'll have one of those, while you're at it. And, yes, I'm off. Going away...'

Sandra looked shocked. 'What moving right away?'

Luke laughed. 'No, just a month or two. I'm hoping Ellie and I will head off for some sunshine for a while and maybe we'll finally get out to Gozo to see Jake and meet his girlfriend at long last.'

'He dives, doesn't he?'

'Yes, he's an instructor. Loves it.'

'Oh, nice. Great place for diving. Malta and the islands are lovely, and the sea's that gorgeous turquoise and crystal clear.' She smiled as she handed him his coffee. 'Good for you.'

'You've been there?'

'Yes, Jim and I have been a couple of times.' She picked up her mobile phone and flicked through some photographs. 'Here. This is the round the island cruise we went on last time we were there. This is coming into the Grand Harbour at Valletta. Very imposing.' She flipped through the photos again, and passed her phone back to Luke. Those two photos are of the Blue Lagoon at Comino. Just look how clear that water is ....and that's Mosta church, where the bomb fell through the roof during World War Two, when the church was full of people, but it didn't go off. Talk about a miracle.'

Luke nodded as he handed the phone back. 'It does look a bit special.'

'It is. You and Ellie get over there and see it for yourself.' She took a sip of her coffee. 'How soon are you thinking about getting away?'

Luke blew his cheeks out and exhaled. 'Not sure. Haven't really planned anything yet. I suppose it depends on when Ellie can get away. She doesn't know yet but I'm taking her out to dinner tonight. I really only decided what I'm going to do when I saw the offer letter, so haven't had much time to think about plans and so on. But I hope it'll be soon.'

'Well keep me updated, and make sure you pay us a visit before you vanish into the wild blue yonder.'

'I will. And there's one thing bothering me about my travel plans.'

'What's that?'

'I hate flying. It scares me.'

Sandra left the room chuckling.

Chapter Two

Birmingham – The Break Up

The atmosphere in the second floor apartment, was volatile. The woman pushed her blonde hair out of her eyes, then she hauled down two suitcases from the top of the wardrobe, one large, one medium sized, and threw them down onto the bed. The second one bounced and tipped over onto the floor.

'Shit!' She reached down to pick it up, just as the man got to it before her.

'Here, I'll do that,' the man said. She scowled and mumbled something that sounded like another expletive, as he placed the case more carefully on the bed. 'Ellie, let's just sit down and talk about it.' Again, she ignored him. He tried again, moved towards her, his arms outstretched, pleading. 'Come on, love, why can't we talk about this? I can't believe you really want to throw four years down the drain just because I've been made redundant?'

Ellie went back to the wardrobe for the … Luke had lost count of the number of times that, avoiding his eyes, she flung open the doors, grabbed an armful of clothes and stormed back and forth to the bed, each time with more jeans, jumpers, dresses, underwear, tore them roughly off the hangers and threw them haphazardly onto the duvet.

He almost smiled as she then took her time in folding blouses and jumpers in a laboriously slow, and pedantically tidy manner. Not like Ellie at all.

Having emptied the wardrobe of most of her clothes, Ellie started on the chest of drawers. Stubbornly silent, she threw pants and bras into her big case; she wasn't so particular in how she packed them.

'For God's sake, Ellie, speak to me!' Frustration was turning to anger. What was he supposed to do?

She said nothing, but her withering glare gave him his answer. He turned away towards the window, ran his right hand through his hair, inhaled, and stormed out of the bedroom. In the kitchen, he paced back and forth, trying to think of something he could say that would make her stay. He had thought, wrongly as it was turning out, that they would be together for life. He had to admit things hadn't been too good between them for a while, and recently they hadn't had much to say to each other. Even so, he always felt that soon things would go back to how they had been. Had he left it too late? Had he just taken it all for granted? Or had the catalyst been his redundancy? He looked out of the kitchen window. There was movement in the street; cars, people walking by but he wasn't really aware of what was outside. He was more aware of the sounds of drawers banging shut, and Ellie stomping around in the bedroom, then slamming the bathroom cabinet closed.

The redundancy? Was that the issue? He knew she was disappointed the firm was cutting staff; but that was a fact of life. Contracts were lost, companies folded, these things were happening every day, but the benefit was that he would have a really good payout. He had talked to her before about taking time for themselves and travelling for a few months. He could look for another job when they got back. He would have enough money for both of them and getting away from everything was just what they needed; it would bring them closer together. A new beginning. An image flashed into his mind of them on a beach, somewhere like Bali, with white sand, palm trees and crystal clear turquoise sea. He was barefoot, wearing a loose blue shirt and white linen trousers. Ellie walked towards him wearing a long white dress and she had a circle of flowers in her hair, around her neck and on both wrists. Her blonde hair was loose, flowing across her shoulders. She smiled as she approached him. He had never seen her look so beautiful. People were gathered around them and a local priest stood before them. The sound of the suitcase snapping shut, drove that vision out of his head.

He went back into the bedroom. The first thing he noticed was that Ellie had now taken all her 'things' out of the bathroom and set them down beside her overnight bag; shampoo, conditioner bottles, deodorant, contraceptive pills, electric toothbrush. There were other things there as well, but his attention shifted back to Ellie. She was crying. Trying to hide it she quickly wiped the tears away with the heel of her hand and ignored him. He walked towards her hopefully, his arms reached out to hold her; the image on the beach still imprinted on his mind. She moved away from him. The dream shattered.

'Oh, come on, Ellie, If this is about the redundancy, It's not my fault the firm's failing you know it was the mismanagement by Ted and his team that lost us a couple of big contracts, and they're all of us who worked on them. I didn't choose for this to happen, but I'd like us to take advantage of it now that it has. It that so wrong? Some of the guys have only been there a few months and they'll get bugger all in redundancy pay...'

'... Luke!' He turned to look at her mascara-trailed tear-stained face. 'Luke, it's not that you've lost your job. I know you're going to get a good payment after all the years you've been with them ...'

'...Then what the hell is it? Ellie, talk to me ... I don't know what to do to make this right.'

She walked up to him, placed her hands on his shoulders. Her usually lovely blue-grey eyes now bloodshot and red-rimmed with crying. 'You know. You know how I feel, Luke. Please try to understand.' She moved away, looked down at the floor. 'Yes, you'll have money in the bank ... thousands.'

He nodded. 'That's what it looks like, then there's my holiday pay and the government's statutory redundancy payment, and ...'

' ...That's exactly what I mean ... but you want to give everything up here and travel ...'

'Not forever, I don't. Just a few months ... I'll keep paying the rent, so we don't lose the flat.'

'But you should be holding onto that money, getting another job so you can keep ...'

She looked so miserable, but did she not understand that he needed a break. It wasn't just a "Oh let's go have a holiday" thing to him. He'd had enough of the city, the office, and the bullshit that went with it all. He turned to her. 'With what I have in the bank already, plus what I'll have next week, for the first time I'll be secure enough financially for us to travel, see something of the world and still have money left when we get back. I've always wanted to see Rome, Prague, the Greek Islands ... Gozo. We could go and see Jake.' For a moment he was stumped. 'How about New York? You said you wanted to go to Broadway, and the Empire State Building. Or Florida, Niagara Falls?' He looked at her, hopefully. 'We're not getting any younger, Ellie. Time's passing. I'm almost thirty-three now. I haven't seen Jake for years. We could go to the Maltese Islands, catch up with Jake, meet his girlfriend, Anjelika.' It sounded as though he was begging. That wasn't his intention; he wanted to persuade, not plead. Ellie had no time for anyone who lost their self-respect. Enough now.

Ellie grimaced..

'Oh, come on. She can't be that bad. Jake's been with her for quite a while ...'

'What, six months is a long time? Hmm.'

'Okay, maybe not. We know very little about her, but Jake seems happy enough, and all that sunshine, clear blue sea, all that history ...'

'... Okay Luke,' Ellie cut in. 'You've made your point, but it's you who doesn't understand. I don't want to travel, at least not yet. I want to be secure first. I can travel when I have everything in place, an established career, my own home...with, or without you. I have a great job here and there'll be a promotion within the next year. My family and our friends are here ... and if we keep working, we can buy a house in another few years. We'll have enough money for a fifty percent deposit.'

Luke turned away towards the window. 'Hmm, and I could die of a heart attack or stroke, fall under a bus, or be suffering with ulcers by then.'

'My God, Luke, don't be so bloody melodramatic. When did you become such a pessimist? You're not an old man, but you sound like one!'

Luke turned again and leant against the window sill. He looked at Ellie and understood, for the first time, that they were two separate people who wanted completely different things. He had always thought of them as a couple, forgetting they were individuals with their own hopes and plans. Was there ever anything other than lust that had brought them together. Had it ever been love, or did he just want it to be? Had he just assumed that Ellie would want the same things he did? Had they ever really talked about taking time away just to see what was out there? No, he could not recall a time when they ever really discussed the future. They just worked for long hours, very often six days a week with late evening finishes and then collapsed on the seventh. When they did take time off together they visited relatives, Ellie's in Devon and his in Northumberland. They never did anything that took them away for a few days alone. Project Management and the flat was all they really knew of each other. Their sex life was practically non-existent; it had slowly eased off after the first ecstatic six months, and now he could not remember the last time they made love.

Ellie walked away to the bathroom again. He heard her blow her nose, the cistern flushed, then the sound of running water. She came back into the bedroom holding a face flannel to her eyes, to take the puffiness down, to soothe.

She looked at Luke. He had not moved from the window. 'Well, what's it to be, Luke?'

As he looked up her, she saw the resigned look in his eyes and knew the answer before he spoke.

'You're a beautiful, funny, highly intelligent woman, Ellie, and I think the world of you, but it's not enough.'

'Ooh! You think the world of me?' She sat on the end of the bed, clearly shocked by his words. 'Thanks for that.'

He gave a sad little chuckle. 'I can see you didn't expect that. You thought I would give in. I'm sorry, Ellie, but if you're honest with yourself, you know we don't love each other, we're a habit. We want different things, and if we didn't work so much we would have seen it before. I want … no, need to get a life before I'm too fuckin' old to enjoy it. Pardon my language.'

'But I …'

'Ellie, you started this argument, remember? But it's made me see the reality of … well … who we are.' He stood up and walked towards her. 'You wanted me to keep working, sorry, I mean you wanted *us* to keep working, but there's a lot more to life than constant work. We're in our early thirties, we drink too much to help us cope with the stress, and we've both been working since leaving university. That's twelve years for me and eleven for you. Jake's got it right. He got out of working with computers and sitting in crappy meetings that in the end meant nothing, working long hours, with all the office politics and pressure. Now he's having a great time in the sun teaching people how to Scuba dive. You and I both know the people who play 'the game', walk around carrying a folder making sure they look as though they're busy, shmooze the bosses, know all the office gossip, and make it to the boardroom by being 'yes' people. I don't want to see that any more. I don't want to be a part of that world any more. So, the choice is, we stay together, see just how real this relationship is and get to know each other again while we're travelling...see some life before we're too old, or burnt out.'

'Or ... ?'

He looked down at her red-blotchy face and swollen eyelids. He hadn't wanted to hurt her, but if there was nothing to go on for ...

'Or, we call it a day.'

'Now?'

'Yes, now. There's no point in dragging it out.'

Ellie took a deep breath, stood up, walked around the bed to her cases, her expression said it all. She reached down to the pillow where she had placed several neatly folded tops and laid them in the case. She turned to Luke. He saw anger, perhaps sadness in her eyes, and he thought he saw something else there – defeat, perhaps.

'I'm going to stay with Sean for a while. I phoned him earlier to say we might be breaking up, and he's offered me their spare room until I can get sorted out. He said Matt won't mind as he thinks of me as his little sister too. So leave me in peace to finish packing. I'll be gone in an hour. I'll get Sean to pick me up.'

Luke nodded. 'Right. I'll just go for a walk then and get out of your way. Just leave your key on the kitchen table.'

He was almost at the front door when he stopped and walked back to the bedroom. He leaned against the door frame watching Ellie. She knew he was there but ignored him and carried on packing.

'Ellie?'

'*What?*'

'I'm sorry things didn't work out. I hope once a bit of time's gone by, we can be friends again.'

'Huh! I shouldn't think so. You'll be off travelling, doing whatever it is you think you want to do, and I'm sure we'll lose touch. Shut the door on your way out, please. Oh, yes,' she said, an acid tone in her voice. 'I promise I won't steal or damage anything.' 'but Sean and I will be back in a couple of days to pick up the last of my things. I'll phone you to arrange when. Goodbye, Luke.'

Chapter Three

Birmingham – Making Plans

'Hi Jake. How're you doing, Bud. My message a surprise, was it?'

'*Yeah. Good to hear from you, Bro. Can't remember the last time we spoke, you two are always so busy.*'

'Ah, yeah. Well things have changed a bit. How do you fancy a house guest for a few weeks, maybe a month?'

'*Uh, great, yeah.*' Luke noticed a slight hesitation. '*It'll be good to see ya, but only one house guest?*'

'Hmm, Ellie and me have split up.'

'*Oh, sorry to hear that. I liked Ellie.*'

'So did I but it turned out that was all there was. We'd burnt out.'

For a few seconds Jake said nothing, then: '*You know I did think that might happen at some time. You both spent too much time apart working, no time just to relax together. That's a relationship waiting to fall apart. I thought a while ago that you weren't sharing a relationship, just a place to live. So what's this about you coming over?*'

'Yeah, that's the other thing. I'm being made redundant. Two contracts have been dropped. Ted and Co fucked up again, and there's a few of us being laid off.'

'*I'm sorry to hear that …*'

'No, don't be. I'm sick of the grind to be honest and will be glad to take some time away from everything.'

'*Can't fault you there. So what's the plan?*'

'I'm going to travel, see something of the world. I have made quite a bit of money which is sitting nicely in the bank, plus there's a nice little … or not so little redundancy payment coming. Even after tax I'll still be pretty comfortable. So I …'

'How long are you planning to be away?'

'That's open-ended. I'll see how things are going, and where I fancy going on to while the money I'm going to set aside lasts.'

'What about your flat? Will you sub-let while you're away?'

'No. If Ellie had been coming with me I'd have kept the flat on, but not now. This is city centre, the agency will find another tenant in no time, and I only have to give a month's notice. I'll put all my stuff I won't need for a while into storage. Right now, I don't even know if I'll come back to Birmingham. The world's my oyster, as the saying goes. I can probably come out to see you, if you'll have me, in two or three weeks.'

'Sounds great. Yep, get yourself over here. We only have a small place, a one-bedroom flat but we have a sofa, a decent sized living room and a balcony that looks out over the village, it's a fair size for a village. You'll love it. Just one thing though, I thought you hated flying.'

Luke chuckled. 'Yeah, You're right, I do, but if I'm ever going to see anything of the world, I'm going to have to deal with that, and just go for it.'

'Okay, but just a couple of tips for you. Have a rum or something before you fly or on the plane, but leave it at one. Avoid coffee and tea as well. Both dehydrate. The flight's only about three and half hours, so not too long, take a bottle of water that you buy after checking-in, and whatever you need to keep you distracted on the flight; newspaper, a book, electronic reader…you'll have to put that on flight mode, or something else to keep you occupied, take your mind off flying.'

'What? No films?'

'Ha ha … no, that's on longer flights.'

'Okay. Right I'm going to head off and start getting organised. I have a fair bit too get sorted out. I'll let you know about the flight details as soon as I've booked up.'

'Hey, fancy coming diving with me while you're here? Unless that scares you too.'

Luke laughed. 'I'm not scared of everything, idiot! And, yeah, I think I can manage a dive or two. I'm a pretty good swimmer.'

'Now that's where people make a mistake. You don't need to be a good swimmer underwater. You just need to follow instructions and kick your legs. The rest is easy, and you'll have plenty to see. The diving around here is fantastic. There's so much to see, and there's teams out here trying to make sure the crap left by thoughtless people, or careless fishing boats, is cleared up and I'm in one of them. We go down with net bags and clear the plastic and other crap from the harbours, while another group clear the beaches...it's pretty sick what people dump in the sea.'

'I can kick my legs. No worries, Jake, and maybe I can give you a hand while I'm there. Look forward to it. Right, I'm off. Be in touch soon.' He was about to end the call when, he remembered something. 'You still there, Jake?'

'Yeah ... what's up?'

'I just thought. How do I get from Malta to Gozo?'

'I'll be at Luqa Airport to meet you, so you don't have to worry about that. We drive from the airport to Cirkewwa, the ferry port, get the car ferry across to Mgarr harbour. The crossing takes about half an hour. They're not particularly new ships, work horses really, but they do a great job and the crossing's fine. Drive off the other side and then up to Xaghra. You'll like the journey from the airport as you get to see a fair bit of the island on the way.'

'Brilliant. Catch you soon. Bye Jake, and say hello to Anjelika for me. Looking forward to meeting her at last.'

'Um, yeah.' There was that slight hesitation again. *'She'll be made up when I tell her you're coming. She's been wanting to meet you.'* He laughed. *'She going to be narked with me, though. I've been telling her I'm the handsome one of the family, and that you're the ugly brother.'*

Luke laughed too. 'Why doesn't that surprise me, brother. You shouldn't have done that. You must have known the truth would come out sometime. Right, this time I am going. I'll call you soon.'

'Bye, Luke. Good to talk to you.'

'Bye, Jake.'

Chapter Four

Birmingham – Arrangements Made

Luke walked up the stairs to the office of the letting agency, walked through the door and found the room buzzing with activity. All four agents were either on the phone, or already sitting with clients, there were already two people waiting to be seen, and the phones rang non-stop. He was in no hurry, so he helped himself to a free cappuccino from the machine that provided complimentary drinks for waiting clients, settled himself in one of the comfortable armchairs, and picked up a travel magazine from the small table.

He sipped his coffee as he flipped through the pages until, as luck would have it, he came across an article on Malta, Gozo and Comino. The first glorious photograph was of the Azure Window that had stood since time immemorial at Dwejra Bay, near the Inland Sea, Gozo, until 2017 when it finally collapsed due to erosion. The other images of Gozo were The Citadel at the capital city, Victoria, also named Rabat, a ferry heading into the pretty harbour at Mgarr, the neolithic temples at Xaghra. But the photographs that particularly caught his eye were those of diving. He had just found the section where details of the marine life were mentioned, when the agent he was due to see, Jahnavi Banerjee, called him over.

'Good article, Luke?'

He looked up and realised that the other two waiting clients were now with agents. 'Yes, sorry, Jahnavi, it's pretty interesting ...'

'... I thought it must be, I called you twice,' she said with a huge smile. 'Come over and we'll get your notice sorted out.'

Luke was about to put the magazine back on the table when he asked: 'Would you mind if I took this?'

'It's a couple of months old, so I don't think anyone would mind.' As they walked over to Jahnavi's desk, she said: 'There's a couple of forms, as usual, that you need to sign but it shouldn't take too long. How's Ms Patterson?'

Luke looked down at the floor, then back at Jahnavi, his eyebrows furrowed. 'Hmm, well that really why I'm here. We broke up.'

'Oh I'm sorry to hear that,' she said, as she sat behind her desk and gestured for Luke to take a seat in front.

He shook his head. 'No, don't be. We should've done it well before we did. Work got in the way and we drifted apart. It happens. It's not unusual and no-one died, I just guess it feels a bit weird though, being completely on my own, but it's better this way. So how are your children? Your boy must be almost school age now?'

'Yes, he starts in September. He's done really well at nursery and he's ready for pre-school. Meena's just started her thirty hours at nursery and she's loving it. I'm not sure how she's going to feel when Rahi isn't there anymore. She's used to having him around. Thank you for asking.'

She opened a drawer on the right side of her desk and pulled out some documents. 'So, let's get your notice on an official footing, Luke.' She pushed the papers across the desk towards him. 'You might want to read through these first. You can take them away if you want, or, as I don't have another client after yourself before lunch, I have time to go through everything with you now, if that suits you. I have to ask though, why are you leaving? I thought you liked the apartment.'

'Yeah, I do ... did, but circumstances have changed and it's time to change with them. I've been made redundant and decided, now that Ellie and I aren't together any more, to do what I've wanted to do for a long time. I'm going to travel for a while and first,' he lifted the magazine up, 'I'm going here, to Malta and Gozo. That's what I was looking at in here. My brother's lived out there for about four years and I haven't seen him in all that time. So it's time to do something about it. We were always close but work got in the way, and time's just rushed on and I didn't really notice it, until now that is.'

'Well, good for you. I'm envious,' Jahnavi gave a wide smile and sat back in her chair. 'Of course, Raj and I go back to India to see our families every two years, and we try to see somewhere new each time we go. We want to make sure the children know their families and their home area and heritage. They mustn't grow up only knowing Birmingham. Although it is a great city and has a lot to offer.' She handed Luke a pen. 'Just ask me anything you need to know about the documents. Are you staying on in the apartment for the full notice period?'

'No, I won't be at the flat for the whole month, I plan to leave in the second or third week of the notice period. I'll let you know my arrangements, once everything's confirmed. I'm guessing you'll be sending someone around to see the condition I'm leaving the place in and, as of Monday, I can be available when you want to send someone round to inspect.'

'That's fine, Luke. We're not anticipating there will be anything that will need dealing with. We know how you and your now ex-partner worked long hours, and well, to be honest, I can't see how you could have had time to mess anything up.' She smiled. 'You should see the state of some of the places we let, but as neither of you smoke, there weren't any pets and so on, I'm sure the apartment will still be pretty pristine.'

'I certainly hope so. It's a nice flat in a good central area, close to everything, so you should have someone take it over pretty quickly.' He signed the two documents Jahnavi passed over the desk to him, and returned them to her.

'Ah, well, I think we already have. There's a bit of a waiting list for apartments with secure entry and parking like yours, so we'll have no problem filling it. That's why we only ask for one month's notice. As long as everything's as it should be, we can give you your deposit back within a couple of days of the notice period.'

'Great. I'll drop the keys in here the day I leave. Is that alright.'

'Yes, of course, thank you.'

Luke stood up to leave. 'Is that everything? I have rather a lot to get done still.'

Jahnavi stood up as well and reached out to shake his hand. 'I hope you enjoy your travels.'

Luke smiled. 'I'll let you into a little secret, I'm scared stiff of flying so my first flight will be a relatively short one.'

She shook her head. 'I completely understand. I'm not too keen on it myself, I often say to Raj that, if Brahma had wanted us to fly, he would have given us wings. So you're going to Malta?'

'Yes, well, flying to Malta, then staying on the smaller island of Gozo where my brother is. It's a nice place by all accounts. As I mentioned, he's been out there for four years, but I've never been there.'

'And now you're finally going,' she smiled. 'Well, I hope you enjoy your time away and, don't forget, we're here if you need us when you get back.'

Luke smiled again. 'Thank you, Jahnavi, but I'm not sure what I'm doing when I get back. I'm not even sure that I'm coming back to Brum.' He turned to go. 'You know, it's a great feeling not to have any pressures any more, no responsibility for a while. Freedom for the first time in years.'

'It sounds like heaven. I might try it myself sometime. Bye, Luke and thank you for being our least troublesome client. I'll probably see you when you bring in the keys and I hope all your arrangements go smoothly.'

'Bye, Jahnavi. Many thanks and I'll see you then.'

'You can let me know how all your plans have gone.'

Luke walked out of the agency into the busy street, and for a short while he just stood by a zebra crossing, surveying with increasing discontent the buses, cars and people rushing by creating a cacophony of noise that he realised he would be very pleased to leave behind for a while. Engines, horns, people talking, mobile phones, a crying baby, the sirens of an ambulance, flashing blue lights and a hurtling police car, almost drowned out the sound of a low-flying helicopter hovering overhead in the almost cloudless blue sky.

It was at that moment, Luke realised he had left his cappuccino half finished, on the small table at the agency.

'To hell with this. Enough!' he said aloud, as he turned away. 'Another coffee and a paper, then there's some calls to make.'

Chapter Five

Birmingham : Flight Details

'Hi Jake. Just wanted to give you my flight details.'

'Where in God's name are you? An echo chamber?'

'No. I'm sitting on the floor in what was our sitting room and is now an empty space, my back against the wall and a take-away caramel latte by my side.'

'So everything's gone now?'

'Yep, and I drop the keys into the agency on my way to Phil's.'

'So Ellie's got all her stuff now.'

Luke took a gulp of his latte. 'Yeah. She and Sean came around with Sean's partner, Matt and collected the rest of her clothes, her microwave, sofa, etcetera, two days ago.'

'How did that go?'

'Better than I hoped. I thought Sean would be an asshole, but he was pretty cool with the split. Ellie was a bit distant but she gave me a hug when she left. She said we should meet up when I get back, when we've both had some time to get used to being apart, and maybe see how we feel then. I said yes, but I don't think time will make our hearts any fonder. It'll probably just prove we were right to split. It was Matt who kicked off though, and I didn't expect that. He's normally pretty quiet, but anyone would have thought I'd cheated on Ellie and mistreated her. He was really in my face. I think he'd been drinking. Threatened to kick the living shit out of me at one point, but Sean pulled him off and apologised, and Ellie pushed him out of the flat.'

'Ah, well you'll be away from it all in a couple of days. Where are you staying now the flat's gone?

'At a Travelodge for now. It'll do until I fly out and I don't really need anything else right now.'

'Yeah, I suppose that's true. You don't really need much, do you?'

'Yeah. I've got what I need with me. So, as long as there's no delays, air traffic control strikes, I'll see you on Sunday. My flight lands at Luqa at 20.35. Are you still alright to meet me?'

'Absolutely. No problem. It only takes about half an hour to drive to the ferry port and the ferries run late. So all good.'

'Are you sure Angelika's happy about me coming to stay?'

'Yeah, er yeah. She's fine with it. She's looking forward to meeting you?'

'What is it now...six months you've been together?'

'Yeah, about that. She's a ... she's a great girl, funny, gets on well with my mates, good cook, very bright, loves the sea and helps with the clean-up. We have a lot in common and we're tight. She's a bit flirty with some of the lads at the diving club, but it's all ... well ... harmless.'

Luke thought he sensed something a little offbeat in the way Jake finished his sentence, but then thought he might have imagined it. He hoped so. 'Great. Glad to hear you're happy, Bro. But I'm going to head off now. Got to get the keys handed in. Haven't done that yet and then I'm meeting some mates from work for a farewell dinner tonight. If I don't speak to you before, I'll see you on Sunday at Luqa Airport.'

'All good, See you then. Enjoy tonight.'

'I will.'

Chapter Six

Arrival : Malta and Gozo

The aromas of coffee, beer and wine were still hanging around in the cabin from the last drinks and snacks round, as the plane descended towards Luqa airport. The closer they were to the ground, the more Luke's anxiety kicked in; although he remembered someone saying that the nearer you were to the ground, the more chance of surviving if anything went wrong. He tried to hold on to that thought.

From somewhere a few rows back, a little boy who had been giggling just a short while ago, began to cry loudly. Luke could hear the child's mother trying to soothe her troubled toddler, but his screams grew a little more shrill with every passing minute. Luke guessed the pressure was hurting his little ears. You can't teach a young one to hold their nose and blow to help clear the pressure, and there had hardly been a peep out of the child during the flight. Well not since take-off anyway. Luke felt some sympathy for the little one. He knew from experience how painful the build-up of pressure in the ears could be, and right now his ears were continually popping as they descended.

Luke felt the plane was descending too fast, and his ears crackled again. His hearing became dull. He held his nose between his index finger and thumb and blew to normalise the pressure. It worked and he could hear again, but then he heard something he didn't like. The engine noise was different. Was something wrong? When would the undercarriage roll down?

He could see the back of the wing from where he sat; it looked okay; flaps opening downwards to slow the descent. So far, so good. But it was not a good idea for him to look down at the fast-rising ground. Ill-defined shapes of buildings were shadows amongst the bright flickering lights of houses, cars, boats, as they gleamed in the blackness of the starless night sky.

The plane banked to the left and he could see the runway lights. Luke turned away from the window and sat, rigidly facing straight ahead, eyes closed, tight lipped.

'Are you alright,' said a soft voice. The red-head in the seat beside him was very attractive, but neither of them had spoken to each through the flight.

Without turning round, and through gritted teeth, Luke managed to mutter: 'Yes. No ... um ... I mean I'm fine. Thanks.'

'I'm afraid you don't look it. Here, take my hand.' Luke could hear the smile in her voice, and realised he was talking himself into being scared. He looked around at the green eyes that held a look of gentle amusement at his discomfort; it was the kind of smile you would give a frightened child. No, he could not let her hold his clammy hands. Get a grip. He managed a grimace, which was nothing like the casual grin he hoped it would be. 'I guess it's not very manly to be scared of flying.'

'I don't see why it should be the preserve of women and children only. There is no rationalising fear or phobias.' It was kindly said, but he still refrained from giving her his hand.

With the main lights having been turned off in preparation for landing, and only being able to see a few people over the tops of the seat, Luke realised that those he could see seemed at ease, conversations carried on, people were laughing, the cabin crew were still relaxed and were walking up the aisle with large plastic bags collecting rubbish. Okay, so maybe he should just take Jake's word for it.

He glanced out of the small window again. They had descended further than he realised and now he could make out the terminal building. Why the hell did they have to call it a Terminal! He had never been comfortable flying and, having heard that take-off and landing were the most dangerous parts of a flight, he averted his gaze from the window to the cabin crew. Watching their movements and facial expressions, he controlled his breathing, but gripped the armrests tightly until his knuckles turned white.

Jake had assured him that, if the cabin crew were relaxed and following normal procedure, then everything was okay, and there was nothing to worry about. The call went out for the cabin crew to take their seats for landing, and Luke watched the four he could see walk casually to their seating points; no hurry, no worried looks, no sweat-beaded brows, no panic. Luke allowed himself to breathe a little more easily, but he kept his grip on the armrest.

It was alright for Jake to tell him how to take it easy, he hadn't flown since he had arrived in Gozo. He had probably forgotten that some people get anxious being on a plane thousands of feet in the air. Luke recalled a couple of times when Jake had admitted turbulence scared him witless, and for all he had said about flying generally, perhaps that was the reason he had not been home, or gone anywhere else for that matter for the last four years.

Luke braced himself for an uncomfortable landing but when the wheels finally touched down, there had hardly been a bump. It had been surprisingly smooth, and he grinned widely when a round of applause from the Maltese passengers erupted through the cabin, some of them even crossed themselves in relief at having landed without incident. He understood exactly how they felt. The plane taxied to the terminal – there was that word again – but the passengers were asked to stay secured by their seat belts until the plane had stopped.

After a few minutes of rumbling along at a steady pace the plane approached the building, stopped, the seat-belt lights went out and, as Luke saw the buses arriving to take the passengers to the building, there was the usual mad scramble of passengers trying to get their bags and anything else that belonged to them from the overhead lockers. Everyone wanted to be ready to get off the plane. The problem was that those people in the aisle who had beaten their neighbours to get to the lockers, were now standing in the aisle preventing others from retrieving their possessions. It was obvious from the facial expressions, that impatience was causing considerable frustration, but thankfully no-one verbally complained, so no actual arguments broke out.

Then a senior member of the cabin crew opened the door and a rush of warm air blew through the cabin. It had been a pleasant nineteen degrees Centigrade at Birmingham when the plane took off a little under three and half hours before. So, as a twenty-nine degrees Centigrade waft of air blew into the cabin. Luke heard a woman comment, 'Oh wow! See, this is what we've come for.' But a man a couple of rows back said very loudly, 'I told you Malta would be too bleedin' 'ot for me, but you wouldn't listen. Now what am I supposed to do for the next two weeks if it stays like this? We should have gone to Cornwall, like I said.'

Luke grinned, and, as he pulled his cabin bag down from the overhead compartments he briefly wondered why the couple hadn't checked the average Maltese temperature for late May before booking the holiday. It didn't sound as if that holiday was off to a good start.

The queue was now moving down the aisle to the exit and Luke looked along the line to see where the redheaded woman who sat next to him was in the line. The man in the aisle seat on their row of three seats, had stood aside to allow her out, but then stood in Luke's way making him wait. She had been very quick to get her bag from the locker and had squeezed in before an elderly man who had stood aside to let her into the queue.

Being the last one in his row to collect his bag, Luke was now some way behind her, and the line was disembarking quite smoothly.

Two young women who had drawn level with his seat, indicated that he could move into the aisle in front of them, but, impatient though he was to catch up with another young woman, out of common courtesy he declined, but moved in behind them to the annoyance of a middle-aged man and his wife.

'Excuse me ... sorry,' Luke said. 'I'm trying to catch up with a friend of mine. I'm sure you understand.' The man said nothing. His wife tutted. As soon as movement allowed, Luke headed towards the door, keeping an eye on who was going through the door. He saw her reach the head of the queue and stared at her, willing her to look around. At the door, she hesitated and he thought his luck might be in, but she just thanked one of the cabin crew and vanished through the exit. Bending, to look out of a nearby small window, he caught a glimpse of her getting on the first bus, but before he reached the exit, he saw the doors close, and watched as the bus headed for the terminal. Unless he caught up with her at Passport Control or at the luggage carousel, it was unlikely he would ever see her again and, for some reason that really bothered him. He had only shared a few words with her, knew nothing about her but he really wished the line would move faster.

The queue at the ten Passport Control EGates went through quite quickly and soon Luke was hurrying through to the luggage carousel hoping the redhead would be there. But he arrived there just in time to see her pull a small case off the carousel, walk briskly towards the Customs area for people with nothing to declare, and vanish through the doors. He scanned the bags on the carousel. His had still not appeared. He was too late, but he hoped there was still a chance of catching up with her in the main hall. Perhaps she was waiting for someone, or had booked a car, talking to a holiday rep. There might still be a chance.

A little over ten minutes later, Luke followed the direction the redhead had taken and found himself in the bustling main area of Luqa Airport. He weaved his way between groups of holiday makers looking for the reps of their holiday operators, drivers holding placards displaying the names of people they were booked to collect, and the car hire reps dealing with families wanting to pick up the cars they had booked, and get off to start their holiday. Focused on finding Jake amongst the crush of people, Luke almost fell over a case being dragged along behind a teenage girl, who was fixated on her phone and not looking where she was going.

'Luke, hey Luke,' Jake's voice reached him over the melee. Jake was standing beside the WH Smith shop doorway, waving and smiling. Luke pushed his way through the crush and the next moment the brothers hugged. Jake pulled away first.

'My God, Luke, you've filled out a bit.'

'Nice greeting brother dear, but yeah, I know,' said Luke with a huge grin, as Jake led him towards the car park. 'That's what happens working in an office for all hours for the last few years, eating junk food at the desk, and too bushed to get to the gym.' While they walked, Luke scanned the crowd, still hoping to catch sight of a head of abundant auburn hair. 'But I have time to do something about it now.'

'Good. I'll take you diving with me. You burn up eight calories a minute Scuba diving.' Jake noticed that Luke seemed a little distracted. 'Looking for something?'

Luke turned to him and grinned widely. 'Not something…someone.' They were at the Arrivals exit door and Luke stopped to take a last look around. 'No, can't see her. She must have gone through already.' As he walked beside his brother, he said: 'Shame. She was lovely…nice too, not just gorgeous. Green-eyed redhead with a throaty, kind of sexy voice, you know like Mariella Frostrup.'

'Oh Yeah. Hmm, how old d'you reckon?'

'No idea, and doesn't really matter, does it? She's nowhere in sight.'

'True. Oh well, no wonder you're trying to find her … but it looks as though you've struck out there, bro. Right, the car's over there.' He pointed to the right side of the long car park. Here, let me take your bag. We have a drive … about thirty, maybe forty minutes to the ferry port at Cirkewwa, but it's mostly a pretty good road, a bit narrow and winding in a few places, but there won't be much traffic around now, so we should make good time. It's a pity it's late as you won't get to see much of Malta in the dark, but you'll have plenty of time during your stay for me to take you around both islands.'

'I'll need a bit of time to get used to this heat. What's the temperature now?'

'I haven't checked, but I guess about twenty-five degrees Centigrade. Should have warned you about that, you'll be glad of the aircon in the apartment, and it does feel cooler when you get to the coast. Sea breezes help.'

A few minutes later, they were driving towards the ferry port, catching up with Luke explaining what had gone wrong between Ellie and himself, and how the redundancies came about. While Jake talked about how settled he was on Gozo and how much Anjelika was looking forward to meeting him. The journey time went by very quickly, and soon they were waiting at the port for the nine-fifteen evening ferry to Mgarr, Gozo's port.

Although dark, it was still very warm and while they waited in the queue for the ferry, Luke got out of the car and took a look around the harbour, and saw the ferry about hallway across the channel between the islands. He thought back to the bustle of Birmingham, the tall office buildings and hotels, the noise at night from the pubs and clubs, and inhaled deeply.

Jake walked over the join him. 'Now you know why I'm here and don't have any plans to go back to the UK.'

Chapter Seven

The Malta Gozo Ferry

With the ferry not being particularly busy, loading was achieved quickly, and the vehicle deck had plenty of room. With the car safely parked close to the exit, Jake led Luke up the steps to the main deck, where they leant on the guard rail watching the prow cut through the calm purple-black water of the channel. The V-shaped surf rippled outward and gradually decreased as they moved on, and Luke was entranced by the tranquillity of the night and the fresh-air smell of the sea. He could feel the tension in his shoulders and neck easing, as he breathed in the clear air. Jake had been right. The sea breeze did make the temperature more comfortable, even if it was still pretty warm.

What Luke noticed very quickly were the colours everywhere he looked. The silvery-white light from the moon reflected on the water, the yellow and orange beams from other shipping, the floating buoys, and the lights from homes across the channel and around the harbour, cast a warm golden glow that shimmered on the surface of the rippling sea. It was spectacular whichever way he turned his head. If he had been the type of person who read fantasy, or even romantic books, he might have described the scene as magical. He smiled. That wasn't like him at all. He was far too practical, a matter-of-fact sort of bloke, not given to fanciful notions, but then how else could you describe how the scene made him feel? He had no answer for that.

'Is it always this peaceful?'

In the light coming from the onboard café Luke saw Jake smile.

'No, sometimes it can be rough. We do get storms, but knowing you're not the world's most comfortable traveller, I ordered this weather for you tonight. Can't guarantee what it'll be like for your return trip though.' Jake turned towards Luke and leant his back again the rail.

'Good of you, Bro.' Luke shook his head. 'I don't remember seeing anything like this before. Much as we loved our beach holidays in Whitby and Scarborough, this is something else again. I definitely made the right decision. I needed to travel.'

'Pity it split you and Ellie up though.'

'No, not really ...'

'Hi, Jake.' They both turned as a young couple, hand in hand, stopped beside them. They had their backs to the cabin windows with the cabin lights behind them, and Luke was unable to see their faces clearly. One thing he did notice though, was that where Jake had been relaxed and cheerful, his manner had changed, Luke thought he seemed stand-offish, with the man, giving him a cool, quick handshake, and then turning to the woman in a much more friendly fashion.

'Hi Irina, George. You're looking really well, Irina. Everything going okay?'

Jake asked with what Luke thought was genuine friendliness, but he was right. Although subtle, Jake's body language had changed. It was as if Jake had braced himself to deal with something unpleasant, when he looked at George. Even though they had not seen each for years, Luke knew Jake well enough to detect when something was wrong that others might not notice. Although, on the face of it, Jake was still being sociable, Luke felt a tension in the air. There was clearly something between George and Jake, although it vanished when Jake spoke to Irina.

'Yes, good, thanks,' said Irina.

'This is my brother, Luke. He's over to stay with us for a month or so, so you'll probably see him around from time to time. And, Luke this is George and Irina Camilleri, plus bump.' The couple reached out to Luke to shake his hand.

'They're a pretty nice couple when you get to know them. Actually, I take that back. Irina's great but George is a pain in the ass, and I would stay right out of their way if I were you.'

'Don't you believe a word of it, Luke. Jake and I are always like this. He gets as much as he gives. There's always plenty of banter when we're together, isn't that right, Jake.'

'Yeah, of course. Just joking,' he laughed, but Luke was not convinced.

'Jake and I are old friends, and I help him find somewhere to hide when he's upset Anjelika. Isn't that right, Jake?' said George.

It was at the mention of Anjelika that Luke noticed a flash of anger in Jake's eyes.

'Yeah, I guess so, if you say so, George.' He turned to Irina. 'Changing the subject, how are you keeping, Irina. Haven't seen you for two or three weeks.'

'Yes, I'm fine thanks.' Irina ran her hand over her swollen belly. 'He's kicking quite hard now.'

George put his arm around her shoulder and she nestled against him.

'She's keeping really well, and we can't wait to meet our little one, can we, my love.'

Irina looked lovingly into George's eyes. They seemed happy together, and there was certainly no sign of any animosity between Irina and Jake. Whatever the problem, it was clearly between Jake and George.

'So you know what you're having now?' said Jake.

George grinned widely and his eyes gleamed with joy and pride. 'Yes, it's been confirmed now. We're having a boy...'

'But we would have been just as pleased to have found out we were having a little girl, wouldn't we?'

'Indeed we would, my love. Just so long as you and the baby are fine, then I'm happy ... and as long as we have a good mix of boys and girls amongst the eight children we are going to have ... '

'What!' Irina pretended to punch his shoulder. 'Eight?' she said, laughing. 'If you want that many children, husband, then you can have the babies. My limit is two!'

'Yes, yes, my darling, I understand … and agree. But no domestic issues in front of the neighbours, please, Irina. Come on, we'll leave Jake and his brother in peace.'

'Bye, Jake. It was nice to meet you, Luke. I'm sure we'll see you again soon,' said Irina as George gently led her away. They had only gone a few steps along the deck when George looked back and whispered, loudly enough for the brothers to hear, 'It'll be eight.' Followed by 'Ow!'

'Our neighbours, George and Irina Camilleri. Nice couple, only married about ten months ago. You'll probably meet them at one of the weekend parties in the apartment block. Anyway, back to what we were talking about. How d'you mean, not really? You know, about you and Ellie.'

'Is there some problem between you and George? I thought I sensed a bit of…tension between you.'

Jake shook his head. ' No, nothing for you worry about. I just don't particularly like some of the people George hangs around with.'

'Why, who are they, and why does it concern you? '

Jake turned back to lean on the rail and look out towards the approaching harbour. 'It doesn't really concern me at all,' he looked around at Luke, 'I just wish he was more careful about the company he keeps because Irina's a good friend and I don't want her to get caught up in anything,' he sighed.

'She seems pretty happy with him … hold on a second … you have a soft spot for her, don't you?'

Jake turned away again. 'I wouldn't say that, I just like her, that's all. Nothing more than that. We're friends.'

Luke gripped the railing with both hands and pushed his shoulders back. 'Hmm… you always did look away when you were trying to hide something.'

Jake gave no answer. 'Come on, it's a great sight coming into harbour, especially at night with all the lights. We'll be home soon.'

Luke understood the conversation was closed, for now, anyway. The prow of the ferry, where the mooring winches, bollards and ropes were positioned, was shut off to the public, so the brothers stood on the port side of the ferry, and as close to the prow as they could. With the mild sea breeze blowing in his face and ruffling his hair, Luke had a sudden realisation that he was very far from home, friends ... Ellie, and that his life from that day on was going to be very different. This was real. He was finally seeing something of the world, and the feeling of liberty it gave him sent excited shivers down his spine.

'Well, glad you're here?'

'Oh yeah, but I can't quite believe it.' Luke pressed his lips together for a moment, trying to gather his thoughts. From the day he and Ellie had decided to call it quits, he had been so busy making plans and hadn't really given a great deal of thought to the actual break up. Now those plans were a reality. 'I suppose I do miss Ellie. We'd been together for so long, I was used to having her around, and I suppose she felt the same about me. I guess we still had some kind of love for each other, but ... and, I can only speak for myself, I wasn't in love with her any more, we'd become nothing more than a habit. The break was probably going to happen at some stage. We'd just grown apart concentrating on our careers with nothing to bring us back together again, nothing shared ...'

'Like kids, do you mean?'

'Yes,' Luke nodded, 'but thank God, that didn't happen.'

'Don't you want a family?'

'Oh yes, don't get me wrong, I suppose I've got to an age when I can see that happening, but it wouldn't have been right for me with Ellie, or for her with me. In the long run we both wanted different things, lives ... you know what I mean.'

Jake nodded. 'I think so.'

'Ellie was all about her career. She said she wanted a family, but not for a long time in the future, but the clock was ticking for both of us. I knew there was more to life than project management, and the redundancy came at the right time for me. Now I want to find something more satisfying to do, see something of the world and, if I'm lucky, find someone who's right for me and vice versa.'

'Hmmm. Yeah, I can understand that.'

'So what's the situation with you and Anjelika?'

The engines slowed as the ferry entered Mgarr harbour, distracting Jake for a moment. 'It'll be time to go below to the car soon.' Jake gave a little chuckle. 'Hmm. What to say about Anjelika and me.' He took a breath. 'Well, first of all, she's gorgeous, and yeah she's cool. She's more of a party girl than a family person, although she's close with her parents. Her family's pretty big, but she's twenty-six and enjoying life too much right now, so not really ready to settle down.' He sounded resigned rather than happy about that. 'But, yeah, we get on and she's fun.' He shrugged. 'I guess with me being that bit older, I've done my partying, but yeah, like I said, she's cool.'

The engines stopped, the ferry eased into its mooring, the bow doors opened and began to rise.

'Come on, let's get to the car,' said Jake. 'We'll be disembarking soon. It won't be long before you meet Anjelika now, and you can make up your own mind about her.'

Chapter Eight

Gozo : Anjelika

Jake opened the refrigerator door, took out two cans of a local beer, and bottle of Ulysses white wine. He handed a can to Luke, and poured a glass of wine for his girlfriend, Anjelika. As she reached out for the glass, Jake said: 'There's only a couple more cans in the fridge, honey, would you mind going to the late-night store? Then I can stay here and show Luke around.'

'But, I'm just starting on the dinner, Jake. No, you go, this time. I'll stay with Luke. Now he's here, we need to get to know each other.' She gave Luke a wide smile.

'Okay, I'll just be about ten minutes,' said Jake, as he grabbed his keys. At the door, he turned to grin at Luke. 'Anything else either of you want?'

'How about some Pastizzi?' said Anjelika.

'Okay, no problem. Just look after this little brother of mine till I get back. Won't be long.' As Jake went out to the local store, Anjelika sipped her wine as she turned away towards the kitchen. Luke stepped out onto their small balcony to look out over the town under the shade of the striped awning. In the moonlight glare, Xaghra's honey-coloured stone houses shimmered. From the small second floor apartment, with the village of Xaghra situated at the top of a plateau, Luke had a great view over the houses, and across to the Mediterranean with its silver-tipped waves. In the distance, the Gozo ferry was about to pass the tiny island of Comino on its way back to the Maltese ferry port at Ċirkewwa.

He became aware of Anjelika's presence beside him. He looked around and smiled, but looked away again, as he realised she had slid the wide straps of her top off her shoulder, and undone the top two buttons revealing far more cleavage than she had before Jake left. She moved closer, her musk-based perfume was warm and subtle. Luke stepped away, unnerved.

'Luke, it is good to meet you at last, and to find out that Jake has such an attractive brother,' she purred.

'Um...yes, it's good to meet you too, Anjelika.' Luke felt his hands grow clammy as she moved nearer. He could feel her warm breath on his face. He backed away, took a swig from the can, holding it as a barrier between them.

'Is something the matter, Luke?'

'Jake said you ... you and ... er he have been together for quite a while now.'

She didn't answer. 'It would be nice to be friends, wouldn't it, Luke?' Her breasts were now very close to him. 'After all Luke, Jake told me to look after his little brother, but you are not so little, I think.' She laid her hand on his chest and began to slide it down over his stomach to his belt.

Luke grabbed her hand and held it, confused and angry by her attempt to seduce him. He reached out to her shoulder and roughly pulled up the straps of her blouse.

'What the hell do you think you're doing?' He was sickened, appalled by her bold, and shameless attempt at seduction than angry. He went back into the living room, turned and snapped at her, as she followed him, far too closely. 'You know ... right ... this stops, right now ... and, get that top done up now! I'm sure you don't want Jake to see you like that!'

Without taking her eyes off him, she slowly raised her hands to the buttons on her top and took her time about doing them up. Even that action seemed provocative to Luke. He walked by her and returned to the balcony. Took a very deep breath to control his anger then turned to find her staring at him, with a leering smile on her face.

'Right, this stops now.' Luke struggled to control his anger and swallowed a few times, trying to get some saliva into his dry mouth. 'Let's get a few things straight. Firstly, I did nothing to let you think I had any interest in you. Secondly, you're my brother's girlfriend ... and I wouldn't touch you with a barge-pole and, well...and thirdly, how could you have been so stupid … he'll be back any minute. How …' He turned away and shook his head. 'How do you think he would have reacted to me … or to you, if he's come back in time to see what you did just now?'

She gave a sultry, brazen smile, looked at him from under long, black eyelashes. 'Why do you think I asked him to get Pastizzi? Our usual bakery here in the village is closed. He will have to go back to Mgarr to get them. He will be some time yet.' She was being wantonly coquettish. Luke just wanted to get away.

'I'm not saying you're not attractive, you are, but you're Jake's partner. If you weren't I might have been interested. But, even if you weren't with Jake, I'd have been put off by how quickly you came on to me. I like to get to know someone first. I'm not a wham-bam-thank you-mam, kind of man. If I go to bed with someone, it has to be worth it. Has to mean something. My days of quick screws are long gone, Anjelika, so I have no intention of allowing you to make out with me.'

Anjelika glared at him. 'Okay, but you don't know what you're missing.'

'Yeah, well I'm sure I can live with that.'

'If you tell Jake, I will say you came on to me.'

Luke shook his head and looked away. 'Oh, so you don't play nicely then. What a piece of work you are. I wonder if Jake realises what kind of viper he has in you, huh … I guess not.' He walked back towards the balcony, stopped, turned round and scowled at Anjelika. 'You know, you're a looker, Anjelika, beautiful even, but you're rotten. No, I'm not going to tell him. I'm not going to be the one to hurt him. He'll find out what a little tramp you are in time I'm sure, but it won't be from me.'

Anjelika looked relieved. 'So, will you stay here?'

'No, with this place being so small I wasn't sure it would be right for me to stay, anyway, but now I know I can't.'

'But what will you tell Jake?' To her credit at least her look of concern seemed genuine.

'Oh, don't worry, I'm not going to make things difficult for you. Don't get me wrong. I'd like to let him know what a little bitch you are. I'd like him to dump you, but you'll slip up one day.' He paused, staring at her for a moment. Silent. Then he stepped closer to her, stood tall, looking down at her. 'Did you honestly think I would do that to my own brother?' He shook his head again. 'What kind of people do that? And no ... I won't say anything, but don't go thinking I'm doing it for you. It's for his sake, not yours.' She looked away, unable to meet the loathing in his eyes. Luke walked back out to the small balcony. Anjelika didn't move, she just stared at him, her face pale, her eyes glistening.

Then something occurred to him. He stood in the doorway and the look on his face brought tears to her eyes.

'You look at me as if you hate me,' she said.

'Perhaps I do. Something tells me this isn't the first time you've done something like this, is it? It was too smooth, too easy and you expected a different reaction from me, didn't you? Do the men you target usually give in? You've cheated on Jake before haven't you?'

Her cheeks began to burn, but still Anjelika tried to bluff it out and resolutely lifted her chin and glared back at the furious Luke, arrogant and proud and refusing to apologise for her flirtatious behaviour. She stood, unabashed, as Luke approached her again. With his face just inches away from her's she tried to stare him down but eventually broke her eye contact and look down at the floor, silent.

'I'll just tell Jake that it wouldn't be good for you both to have me staying here for a month or two. That I like to sleep naked, or scratch my arse when I wake up.' He paused, thought for a moment then said: 'I'll tell him that it wouldn't be right to deprive you both of your living room when I sleep late, so I've decided to look for a hotel nearby.'

Footsteps echoed along the corridor and Anjelika darted back to stand in the kitchen doorway, with her glass of wine, while Luke quickly began talking about his flight from Birmingham Airport to Luqa. Jake kicked at the door to be let in, and entered with both hands holding a cardboard box containing several cans of the local lager called Cisk, another bottle of Ulysses, and a paper bag from which came the aroma of warm pastry and ricotta cheese. If he sensed a strained atmosphere between his girlfriend and his brother, he did not show it.

'Okay, guys, it's time to party and welcome my favourite brother,' said Jake.

The rest of the evening went smoothly, although Luke avoided looking at Anjelika unless he had to, and Anjelika played her part by snuggling up to Jake as though nothing had happened, and she really made it look as though she adored him. Luke thought her performance that night was worthy of an Oscar.

Although he had been invited to stay with them, even before the dangerous incident with Anjelika, Luke had not been greatly enthusiastic about the idea as soon as he saw the apartment. It was a little on the small side and only had one bedroom. The idea of sleeping on the sofa for a month, and having to be careful about making sure he had his boxer shorts on when he got up in the morning, or in the middle of the night when he needed a pee after a few beers, in case Anjelika appeared, didn't really appeal. But now the less he saw of Anjelika, the happier he would be.

Later, when they had all gone to bed, Luke searched online for nearby hotels. There were plenty in the capital city of Gozo, Victoria, but Luke looked for somewhere quiet, preferably without too many children around. It wasn't that he didn't like kids, but just wanted somewhere to relax, read a book by the pool, and get up when he wanted without being awoken by little ones splashing in the pool at eight o'clock in the morning.

As luck would have it he came across what looked like the right place, the four-star Cornucopia Hotel, and it was only about ten minutes away from Jake's apartment. Luke checked out the reviews, all of which appeared really good. There were only two floors with just forty-eight rooms, plus the pool terraces looked fine. So far so good.

Chapter Nine

Gozo : Sleepless Night

Luke barely slept that night, he had lain awake long after Jake and Anjelika had gone to bed. It had been a long day of travelling and, although he was dog tired, the situation with Anjelika was on replay in his mind. Jake was only just out of the door before she had hit on him. It was almost predatory. As he asked himself whether, if she had not been his brother's girlfriend, would he have given in? The answer was, yes ... maybe, although he would have preferred a little more time to get to know her before he slept with her. But, fuck it, she was his brother's girlfriend and she had no right to put him in the position he now found himself. Several times he looked at his phone to check the time. A little after two o'clock, he poured himself a glass of water and sat out on the balcony watching the lights of boats in the harbour. It was a lovely night, with an immense purple-blue sky, thousands of stars had appeared and the full moon was larger and looked closer than he had ever seen, anywhere. The air was warm and the occasional bat flitted by. There was very little traffic and he could hear the occasional snatch of conversation, or laughter, and from somewhere in the surrounding streets a dog barked incessantly for about five minutes. It stopped when someone shouted at it followed by the sound of a closing door. He sat there, looking at the stars, and wondering whether he should say anything to Jake about what had happened. After about fifteen minutes, he went back to his sofa bed, but was still unable to sleep. The last time he looked at his phone to check the time, it was three forty-two. He must have drifted off to sleep, but awoke a couple of hours later to see pink rays of dawn peeping through the beaded window blinds. He turned over and tried to go back to sleep, but after another thirty minutes of fidgeting, he got up, quietly made himself a cup of coffee, took a croissant from the packet on the worktop, and headed for the balcony again. The sunrise was spectacular. Soft shades of pink, gold and almost a lilac tone were reflected in the glassy unruffled ocean, as the sun leisurely climbed higher on the horizon. Its rays, like golden fingers reaching out to seize the land, edged metre by metre, street by street, further into the town, giving honey-colour stone of the buildings a warm golden lustre.

For those few moments Luke forgot Anjelika, forgot home. He had not a care in the world. He inhaled the fresh clean air, and took in the aroma of fresh bread coming from the nearby bakery. He was going to enjoy his time on Gozo.

He heard the clattering of crockery in the kitchen. Someone else was awake and up and about. He hoped it wasn't Anjelika. He had hoped to be out of the apartment before she surfaced. The blinds rattled and he turned to see Jake, leaning against the door frame, a coffee in one hand and a half-eaten croissant in the other. Luke was relieved. With a bit of luck, he would be out of there, before Anjelika made an appearance.

'Morning, Bro,' Jake said as he pulled out a chair from under the table. 'Are you sure you want to go to a hotel? I mean it's only for a month, and we'll manage. I know the apartment is small, but ...'

'No. It just wouldn't be right ... I'

'But what about the cost? You were supposed to be having an easy time of it with us, saving some money.'

Luke laughed. 'But that's not a problem, not right now anyway. For the first time in years I don't have to think about rent, bills, fuel costs. My redundancy money is sitting in my bank account and I'm travelling. I don't have to think about getting out of bed in the morning if I don't want to. My time ... and my money is my own to do as I please, and I'm going to make the most of it, to Hell with the cost. Life's good right now. I'll worry about money later. Anyway I've already called a local hotel and they have room for me.'

If Jake was surprised that Luke had been so quick to get organised, he didn't show it. 'Which one?'

'The ... um ... Cornucopia. D'you know it?'

53

'Oh Yeah. It's not far from here. Good choice. I know a couple of the guys who work there. Some of the people who come diving with us stay there, and I've never heard anything wrong at all, in fact some of our guys recommend it when they have family or friends coming over. They get a lot of repeat business which says a lot for them. Food's good, it's clean, comfortable, good staff, a couple of really good pools, nice looking place. It's expanded over the years, to bungalows and farmhouses, but it's not one of those big impersonal hotels. It's a relaxed, friendly place. Yeah, you should be fine there.'

Luke smiled. 'Good. That's settled. Can't check in until later, but they've said I can take my case there earlier, have lunch perhaps, and if the room's ready before, then it's all to the good. We'll see what happens.'

'What's the hurry?'

Luke had to think on his feet. 'Um … no real hurry, it's just that I'd like to get settled, get unpacked, then I can get on with taking a look at Gozo.'

'In that case, you have the time to come diving with me today and check in afterwards.'

Luke had to think quickly. How did he get out of that one?

'Er … no. I draw the line there. Much as I want to see the world, I'd rather see it from the land. Thanks. I guess I belong to that group of people who believe that if God wanted us to go underwater, he'd have given us gills. There's still a few of us dinosaurs around.'

Jake grinned and turned away shaking his head, then turned back, put his right foot on the other chair, leaned forward, rested his right elbow on his leg and stared down at his brother.

'You're not going to tell me that you travel all this way, look at the glorious crystal clear sea we have here, and you're not curious about the marine life?'

Luke nodded. 'Yep, I am going to tell you just that. If I want to look at marine life I can look it up online or at an aquarium.'

Jake looked down at the floor and shook his head again. 'That's nuts. You flew here yesterday, but you didn't grow wings. Come on, where's your sense of adventure? You're thirty-three, not ninety-three.' Jake had stopped smiling. Luke's reluctance to try something new worried him. It was time for calm persuasion. 'Look, you've already broken away from your mundane life, and now's the time to do things you've never done before.'

Luke was obviously thinking about it and trying to find an argument against diving, but was struggling to find anything valid, other than he was terrified.

'Look, I'll tell you what,' Jake said. 'Try snorkelling first. I'll take you out to the Blue Lagoon at Comino. You wouldn't believe how clear that water is. It's not too deep. I can ask to borrow the smaller boat.'

'But haven't you got to work today?' Luke seemed to be swaying.

'No. Because you were coming out I booked three days off to spend time getting you settled and showing you around.'

Jake was very persuasive. Snorkelling. Luke had to admit that was something he had often thought of trying. 'Okay, but not today. I'll go snorkelling with you tomorrow, but I don't have a mask and stuff.'

'No worries, I do. I have all the gear you'll need. Did you bring trunks, swimming shorts.'

Just then Anjelika came out of the bedroom wearing what Luke guessed was one of Jake's company T-shirts. On her slim frame, the T-shirt was oversized, baggy and almost long enough to reach her mid-thigh, exposing long shapely, tanned thighs and two silver ankle chains on her left leg and crimson painted toenails. Her long hair was loose and tousled from sleep, she wore no make-up. It was obvious she was braless, and Luke suspected the T-shirt was all she was wearing. He glanced at Jake, whose frown confirmed Luke's suspicions.

'Good morning, Luke.' Her smile was flirtatious. With the grace of a cat she glided over to Jake.

'Hello, my darling.' Her kiss was long and passionate She lifted her arms to reach around his neck, causing the T-shirt to ride up exposing her small, firm buttocks. Luke was right and he turned away in embarrassment and disgust. Jake saw Luke's reaction and understood. He reached behind his head, grabbed her hands and pulled them down.

'Go and get dressed, there's a good girl.' Jake glared at her, but Anjelika just smirked, whispered, 'Okay'. She was being deliberately provocative, playful. She fluttered her eyelashes at Luke as she sauntered back to the bedroom, seemingly blasé about Jake's disapproval and humiliation.

Jake and Luke looked each other in the eye for a few seconds. There was no need to say anything, but as soon as the bedroom door had closed behind Anjelika, Jake said, 'Are your things ready?'

'Pretty much. I just need to get dressed, then I'm done.'

'Okay, so it's ten-fifteen now. Let's get you to the hotel, and then we'll get some lunch.'

Anjelika came out of the bedroom, fully dressed and ready to apologise, but there was no-one there. Jake and Luke were already on their way to the Cornucopia.

Chapter Ten

Gozo : Drive Angry

There was a leaden silence in the car on the short trip to the hotel. Jake burned with humiliation, anger and embarrassment, while Luke struggled with guilt. If he had not been there, Anjelika would not have behaved that way. It was quite clear, from the brazen look she had given him in front of Jake, that she knew exactly what she was doing. She could walk around stark naked all day if they were on their own, but Luke had never known any woman flaunt herself like that. It was calculated. Cruel.

Luke glanced at Jake. Since getting into the car Jake had never taken his eyes off the road, but his mind was on Anjelika's conduct, and he almost hit a car coming the other way, when taking a turning. The driver shook his fist and swore at Jake, who simply nodded and raised a hand as a gesture of apology, and the other car went on its way.

Although wearing his seat belt, the abrupt stop, forced Luke forward with a sharp tug. Jake swore, called himself stupid, cursed, apologised to Luke but still did not look at him, and drove on. His hands gripping the steering wheel so forcefully his knuckles were white, reminding Luke of his grip on the arm of his seat on the plane. The way Jake was dealing with this situation reminded Luke of when they were children. Jake would never shout or scream when he was angry. There were no tantrums, he would become very quiet, and would usually head off to his room preferring to deal with the intense emotion alone. Both of the family cats, who generally seemed to prefer Jake's room to sleep in, would skulk away. Jake would be silently seething, would spend the next half an hour or so away from everyone, closeted in his room, until he had his temper under control. Then he would calmly rejoin the family as if nothing had happened. Later he would pour out the reason for his anger to their mother, who would help him understand or resolve the issue that had riled him. Luke, however, was completely different. As a child, he would throw things when he was upset, and was difficult to reason with at times. In his late teens, once the hormones had settled down, and he found working out at the gym helped keep the testosterone in check, his anger issues generally subsided. However, like most other people, if pushed too far, he could still become irate, enraged, but he handled it better now. He was angry with Anjelika and sympathetic to Jake, but unsure how to show it, or if Jake would want it. What the fuck was Anjelika playing at? More to the point what did she think was going to be the result? That wasn't flirtation. It was deliberate provocation. Did she think they would *perform* as a family? No matter which way he looked at it, he couldn't fathom the answer to that one.

A few minutes later Jake pulled in between two parked cars beside a wall covered by a pretty pink-flowering climbing plant.

Jake turned off the engine. 'Right, we're here.'

Luke looked around him but, from where he was sitting he couldn't see anything that looked like a hotel. 'What? Where's the hotel?'

But Jake was already out of the car and had pulled Luke's case off the back seat. 'It's just down there.' He pointed towards the corner of the road.

'Where?'

'There's a gateway just beyond that third car. Come on. Let's get you checked in and then we'll have a beer.'

Chapter Eleven

La Gomera : Mateo Moreno

It was a little after dawn and already twenty degrees Centigrade, when a small team of gardeners tramped down to the neglected sloping garden of the ruined villa. Their elderly supervisor, Mateo Moreno, paused beside of the remains of the villa's stone wall, stroked his stubbly chin, and felt a great disappointment. After four days of twelve men working for eight hours a day, with the use of a mechanical digger and chain saws, he would have expected to see more progress, but there was very little to show for their efforts in the entwined mass of laurel trees, junipers, willows, canary palms, agave, sedges, and whatever else was concealed within the interwoven tangle of plants. But then, what did he expect when the garden had been left to grow wild for three hundred years, on fertile land with no-one keeping it controlled. He shook his head, not exactly in despair, but more in contemplation of how, in God's name were they to clear what could only be described as a jungle, and prepare the ground for planting the required ornamental garden, within the thirty day target they had been given. It had taken Madre Naturaleza three hundred years to get the garden into this state, and they only had a month.

'Do you want one of these, Mateo?'

Javier Garcia, the youngest member of the team walked by Mateo, carrying two chainsaws. Mateo chuckled, and the white laughter lines around his eyes disappeared, concealed within folds of nut-brown, weatherbeaten skin. He reached down to pull a pair of heavy duty secateurs from one of the several pockets of his gardening apron.

'No, these will do for me. Those heavy machines are not for the likes of me, they are for young men like you to use. My old shoulders will not cope with the weight of them. Give one to Ramon, and you use the other. Go to the patch where I was working yesterday. I have snipped off the smaller stems so the laurels there are ready to have the branches lopped. If they are long, halve them, and the same with the trunks, so they will fit into the skips. They can be used for firewood once they are seasoned. I will be working over there by the dividing wall today, but first I'm going to check the roots situation inside the villa walls.'

'Yes, Mateo.'

'And be careful of the wildlife,' he called to Javier, who continued walking away, and did not turn around. 'Make sure you warn them before you start cutting into their homes. Give them time to get away.'

Javier waved. 'Yes, Mateo,' he shouted his reply.

Mateo watched his teenage protégé walk down the slope to join Ramon. Javier was a good lad, and reminded Mateo of his son who was now living in Madrid with his family. He had not seen Carlos for a couple of years, and he had not yet met his little granddaughter, Alina. Although Marta and Carlos sent lots of photographs, it was not enough. It was nothing like enough for Mateo. He needed, no, desperately wanted, to meet the little girl, let her know who her Grandpa, her Abuelo, was. It was time he took a holiday.

The villa had been destroyed by fire and, until recently when the land had been bought to build a hotel on it, it had remained abandoned and forgotten. To have someone who clearly had a lot of money to spend, finally find the site of interest, came as a very pleasant surprise to most people. Mateo didn't know who the buyer was, and nor did he care. As far as he was concerned, it gave his men work for which they were getting well paid. That was all he needed to know. Conversely, he wasn't entirely comfortable about the renovation. It would be a shame to do away with this almost mystical reminder of the past, and the attachment that many people locally had for it. On the other hand, maybe it was time to bring the place back to life.

As a child, Mateo had played on this land with his brothers, and he had very fond memories of those days. They hid amongst the trees, caught rabbits and butterflies, bird-watched for the spotted woodpeckers, beech finches, kestrels and ravens, and if ever they were lucky enough, small eagles. They searched for lizards, the black Gomerian and the giant lizard, and sometimes stayed out late in the evening to watch the bats. He looked across to a corner of the garden where they had built a camp and invited only a few selected friends. He smiled at the memory. And after fifty years, that's all it was now, just a lovely memory. The simple wood and string construction had been buffeted by strong winds and rain and, with no-one to repair the damage, it had simply blown away.

It was this place that sparked his interest in gardening, and he loved walking around inside the shell of the burnt out villa, trying to imagine who had lived there. He and his brothers, Juan and Pedro, four and two years older than Mateo respectively, had spent many hours hiding inside the villa, or in the undergrowth when they had done something wrong, and had run away to avoid a scolding from their mama.

But, now he was the last of the brothers. Juan, a horse-mounted picador in bullfights, had died at just twenty years old, in the bullring in Huelva. Pedro had contracted pneumonia and died nine years ago at the age of sixty-five. Now Mateo, a widower of five years, was looked after by Maria, Pedro's widow; they shared a house, but not a bedroom. He earned the money and she cooked and cleaned for them both. She was a good woman, they got on well together. It worked well for them both, Maria had no children, and since Carlos, his son, had moved to Madrid and rarely came home, they were good company for each other.

From the top of the garden Mateo watched the team spread out returning to the patch of ground they had left the day before, all except Javier and Ramon, of course, who had begun to work where Mateo had last been.

Mateo was not looking forward to working at the wall that divided two sections of the garden, and dragged his feet as he trudged to the spot as slowly as he could without drawing attention to himself. He was getting too old, the work was becoming too hard for his shoulders and knees, and although they could use hand-powered rotavators, they were of no use until the all the long-established trees, shrubs and tangled, stubborn roots had been cleared. They had a small tractor arriving in a day or so, but it would have been so helpful to have had diggers to get down to the roots of the larger plants to get them out of the ground. But the new owners had refused them that help, saying they could not afford the insurance for machines to work on such an incline. One false step and a digger, and perhaps its driver, could end up going over the cliff, and therefore it was too risky to agree to their use. Well, if the owners insisted on sticking to that, then they only had themselves to blame if the work took longer than scheduled. At least they would not be starting to build until the following Spring.

Mateo stepped gingerly over the remains of the stone wall at the front of the villa and into what he took to have been the long hallway. He never felt alone within the boundary of the villa. He sensed the ghosts of previous residents watching him, and he had a compulsion to show respect for the long gone. Taking off his wide-brimmed straw hat he noted that some more of the straw strands had broken off again. Ah well, it had served him well for many years, but there was still enough life in it for this summer.

Within the shell of the building he tried to imagine what each downstairs room was used for. It was no good thinking about the upper floor as it was no longer there; just the shards of a few red clay roof tiles that lay broken on the ground were all that was left.

How many times had he stood in the same position trying to imagine the face of Don Alphonso Ruis de Casals? Everyone locally knew the legendary account of Don Alphonso. Maybe the story had changed over the years, like Chinese Whispers, growing and changing with each re-telling, but what if it had? It made no matter. What they did know was that Don Alphonso had existed, they knew he had taken his own life, that at least was all true. That much of his story had been written down. Don Alphonso's friend and Servant, Miguel Flores, had dictated his story to his daughter as he lay on his death bed. Two of Mateo's closest friends were descendants of that very Miguel, and almost three centuries later, they still kept his writings safe for handing down through the generations. They knew that Miguel and his family had been sent away and into hiding by Don Alphonso, in fear of retribution from his uncle, but why was still a mystery.

Mateo took a good look around the ruin and noted where the vines and roots had broken through the floor, or twined around the walls, and he sighed. It would all be gone soon. He pressed his lips tightly together, gave a little nod, crossed himself, and reluctantly stepped back over the crumbling wall to trudge half-heartedly down to the tough old Granadillo shrub by the collapsing low stone wall that divided the one-time ornamental garden from the less tidy one. He often tried to imagine where members of the family would sit on the grass having picnics, or just lazing in the sun. At least, that was how Mateo imagined the two sections of garden would have been used; the formal area for entertaining, and the relaxing family area where they could just be at ease.

A few minutes later he was on his aching knees wrestling with the Granadillo bush he had begun digging out the day before. He was determined it would come out today. It had to, he had already spent too much time on it. If he could not get it, he would ask for someone to help, but one way or the other, the damn thing would be out of the ground before they left that day. Although the new owners may not be in a hurry to have the ground cleared, spending too much time on one thing was a waste of his time. There was still so much clearing out to do in preparation for the when the landscapers were able take their measurements for the new garden design. Hopefully he would be employed again when they took over. In the meantime, the architect was already working on designs for the new hotel where it would overlook the channel between the islands of La Gomera and Tenerife. The remains of the villa were to be demolished as soon as the garden had been cleared.

An hour later, hot and tired from his efforts, the shrub still stubbornly refused to budge, but Mateo had brought a mattock with him this time. The tool had a wooden handle and a metal head with two different ends, one wide and flat, the other thin and pointed, and was ideal for breaking up hard dry ground.

Having snipped back the foliage of the overgrown shrub as much as he could, Mateo began gouging out clumps of earth with the thin end of the tool. When he guessed he had broken up enough dirt to loosen the roots this time, Mateo decided to use his spade instead and began shovelling loose earth away from the hole. Then his spade connected with something hard. Expecting it to be just another rock, he sat back on the low wall that divided the two sections of the garden to catch his breath, took a plastic water bottle from his cool bag, took off his straw hat and wiped the perspiration from his brow with his sleeve. From a few metres away below him on the steeply sloped garden, Javier returned to check on his mentor.

'Are you alright, Mateo?'

Mateo batted a wasp away with his hand. 'Yes, Javier. I am okay, thank you for asking. How are you and Ramon getting on?'

'It was hard going, but it looks as though we are winning. We are getting through the laurels and a few palms. I was just taking some of the chopped branches to the skip, and thought I would see if you need anything.'

'That is kind of you, my boy, but I am alright, thank you. I have my water bottle, I have a little strength left to keep working on this bastard of a shrub. I may call you if I cannot get it out within the next half hour. But, the more I fight with it the more I think maybe I should retire. I am getting too old for this kind of work. Maybe I should only work in a greenhouse now, potting small plants.'

'No, not you, Mateo. You will never retire. You enjoy your work too much ... and you have so much knowledge to pass on to us younger people. But, be careful in this heat, the sun is burning, perhaps you should work less hours when it's this hot.'

'Huh. Maybe you're right, but also maybe not. You're a good boy, Javier, and a good worker. I will be happy for you to take over my business when I do retire.' He looked up into the sky. Not a cloud to be seen other than a few faint white streaks over Mount Teide on Tenerife. 'At least it is early still, and cooler than it will be in another two or three hours. We will stop for the day then.'

'Yes, Mateo.'

'Right, now I need to get back to digging out the rest of this damn Granadillo.'

'Do you need my help?'

'No. No, you have enough to do where you are.'

'Just let me know if you do.'

'I will. I promise.' Mateo smiled as he watched Javier walk away. He was a good boy. His mama could be proud of him.

Using the sharp end of the mattock, Mateo loosened more earth, and again it connected with the 'rock' he judged was just a few centimetres further down. If the rock, if that's what it was, was preventing him from getting to the more established roots of the plant, then it had to go. Carefully lowering himself onto his arthritic knees, Mateo's gloved hands scraped away more of the earth from the hole. He reached for the mattock and broke up some hard chunks of earth and stone, and scraped again with his hands. Then he saw it. This was not a rock, it was something hard wrapped in cloth.

'Javier!'

'Do you need me?'

'No, I don't, but it seems like a good time for you and Ramon to distribute the water bottles around the team. They are in the big blue cold bag in the van. Be a good lad and see if everyone is ready for a break. You'll find a tin of Florentine biscuits that Maria baked last night in a box in the back as well.'

'Yes, Mateo.'

Mateo peered over the shrub at the two young men, silently urging them to go away. Javier lay his shutdown chainsaw on the ground, nudged Ramon and pointed to the top of the hill. Ramon nodded, turned off his chainsaw and set it on the ground beside Javier's. Mateo was relieved to see both his young workers, walk at a brisk pace to the top of the hill and head to where the vehicles were parked. Mateo envied them their pain free youthful fitness, and that the heat did not seem to affect them at all.

'Now let's see what this is.'

A few moments later, having checked every few seconds that no-one was coming his way, unobserved, Mateo unwrapped the linen to find a second wrapping of leather. He peered over the shrubbery again. Pulling back the leather, he cut the leather strips that bound the package, with his pruning knife, only to find another layer of linen. 'Whoever buried this wanted it protected from damp.'

Removing the final layer, Mateo discovered the ornate wooden box, and was about to open it when he heard Ramon and Javier talking as they returned. They were close, too close.   Ramon continued towards where they had left the chainsaws. Javier walked towards Mateo.

Mateo quickly re-wrapped the box in the leather and linen, stuffed the thongs hastily into his pocket and hid his discovery under the remaining foliage of the Granadillo shrub. As Javier approached with the bag of florentine biscuits, he found Mateo back scraping earth away from the shrub. Everything looked perfectly normal.

'I will not have one of those right now, thank you, Javier.'

'There are just four left. Would you like me to take them back to the van?'

'No. No, it's okay. You take them home to your mama and brothers. We'll be packing up for the day in an hour, and I can manage until then. After one of Maria's paellas I shall sleep in my hammock the shade of the banana palms in my garden. This kind of outdoor heavy work is better done in the autumn months, not high summer. Go, tell everyone that at midday we will finish for the day. Back tomorrow at six o'clock as usual.'

Mateo waited until Javier was back with Ramon, slipped the box into his cold bag, and used the wall for support as he struggled to his feet. He stood for a moment, allowing the blood supply in his legs to circulate again, then sat on the wall looking out over the channel while the cramp in his legs eased. Behind him, a little further up the hillside, his team were back at work after their short break. He smiled as he heard them whistling to each other using the language of Silbo Gomero, unique to La Gomera. It was good that the young people were keeping it alive. Too many old customs from his youth had already gone by the wayside.

As he sat, he saw a ferry leave Los Cristianos on its way to San Sebastian harbour. He loved to watch their progress across to his island. It took about an hour for the journey, and on this day the channel was calm; it would be a good crossing. He found it relaxing to observe the boats in the channel, but watching was one thing, being on them was another. He had no love of being on a boat of any kind. He much preferred to be on dry land where he felt safe. It wasn't that he suffered with seasickness, he was just frightened that the boat would sink and he would drown. He had never learned to swim. That was stupid. He knew that. Both his brothers could swim and always encouraged him to join them in the sea. He shuddered at the memory of Juan trying to pull him into the ocean. No, if God wanted him to swim he would have given him gills and fins. And, although he loved watching the boats, there was always a hint of dread. There were already plenty of wrecks on the sea bed, and he was always relieved when the ferry pulled into port.

However, if the box did contain anything of interest, he would have to take a ferry to Tenerife, and a bus to Santiago. Senor Taylor-Owen, the historian, had paid him well for special items he had dug up before. If he was right, and the box was at least three hundred years old, and found in the grounds of this particular villa with its legendary reputation, there must be something very precious in it that someone wanted to preserve, otherwise it would probably have been destroyed in the fire, wouldn't it? Perhaps this would be the one find that would provide him with enough money to finally retire. If there was anything of value he would use some of the reward money to buy Maria a lace shawl to wear to church on Sundays. She would like that. The one she wore now had a few holes in the lace and was becoming discoloured with age. Yes, that would be a very nice gift.

He looked down at the stubborn Granadillo. Damn the thing. It could stay there until tomorrow, and then he would only spend a few more minutes on it. If it didn't come out after that, someone else younger and stronger than him could pull it out.

How quickly an hour went by. While he had been sitting there looking out to sea a whole sixty minutes had flown. He gave a sad little laugh. His life had been like that. It seemed like just a moment ago that he was a boy running around in this garden with his brothers. Those were happy days.

The sound of a van door being slammed shut broke into his thoughts. Ah, the lads were almost ready to leave. Luis Garcia, Javier's cousin, was standing with Ramon and Javier waiting patiently for him.

'Yes, yes, I am coming, but do not expect me to walk uphill quickly. You young people always want to do everything in a hurry. Well, my old bones will get there but in my own time.'

'Would you like me to carry your bag, Mateo?' Javier called down.

Mateo struggled to his feet. 'No, I am fine. I can carry a few tools. I am not spent yet, but thank you for the offer.' No. He would not like

Javier to carry his bag. He clutched the cold bag a little closer to his side as he plodded up the path to meet them. At the top, Ramon held the passenger side door of the van open for Mateo to climb in. Luis and Javier clambered into the back to sit on wide cushions on the van floor amongst the gardening tools, sacks and coils of rope. Ramon started up the engine and they headed down the rough track that joined a serviceable road halfway down the hillside. Mateo looked out of the window and smiled. He would be home soon and could open the box away from prying eyes.

Chapter Twelve

Gozo : The Cornucopia Hotel

Jake put on his sunglasses then lifted Luke's case and walked alongside the wall until he came to a doorway, but instead of going inside, he beckoned to Luke to follow him across the road.

'Here, come and take a look at this. All you've seen of the island so far is the harbour, streets and houses.' Jake crossed over to the other side of the road, put the case down and leant against a railing. 'This is Gozo. This is why I stay.'

Luke, was not wearing his sunglasses. With the car having a very efficient shaded windscreen he had not needed them. But, on getting out of the car he realised very quickly that now they were necessary, and slipped them on. As he joined Jake at the railing, and looked at the view without squinting, it momentarily took his breath away. He knew Xaghra was on a hill but had not appreciated just how high they were until he looked over the railing and saw how much the land dropped away beneath them. Across the valley, he could see a small town with a very large church and to his right, he could see the sea. It was as though he was on a high balcony from which he could see over a vast area of the island, with its numerous terraced fields separated by dry stone walls constructed with the same honey-coloured stone as the buildings. In some fields he could see sheep, and goats, one had a small herd of cows, and several allotments had chickens scratching around. Cacti grew in hundreds of clumps around the fields, and there were more trees than he would have imagined on a mediterranean island that had little rainfall over the year.

'What's the hill over there with the statue on it?'

'That's the hill above Marsalforn. It's only a little over a couple of miles away. I'll take you there, tomorrow if you like. It'll only take about ten minutes. But first we'll go to Xlendi. It's a great little bay, sheltered, so it would be a good place to let you have a crack at diving.'

' I thought we were going somewhere else, the Blue ...'

'Oh, yeah, I forgot that. Hmm, the Blue Lagoon's probably better, snorkelling will be easier for you. We'll do Marsalforn and Xlendi the day after.'

'Huh, and I came here for a rest.'

Jake laughed. 'You'll still get your rest, Bro. It'll just be different ... and you also came here to see the sights, remember?'

'Yeah, we'll see.' He pointed at some trees with twisted trunks. 'Are those olive trees?'

'Yes, most of them, plus there's tamarisks, carobs, almond, palms, of course, pomegranates, figs and a few others.'

'I'm surprised it's so green.'

'Oh yes, there's plenty of vegetation here. At this time of year there's still water in the reservoirs from the winter months,' Jake said still looking into the distance. Luke was glad the conversation had not turned to Anjelika. 'Farmers grow cauliflowers, artichokes, fennel, potatoes, lettuce, onions, cereal crops, mostly for their livestock, and quite a lot of farmers keep beehives. The island is self-sufficient. You know if it hadn't been for the people of Gozo, Malta might well have had to yield to the Germans in World War Two?'

'No, I didn't know that. I knew the Maltese people had a really hard time of it, but they held out, and the whole island was awarded the George Cross, but I didn't know that.'

'Okay, let's get you checked in and settled, get that beer and some lunch. I never got around to having a proper breakfast.'

A short while later, having been welcomed by the reception staff at the hotel, with his case stashed in the office while he waited to check in, Luke ordered a couple of hamburgers and two Cisk lagers which were served at a table on the lower pool terrace. A small ginger cat, padded up to their table, purred around Luke's legs for a few moments, then settled down in the shade of the table to sleep.

There were a few people on the upper pool terrace, but apart from the occasional snatch of conversation, laughter or the gentle lapping of water against the side of the pool, the terrace area, surrounded by the sides of the hotel, was quiet and peaceful. Two blocks of two-storey buildings in an 'L' shape contained just forty-eight rooms. The other two sides were the main building of the hotel and the high wall at the far end of the upper pool terrace. The overall atmosphere was one of complete relaxation. As he sipped his lager, Luke looked across to the block of rooms on the other side of the pool where a member of staff was servicing a room at the end of the veranda that ran along the length of the block.

'You know, you haven't changed a bit in the four years since we've seen each other,' said Luke, 'and I realised when I was in the bathroom this morning, that the face in the mirror was really like dad, but you're more like mum. The shape of your eyes, and the colour ... hazel, I think they call it, is just like hers, and you've got her fair hair. My hair's starting to go grey at the sides, just like dad's. His brown hair started to go grey in his middle thirties too, and I have his brown eyes.'

'Yeah.' Jake took a gulp of his lager. 'I noticed you'd grown older, since we last met.' He laughed at Luke's frown. 'Got a few of the old grey bits in your eyebrows too, and what's with the glasses? You never wore glasses before.'

'Too much close work and being on computer screens for too long.'

'And you've definitely spread a little.' He patted his stomach. Is that what work's done to you too?'

'What is this, make Luke feel old time?' He grimaced. 'But you're right. As I said before, working all hours, no regular eating times, take-aways at the desk, and precious little time for exercise. I suppose it was only to be expected that I'd get flabby, but all that's going to change over the next month or two.'

'You definitely need to go diving. On average you burn around six or maybe seven hundred calories every hour while you're diving. The amount of calories burned can vary depending on the temperature of the water, and how deep you go, due to the hard work your body's coping with. Obviously, you lose more body heat faster in colder water, even with a wet or dry suit. Then there's the activity of getting into and out of a boat, if you use one. Swimming against a current takes effort, and you've got heavy dive kit, plus you're swimming.'

At the sound of a door closing, Jake looked up at the veranda. The staff member who had been working on the unoccupied room, was now heading to the steps that led down to the terrace.

'That could be your room ready now,' said Jake.

'Could be. They'll let me know ... but I hadn't realised diving ...' Whatever he was going to say was interrupted by the unexpected arrival of a small squadron of bickering sparrows that flew at breakneck speed into the abundant tangle of the same, pink-flowered climbing plant that grew on the walls outside. One or two at a time, the birds darted out to land on the tiled terrace and hopped around the table legs, clearly looking for any lunchtime crumbs that might end up on the floor, and seemingly unconcerned by the humans. Luke tried to count them, but gave up as they flew in and out, and refused to settle in one place long enough. Jake nudged him and pointed towards the floor just in front of Luke's chair. The cat had crawled out from under the table, low to the ground in a normal feline hunting position, and was watching the sparrows, wide eyed, tail lashing. Head low, it chattered at the birds, waiting for one to come close enough to catch. Of course, none did. They were off before he could get close enough.

Luke laughed as the cat sat up with a definite look of frustration etched on its face. 'Apart from the sparrows, and the few background noises, it's amazing how quiet this place is, bearing mind there's a road out the front. After all the years of working sometimes from seven a.m. to midnight, weekends too, this is exactly what I need. Stress free, warm, quiet.'

'Speaking of stress, Luke, I guess we need to talk about the elephant in the room.'

Luke turned away from watching the cat, set his elbows on the table, clasped his hands together and rested his chin on them. 'Hmm, yes, I suppose we do.'

'I thought I noticed an atmosphere in the apartment when I got back last night. What happened?'

'I wouldn't have said anything if you hadn't asked, but almost as soon as you went out the door, she came on to me.'

Jake turned away, sat back in his chair, and gnawed at his bottom lip. Luke noticed Jake had tightened his fist. Tense, Jake nodded and turned back to Luke.

Pre-empting Jake speaking, Luke said, 'I turned her down flat. I hope you know that.'

Jake nodded again. 'Yeah, of course I do.' He swallowed the dregs of the beer in his glass and stood up. 'I'm going to the bar. Want something stronger this time?'

'Why not.' Luke handed over his empty glass, and watched Jake walk back into the hotel bar. Did Jake really believe him? If so, why was it so easy? He was pretty sure it wasn't the first time Anjelika had behaved that way. She was too confident, but if she had then why was Jake still with her? It didn't make sense.

Jake returned with two double single malt whiskies. He sat down, head downcast looking into his glass. He held it between both hands as if trying to warm it. Luke waited for him to speak. Jake opened his mouth and closed it again as a couple walked out of the hotel and across to the outside staircase. Once they were too far away to hear, he said, 'I do completely believe you. It's not the first time she's tried it on with other guys,' he took a mouthful of whisky, 'and I'm pretty sure she's had an affair ...'

'... But you've only been together how long ... what, maybe six months?'

'Hmm, a little longer. It happened soon after we got together. You'd think with a new relationship we'd both be so ... you know, into each other that we wouldn't want anyone else wouldn't you?' He pressed his lips tightly together, and looked down into his glass again. 'I think we'd been together about a month, when she started seeing an old boyfriend again behind my back. He had money, a yacht, a fancy apartment in Victoria, you know all the fuckin' trimmings. There'd be times when I couldn't get her on her mobile, or when she'd say she was going to see her ... uncle,' he looked up at Luke, 'she does actually have an uncle in Xewkija, but when she came back, she told me the truth, cried, said she was sorry and begged me to forgive her.'

'So you took her back, but why?'

'God only knows. I spent a couple of days away from her. Looking back, I … well, I suppose I had too much time to think, and I missed her, I thought I loved her. So yes, like an idiot, I forgave her. She behaved herself for a while, but then, the flirting with other men began again, little things to begin with. You know, the odd eyelash flutter … you know, you've seen it. Then there were the little *friendly* hugs with other men that lasted just a bit longer than necessary.'

'But no more going to see her uncle, or not being able to get her on the phone?'

'No.' Jake shook his head. 'No, none of that, but what she did this morning was just not on. I'm sorry she behaved like that with you, and I really don't know what got into her. I've never seen her do anything quite so … so … blatant.'

'So what are you going to do …'

'Excuse me, Mr Rutherford …'

A young woman from the reception team appeared at Luke's side. 'I'm sorry to disturb you both, but your room is now ready. You're in Room Twenty-Seven. I'll have your case taken up to your room for you.'

'That's great, thank you,' said Luke as she handed him the key, and walked back inside the hotel.

'Well, it looks as though I'm settled.' He looked across the table at his forlorn brother. 'But what are you going to do?'

Jake took a moment to think, then stood up. 'I'm going back to have it out with her. Find out just what the hell was going through her mind when …' He walked towards the door leading into the hotel. He stopped, turned around. 'It's good to have you here, Luke. I'm just sorry that this has happened. It's been embarrassing for us both. Hmm … anyway, I'll leave you to get unpacked. Get some rest, you look tired.'

'Yeah, well, I didn't get much sleep last night.'

'Will you be okay on your own tonight? I think Anjelika and I might be having a long conversation.'

'Yeah, I'm fine. You get off, I'm all grown up now and I can manage my unpacking, and it's pretty warm, what d'you reckon, twenty-eight Centigrade? I'm thinking maybe a swim before dinner, then get an early night …' He paused as a couple he estimated to be in their fifties, draped with towels over their swimming costumes, nodded a greeting as they went by, and headed up the stairs to the second floor rooms. 'You just do what you have to and I'll see you in the morning.'

'Yeah, but not too early, eh? I'll pick you up say ten-thirty.'

'Sounds good to me, and it's Comino?'

'Yeah, I think so, I'll remember the snorkelling gear.'

Luke frowned. 'Oh whoopie-sodding-do. I'll really look forward to it.'

'Chicken.' Jake chuckled as he walked towards the exit.

Chapter Thirteen

La Gomera : Mateo Takes the Ferry

It was a little before seven o'clock on a bright, clear morning when Mateo parked his old SEAT Arosa at San Sebastian harbour. He was there to board the seven-fifteen ferry across the La Gomera Channel to Los Cristianos, on Tenerife. The ferry engines were running and car passengers were already driving on board through the huge sea doors at the rear. Mateo had decided not to take the car on the ferry. He rarely crossed to Tenerife but knew that the roads were much busier over there than they were on La Gomera. No, the bus was better for him. Let someone else have the responsibility of driving in fast-moving traffic.

Anxious about the crossing, Mateo hesitated for a few moments before getting out of the car, but seeing people walking up the steps onto the ferry, he knew if he didn't go then, he never would. He looked down at the bag containing the box he had discovered in the villa garden. He had not opened it, that would be for Senor Taylor-Owen to do, but he was intrigued by what it might contain, and what his reward might be. That thought spurred him to get out of the car and head to the ferry. A few moments later he stood in the queue of workers and sightseers, at the bottom of the ferry steps waiting for his turn to board. He could hear his heartbeat pulsating in his temple, and took a handkerchief out of his trouser pocket to wipe his sweaty palms. The rubbery smell of the diesel biofuel, made him feel nauseous, but he suspected that his anxiety about being on deep water had probably added to that. He had never been able to conquer that fear, and he wondered whether whatever was in the box was really going to be worth all this distress.

Maria had tried to get him to have some breakfast earlier that morning, saying that a little bulk would stabilise the acid in his empty stomach. She thought he was stressed because of the work on the villa garden, that it was too hard for him. He had not told her about the box or his plans for the day. He had snapped at her for fussing, but was now sorry for it. She was only trying to help but he just couldn't face eating anything at that time. But she was probably right. He managed a smile. He had to admit that Maria was usually right, and he owed her an apology, and perhaps a box of her favourite almond cakes, tortas chasneras, as a peace offering. Yes, that would do very well.

His thoughts turned to the purpose of his trip. Senor Taylor-Owen sounded quite excited about it when they had talked on the telephone. Although the Englishman was aware of Mateo's anxiety and had offered to go to see him at his home in the pretty clifftop village of Agulo, Mateo did not want anyone to know his business. He was well known around the island and, no matter where he went, he could always bump into someone he knew. No, he may not like being on water, but his business was private and it suited him better to go to Senor Taylor-Owen.

The queue had moved along and he was almost at the steps. He thought about turning back, but resisted the urge to run away. Instinctively, with his right hand, he touched his forehead and his stomach, then from the left to the right of his chest, making the sign of the Cross, and muttered a little prayer asking God to keep him safe, as he joined the other foot passengers queuing to embark. At the steps he hesitated, a moment of panic, but behind him people were waiting for him to move. With a deep breath, he forced himself onto the steps, and just kept putting one foot in front of the other, steeling himself to think about nothing else other than taking the box to Senor Taylor-Owen, and what he hoped to gain from the journey.

On deck, he told himself that he was being a stupid old man, and that the ferries were perfectly safe, the sea was calm, the morning was already warming up and the sea breeze was gentle, but on deck he could not avoid looking down at the gently lapping water and he froze, wishing he was anywhere else.

A few moments later, the engine noises changed, the sea doors closed, the hawsers mooring the ferry to the harbour bolardos, were released and pulled on board by members of the crew, and the ferry slowly pulled out of the harbour.

Mateo wanted to be on deck where the air was fresh, but wherever he stood he could see the reflection of the sun on the calmly shifting wavelets. He had to agree that the water, in all its changing blue and green with flashes of gold, and ripples of white foam, was beautiful. But enough was more than enough, and he decided to go inside for the fifty minute trip for a coffee and a cake; maybe a donut or a croissant (cruasán), either would do.

Having bought a newspaper before he drove out of Agulo that morning, once he had bought his coffee and, not being able to make up his mind between a donut and a croissant, he bought both, Mateo found a vacant table in the restaurant in a line of several all served by one long bench seat. At the next table, a man was typing furiously on his laptop, and on the other a young couple sat staring into each other's eyes and holding hands. The queue at the food counter was growing, and Mateo was pleased that he had gone inside when he did. He put the bag containing the box down under the table between his feet, where it would be less conspicuous, opened the newspaper and settled down to read it while having his coffee and breakfast. The time went quickly and before he knew it, an announcement over the public address system notified passengers that they were coming into Los Cristianos, and should collect their belongings together.

Mateo, picked the bag up from under the table, slipped his newspaper inside and joined the throng of people heading to the exit as the ferry stopped at the quayside. That was when he heard a voice he recognised.

'Mateo! Hey, Mateo.'

He turned to see his neighbour, Enzo Flores, pushing through the crowd to reach him. Mateo swore under his breath. He had hoped to travel to Tenerife and back without meeting anyone he knew, even though he knew it would be unlikely. Oh well, he would be friendly, but ditch Enzo as soon as he could.

'Have you absconded for the day, Mateo? Should you not be at the villa again today?'

'No, no. I am giving my old back a rest today. My team are there and they can work faster than me these days.'

'So what takes you to Tenerife?'

Mateo gave a little laugh and gave a conspiratorial wink. 'I think I may have found a lady friend, Enzo, but do not tell Maria, or I will never hear the last of it. She will start nagging me about another woman in my life and that I will want her to move out, which is nonsense.' Mateo leaned in towards Enzo. 'To be honest, I'm not sure about this anyway. I am probably too old, too set in my ways for a romance, and even if it does go well, I would not want Maria upset. She is seventy-five and I am seventy-two, don't know that I could live with another lady now.' He grinned. 'But it is an adventure.'

'Well I am heading to Puerto de la Cruz to see my daughter, you know, Gabriela, she is married to the doctor. I will be staying there for a few days.' He looked at his watch. 'I am sorry, Mateo, I will have to rush or I will miss my bus.'

'That's fine, my friend. Off you go. Enjoy your visit and give Gabriela my love.'

Enzo began to push his way through the crowd, then turned back. 'I will. Enjoy your date.'

Mateo just smiled and waved to Enzo, relieved that he was not going to have to spend any more time with his friend. Having to keep answering questions about this invented woman might have become awkward, but it was the first thing he thought of. Enzo might have been in a hurry, but Mateo had about thirty minutes to wait for his bus to Puerto de Santiago. So no rush, he would stroll to the bus station.

Disembarking from what had been a cool and shaded restaurant area and walkway to the exit, Mateo realised how much warmer it had become while he was on the ferry. Yes, he would take his time, buy a bottle of water and finish reading his paper during the journey on the bus which would take a little over an hour. Senor Taylor-Owen was expecting him about ten o'clock, and he was running on time.

Chapter Fourteen

Comino : The Blue Lagoon

Looking down from the top of the hill at Mgarr, Luke gazed at the pretty, colourful and incredibly busy harbour. Within the shelter of the breakwater constructed of huge boulders, were several pontoons for mooring yachts and other pleasure boats, and numerous brightly painted fishing boats. For a moment his view of the harbour was blocked by shops and houses, but a little further along, he had a clear view.

'What's the catamaran?' Luke pointed to a long, mainly green and white painted twin-hulled vessel that was leisurely coming into the harbour.

'That's the fast ferry. It goes directly into Valletta Grand Harbour. Takes about forty-five minutes.'

'But, if it's the fast ferry, why does it take longer?'

Jake frowned at his brother. 'How long did it take us to drive to Cirkewwa from the airport last night?' They had reached a car park on the other side of the harbour from the ferry quay.

Luke nodded. 'Got ya. The Channel ferries take around thirty minutes or so, but then you have to drive across the island.'

'Yep. The fast ferry's pretty good.' Jake got out of the car and Luke followed. Over the roof of the car, Jake said, 'There's a café on board, it's comfortable...only costs about seven Euros, and if you're lucky you can get out on the sun deck.' He walked around to the back of the car while Luke put on his sunglasses and gazed across the harbour. So many boats, so many colours, the sun shining down onto the clear, and as far as Luke could see, clean harbour, it made for a breathtaking sight.

'Are you ready?' Jake handed Luke one of three bags he had taken from the boot. One that he had hoisted onto his back, looked quite heavy.

'What's in there?' Something about Jake's grin made Luke suspicious. 'Do you have the snorkelling stuff?'

'Oh, yeah. Course I do?' Jake walked ahead of Luke, who followed wondering what his brother was up to, onto a long pontoon where expensive looking speedboats, motorboats and yachts were moored. They were about halfway along when Jake stopped at a small, white-painted motorboat with a blue canopy.

'This is us.' Jake climbed on board and dumped the bags on the floor. The heavy one made a clanging noise as it landed on the floor. Luke frowned.

'This isn't yours, is it?'

Jake 'No. I've borrowed it from the dive centre for the day. There's some food, a bottle of water and a couple of cans of lager in the cold bag, there's sun cream and the snorkelling gear is in the black plastic bag.'

'And what about that one?' Luke pointed to the large heavy bag.

'Nothing much. Just some safety stuff in case we need it.' Jake turned away, switched on the engine, checked a couple of the dials, asked Luke to untie the mooring line, then took the wheel and slowly drove the boat away from the pontoon, and out of the harbour towards the open sea. 'It gets a little bumpy as you lose the shelter of the harbour walls and go out into open water. But it's a good day again, the sea's calm, and it's only a short trip to Comino.'

Luke made himself comfortable on the seat at the back of the boat, his arm resting on the side of the hull being splashed by sea spray. While Jake was occupied with driving the boat, Luke suddenly realised that they had not spoken about how things had gone between Jake and Anjelika during the previous evening.

On going to his room, Luke had been very pleased with the cleanliness and the comfort, and having booked to stay for a month, he was confident that there was nothing he had seen, that would make him want to move elsewhere. After unpacking, he had gone for a swim in the larger pool on the upper terrace. The water was cold, but the pool area was spotlessly clean. He showered afterwards, changed into a smart pair of chinos and a clean T-shirt, then headed to the bar for a drink before dinner. Not really wanting a beer which would bag him up before his meal, he asked the barman, Zephaniah, for a Glenfiddich with ice, which he took out to the lower pool terrace again, and soon found himself chatting with a very nice couple, also in their middle thirties. Janice and Ian were from West Bromwich, a neighbouring town to Birmingham, and supported rival football teams, so they had plenty to talk about.

When the couple went in to the hotel restaurant, an unusual but very attractive, circular high-vaulted stone ceiling room, Janice and Ian invited Luke to eat with them rather than having to sit alone, and the conversation on Aston Villa continued for another half an hour or so, before Janice asked Luke why he was there alone. Normally reticent to discuss his personal life with strangers, the Glenfiddich and the excellent local red wine, loosened Luke's tongue and he told them all about his break up with Ellie, his redundancy, his plan to travel and meeting up with his brother again. He omitted the incident with Anjelika. There was no need to talk about that.

After dinner, the trio finished their wine on the lower pool terrace and got into conversation with another couple of similar age, Dave and Rosie from Glasgow. As dusk fell, the ginger cat appeared on the terrace again, and they all made a great deal of fuss him before he sloped off to another table where a woman dropped little bits of cheese on the floor for him. By the time Luke went to his room at ten o'clock, he knew that Janice was a nurse, Ian a car mechanic, Dave worked in project management and had a job similar to the one Luke had just left, and Rosie worked in the John Lewis store at Princes Square shopping mall in Glasgow. Neither couple had any children yet, but thought the time was getting closer for them to have their families.

Luke fell asleep very quickly that night due probably to a combination of travelling, the lack of sleep the night before, the very good dinner, and red wine. Even though the hotel was busy, when Luke's head hit his pillow, he slept right through the night completely undisturbed by anyone, until eight o'clock the next morning.

Now here he was on his way to Comino and to snorkelling for the first time. He looked across the channel and saw the ferry leave

Cirkewwa heading for Mgarr, and there were quite a few other boats nearby. In the distance he saw a paraglider. That was not for him. Being that high up and tugged along by a tiny boat below, was not his idea of fun.

Ahead he could see the opening of the channel between Comino and what looked like a huge rock wall on the other side. There was a clear demarcation in the colour of the water that seemed to glow in the sunlight; it was truly turquoise. As they turned into the lagoon, Luke was surprised to see so many other boats. He guessed there were about thirty of various sizes. There were two fairly large tourist-trip vessels, displaying the same company logo, moored side by side. Several other small boats had docked against the rocks, but many more were anchored out in the open water. People were snorkelling, swimming, diving in from boats or off the jetty, sunbathing on towels, airbeds, and deckchairs and little ones were paddling holding adult hands as they splashed and giggled on the edge of the shore. Across the water, the islet known as Little Comino, had a soft, golden sandy beach, and a passageway that led through to the open sea.

Jake slowed the boat to navigate between the other boats and swimmers, a pair of scuba divers, and the engine sound decreased to a slow chug rather than a growl. He eased the boat into a free space, cut the engine, leapt onto the jetty and secured the boat by rope to a metal ring.

'There's a lot of people here. I don't know why but I imagined it would be quieter than this,' Luke said looking around at the activity in the lagoon.

'You get a lot of tour boats here, from Mgarr, or Xlendi, Cirkewwa and more, and if you think this is busy, you want to see it in the holiday season. It's a popular tourist spot. The tour boats bring people out, let them splash around for a while, provide lunch, then they'll stay on for another hour or so to let them back in the water for a while, then take them back. Typically, you're talking about a three-hour visit. On the way back they'll make stops at bays that are more convenient for their passengers. Some may have boarded at Xlendi but they stay nearer to Mgarr, so they'll get dropped off there instead.'

Luke pointed across to Little Comino. 'That little cave, kind of tunnel across there, where the sea comes in to where the sand seems lower, and leaves a little pool, looks familiar but I can't think why. I just feel that it I've seen it somewhere.'

Jake hunkered down, unzipped the bag with the snorkelling kits and tossed a mask with attached breathing tube to Luke. 'Yeah, you probably have seen it before. Did you ever see that film Troy, with Sean Bean, Julie Christie, Brad Pitt...?'

'...Brian Cox, Orlando Bloom, yes, I did.'

'That scene with Julie Christie and Brad Pitt was shot there. You know, when his character, Achilles, goes to talk to his mother about whether he should go to Troy or not.'

'Yes, I remember. Isn't she collecting shells or something like that.'

'You got it. Malta and Gozo are used a lot for film settings. Films like Gladiator, Robin Williams' Popeye...the film crew built Sweethaven village at a small bay just outside Mellieha, and it's still there for tourists to visit. World War Z, one of the Jurassic Park films, even some scenes in Game of Thrones were filmed on the Maltese islands.'

Luke looked around, 'I think I can see why.'

'Anyway, ready for snorkelling?'

Luke looked a little reluctant but said, 'Well, I said I would, so let's do it.'

'Right. So here's your mask. When you get into the water, spit into it then rinse it with seawater, that will help stop it from steaming up. Make sure the strap is tight enough not to slip off or allow leaks, but not uncomfortable. The pressure of the water against the mask will help it stay on. You don't have to swim as such, just keep paddling your legs like you would if you were doing the crawl stroke, and you'll float along, you can give yourself a little push along with your arms if you need to. I'll be right alongside you. Oh, yeah, remember, the water's cold. Probably better to jump straight in instead of walking out, or you might change your mind.' He rummaged in the bag again and brought out two pairs of, what Jake called, wet shoes. 'I guessed on your shoe size, as I thought you're about the same size as me. We're going to be walking over some rocks before we get to the water. The soles are good for gripping slippery surfaces and you won't get cuts.'

'You think of everything,' said Luke, trying on the fabric and rubber shoes.

'Experience, bro. It helps to be prepared.'

Luke looked around at the number of people who were already in, and seemingly enjoying the water, so it didn't look as though it was too cold and thought Jake was joking. A few moments later Luke discovered he wasn't. Although getting into the water was a bit of a shock to the system, Luke soon became accustomed to the temperature, and although there were boatloads of people there, there was still plenty of room to swim about freely without getting in anyone's way. Luke allowed himself to float, face down on the surface of the water, and found breathing through the snorkel tube was not as difficult as he thought it would be, but he was pretty sure it would not be so easy diving.

Jake appeared at his side and handed Luke a disposable underwater camera. That got a thumbs up from Luke and for the next fifteen minutes, he lost himself in the sheer enchantment of the marine life below. The freedom he now had to try things he had never done before, convinced him he had made the right choice in making this dramatic change in his life and, wished he had not devoted so much time to work; he was learning that career wasn't everything.

At that moment, he wished that Ellie had been brave, or spontaneous enough to have been there to enjoy what he now had. But her practical, pragmatic, nature denied her all this scenery, this joie de vivre, as the French called it.

Jake nudged him. 'Come on, water baby, let's get some lunch. Your toes are probably wrinkling. There's time to get in again later, if you want.'

Luke followed Jake out of the water to the jetty and onto their boat, while trying to avoid making it sway as they boarded. Jake threw him a towel.

'If you're not going to sit under the canopy, cover your neck, back and shoulders with the towel and that beanie hat, for now. You'll burn in this sun pretty quickly without sun block, especially with the salt from the seawater on your skin.' Luke did as he was told. Jake was right, the temperature had risen while they were in the water. It was certainly hot.

Jake opened the cold box, took out two cans of Cisk lager, and two packs of cheese and pickle sandwiches. They sat back, relaxed and content just to watch the world and his wife having fun in the water.

'So how often do you take people diving, and does it make a good living?'

'I work mostly with one dive centre, and the money's not brilliant, but it's enough to survive on. Anjelika's money helps of course.' He paused, looked down at his feet, then out across the bay. Luke wondered at the hesitation.

'There are other ways of making money if you want to through diving, and knowing the right people, which I do.' He looked away again.

'How d'you mean?'

'Oh, ways and means. I help out sometimes when…stuff needs moving, let's put it that way. Better you don't get involved, but it's helped me to put some money aside, and I've made contacts that are…useful.'

Luke said nothing for a moment, troubled by Jake's almost confession.

'I take it moving this stuff isn't exactly legal?'

'Hmm. Well, I did have some problems, money problems a while back, and…well, a mate of Anjelika's kind of helped me out, so I owed him a favour or two.'

'Is this dangerous?'

Jake looked down at the beer can in his hand, took a last gulp, crushed the can and threw it onto the deck. 'Probably not. Anyway, d'you want to go in again or, should we head back?'

No longer in the mood for going back into the water, Luke said they should head back to Xlendi. The brothers said very little to each other on the return journey, Luke confused and worried about what Jake had told him, and Jake wondering whether he should have kept his mouth shut.

Chapter Fifteen

Tenerife : Edward Taylor-Owen

Mateo was the first traveller to board the route 460 bus to Consultorio via Estación Costa Adeje. Not having the App on his mobile phone, and planning to return home to Agulo later that day, he had bought a round-trip ticket. On boarding he showed his ticket to the driver, then moved along the bus to take a seat at the rear, where he felt he would have more privacy. Taking a window seat, he placed his bag, containing the precious box between himself and the side of the bus. With the aid of efficient air conditioning, the bus was very cool. Usually, Mateo would keep his jacket on when travelling on the new buses, but this time he was more concerned with keeping the box safe, than the temporary discomfort of goosebumps, and he removed his jacket to conceal the bag. While people boarded the bus, Mateo watched other buses enter and exit the bus station, and looked at his watch a number of times eager to get on their way. He was impatient to see Senor Taylor-Owen. He sighed peevishly as a few more people boarded the bus; a young couple, two single men, a woman with two young children, one in a pushchair, and an elderly lady carrying two full shopping bags who struggled to get on board. She was helped by a passing young man and the driver, who took her bags from her and helped her to a seat at the very front of the bus. No-one sat near Mateo, for which he was very grateful. At last the driver started the engine and the bus slowly headed out onto the main road and into the fast-flowing traffic for the journey which would take a little over half an hour.

As they passed through the town and out onto the dual carriageway, despite the cool air, Mateo's eyelids grew heavy and he dozed as they drove through the busy traffic, passed Siam Park, the huge water kingdom at Playa de las Americas, and he only saw one coastal town, Torviscas, on the way to Costa Adeje. The other villages he slept through until they pulled in to the bus station at Costa Adeje. On exiting the bus, he looked for the 477, which would take him on to Puerto de Santiago, and then terminate at Los Gigantes a little further along the coast. His short wait for the second bus gave him enough time to buy a take-away coffee, which he took on board and drank to keep him awake for the slightly longer part of the journey, which took a little under an hour.

They drove by the imposing pink Abama Hotel, which he had heard celebrities visited, and he knew someone who married on the beach there a couple of years ago. By all accounts, it was a wonderfully planned occasion, with fireworks when it grew dark. A little further along the coastal road they passed through villages San Juan and Alcala, with its pretty little bay, through Playa de la Arena and finally into Puerto de Santiago, and to the Bus stop in Avenida Oceano.

Clutching the bag tightly, Mateo alighted from the bus and into the warm air again. He stretched. His old body quickly stiffened if he sat too long. The bus drove off and Mateo turned to the right and walked along to the third white painted villa, then down the long, red-tiled driveway surrounded by gently swaying palm trees and variegated American agaves with their long broad leaves edged with yellow. The door opened and a young man Mateo had never seen before stood waiting for him. As Mateo reached the door he opened his mouth to speak, but the young man pre-empted him.

'You must be Mateo Moreno.'

Mateo nodded.

'Please come in, Mateo. Edward, I mean Mr Taylor-Owen, is expecting you. He is waiting for you on the terrace.' Mateo entered into a long, cool hallway, and waited for the young man to close the door behind him.

'It is good to meet you...you don't mind me calling you Mateo?'

Mateo shook his head. 'No, as that is my name.' He was a little wary of this young, and very handsome young man, with his medium-toned almost olive-coloured complexion, dark curly hair and surprisingly green eyes. He certainly worked out though, his clinging white T-shirt and knee-length frayed denim shorts revealed plenty of muscle.

'Thank you, please follow me.' He gave Mateo a wide, welcoming smile, and gestured towards the glass double doors at the far end of the hallway. Mateo was impressed by the ornate blue and tan patterned floor tiles, and several floor-standing plant pots with a variety of tall plants Mateo recognised as *ficus benjamina* (weeping fig), *Chamaedorea elegans* (Parlour Palm), and *Monstera deliciosa* (Swiss Cheese Plant). As they headed towards the rear of the villa, the young man said, 'My name is Antonio Martin, and I am Edward's assistant.'

Mateo just nodded, but wondered if the title of assistant was another word for a different kind of relationship.

'Thank you, Antonio, I am pleased to meet you.' Mateo paused. 'How long have you been with Senor Taylor-Owen? I know we have not met before and I have seen Senor Taylor-Owen on a few occasions.'

'A little under three months now. We met at a fascinating talk that Mr Tay...Edward gave on local shipwrecks at the British School.' Antonio opened the door and stood back to allow Mateo through to the pool terrace where Edward Taylor-Owen appeared to be reading one of several documents on the table in front of him.

'Edward, Mateo is here,' Antonio said, as he walked a little behind Mateo.

In the shade of a blue and white striped awning, the historian was so engrossed in the papers spread out on the table, that he momentarily seemed a little surprised at the interruption. He frowned as he looked over his glasses at the new arrival, then recognising Mateo, he gave a wide smile and stood up to welcome his visitor, clasping Mateo's outstretched hand with both of his.

'Mateo, my friend. It's been ages.'

'It certainly has Senor Taylor-Owen.'

'Oh, come now, we have known each other long enough now for you to stop calling me Senor Taylor-Owen, it's too much of a mouthful, please call me Edward. Come, take a seat...or would you like to take a look at the new scenery?'

Mateo looked across the terrace with its kidney-shaped, small but very adequate pool, and the surrounding garden. He was impressed that the blue and tan tiles extended from the house to the pool terrace and were edged by low, white-painted kerbstones.

'If it is alright with you, Sen...Edward, I would like to have a look around the garden of your new home. Your previous house was bright and well decorated, but this seems a step up from that one and, from what I can see so far it is very beautiful. How long have you been here?'

The light sea breeze ruffled Edward's bristly greying hair, and he stroked his beard that still had streaks the dark hair of his younger days. His hair and beard reminded Mateo of a badger.

'Next month it will be a year since I moved in. As you know, I had always kept an eye on the villas in this avenue, and when this one came up for sale, I was in a position financially to be able to buy it. You will remember, Mateo, my previous home here was in the middle of the town, but I always wanted to wake up and see the sea. A couple of my books have sold very well over the last few years, and I put the money aside for when I found the right property, and here we are. Come, let me show you around.' He turned to Antonio who was still standing by the table. 'While I am showing Mateo around, would you get lunch ready, please?' Mateo turned to see Antonio heading back into the house.

Edward said, 'I am sure after your long bus journey, you must be ready for some refreshment.'

'Thank you, yes.' He was more than happy to accept the historian's hospitality. Yes, he had travelled a long way to see him, but he also had that long journey back again. As they walked on, he realised that the piece of ground where the agaves and palms grew was not the garden boundary, there was more of the garden. Behind a wide agave was a path edged by a clear fibreglass barrier, topped with a chrome railing. Beyond that barrier was a slope that ended a few metres away in a sheer drop to a rocky beach. Local plants grew on either side of the path, and Mateo was overjoyed to find *Echium wildpretii* (Tajinaste rojo or The Tower of Jewels) with their thick trunk-like spikes that can grow up to three metres high, and their raspberry-pink flowers. Edward had four of these that Mateo estimated were about half the size they could grow. They produced lots of seeds and he could imagine a magnificent wall of these strange and wonderful plants in the future.

'I understand you have something you wish me to take a look at, Mateo.'

'Indeed I do. We are clearing the land at the ruined villa where Don Alphonso Ruis de Casals lived, you know the one I mean.'

'Yes, I know it. So, what did you find?'

'Edward,' Antonio called from the patio. 'Lunch is ready.'

'Come, Mateo, we'll have lunch and you can tell me more afterwards. We can go to my study and you can show me what's in the bag you are holding so tightly.'

Set out on the table were plates and bowls of cold cuts of chorizo sausage, Manchego cheese, olives, soft, buttery bread rolls and slices of Pan Rustico bread, grapes, huge slices of beef tomatoes, slices of thick Spanish omelette, called Tortilla de Patatas, made with onions and diced potatoes, parsley and olive oil. There was also a bottle of Viñátigo Tinto, a red wine that Mateo was very fond of, but was rarely allowed due to Maria's frowning disapproval. She no longer drank alcohol of any kind, other than Communion wine, of course. Mateo gulped. To him it looked like a banquet. He hoped Edward didn't expect him to eat half of what was on offer. But then he realised there were three places set, so Antonio was obviously joining them.

During a relaxed lunch Edward talked more about how happy he was now that he could see the sea, but did admit that perhaps a three bedroom villa was possibly too large for his needs. He had no family other than a sister who lived somewhere in Devon, and who hadn't seen in several years, and other visitors were a rarity. However, since Antonio had moved in, that took care of one of the bedrooms, and Edward, having needed somewhere to stock his vast number of books, had converted the other into his library and study. Antonio asked Mateo about La Gomera. He had never been to the island, but having seen it on his journeys to Tenerife South La Reina Airport, or to Playa de las Americas, had seen the ferries in the channel, he had promised himself a visit.

When Mateo began to talk about the villa, Edward looked at his watch, pushed back his chair and stood up. 'Have you seen what time it is? Gentlemen, we have been talking and eating for almost two hours.' He looked down at Mateo. 'My dear friend, we have business to complete and you have a long journey home. Come, we will go to my study where you can show me what you have found. If it is anything like the other treasures you have brought me, I am sure this one will be worthwhile taking a look at.'

Mateo's legs had stiffened after having been sitting for so long and he struggled to rise from the chair. Antonio walked around the table to help him up, but his grip on Mateo's arm was a little too rough for the old man, and he quickly pulled away. He glowered at Antonio who met Mateo's eyes for a little longer than necessary, as if daring Mateo to complain. Edward, having turned away towards the door, saw nothing of this exchange, and Mateo decided to remain quiet about what could have been an accident, or the imagination of an old man. Besides, he would be leaving soon and on the bus journey to Los Cristianos and home. But, he was pretty sure there would be bruising on his arm.

'Antonio, while Mateo and I are busy, could you clear the table, please? It would not do to invite the cockroaches in to enjoy our leftovers. Come with me, Mateo and let's see what you have for me.'

Chapter Sixteen

Tenerife : The Contents of the Box

Antonio's smile reached his mouth only, it was not reflected in his eyes, and his, 'Of course, and let me know if you need me,' sounded resentful, but Edward appeared not to have noticed. There was something in the atmosphere between the two men, that Mateo could not put his finger on, but he decided to put it out of his mind as he followed Edward back into the cool villa, taking one more backward glance at the brooding Antonio.

The library had, of course, the obligatory two walls of book shelves from floor to ceiling, what looked to Mateo like an antique oak desk, a grey fabric covered armchair with two more similar but smaller, more functional chairs, one in front of the desk and another in the corner of the room. The blue and tan floor tiles followed through into this room as well, leaving Mateo to assume that they covered the floors throughout the villa.

A soft warm breeze fluttered the floor length net curtain which, as it gently moved revealed more garden space beyond the patio doors, with several of the same Tower of Jewels plants.

As Mateo looked around, he noticed one thing he would have expected to see was missing; family or friends photographs. There were a few abstract paintings on the walls, mostly in the same colours as the floor tiles, which Mateo assumed were bought for their colours rather than their content.

'Take a seat, Mateo, make yourself comfortable and then let me see what's in that mysterious bag.' The old man did as he was told, and handed over the bag.

'Whoever wrapped this was being very protective of it.' Edward, said as he removed the thongs, and layers of cloth and leather. As he removed the final layer, he looked up at Mateo, who had been sitting quietly studying the historian's face. 'You have not opened the box?'

'No, Sen...Edward. I thought you should be the one to do that, and to be honest, I was a little worried that whatever is inside might be damaged if the air got into it...'

'...I don't think...I hope that won't happen. Some materials can be affected that way, but I think we have to take a chance.' With the last protective layer gone, both men had their first sight of the ornately carved box. 'My God, Mateo, this is beautiful craftsmanship.' He turned the box this way and that inspecting it from all angles, aware of the shifting weight of whatever was inside with each movement. 'It feels quite heavy.' He held the box to his ear and gently shook it to be rewarded with a clinking sound. Mateo sat forward on the edge of his seat trying to hide his impatience, and chewing the end of his moustache.

'Well, whatever is in here, Mateo, we shall soon discover, but I think I would be correct in saying that this box is eighteenth century.' He turned it over, and again the contents moved. He tried to push the lid up, but it proved reluctant to open. 'I am not really surprised that the lid seems to be stuck after all these years, but I will not damage it by using some tool to prise it open. We must be a little patient with it being unwilling to open. 'I will be careful. I'll just manipulate it a little. One must not be cavalier with something so precious.'

Mateo wondered why the historian was talking about horses. 'What means cavalier, Senor Edward?'

Edward looked up and smiled at the quizzical expression on Mateo's face. 'Oh, yes, sorry, Mateo. It has nothing to do with horses in this regard. It just means...um...careless, or irresponsible.'

'Ah, I see.' Mateo was growing nervous at the wait. Nervous or excited, he wasn't sure which, but it didn't really matter; the box was about to be opened.

After some nerve-wracked moments with Edward gently easing the lid one side, then the other, the lid creaked upward. From where Mateo was sitting he could not see the contents, but the look on Edwards face told him he had found something very special. He stood up, walked around the desk and looked over Edward's shoulder.

'My God, Mateo,' Edward lifted out the jewelled crucifix and stared open mouthed. 'You have really excelled yourself this time, my friend.' Mateo crossed himself. This was the most beautiful thing he had ever seen. As far as he knew none of the churches on La Gomera had anything so fine. The emerald in the centre alone he guessed would be worth thousands of Euros.

'You think it might be valuable, Senor Edward?' Mateo could hardly contain his delight.

'Oh I think...think, mind you, that this could be very valuable, but I won't know exactly until I do some research.'

Mateo looked crestfallen.

'However, don't be downhearted. I am certain there is some wealth in it, I just don't know how much, but you will be the first to know when I find out.'

Mateo smiled and sighed. 'Thank you. It would be good to know. I promised myself I would buy Maria a new silk shawl for her to wear for church, if the reward for my find was worth anything, but if the value is higher, then she can have a new dress and shoes as well.'

Edward chuckled. 'I promise nothing, Mateo, but if it's worth what I think it is, then you may be talking designer dress, shoes and even a decent handbag.'

Smiling, Mateo looked down into the box and saw two wooden boards smothered in some kind of waxy substance, and there was something underneath. He reached in, and brought out the miniature painted image of a very pretty lady. He handed it to Edward.

'Oh this is nice. It's beautifully painted. If this is a true likeness, she must have been a beauty, Mateo.' Edward held the miniature in his right hand and the crucifix in his left. 'These are superb treasures. They are the kind of relics that historians always hope they will come across. Let's hope there's something here that explains more about who she was, and who buried this box. Maybe this will tell us.'

Edward lifted out the beeswax-smeared boards, bound with a length of linen, but with the soft wax on his fingers he just could not grip the knots. He reached into the right hand drawer of the desk and pulled out a small pair silver scissors and carefully, snipped the linen away from the boards. Separating them from the parchment was not as easy though.

'This is where I have to be careful. I can see there's a document within and, after all this time it may be stuck to the wood. It may tear.' He looked up at the anxious Mateo. 'Plus, you do understand there's the possibility that any writing may have faded…, or simply bled, making it difficult, if not impossible to read. The only good thing is that the beeswax seems to have softened the wood a little.'

Mateo winced, but nodded to show he understood.

Just at that moment, the door opened and Antonio broke the suspense in the room. 'Anyone want coffee?' From the doorway he spotted the open box and joined Edward and Mateo at the desk. Wide-eyed, he fixed his gaze on the crucifix.

'Madre de Dios! Glorious! Where did it come from?'

'Mateo found it in a garden he was clearing on La Gomera.' Edward held the crucifix to the light revealing the brilliance of each of the gems.

'Can I touch it?'

Edward handed him the crucifix.

'It's so beautiful … and it weighs more than I thought it would. Is it real gold?'

Edward raised his eyebrows and nodded. 'I'm pretty certain it is, and my guess is eighteenth century. It's a particularly lovely piece of history, and we may find out more about it if I can just get the document inside here out cleanly.'

Antonio handed Edward a box of tissues. Edward pulled a few out and wiped the rest of the beeswax from his hands. Then little by little he painstakingly eased first one corner, then another, then the third and fourth, prising them steadily away from the parchment. Mateo did not realise how tense he was until he felt something wet and warm in the palm of his right hand. He opened his tight fist. Blood was seeping from the wounds he had caused by pressing his fingernails into the palm. He looked at the left hand. It too showed marks where his nails had dug in, but they were not so deep that blood had been drawn.

Antonio had seen and gave him a sympathetic smile, and a few tissues to staunch the bleeding. He leaned closer to Mateo and whispered, 'It will be alright. Edward knows what he is doing?'

Without looking up Edward, his eyes still fixed on the delicate operation, and said: 'I do hope you're right, Antonio. Now, I need to concentrate.'

Antonio watched as Edward went back to the first corner and repeated the process inching the board away from the parchment a little at a time. Trying to separate the board from the parchment without damaging it was a nerve-wracking moment for the historian. One slip and the entire document could be ruined.

As the seconds ticked by, Edward wiped away the beads of sweat, that had formed on his bristly eyebrows, with more tissues. Focussing solely on what he was doing, he was aware of the responsibility resting squarely on his shoulders, or rather hands, as he continued with the delicate task of releasing the parchment from its wooden covers. As more and more of the document was safely exposed, Edward stopped, sat back in his armchair for a moment and looked up at his audience.

'I need a moment to breathe, but I think we may be in luck, my friends. So far the document is undamaged. I just hope that if I am fortunate enough to release it from its protective cover in one piece, it will still be decipherable.'

'I do not know that word,' said Mateo. 'Please, what is decipherable?'

Edward smiled. 'It means that we are able to read what it says. Of course, having been found on La Gomera, it is unlikely to be written in English, but I can translate Spanish language documents. Antonio, could you bring me some cold still water, please.'

'Yes. Back in a moment.'

Edward looked up at Mateo. 'How are you? You look as tense as I feel.'

Mateo opened his right hand to show Edward his bloody palm. 'And I thought I was anxious. Hmm, for your sake, Mateo, I think I had better get this over with. You don't need any more injuries.'

Edward turned back to the document. The board he was working on had loosened around all the edges; there was just a section in the centre of approximately twelve centimetres square, that still need to be released. Edward took a plastic paperknife from his right hand drawer and gently held the document in place with it, as he methodically withdrew the board away on the left side, then repeated the process on the right.

Mateo, unable to watch any longer went out to the terrace, just as Antonio returned with a glass of water. Antonio then joined Mateo and together they paced around the pool while they waited for Edward's call. To Mateo it seemed as though time had stopped, but strangely it also felt as though he had been pacing for hours when Edward finally called them from the study.

On returning to the study, they found Edward sitting back in his armchair, a huge smile on his face and holding a long piece of parchment for them to see; mercifully, there appeared to be very few signs of damage, but here and there some of the ink had become smudged. However, Mateo's old eyes strained to read the antiquated writing style.

'Senor Edward, what does it mean? Can you read it?'

'We are in extreme good luck, Mateo. Fortune has smiled on us. Although there are patches that I cannot read, they are fewer than I would have expected and thankfully, they are small-scale, minor. I can certainly read most of it, and I now know who the lady is in the miniature painting. I also know who buried the box, and why. He protected this document very successfully. Where did you say you found it?'

Mateo explained as Antonio moved to stand behind Edward to look at the parchment over his shoulder.

'And you showed it to no-one, you spoke of it to no-one?'

'No, not even Maria. I wanted you to see it first.'

'That's good, Mateo, thank you.' He sat back and glanced at Antonio still standing behind him. 'I believe you know, Mateo, that one of my main interests is shipwrecks. I know of many around these islands and, in addition to my historical interests, my other hobby is Scuba diving to the wrecks. As you know, I am quite well known as an authority on local shipwrecks. The crucifix and the miniature are of great interest, especially as, from this document, we are able to authenticate their original owner, and today I will give you five hundred Euros...'

Clearly shocked, Mateo's mouth dropped open. Edward grinned.

'But I believe that will just be the first part of your reward. I cannot tell you exactly how much you will earn from this, but I can tell you that Maria will certainly be very well dressed for church, and you will be able to buy that new car you have been talking about. You certainly will not have to continue working unless you wish to retire, that is, but I think I can honestly promise you a life of comfort as you and Maria grow older.'

Mateo could not hold back the tears. Antonio looked at the desk for the pack of tissues, but it was empty. He ran out of the room and returned with a roll of kitchen tissue paper, and handed to the jubilant old man.

'Thank, you,' Mateo laughed, 'but I will not need all that.'

'There is more, Mateo,' said Edward as he leaned forward, rested his elbows on the desk and steepled his fingers under his chin. He told Mateo about the storm, the sinking of the *Katarina-Thereza* which had brought about the ruin of Alphonso Ruis de Casals and his subsequent suicide. 'So, somewhere close beneath where the villa was situated, that ship carrying untold wealth in modern day values, crashed onto the rocks and was sunk. With all my knowledge of wrecks around the islands, I had never heard of her. My guess is that with time, tides and underwater currents, whatever remains of the *Katarina-Thereza* will have drifted over time and I will need to carry out some investigations to find out where those remains are likely to be now. When I have that an exploratory dive will be carried out to see if we can find her…or what's left of her anyway.' He turned to Antonio.

'Antonio, you know the combination to my safe. Please take out five hundred Euros and give them to Mateo.'

'Yes, Edward. Mateo, as I understand it, you could be a very rich man once all this is confirmed and that's just from the artefacts you have here.' He left the room and a few moments later they heard music, the voice of Enrique Iglesias, reached them from the portable radio in the kitchen.

Edward chuckled. 'Antonio loves music, popular music that is. I prefer classical music myself, but why he's put the radio on now beats me, but he'll be back in a moment with your money, Mateo.' Edward stood up and walked around to lean his backside against the desk.

'For now,' Edward began, 'I would continue to say nothing to anyone, especially Maria. You never know, she might let things slip if she knows.'

Mateo nodded. 'I do trust her, but I will do as you say but, and please don't think me ungrateful or impolite, but as you haven't known him long...'

Edward turned away and walked back behind his desk again, sat down, rested his elbows on the desk, his hands together and fingers steepled. '...I understand what you are going to ask, and no I don't think you are either of those things, Mateo. I am asking you not to trust Maria, who you have known almost all your life, and to you I appear to be putting my trust in someone I have only known for a short time. Your question is relevant and understandable.'

'Perhaps I should not ask as you seem close, but he was not with you when we did business together before. Then, it was just between you and I. No-one else was involved.'

Edward seemed fidgety. He rose from his desk again and walked around to the front. ' I hear what you are saying, Mateo, and I can understand why you might feel a little...let's say uncomfortable with having a stranger around. But, let me assure you that Antonio has been with me for long enough for us to gain a trust in each other, just as a trainer trusts his apprentice, and vice versa. In fact, he and I have...grown quite close.' He paused. 'So please do not be uneasy over Antonio.'

'I understand, and if you think he is dependable, then I will be guided by you.' However, although Mateo may not have been particularly well-educated, but he was a shrewd judge of character generally, and the little voice in his head, his instinct, spoke to him now. There was something about Antonio that said all was not as well as Edward believed it to be. Had Edward become blinded to any failing in Antonio? Mateo was not done with his probe into the relationship between Edward and Antonio. 'So where did you two meet?'

Edward blushed. 'He was a waiter at a restaurant I go to regularly, the Bar Felipe. I was working on some details for my next book at an outside table one evening, when he served me. I recall asking him if he was new at the bar as I had not seen him before. He said he was and that he had come to Tenerife for two reasons. One was to help an old friend with a project he was working on, and the second was to try to escape an ex-girlfriend who had made his life a misery. Over the next few weeks we got chatting, and he expressed an interest in my work with the maritime history of the Canary islands. 'He was intrigued by my work and asked a lot of questions, so I invited him to take a look at my library. After that he became a regular visitor and began helping with my research.'

'That's very nice.'

'But you're frowning, Mateo. Is something wrong?'

'Only that I am worried about what I say to Maria when I go home with five hundred Euros that I did not have when I left home this morning.' He shrugged.

Edward laughed. 'Tell her you won it playing Bola.'

Mateo grimaced. 'But then she will scold me for betting.'

'Better that than having other people find out what's going on, until we succeed in finding the wreck...and whatever was on it. You know people won't leave you alone if they find out about your discovery, which is why you hid it in the first place.'

Mateo nodded. 'Yes, you are right, but I find it hard to keep secrets from Maria. As you say, though, a telling off for gambling is better than everyone knowing my business. And, if she thinks I have won all that money, perhaps she will not reproach me too badly.' He took out a shabby brown-leather wallet with the embossed emblem of La Gomera, in the shape of the island with the faded red and yellow motif of the Spanish flag.

'I see you still have that old wallet, Mateo.'

Mateo looked down at the wallet and his eyes lit up. 'I will use it until it falls apart...or I do. My Ramona gave me this wallet. I have a few things, keepsakes, to remind me of her...no, no...they mean more than that, more than keepsakes, Edward. They keep her with me, and this one is special, I remember the day she gave it to me.'

-o0o-

In the kitchen, Antonio dialled a foreign telephone number, took a glass from the cupboard, walked over to the water cooler and filled the glass almost to the brim, while he waited for an answer.

'Hello Anton. I wondered how much longer it would be before you called. What have you got for me?

With his voice low, almost a whisper, Antonio kept an eye on the study door in case Edward came looking for him.

'Papa, I can only talk for a few seconds. There is an old man here who has told Edward about a shipwreck off La Gomera.'

'Ha! There's always talk of shipwrecks, rumours and legends that have been blown...'

'No, Papa, not this time. He has documents, details of the ship, everything, and they're talking of much treasure that was lost with her. It's what you have been waiting for.'

'Documents, eh? That sounds more like it. Good boy, Anton. I knew if you grew close to Taylor-Owen something worthwhile would come of it, eventually. Do you know how much the treasure might be worth?'

'Not yet. Edward is going to research it, but it certainly sounds significant. I have to go. I was only going to be out of the room for a few moments. Edward wanted me to get some money for the old man.'

'Then go, but remember, you will have to find a way to make sure this information goes no further than Taylor-Owen and the old man. Do whatever you have to.' The line went dead.

Anton closed the safe door, entered the code again, checked it was locked, then pausing to make sure Edward and Mateo were still talking in the study, he raced on tiptoes to the bathroom where he pressed the button on the cistern to flush the toilet, took a breath, and dashed back to the kitchen where he collected the glass, gave himself a moment to calm then sauntered back to join Edward and Mateo.

-oOo-

'Ah, there you are, Antonio.' Edward smiled as Antonio entered the room carrying a large glass of water, and ten fifty Euro notes which he handed to an emotional Mateo, who quickly slipped the money into his wallet. 'I was just wondering why you were in the kitchen.'

'My apologies, Edward, I needed to get some drinking water from the kitchen, and popped to the toilet.'

The affectionate smile that passed between Edward and Antonio was not lost on Mateo. He raised an eyebrow as he looked down at his wallet. If Antonio wanted a drink of water, there was a jug of iced water on the table on the patio just outside the study. But, perhaps he forgot. Mateo wondered if he was just being suspicious for no reason, and decided to give Antonio the benefit of the doubt, but it feel that something … was wrong, or rather just not right, about Antonio. Or was it just his imagination? Edward clearly liked and had faith in him, so perhaps he should just accept that.

Mateo nodded his thanks to Antonio, then turned to shake Edward's hand. 'Thank you, Edward. I did not expect anything like this when I found the box, but I am certainly glad I did, and Maria will be too when I give her that new lace shawl. I know that will please her. But, now I have a long journey home and must catch my bus. Thank you, again and I look forward to hearing from you when you know more about the shipwreck.'

Edward stood up. 'Come, my friend, I will see you out. You have my word that I will keep you updated on progress. Stay safe, stay well, and I will see you soon.'

At the door, Antonio said, 'Mateo, I was going to Los Cristianos later today. Edward, is there any reason why I should not go now? I could give Mateo a lift to the harbour.'

'That's a good idea. No, there is no reason why you need to wait until later.' He smiled at Mateo, who although not entirely happy with this new arrangement, could see no logical reason to turn it down. 'There, and now you don't have that long bus journey. You can be at the port in about half an hour. Great idea, Antonio. Mateo, have a good trip home and I'm sure we meet again very soon. I will be in touch. Goodbye for now.'

'Come along, Mateo, the car is parked just a few doors along from here,' said Antonio, he put his arm around the old man's bony shoulder and led him to the car.

Chapter Seventeen

La Gomera : Mateo Goes Missing

Maria stood at the entrance to the Comisaría de Guardia Civil in Calle las Escuelas in San Sebastian, seemingly unsure about going in. Mateo had been missing for two days, but Maria had never had dealings with the police before, and was nervous about how to talk to them.

In a café across the road, Corporal Paloma Perez, watched the old lady as she paced up and down in front of the building occasionally stopping, walking towards the door, then backing away again. With her slouched shoulders and worried expression, it was easy to see the lady had a problem, but still she hesitated.

When she finished her coffee, Paloma took her empty cup back to the counter, bought her lunch of a large croissant filled with slices of chorizo sausage, cheese and tomato, and paid her bill. From the doorway Paloma, transferred to La Gomera from Madrid almost a year before, speculated on whether to approach the lady, or let her decide for herself what she wanted to do. There was a chance that if she attempted to talk to her, the lady might just walk away. So she waited, observing only, not wanting to scare the old lady away, but aware something was very wrong. But Paloma was forced into action when, with her mind clearly preoccupied with whatever was worrying her, the old lady crossed the road right in front of an oncoming car, and was lucky the driver had excellent reactions. Had he not braked in time, she would certainly have been injured, perhaps even killed. The driver shouted at the old lady, who put her hands up in apologetic horror, at what might have happened to her, and crossed to the refuge of the pavement as the driver, cursing, drove on.

When Paloma caught up with her, the old lady was sitting on a low wall, sobbing, her spectacles on the wall beside her. Paloma sat next to her and handed her a tissue.

Maria Moreno looked at the uniformed young officer sitting beside her, and between sobs, gulped for air, but said nothing. Paloma waited until she had controlled her tears.

'Would you like to come into the station and tell me what's wrong. I could make you a cup of coffee. It's not very nice, so if you prefer, I will get you one from the café and we can sit on the bench by the trees and you can tell me what's wrong. Would that be alright for you?'

Maria nodded. 'Yes, thank you. That is good of you, and thank you for your kindness. No sugar, please. I will go over to the bench to wait for you there.'

'Excuse me, I believe these are yours?' Paloma picked up the spectacles and handed them to the lady.

'Oh yes. I am sorry, but my head is spinning at the moment.' She took the glasses and put them in her pocket, with an absent-minded, 'Thank you.'

A few moments later, as the lady sipped at her coffee, Paloma discovered she was talking to Maria Moreno, a widow from Agulo, and that she was very worried about her brother-in-law, Mateo, with whom she lived and looked after, and that he had been missing for two days. She had no idea where he was going when he left the house. No, he had never gone missing before. No, he drank very little alcohol. He was seventy-two years old, worked as a senior gardener, and had a small team who he supervised, but had few real friends. No, he didn't gamble, well as far as she knew anyway.

After a while, asking basic questions as gently as she could, Paloma suggested that Maria accompany her to the police station where they could both talk to a senior officer. Maria seemed reluctant, scared, saying that she had never been in a police station, but Paloma promised she would be with her the whole time. Ten minutes later, Maria and Paloma were sitting in the office of the Guardia Civil's Sergeant Emilio Alvarado.

'It has been two days since Mateo left the house, Sergeant. It is not like him at all.' Maria took off her spectacles and wiped her tears. Paloma reached out to lay her hand over Maria's. 'He never stays out overnight.'

The Guardia Civil officer listened to the lady's concerns with sympathy. 'I regret, Senora Moreno, that without knowing where he was going, we do not know where to start looking for Mateo. However, that does not mean we are unable to help you. It is just that searching for him is made more difficult because he gave you no idea of where he was going.'

Maria's hands trembled as she groped in her pocket for her handkerchief, but Paloma handed her a tissue. Seeing Maria's little body shuddering with grief and desperation was distressing. 'Then … um … is there nothing you can do to help … me … um find him?' Maria stammered as she gulped for air.

Paloma clasped Maria's bony hand in both of her's to give comfort, and as Maria wiped her eyes with her free hand, Paloma mouthed to the Sergeant that there must be something they could do. He too wanted to help the lady and gave Paloma an encouraging nod.

'Senora Moreno, we will need your help to find Mateo. As I explained, without knowing Mateo's plans, it is true that we do not have a starting point. However, if you can give us a list of his friends, acquaintances, your neighbours, then we may discover something. Someone may have seen him, or he may have told someone where he was going.'

Maria shook her head, her eyes filled with tears again. 'I am trying to think if anyone …' She looked up at the sergeant. 'Yes, yes, maybe I do. There is a young man Mateo is always talking about … Javier.' She paused. 'Yes, Javier, Javier, yes, Javier Garcia.' She smiled for the first time. 'Javier is always helpful, Mateo told me. Mateo always said that when he retires, Javier should take over from him. He is not just a labourer, he knows his plants. Mateo has been training him.' She turned from Paloma to the sergeant and back at Paloma. 'Will that help? Will that help you find Mateo? I don't remember the other names, but if Mateo confided in anyone, I believe it will be Javier.'

'It may well do, Senora. Do you know where this Javier lives? If you don't I am sure we can find him.'

'I believe he is from Agulo too, or just outside. I am sorry, but I don't know any more than that.'

'We will look for him and there will be other things we can do to try to trace Mateo's movements.'

Paloma joined in. 'We can take a look at the CCTV records around the town and harbour. Do you think there is any chance that Mateo may have taken a ferry to one of the other islands.'

Maria shook her head. Her tears had abated a little. 'It is unlikely. Mateo was frightened of deep water and would avoid taking the ferry unless it was really necessary, and I cannot think of any reason why he would need to take the ferry.'

'Very well. I will speak to my captain and we will send someone to find Javier Garcia to see if he knows anything, but for now, I want you to go with Corporal Perez, Paloma, to a more comfortable room where she will make a list of any other people you can think of who may be able to help us. I would also like you to give Paloma a full physical description of Mateo, and if you have a recent photograph, that would be very helpful.'

Paloma stood up, held out her hand to help Maria up from the chair. Maria turned to the sergeant. 'Unfortunately, I do not think there is a recent photograph of Mateo.' Maria's smile was forlorn. 'When you get old like us, you do not take as many photographs as you did when you were young, but I will try to find one that looks something like he does now. Thank you for your time, Sergeant.'

Paloma put her arm around Maria's shoulder as she led her to the door, but in the open doorway Maria turned to the sergeant again. 'I am grateful for your help, but in my heart I believe Mateo is dead. Something awful has happened. He would never stay away from home for so long.'

'Let us hope you are wrong, Senora Moreno.' Sergeant Alvarado replied. 'Until we know for certain what has happened, we will hope for the best, dear lady.'

'Come, Maria,' said Paloma, 'let us go through those details the sergeant asked for, then I will take you home.' She looked at the sergeant over Maria's head, silently seeking his permission to escort Maria home. He nodded his agreement.

A little under two hours later, to the astonishment of her neighbours, Maria arrived home in a police car. A small crowd gathered as Paloma assisted Maria out of the car and walked her to her door. 'Would you like me to stay while you get settled indoors, and if you want me to send away your inquisitive neighbours, I can do that.'

'No, thank you, Paloma. You have been extremely kind and I do appreciate it, but you do not have to stay. However, yes please ask the neighbours to leave. I do not feel like talking any more today, and would be glad of some peace and quiet. So, if you could ask them to leave me be today, I would be grateful. I know they mean well, we have all looked after each other for years, and have been through many events, happy and sad together, but now I need to rest. I will see them tomorrow.' Maria slumped into an armchair near the window at the back of the room and closed her eyes, but remembered something she had not done, and opened them again. 'Paloma, before you go, you wanted a photograph of Mateo.'

'Yes, I did. I should have remembered that. Thank you for reminding me. I would have been in trouble with my sergeant if I went back without one.' And there's one more thing, Maria. Would you mind if I had a look in Mateo's room? There may be something helpful, notes, an address book, a business card, anything at all that gives a clue as to where he may have gone.'

'Yes of course, but I warn you. it may be a mess in there. He's not particular about keeping tidy. Do you need me or shall I look for that photograph while you're taking a look?'

'No, I can do that while you look for a photo.'

Mateo's bedroom was small, with a large window that extended from almost one side of the room to the other, with white, plastic venetian blinds and long dark blue curtains on either side. It was a simple room. On a hook on the back of the door hung a man's blue towelling dressing gown, and a pair of blue slippers peeped from under the single, unmade bed. Paloma guessed that Mateo must have been in a hurry to leave that morning. Everything else about the fairly spartan room was tidy, but he had not made his bed. The rest of the furniture comprised, one tall chest of drawers against the wall opposite the window, a single wardrobe, a small hand basin with a single bar of soap, a blue hand towel hanging from a chrome ring on the wall to the right of the sink, and a bedside cabinet with a lamp and a book. Paloma picked up the book. It was *Don Quijote de la Mancha* by Miguel de Cervantes. She smiled. The book was a classic, but she had not seen a copy in a very long time. She opened the drawer of the bedside cabinet. Inside was a pen, two neatly folded handkerchiefs, a closed pen knife, and a notebook that as far as she could see contained information only about plants. After checking through the chest of drawers and the wardrobe and finding nothing remotely helpful, Paloma joined Maria in the living room.

'I hope Mateo won't mind that I have been in his room.'

'We won't tell him, will we?' Maria gave a gentle smile. 'I have found some photographs. Let's take a look through.' With both arms she pushed herself up from the armchair and walked over to a wooden cupboard next to the window, and took out a bundle of photographs from one of the drawers. She spread them out on the table and shuffled them around. Paloma noticed one of a middle-aged man wearing a peaked cap, something like she had seen the fishermen wearing. She picked it up. 'Is this him, Maria?'

'No, that is my Pedro, he died a long time ago and I still miss him.' She took the photograph from Paloma. 'He is very like Mateo though, if I cannot find a good likeness of Mateo, this may help. They were so alike, they could almost be taken for twins.' She chuckled. 'Ramona, Mateo's late wife and I used to say, if we swapped husbands, would we notice the difference.' She looked at Paloma with a little smile that reflected in her eyes. 'Not that we ever did you understand.'

It was good to see Maria smile, even though it was fleeting. 'I would never have thought otherwise, Maria.'

'Now, I know you must be busy, and you have to get back to San Sebastian, so let me see if I can find a photograph of Mateo.' She began fumbling through the photographs again. 'Ah, this one is Mateo. Yes, I am sure it is. Yes, look he has his gardening apron and gloves on. This one I think would have been taken about three years ago, when he was working in the grounds of a hotel in Valle Gran Rey. Will this do?'

Paloma took a look at the photograph and had to agree that the brothers were indeed very alike, but it was certainly an excellent image of the missing man.

'Yes, this is fine. Thank you. I must go now, but I am on duty again tomorrow and will pop in to see you. In the meantime, we will begin going through the list of names you gave me, beginning with Javier Garcia. Do you have an address for him?'

Maria frowned. 'I think he lives near San Marcos church, in the same road.' She looked down at the floor, frowning. Paloma waited while Maria tried to remember the name or number of the house. She looked up. 'No, I am sorry, I cannot recall which one, but I have been there. I went there once with Mateo. Javier's door is painted yellow. The house is the middle one of three, all joined together, and if the church is on your right, then Javier's house is on the left … oh, yes, and his mother has put a pretty statue of Our Lady on the window ledge. He is a nice boy and worked hard to learn everything Mateo could teach him. Although I know Mateo never mentioned it to Javier, but he had it in mind to make Javier supervisor next year. I'm sure that if Mateo told anyone where he was going, it would have been Javier.'

'That's really helpful, thank you, Maria. On my way out, I will ask your neighbours to leave you in peace today. Is there anything else I can do, or get you before I leave.'

As Maria sat back down in the armchair, a grey and white cat appeared from nowhere to jump onto her lap. She stroked the purring cat who circled twice then sat down to look adoringly at the old lady. Paloma sensed that the cat knew Maria was distressed and was trying to give comfort.

'Thank you, no. I will be fine here with Gato.' She smiled at the cat, then looked up at Paloma. 'We never gave him a name, you see.'

'Then I must go, Maria. I will see you, and perhaps Gato, tomorrow.'

Outside, Paloma talked to the neighbours and explained that Mateo had gone missing. She also informed them that although Maria was resting and was not up to speaking to them at that time, she would see them tomorrow. She also explained that members of the Guardia Civil would be interviewing them in case anyone knew anything about Mateo's disappearance, or had seen him.

One lady came through the group. 'Excuse me, officer. I am Juana Flores. I live two doors down. I may be able to help.' The group parted to allow Juana to talk to the officer.

'Senora Flores, any information you can give us will be really helpful.' The group moved closer, every one of them wanted to hear what Juana had to say.

'Well,' Juana began, 'my husband, Enzo had to go to Tenerife two days ago and he told me he saw Mateo on the ferry to Los Cristianos.'

Paloma could have kissed the lady. That was exactly the kind of information they needed. 'That's great news. It gives us a start and cuts the time taken in looking in the wrong places. You have saved us a lot of time and manpower, Senora Flores. By any chance did Mateo tell your husband where he was going?'

Juana shook her head. 'No. Enzo said he thought Mateo was going no further than Los Cristianos. He said something about having maybe found a lady friend.' There was a collective gasp from the gathered crowd. Juana looked around at her neighbours. 'Yes, that does seem strange doesn't it. I don't actually believe it, do you?' she asked them. Several shook their heads, and there were many negative responses, but only one said. 'Why not? Mateo has been alone for many years. Perhaps somehow he did find a girlfriend.' But he was drowned out by the many who did not believe it possible.

'Is your husband at home, Senora Flores?'

'No, officer, he is visiting his mother in Valle Gran Rey today, but he will be here tomorrow.'

'Thank you, please tell him that I, or one of my colleagues, would like to talk to him. Would it be possible for him to come to the station sometime tomorrow?

'Yes, of course. I will make sure he comes to see you in the morning.' Juana walked with Paloma back to the car.

'Thank you, Senora Flores. You have been very helpful. Please tell your husband to ask for Corporal Paloma Perez when he comes to the station.'

At the car, she remembered something she had meant to ask, and returned to the concerned group of neighbours. Some were looking towards the Moreno house, speaking in soft tones, but Paloma heard their comments. Every word uttered showed their concern for Maria and their worry for Mateo. It warmed her heart to see just how close-knit and supportive this little community was, and she knew they would all be taking care of Maria, but she had one more request of them.

'I would ask you all not to mention any of this to Senora Moreno, please. For the moment we know nothing more, and I would not like any speculation to give her any false hope by telling her Mateo was seen. Let us follow this up to see if it leads us anywhere first. We will check CCTV records both here, at the harbour in Los Cristianos, at the bus station and any other areas where CCTV may have picked up signs of Mateo. I will see her again tomorrow, but in the meantime, thank you all for your help.'

Chapter Eighteen

Tenerife : Anton Confesses

Anton made the call he knew his father was waiting for. 'I did as you asked, Papa. The old man is dead.' He tried to sound relaxed, nonchalant. His father had a knack of knowing when he was lying even from over the phone and thousands of miles away.

'*What did you do with his body?*'

'Uh...it is...' he paused, swallowed. His mouth dried, he had no spit.

'*What is it? What's the problem? Did you hide him well enough?*'

'Yeah, yeah, of course I did. What's the matter Papa, don't you trust me?'

'*You seem evasive, like you're trying to hide something.*'

'No, no. It is hot here. I just took a drink. 'Don't worry yourself, Papa. Everything's okay. Honest.'

'*You hesitated. Why? Tell me the truth. What did you do with the body?*'

Anton rolled his eyes. Why did his father always put him through a third-degree interrogation. 'I buried him under a hedge on an old, abandoned banana farm.' He prayed he'd get away with that one.

'*You're sure he's not going to be dug up by some local mutt looking for his bone, or something?*'

'No, Papa. It's fine. Look, if you don't believe me, come over and check for yourself.'

There was a brief silence at the other end of the line. '*Don't you snap at me, boy. I think you'd better calm down. You don't tell me what to do! If you're incapable of seeing this through without losing your nerve, maybe I should send someone out there who can. I can always pull you out if I can't trust you.*'

'There's no need, Papa. I'm fine. Everything's under control. I guess it's just that I'm not used to killing people.'

'Then get used to it. It won't be the last time. So, back to Taylor-Owen, he thinks the old man went home to La Gomera?'

'Yes, of course. He believes I took him back to Los Cristianos and he went home. There's no reason for him to think anything else.'

'Is he not going to try to contact him, Anton?'

'Eventually he will, but not yet. Edward gave him five hundred Euros, and told him he would be in touch again once he found out more about the value of the things in the box, and when he knew where the ship, or what's left of it, may have drifted to. He was only going to contact the old man when he had something to tell him.'

'I don't give a fuck for the stuff in the box, it's the ship I want. Nothing must happen to Edward until he has some idea of where the treasure might be. You understand that, don't you?'

'Yes, Papa.' Anton stifled a sigh. He would be so glad when his father ended the call and left him in peace. It had been a difficult day. He had never murdered anyone before.

'So what happened to the money?'

'What money?'

'The five hundred …'

Antonio could have kicked himself. He should not have mentioned the money.

'I said what happened to the money?'

Having made the mistake, Anton could not avoid telling his father the rest. 'Oh, I got that. I took it off his body. Why not? He's got no use for it now.'

'Good, you can hand that over as well when I get there.'

Anton had wanted to keep that money. The allowance his father gave him was minimal, his wages from the restaurant had only just been adequate and although Edward helped him financially, it appalled him that he was a 'kept' man, and even Edward, generous as he was, regularly enquired about how Anton was spending his 'pocket money'. That five hundred Euros would have made all the difference. It would have given him some self-respect, although it was pretty illogical bearing in mind he had taken it from a man he had just murdered, but it was better in his pocket than left with the body.

Why hadn't he just kept quiet about it though? For once he'd had something of his own, something his father didn't control. He had slipped up badly there. For just a brief moment he had forgotten what his father was like. He owned everything, including Anton.

'Okay. So I'll leave you to it. Call me when there's an update. I want that wreck found and quickly. D'you hear me, boy?'

'Yes, Papa, of course I do. That's why you sent me here, isn't? Gain Edward's trust, become his lover, learn as much as I can from him and let you know if he finds another wreck. I have been doing this now for months. Since I moved into the villa, I've been with him pretty much twenty-four hours a day. I've learned how to dive, I've found out where the currents are strong, and I can tell you about when tides are highest, when they're lowest. I can get all the charts you need and...Papa, I want to come home once Edward locates this wreck ... I want ... to ... come ... home, but I know I have to stay until all this is done, finished.'

'Stop fretting boy. Just get on with what you have to do. You will be home soon enough and back with me. I have a pretty nondescript motor boat ready to come across when the time's right. Once we get the treasure from the wreck, you'll come home with us then. In the meantime, life may suck, my boy, but just get on with what you have to do, it'll be worth it. I have found a pair of divers who are used to wreck diving, they'll be in Playa de la Arena quite soon. I've had false passports, PADI documents, flights, hotel bookings made ready for them, and I'll let you know how and when to make contact with them.'

'So, are you okay with how things are going here?'

'Fuck, no. It's taking too long. But I am not stupid. I understand that a plan like this takes time to perfect, we can't continue without all the details being in place, or it will end in disaster. Edward must do his part, even though he won't see his hopes end the way he would like. I shall be sorry when he is gone. It'll be a shame to kill him. He's a distinguished historian, a skilled linguist, and although we've never met I've respect for the man. You know how long I've been following his career, charting his discoveries, what he doesn't know about wrecks around the Canary Islands is not worth knowing, and his...untimely...demise will upset me, at least for a while. It will be a

shock and a loss to maritime research, but there is no other way. When the time comes, he has to die, and it must look like an accident.'

Antonio knew and was resigned to Edward's death. 'I know, and understand. I'll call you again when I've got news.' If his father noticed the sound of dejection in Antonio's voice. He gave no sign of it.

'Good. Make it soon.'

Anton ended the call, sat back and closed his eyes, only to immediately open them again. The memory of driving the unsuspecting old man to his death turned Antonio's stomach. It was late in the afternoon when they left the villa and he had explained to Mateo that he had a quick errand to run, and had to go to Los Gigantes before going on to Los Cristianos. Mateo smiled and said that as he no longer had to take two long bus journeys, and the ferry ran quite late, the detour was no problem. Shortly after, within minutes of setting off Anton realised Mateo had drifted off to sleep. That made things easier for a while. It was only when Anton drove to a remote area a quiet section of road and stopped the car that Mateo woke.

Chapter Nineteen

Cape Town : The Nikolov Brothers

Valko Nikolov craned his neck out of the car window to call out to two girls in bikinis parading along the sea front promenade. As the girls turned round, he slid his sunglasses down his nose to get a better look. 'Hi girls. Looking good,' he called. One refused to respond and loftily stuck her nose in the air, but the other smiled and waved back, only to have her arm grabbed by her friend, and be dragged away down the steps and onto the beach.

Valko laughed. 'Hey, Viktor, did you see that?'

'No, I'm keeping my eyes on the road. I don't have time to fool about like you.'

They turned off the coastal road to head up the hill towards Cape Town's affluent Bantry Bay area. The blue Volvo XC60's diesel engine grumbled as it laboured up the steep cliff road.

'Did you see those girls on the beach back there?' asked Valko.

'No. I was concentrating on the road, not what was on the beach and this bastard car couldn't pull the fuckin' skin off a rice pudding.'

Valko laughed. 'It couldn't do what? What in the name of God is a rice puddin'? And where'd you get that from?'

Without looking around, Viktor chuckled. 'That Scottish man, Sam, at the garage. He's always saying things like that, but you need to get your head off that beach. We've got more important things to think about now. We need this job. There'll be plenty of girls around after we've got paid. So get your mind off your dick for a change.'

Valko sulked, turned away to look out of the window, while Viktor ignored him. It was time his brother grew up.

As they drove up the mountain road, Viktor noticed that the further up the mountain side they went, there was more distance between the houses, they were larger, more impressive, further back from the road with surrounding walls, and longer driveways. Many of the properties had long garages, others had very expensive looking vehicles parked outside them, and a couple actually had swimming pools in the side garden that could be seen from the road. There were differences in sizes and shapes of the homes but, in some features they were all the same; white-washed, glinting in the mid-day sunshine. The higher they climbed, the more glass the houses had affording panoramic views of the bay.

'Will you look at these houses,' said Viktor.

'It's not the houses I'm looking at,' said Valko, 'it's the cars, and them speedboats up on trailers. They're all over the friggin' place.' They fell silent awed by the affluence. Valko was overwhelmed, and not a little alarmed about being in a place like this. He was more accustomed to the more sleazy side of life, and living in cheap hotels. 'Just what the 'ell are we doin' 'ere?' He gazed at the surroundings and slunk down in his seat. 'This old Volvo with its dents looks well out of place here, don't it Viktor? We don't belong here. Might as well have a sign on our heads: Strangers! Thieves! Be on the lookout for these men,' said Valko.

'Yeah,' Viktor laughed. 'And they'd be right, wouldn't they? We're not really the type of people the locals would want as neighbours, but if I've got it right, this job might change all that.'

'Let's just turn round and go back the way we came,' said Valko. 'Yeah, let's just piss off outta here, an' forget all about this Mr Maartens.'

'No, we're going to stick with this. The money we get from this job will set us up nicely.' He grinned across at Valko. 'No, little brother, we're staying for this one. There's no running away. We get the job done, then we find somewhere we like ... maybe go straight.'

Valko thought about it for a moment. 'Yeah, okay Viktor, and let's just say it does change everything for us, what d'you wanna do with your share?'

'Put it together with yours, go back to Bulgaria and spend it on living well in the family home country.'

'Fuck that, brother!' We have nothing to go back for!'

Valko couldn't believe what he was hearing. 'Well, back to London then.'

Continuing to watch the road, Viktor cast a scornful glance in Valko's direction. 'No. We will go back to Bulgaria, but not to stay. You're right, we don't have anyone to go back to, but it would be good to go back with money.' His grin faded, replaced with a dark frown. 'I want to show them that we are wealthy and people to be respected now.' He slapped the steering wheel. 'I want to go back wearing gold rings, have the gap in my teeth filled with a gold one. I want those in dad's village who rubbished me and beat you, to know we have made it. They won't mess with us again, and then we go.'

Valko listened in silence.

'Then we choose somewhere good to live,' Viktor continued, 'we have champagne, steak, cars, girls.' He turned to Valko. 'Then we have anything we want, go anywhere, it doesn't matter. We do what *we* want. And now we are here.' He turned the car through tall open gates and into the driveway of a two-storey, red-tiled rooved, white-washed house with a glass-fronted balcony that stretched the breadth of the house.

Having parked the Volvo, which looked absurdly shabby next to a silver and black Jeep SUV; Viktor promised himself he would dump the Volvo and buy himself a decent car when they got paid, whatever the job was. Walking towards the door, Viktor missed seeing that Valko had stopped to gawp at the green Bentley Continental parked in the shade of the car port.

The front door opened, and a man who Viktor guessed was of mixed race, and who could only be described as a giant, waited with a look of disdainful tranquillity at them. As they approached, Viktor estimated the man was close on two metres tall and clearly muscled. He was not only impressed by his height, but being dressed in full, formal uniform of black evening jacket, black waistcoat, grey pin-striped trousers, crisp white shirt and a black cravat, he should have been sweltering, but showed no sign of sweating. Very cool. But Viktor also realised the man was more than a manservant; he had the build of a bodyguard, and commanded immediate respect. But the butler, if that's what he was, was looking beyond him towards the car port and realised that Valko was still standing by the Bentley.

'Valko! Get over here now,' sighed Viktor. His awkward smile at the butler was not returned. Valko ran over to join his brother and finally the butler spoke.

'Can I help you?' His deep voice matched his physique and his accent was definitely not South African, but Viktor could not place it.

'Viktor and Valko Nikolov, here to see Mr Maartens. He's expecting us.' He nudged Valko whose attention was now directed at a tall, red-haired girl as she walked through the reception area behind the butler, carrying two filled champagne flutes. Valko took in every inch of her shiny gold, thigh length jacket, open at the front revealing a leopard-print bikini. She glanced towards the door briefly, but showed no sign of interest in the newcomers before disappearing down a corridor to the left. The butler raised an eyebrow at Valko's disrespectful stare.

'Valko! That's not what we are here for. Get a grip.' Viktor was getting annoyed and Valko knew better than to try his brother's patience any further.

'Very well. Please come in. I will let Mr Maartens know you are here. You can wait in the library. I will show you where it is.'

Viktor tugged at Valko's arm. 'Pay attention, Valko. We're here on business, remember?'

The manservant opened the door a little wider; enough for single file entry only. Valko followed Viktor into the marble-floored hallway, and they were directed towards a large, well-furnished room, with white walls and ceiling and wood-tiled floor. The far wall was fully triple-glazed with patio doors that were slightly open allowing a soft warm breeze into the room, and the gentle sounds of flowing water and, of more interest to Valko, female laughter.

To their right was the reason the room was called the library. Right along, from one side to the other, the wall was entirely filled with bookshelves from the floor to the ceiling, mostly with hard-cover books, which implied that an awful lot of money had been spent, and someone loved reading.

Intrigued, Valko scanned the room wondering just how much it had cost Maartens to furnish this room, never mind the entire house. To their left was a large black metal rectangle fireplace, with a glass front and laid with logs. In front of the hearth lay a vibrant Berber rug in browns, yellows and greens, the colours of nature, that extended beyond either side of the fireplace. And, in front of the fireplace, side by side were two round black wood coffee tables ornately carved with images of indigenous animals.

'Is that ebony?' Valko asked the butler.

'It's actually mpingo, a very tall tree, very like ebony, that grows here in the south and in central Africa. I do not carve, but I understand it is a particular favourite to our craftsmen as it good to work with.'

'Thank you,' said Valko, turning back to examine the detail of the carvings. 'They are very impressive, must have cost a lot of money.' The butler said nothing.

The tables were bordered by two three-seater sofas covered in textile throws and cushions, matching the colours of the hearth rug; they also appeared handcrafted.

Viktor and Valko gazed around the beautiful room with its strong African theme with several Zulu weapons: clubs, spears, and shields covered in what looked like white and brown patched cowhide displayed around the room, and colourful beaded necklaces and bracelets hanging on hooks on the bookshelves and above the fireplace.

Valko turned to the butler who had clearly been keeping an eye on the brothers. 'I have been trying to learn a bit of the IsiZulu language since we have been here. Am I right that the clubs are called knobkerries and the spears, assegai?'

The butler nodded, and for once gave a hint of a smile. 'Yes, both right.'

'What about the shield?'

'Ishilunga.'

'Ishilunga. Thanks. I'll remember that.'

Viktor frowned. What was Valko up to. He had never shown any interest in local languages anywhere else they had been.

But Valko's questions seemed to have allayed some of the butler's guarded opinion of the brothers. Perhaps there was more to them than he supposed. He turned to leave, but halted in the doorway. 'You will remain here, please, until Mr Maartens is ready to see you. He is currently in engaged elsewhere. Please make yourselves comfortable. There are magazines on the coffee table and I can have some refreshment sent to you. Tea, coffee...a cold beer, perhaps.'

'But he asked for us to be here at this time!' Viktor protested.

'And he will be here...when he is ready. As I stated, Mr Nikolov, Mr Maartens is otherwise occupied at present. Wait or don't wait. The choice is yours. However, for the reason that brought you here, I would advise you that waiting would be most advantageous to you and your brother.' He scowled across at Valko, who was examining the bookshelves, taking a book to look at then replacing it, and moving onto another. 'Here, Mr Butler...sorry, what did you say your name was? Has Mr Maartens read all of these then?'

'No. He hasn't,' the butler ignored the comment about his name, 'just most of them. Mr Maartens is a keen reader, particularly of maritime tales, diving, long sea journeys, shipwrecks, that sort of thing.' He turned to Viktor. 'I presume you would both prefer a cold beer to something hot, yes?' His previously frosty manner definitely seemed to have thawed a little.

Viktor nodded. 'Yeah, that would be good, thanks. You said Mr Maartens was interested in diving?'

'Yes, but I have some concern when he goes on diving trips in the bay here. There are some fairly large sharks, including great whites seen here regularly, and especially in the summer months, like now, when we have shoals of yellowtail snappers coming in. When they do, you can be sure the sharks are not far behind.'

'I didn't know Mr Maartens dived, so do we, and we have experience in being around sharks. Do you dive?'

'Absolutely not. I have to confess to being terrified of sharks. No, a walk along the beach is more than sufficient for me, thank you. Crabs that nip you, sharks that bite you, waves that drown you, are not on my list of fun things. Now, I will get you that beer. Help yourself to magazines, there are packs of cards in the desk drawer, but...young man...' he looked at Valko, 'please return the books to the shelves and then leave them alone. Thank you.' He left the room.

'Is he for real?' said Valko, walking over to join his brother. 'A big guy like that afraid of little crabs.'

Viktor chuckled. 'Well, they say elephants are scared of mice, so maybe. It's interesting that the boss is a diver. I wonder if that's got anything to do with why we're here?' The brothers took seats at the highly polished wooden table, and Valko opened the drawer to take out a pack of playing cards. Female laughter, following by the sound of splashing and a man's voice were heard outside. The brothers got up from the table and went to stand at the patio doors, concealed by the floor length vertical blinds. Valko moved a couple of the blinds, just enough to peep out to the pool area, without being seen. Viktor, slightly taller than his younger brother, stood behind, looking over Valko's shoulder.

The girl in the leopard-skin bikini was lying on a sunbed, giggling, her hand over the top of one of the champagne flutes, while a grey haired, bearded man in the pool was splashing water at her.

'Come on in, Rhonda, leave the champagne.'

'But it will get warm,' she said with a teasing smile.

'Then I'll buzz for Mel to bring a cold box out.'

'But what about your visitors, Andries? They'll be waiting for you.'

'Ah, Mel and Thabisa can take care of them. Thabisa has all the detail she needs. Just press that switch, Rhonda. It rings through in the office and Thabisa will come for instructions. She can tell Mel to bring out the cold box.'

Rhonda, dripping and bare-footed glided over to the push-button on the wall, and pressed it. She heard nothing.

'I didn't hear a buzz, Andries. Is it working?'

'Yes, Mr Maartens?' A tall, slim young mixed race woman, in a sleeveless pale blue mini dress, and gold coloured toe-post sandals, slipped quietly out onto the patio on the other side of the pool. Andries Maartens swam up to the edge of the pool to meet her.

'Ah, Thabisa. The gentlemen we spoke about this morning are here, and I would like you to deal with them for me, please.' He smirked, and looked in Rhonda's direction. 'As you can see, I am a little tied up at the moment, and you know all there is to know about my proposal to them. You have all the paperwork they will require.' He swam over to the steps to haul himself out of the pool. 'Tell them I will be too busy to see them today.'

'Yes, Mr Maartens.' Thabisa was about to walk back inside when he called her back. 'And, Thabisa, ask Mel to bring out the cold box, another bottle of champagne and I think some cheese snacks, please.'

Yes, Mr Maartens.' Thabisa turned to go back inside, but stopped, when Rhonda called her back.

'Oh, and grapes, please, Thabisa,' said Rhonda.

Thabisa did not respond. Viktor had already returned to the table, but Valko thought he saw a flicker of resentment cross Thabisa's face at Rhonda's request, that vanished almost instantly just before she disappeared through the doors.

'So, he hasn't got time for us,' said Valko, back at the table. 'He's busy, huh!' He threw down the card pack onto the table. 'Well, brother, what do we do? Do we wait to see the lady, or leave now?'

The door opened and the butler brought in two pint glasses bearing the name *Castle Lager*.

'My apologies, I meant to bring these before but I was sidetracked. I understand that Mr Maartens will not be long now.'

Valko opened his mouth to speak but Viktor's barely noticeable shake of the head stopped him. 'That's fine, thank you, um...I'm sorry, I didn't get your name?'

'It's Meluzmi, but everyone calls me Mel.'

'Well, thank you for the beers, Mel, we'll wait. After all, we have nothing better to do, have we Valko?'

'Um ... no.' Valko said, puzzled. If Maartens couldn't be bothered to meet them, then why were they going to wait? He turned back to the window and gently parted two of the blinds a little, hoping the movement was not seen by the couple outside. The last thing he wanted for Maartens to know he had been spying on them, but he was drawn to the beautiful and voluptuous Rhonda, she fascinated him. He found it difficult to take his eyes off her, and gazed at her admiringly. If he had a girl like that to spend time with, would he want to leave her to meet up with a couple of low-life types like him and Viktor? He sniggered. Hell no, of course he wouldn't, especially if he had someone else who could stand in for him. He looked behind to find Mel had left the room, and Viktor was relaxing in an armchair in the corner of the room next to the bookshelves, thumbing through an Auto Express magazine.

His eyes were drawn back to the pool. Maartens and Rhonda were now making out on one sunbed in the shade of a large parasol, their champagne flutes standing side by side on a small table. From behind the blinds, Valko studied Rhonda as she kissed Andries passionately on the mouth. He envied Maartens, closed his eyes and imagined it was him Rhonda was making love to. No. Stop this. There was a word for what he was doing. He couldn't remember it, but he couldn't tear himself away.

Maartens left hand stroked Rhonda's hair, then grasping a handful of her auburn locks, he gently tugged her head away to look into her eyes. Rhonda leaned forward, kissed his neck, her tongue flickering around his throat. She slithered a little further down the sunbed to kiss his chest, her right hand moved further down his belly, and he laid back, giving her unspoken permission to continue. Valko was incapable of taking his eyes off the sensual scene playing out in front of him. He wondered how far they would go when they knew there were people about. Surely they would go inside to continue what they were doing in private.

Then two things happened at once. Supporting himself with one elbow, Maartens raised himself up, and as Rhonda moved further down the sunbed, he turned to look directly at the window where Valko was hiding behind the blinds. And, being so obsessed with concentrating on the couple on the sunbed, Valko could not take his gaze away, fixated by the scene by the pool and wondering how far the couple would go. Engrossed, he flinched as Viktor put a hand on his shoulder.

'Come away, little brother. Watching them is not good for you, or for us. It is no way to impress someone we want to work for.'

The door opened and Thabisa entered carrying a dark red leather brief case.

'I am Mr Maartens assistant,' she declared, as she walked towards the desk. 'Take a seat, gentlemen, and we will discuss the reason you are here. Unfortunately, Mr Maartens is otherwise engaged and is unable to meet you personally.'

Valko sniggered, as he sat down on a seat on the other side of the desk from Thabisa. He received a withering look from her, and a kick in the shin from Viktor.

Thabisa ignored the interruption and continued '...and has asked me to go through the necessary details with you.'

'What is the job?' asked Viktor.

Thabisa clicked open the brief case but did not lift the lid. 'You will be travelling to Tenerife...'

'What? Hey, that's cool, Viktor. We haven't ...'

'Shut up and let the lady speak, Valko,' snapped Viktor.

Thabisa gave Valko a frosty scowl. 'Thank you. I'll continue, and if you have any questions, please leave them until after I have gone through everything with you. It will save me from having to repeat myself.' From the brief case, Thabisa took a single white envelope which she handed to Viktor. You have been recommended as qualified and experienced shipwreck divers. The job is to locate an eighteenth century wreck that went down close to La Gomera. We have been given the details of the location but, of course time and currents will have done their damage and she, or parts of her, will probably have drifted. Finding her remains may not be easy. You also need to understand that secrecy is vital. As far as we are aware only three people at present know of her existence. That will be taken care of.'

Valko swallowed. What did she mean by would be taken care of? He looked at Viktor, but his brother showed no sign of concern.

'These are your flight tickets to Tenerife. There are no direct flights from here, so you will fly to Amsterdam and take a connecting flight to Tenerife South. There you will hire a car and drive to Masca where you will stay with one of our associates, more about her in a moment. Your new passports are also in here.'

'But we have passports.'

'Mr Maartens would prefer that you make no contact with people other than our colleagues. We have provided documents to give a false trail if for any reason the Guardia Civil approach you while you are on the island, or try to trace you after you have left. Hopefully you will not need those documents after you have left Tenerife South airport. However, you will need to use them for hiring your car at the airport, where you will have to produce passports and credit cards. In this envelope you will find everything you need, passports, credit cards and car hire vouchers in assumed names, make sure you are familiar with them. If anything did go wrong and the Guardia Civil try to trace you, they will find dead ends with your false identities. In addition to those documents, bank accounts have been opened in your new names as well. If everything goes to plan, you will not need to use any of them again. Keep to Moya's house and the boat trips with Anton, keep your heads down, and hopefully no-one will notice you, thereby avoiding awkward questions. Viktor and Valko Nikolov will never have arrived on the island of Tenerife. Do you understand me? Thabisa's manner was impersonal, business-like to the point of being offensive. It was clear she didn't give a damn about them, they were not worth her courtesy. 'We know the type of people you have worked for previously, and we know the...varied types of...work...you have carried out. You do what you have to, to get the job done, and so do we ... whatever it takes.' She glared, almost with distaste, at them both from under her long eyelashes. Valko was intimidated by her, but Viktor's anger was intensifying. Who the Hell was she to disrespect them. After all, she too was just the hired help, but not prepared to lose a big pay day, he held his tongue.

Thabisa continued. 'There can be no mistakes. Be the professionals we have been told you are, and for which you will be very well paid.'

'But how ...' Viktor began.

'I *said* you can ask any questions you may have when I have finished, Mr Nikolov. I will continue. We have a number of associates we contact when we need to find the kind of people Mr Maartens needs. Their backgrounds and any other details necessary, such as that you were born to Bulgarian parents, and lived in the coastal city of Varna in North Bulgaria into your early teens. That is where you both took up scuba diving. Following the death of your parents in a car accident, you moved to London to stay with other members of your family, and there you became members of a group of people who lived outside of the Law. Whilst there, three years ago an incident took place that went very wrong ... it was not your fault, but you chose to leave the UK, went firstly to Rome, moved on to Tunisia, then Johannesburg, and now Cape Town. Need I continue?'

Viktor nodded. 'I'm impressed. You've been very thorough, but no. I can see you have done your homework.' She was incredibly well informed.

Thabisa then went back to giving them their instructions.

She took out a second envelope from the brief case. 'These are the details of our colleague who will be looking after you. She will give you further updates when you get to Tenerife. Her name is Moya Gibson, and you will find her address in here. You will spend your time with her, and another associate by the name of Anton, at Moya's home. Anton has all the information you need regarding the dive location, currents and tides. Everything you need to know is there. Do nothing to call attention to yourself and if anyone asks, you are there for the diving and whale watching. You will go sea fishing with Anton. I understand the sea can be quite rough in parts of the channel between the islands, but I am sure with all your experience, you will be able to cope with that. Anton and Moya also have everything you require in the way of scuba equipment, and they have access to a fishing boat that is regularly seen taking people on fishing trips. Anton will take you out into the channel from a small quiet harbour each day. If anyone asks, you are on a fishing and diving holiday.'

'How will we get to Tenerife?' asked Valko.

Thabisa took a deep breath and scowled at Valko. Her look said it all. He shut up.

She withdrew a third envelope from the brief case, and handed it to Viktor. 'Inside are your flight details to and from Tenerife South – Reina Sofia Airport via Amsterdam Schiphol Airport. You will fly out in two days. There is a hire car voucher, you will collect the car from the airport. Everything is in your assumed names, so start drilling them into your heads now to give yourselves time to become accustomed to using them. In a distracted moment, it is easy to make a mistake, use your given names and you put this … venture in jeopardy.' She hesitated, looked at them both, as if to give them time assimilate what she had just said. 'However, if all goes well, your only company will be Moya and Anton, and those names will not be an issue.'

She looked down at the brief case. There had been no mention of money. Viktor was beginning to wonder if they were expected to wait until after the job was done to be paid. That would be pretty normal, but he would have liked to know how much they were going to get.

'Now, there are just a few more things.' Thabisa put her hand in the brief case and this time pulled out a white plastic wallet, that appeared tightly packed. 'In here are five thousand Euros in various denominations. This is to be used for your expenses. You do not have to pay Moya for her hospitality. She has already been paid for your food etc. but she is not a maid. While you are there you will respect her home, and not treat her as you would your mother.'

Viktor gave a silent sigh of relief. Valko grinned. Thabisa ignored them both.

'Spend this carefully. Whatever is left at the end of this task will be added to your final pay.'

She reached in to the brief case again and pulled out a mobile phone.

'This is a burner phone. It is not registered, it's prepaid and will be used only for communication between myself, Mr Maartens and you, Mr Nikolov. Now there's one last item. And it is the most important.' From the brief case she produced a blue plastic file.

'This is your task. In this document, you will find the details, as far as we know them and the location of the shipwreck we are seeking.'

'Can I ask a question now?'

'Yes.'

'The registration with PADI is in our assumed names?' asked Viktor.

'Of course,' said Thabisa. The look on her face suggested that she thought that question should not have needed to be asked. 'Exactly the same as your passports. Names, dates of birth, and all other required information is identical. However, only use them if absolutely necessary. However, whenever possible your dives will be kept to yourselves and Anton. Avoid any socialising if at all possible.'

Thabisa sat down on the chair behind the desk, clasped her hands together and rested her arms on the desk. 'Mr Maartens has given me permission to give you background information. He felt it was necessary that you know what is required of you both, and how this came about. Mr Maartens is an enthusiastic marine historian, with an interest in shipwrecks, particularly where Spanish treasure was involved. A short while ago he heard of a Spanish treasure ship, the *Katerina-Thereza,* that sank and, we believe, virtually disintegrated in a terrible storm off the island of La Gomera, in seventeen-twenty-two, across the channel from Tenerife. It seems that until very recently no-one had heard about her, but papers have been discovered confirming her loss.

'A specialist historian, Edward Taylor-Owen living in Santiago, very near Playa de la Arena, came across details of where she is likely to be, although there is a very good chance that the shifting seas, and currents may have moved what is left of her. He also dives by the way and is friends with other divers locally.'

'Hey, you had me at treasure ship,' said Valko.

'Yes, I thought would appeal to your mercenary nature,' said Thabisa.

'So you want us to dive and find her?' asked Viktor.

'Yes. Mr Maartens wants you to find out what Taylor-Owen knows from Anton who works closely with him. Try to locate the *Katerina-Thereza.*'

'Is there anything else we need to know?' Viktor was looking sceptical.

'Yes. La Gomera is an extinct volcanic island. The tallest mountain being Alto de Garajonay. It is believed that the last volcanic activity was around three million years ago.'

'So not likely to be too hot when we get there then,' said Valko.

Thabisa shot him a withering look and continued with what she was saying. 'As the lava flowed downwards it hit the sea and cooled, leaving tunnels, tubes, and small caverns. These are perfect places for hiding anything you don't want anyone else to know you have. You will find a safe, suitable hiding space for any treasure or artefacts, relics you may find. Speak to Moya about how and when you bring anything you find to the surface.'

'So if Mr Maartens wants this treasure, how do we get it to him?'

'He has a motor boat, the *Amahle,* moored at Agadir. When he and Moya feel the time is right, he will come across to La Gomera in the *Amahle* to collect on his investment. In a month from today, he will join you both either at San Sebastian, La Gomera, or somewhere near

Los Cristianos. Those final plans have yet to be decided, but Moya will be kept updated.'

Valko was about to say something, but a sideways glance from Viktor warned him to stay quiet. If Thabisa noticed Valko's cut-off interruption she ignored it. She continued. 'Mr Maartens is limiting the duration of this undertaking to no longer than one month. The longer it takes, the more it increases the risks of you drawing attention to yourselves. So you have one month, no more. Also, with the information you will gain, Mr Maartens considers this optimum length of time to make this undertaking, and his investment in it, worthwhile.'

'You will be notified, via Moya or Anton, when the *Amahle* has left Agadir and Mr Maartens is on his way to join you. At that time you will begin to dispose, securely, of any unnecessary documentation.

'On his arrival, you will have one last dive to retrieve whatever, let's call them assets, you may have amassed, load it onto the *Amahle* and together with Anton you will sail back with Mr Maartens.'

'But you said you had booked return flights for us,' said Viktor.

Thabisa sighed and gave Viktor an exasperated glare, raised her eyebrows.

'The return flight was booked to make it appear that you are both there for nothing other than a diving, fishing extended holiday. It is nothing more than a smokescreen in case you do find yourself in conversation with outsiders, using your adopted names, of course. By making mention of your return flights occasionally during conversations with people you get talking to, you will be leaving a false trail that strengthens your story.

'You look doubtful, Mr Nikolov. Is there something about those instructions you don't like?'

'No, no, it's nothing to do with that. My questions is how does Mr Maartens know for certain that the treasure is definitely there?'

'He would not doubt Mr Taylor-Owen. His knowledge of shipwrecks around the islands is second-to-none, legendary. He has records of sunken Spanish treasure ships off Florida and elsewhere but, as I mentioned earlier, this one is not on the available records, and Mr Maartens wants this explored. So, with your diving expertise he hopes you will find whatever remains of the ship in question, and see what can be...lets' say, salvaged.'

'Why is he so convinced?' Viktor asked, again.

Thabisa rolled her eyes. She was clearly growing impatient with answering the same questions, and was wondering what it would take to reassure these two men, and how quickly she could get rid of them. This was taking far too long and becoming annoying. 'I have already given the answer to that question. If Taylor-Owen is prepared to follow this lead, that is good enough for Mr Maartens. He respects Mr Taylor-Owen's experience, knowledge and instincts. The man is a scholar, a goldmine of information, and certainly does his research. He has found several wrecks in the past few years just through research and cross checking data. Mr Maartens is a big fan of his.'

'And do they know each other?'

Thabisa hesitated and for the first time seemed a little unsure of herself. 'Um...well, Mr Maartens obviously knows Mr Taylor-Owen, but let's say that Mr Maartens has been watching Mr Taylor-Owen from afar, and he certainly appreciates his expertise.'

'So, this will be without this Taylor-Owen's permission or assistance.'

'Uh...yes. I assume that does not bother you?'

'No, not at all. It's just good to know how things stand. Valko and me are used to working in and outside of the law wherever we are. I speak for both of us when I say we are prepared to go through with this, but what do we get out of it besides a month's free holiday in the Canary Islands.'

'You get a flat fee of fifty thousand American Dollars ...,'

'Wow! D'you hear that, Viktor.' Valko sat forward on his chair, beaming. Viktor remained looking directly at Thabisa, trying to read her face.

'...and a percentage from the treasure haul of ten percent. The more you acquire, the more you will earn.'

'And what if things go wrong? How far do you want us to go?'

'It is not what I want. It is Mr Maartens who will be paying you and it's what he wants. As I understand it, for that money he will require you to do whatever is necessary to get the job done satisfactorily.'

Viktor did not react. 'I understand. Now, apart from this man, Anton, and what was her name...'

'Moya Gibson.'

'Yeah, Moya. Is there anyone else on the islands involved who we need to know about, and what are their roles in all this?'

'Anton, is the assistant to Mr Taylor-Owen, but he works for Mr Maartens. He feeds us information on what Taylor-Owen is currently working on. His information is always valuable and timely. Moya has worked for Mr Maartens and carries out a few facilitating jobs for other people. She and Mr Maartens have been ... friends for many, many years, and she is totally reliable.'

'One more question before we go. Are we likely to meet the obviously very busy Mr Maartens today?'

'Not today. You may receive an invitation to meet him before your flight.'

'Good.'

'Then again you might not.'

'Okay. I get it. Don't mix with the guys who are doing your dirty work.'

'If that is what you choose to think, who am I to say anything different.'

Viktor nodded. 'Can I have the brief case to keep all these papers in?'

Thabisa nodded. 'I don't see why not.'

'Come on, Valko. Time to go. We have some reading to do.' He turned to Thabisa.

'He sounds pretty ruthless. Why do you work for him?'

She gave a sad little smile. 'I can't do anything else, neither can Meluzmi. He is our father.'

'Shit! And I thought our old man was bad,' said Valko.

Viktor opened the library door and walked out into the hallway to find Meluzmi waiting to see them out. 'That's some father you have there.'

Meluzmi shrugged his shoulders. 'This is South Africa. You do what you have to.'

Valko had just left the library, when he ran back. 'Thabisa, that trip from Agadir you were talking about when Mr Maar … your father comes to Tenerife.'

'Yes, what about it?'

'Ask him to bring Rhonda with him.' Valko ran back to where Viktor was standing at the door waiting for him, unsure whether to slap his brother, or laugh at him.

Chapter Twenty

Gozo : Diving in Xlendi

'Okay, so now we're here in Xlendi,' Jake pulled up in little square on the other side to where a number of long and sleek green and white buses were parked, and small groups of people waited at the stands for doors to be opened.

The sky was clear apart from the occasional wispy cloud and the air was already warm guaranteeing another very warm day. Luke thought back to the rainy summer days in Birmingham, the tall blocks of offices and apartments. He tried to recall if he ever actually looked up. All he remembered was looking out for traffic, or rushing to the office. In the darker winter months he started work so early and finished so late, he rarely saw daylight, let alone the sky. And now here he was with this vast sky and low buildings, and the world was an entirely different place.

'Hey, daydreamer.' Jake was already at the back of the car hauling two large canvas bags out of the boot. He handed one to Luke. The bags were heavier than they looked. Jake closed the boot and clicked the fob to lock the car. 'This way to the harbour. There's a lot of small boats moored near to the harbour wall, so part of the bay has been roped off for the safety of swimmers. That's where we'll try you out with the Scuba gear.' He led Luke down a short road full of cafés with quite a few occupied tables outside, which surprised Luke, as it was only eight-thirty in the morning, and he only finished his breakfast at the hotel a short while before. There were several shops on either side of the road with carefully displayed local hand knitted jumpers and cardigans and lace, beach towels, blow up water beds, postcards, sandals, snorkelling masks and breathing tubes, a couple of souvenir shops had glass-topped freezers containing more flavours of ice cream than Luke had even seen in one place before. He stopped to look, but Jake tugged his arm and led him away. 'No trying to put it off now. You're going in.'

'Oh great.' Luke seemed less than enthusiastic about trying Scuba diving, even though he had, eventually, enjoyed snorkelling.

'Oh come on, Luke, you big wuss. God knows what working in an office all this time has done to your adventurous streak. You were the one who pushed me into climbing trees, stealing apples, racing our bikes around the village, remember?'

Luke laughed. 'Yeah, I remember. I remember the scrapes you got me into as well.'

'Oh, yeah. Okay well we'll skip over those. Come on, let's get you into the sea again.'

As they rounded the corner, Luke had expected so see a rounded bay like most of the others he had seen, but Xlendi was a surprise to him. The inlet was, he estimated, about one hundred metres across, and the completely straight promenade had cafés, with canvas-covered seating areas against the sea wall.

Looking over the wall, Luke could see the roped off area that Jake had mentioned. Bright, orange-coloured cork floats prevented the rope from sinking, keeping it highly visible to nearby boat users. So it looked safe enough.

On the right side of the harbour was a low jetty that separated a small section of the harbour in which several small boats were moored, but there were a few more that shifted gracefully on the sun-kissed wavelets a little way beyond the rope. Just as Luke had seen at the Blue Lagoon, the water at Xlendi was clean, perfectly clear and, had it not been for the easy-going movement of the sea, he could have been looking through a window.

'We'll go up there to get ready,' he pointed to the far end of the promenade. 'There's steps into the water, and I know Vincent, the café owner there. He'll look after our things while we're in.' Jake introduced Luke to Vincent Fenech, a tall, lean man who, Jake said had owned the café for many years after it was handed down to him from his father. 'Vincent always lets me stow my things at the back of the café when I dive here. Sometimes he comes with me, but you're not a keen diver, are you, old mate? This is my brother, Luke. He's over from the UK on holiday.'

Vincent grinned widely. 'I am happier on land most of the time, but just occasionally I dive when we know the turtles are here, I like to see them, and they like to see me.' He smiled at Luke. 'First time diving?'

'Uh-huh. So I hope Jake keeps me safe.'

'He will. He knows what he's doing and why would he not look after his brother?' He turned to Jake and winked. 'I'll have coffee and lunch ready for you when you finish. Calamari?'

Jake laughed. 'You know better than that, Vincent. Calamari and I don't get on, and it'll be lunchtime when we're out and dried off. Pastizzi and beer, please Vincent.' Vincent walked away chuckling.

In an unoccupied corner of the café, the brothers stripped down to their swimming shorts, and got into their shorty wetsuits, exposing legs from just above the knee and arms from just above the elbow. Jake lifted one of the bags, handed the other to Luke. Jake waved to Vincent and they walked out of the café to sit at the top of the steps with their feet dangling in the water. Jake understood Luke's nervousness. He had been the same on his first dive, before he fell in love with being underwater, but Luke didn't want too much time to think. He reached down into one of the bags and pulled out two masks.

'Right, now, the mask. I brought the one you used before, it just needs a little adjustment of the straps to make it fit correctly, again. One thing to remember at all times, Luke, is when you're going in or out of the water slip the mask down around your neck. You put it on just before you go underwater, but don't leave it on your head when you're not about to use it.'

Luke looked quizzical.

'Okay, so whenever you're getting in or out of the water, there's always a chance you might have a wave knock into you or there may be some drag-back. If you fall over or slip, the mask could be ripped off and lost. There's no such thing cheap good diving equipment, unless you buy low-grade quality, and that's not worth having.' He picked up the mask. 'And don't forget. there's a procedure to go through before you put the mask on to stop it fogging up underwater.

I've already treated this one for de-fogging, so you don't have to worry about that either for now but, as you know, we usually spit into the mask rub it around then rinse it. If you get a mask of your own it'll be as well to remember the processes, but we'll skip some today. I can take you through them fully next time...'

'...If there's a next time.'

'Chicken. There will be. Once you've tried it, you'll be hooked, like me. So back to the mask.'

Jake placed the mask on Luke's face but did not place the strap over his head. 'Okay, inhale through your nose, that will create suction that will hold the mask in place for a moment, and it'll cling to your face.' He looked all around the seal to check the fit was snug enough to prevent water seeping in. 'We'll check it again as soon as you're submerged but the pressure of the water against it keeps the seal...unless it's faulty.' He placed the strap over Luke's head. 'How does that feel? Not too tight?'

'It feels tight, but not uncomfortable.'

'Good.'

'When you were snorkelling, I didn't go through the scuba hand signals. We didn't need to then, but we do now, so I'll go through some basic hand signals, then we'll get suited up. To be honest, the water's warm enough and we won't be in for long, so you could just go in your swimming shorts, but I wanted you to get the feel of the suit, and the BCD...'

'BCD?'

'Buoyancy Control Device. It allows you to maintain a level of buoyancy, so you stay at a level in the water.'

'Okay, so how will I know how to do that?'

'You won't have to today. I'll do that for you. So onto the signals. Now the first one is to show you're happy with everything. Everything's okay. With your right hand, thumb and forefinger make an 'O' the other fingers point upward. That's the okay sign. Next, thumbs go up or down, for up or down. Simple. Got those?'

'Yeah. Of course.'

'Okay next one. Hold your right hand out flat.' Luke did as he was told. 'Now tilt it from side to side. Good. Now remember that's the sign for something's wrong, you've got a problem, like maybe you're having trouble breathing, or you can't balance the pressure in your ears. Whatever it is, after letting your instructor know there's something wrong, point to it. They're not going to know what to help you with unless you indicate where the problem is. Goes without saying really, but I'm used to telling beginners that. The only other one you'll need today is the look at me sign. You'll have seen in films when someone makes a fist turns it towards their own face and points the first and middle fingers towards their eyes then towards someone else implying that they're watching them. Well, that's the same sign we use to show a beginner that they must watch what their instructor is doing, or trying to tell them. Got all that?'

'Yes, I think so, just five signals.' Luke repeated the gestures to show he understood.

'Right, well those are the most important signs you'll need today. If you find you enjoy yourself and want to go again, which you will, we'll maybe go out to a reef, I'll take you through the others then.' He reached into the other bag and pulled out what looked like a dial on the end of a cable. 'Now this is your most important piece of equipment. It's the regulator. It connects to your dive tank, the (BCD), the pressure gauge and the diver. Without this you cannot breathe underwater...unless you're Harry Potter and you've got some Gillyweed handy. Do you want me to go into the technical details?'

Luke shook his head. 'No, it's fine for now but if I do this again, it'll be more important then.'

'Good, it's quite detailed so another time suits me too.' He showed Luke the air pressure gauge. 'This also connects directly to the air tank. When the tank is full, it shows two hundred bars. As a beginner, you may use up around thirty bars very quickly as you control your breathing. Once you relax and your breathing settles down, you'll use your air more slowly. You have two hundred bars showing on the pressure gauge to start. When the gauge shows there's only fifty bars we'll exit the water.

'One important thing to remember is keeping an eye on how much air you are using going out. You have to remember that you need to exit the water when you have fifty bars left on the gauge. Whatever the distance of your dive, you're going to use the same amount of air for your return, and you still need the fifty at the end for safety. So, an example would be seventy-five bars used going out, seventy-five bars going back, which leaves you the safe level of fifty to exit.' They carried the diving gear down the steps where they stood in the shallow water and Jake helped Luke put on the BCD, with a ten litre air cylinder, buckled up the straps and added a few weights into the pockets. Luke grimaced at the sudden heaviness of the BCD.

'The weights help you to go down, but you won't feel the weight so much when you're in the water.'

Jake looked beyond Luke and smiled. 'It looks as though we have an audience.' A group of children, Luke guessed were all about ten or eleven years old, had been playing in the water nearby but were now watching with interest at what the brothers were doing.

'Let's hope I don't disappoint them,' said Luke.

'There's them negative thought waves, again.'

Luke looked around to see if the children were still watching. They were. One little boy gave him a toothy grin and the thumbs up sign. Luke smiled back at him.

'Forget the kids and just concentrate on what we're doing. On another dive, it might save your life!'

'Yes, boss.'

'Okay, you're ready to submerge. At this depth you'll be able to kneel on the bottom with only a few centimetres of water above your head, so remember, any problems, all you need to do it stand up and you'll breathe air again. Just keep your eyes fixed on mine until you're happy with your breathing, then we'll stick around here for a while until you get the hang of things, and then when you're relaxed we'll move further out into the bay, but here, as you can see, you're close to the shore at all times. You're not in danger at any time. Okay with that?'

'I guess so. If Ellie could see me now.'

Together the brothers dropped to their knees and Luke felt the cool sea water seep into his wetsuit, but soon his body temperature warmed the water inside and he felt comfortable. What he wasn't comfortable with was his breathing. His heart thumped in his chest and total panic took over. Jake made the sign for the eye to eye contact, followed by the okay sign. Luke remembered how to answer.

He held out his flat right hand and tilted the sides up and down. No, he wasn't okay. Jake signed they should stand again.

'Breathing?'

'Yeah. It just didn't feel right. You spend all your life believing you can't breathe underwater, and I guess I just panicked.'

'You're not the first. It's a normal reaction, but you can, people do it all the time with the right equipment, and telling your brain that you can. We'll try again, but this time concentrate on steadying your breathing. In and out, focus on it. You have enough air there and you'll be fine, but controlling your breathing will help you calm down, before long you won't even think about it.'

'Okay. I want to try again.'

'So, as you go down, keep looking at me until you feel comfortable, then we'll go side by side. Wherever you are within the first section of this bay, the surface is only just above your head, so you can just stand up if you need to. Just remember, you don't really have to swim, keep your arms to the side and just kick your legs like you were doing the crawl. You must have seen divers in films and the way they move through the water.'

Down on their knees again, Luke did exactly as Jake told him and within a few minutes, they were moving along underwater together with shoals of small fish, the occasional crab, and a small octopus. Luke almost forgot to concentrate on his breathing as within a few moments he was breathing regularly, and being underwater was surprisingly easy and fascinating. He wished he had tried it before, and was quite disappointed when Jake signalled that it was time to go back. The children were still in the water, and the brothers surfaced to applause and cheers, making customers at the promenade cafés turn to see what was going on. The brothers laughed and took a bow.

Later, as they sat back in their seats at a promenade café with a beer and Pastizzi lunch, with the children having left, the brothers looked out over the gleaming, transparent water of the inlet, listening to the gentle rhythmic sound of the ripples softly slapping against the small boats and harbour wall, and the background of quiet conversation from customers at the busy cafés.

Luke agreed the dive had been a very special experience which he would be doing again.

'This bay is peaceful, and maybe I won't be so scared of being underwater again, but how would it be further out where it's not so calm, maybe if you go out beyond the headland?'

Jake leaned in to the table. 'What you have to remember is that, unless there's a strong current or some turbulence, when you're underwater, it's generally just as you found it today. Most of the movement is on the surface unless there's a storm. Of course, sometimes the worst bit is actually getting out of the sea if you're going up onto a beach where there might be an undertow. There are some beaches where the receding waves try to pull you back in. You, and whoever you're with, might need help to get out of the water. In a place like this there generally isn't a problem, which is why I brought you here. As you saw, there are people further out who are swimming, snorkelling and diving. Xlendi is a nice bay, great for kids and beginners, sheltered by small cliffs on either side, and on a day like this when the weather is fine, it's ideal for a first diving lesson.'

Chapter Twenty One

La Gomera : Mateo is Traced

'Buenos días, Senora Moreno, may we come in?' There was something about Corporal Paloma Perez's formality that immediately alarmed Maria. The fact that she was accompanied by her senior officer, Sergeant Alvarado, from Maria's point of view, spoke volumes. This was not going to be good news.

On the path beyond Maria's gate, several of her neighbours who had seen the Guardia Civil car pull up outside Maria's house, gathered waiting for news. Some, who were convinced that Mateo was dead somewhere, were genuinely concerned for Maria. But there were others more concerned with gossip and rumourmongering.

Ashen-faced and shaking, Maria hurried the officers inside and closed the door. Once inside her sitting room, she closed the curtains shutting everyone out, leaving only the light entering from the rear windows that overlooked the garden, and invited the officers to sit. Paloma chose an armchair next to Maria. This time the cat chose Paloma's lap to snuggle down on.

'You have news for me,' said Maria, 'and from the look on your faces, it is not good. Is Mateo dead?'

'Senora Moreno,' the sergeant began, 'I will be honest with you, at this stage we cannot confirm that. However, we do have news of where Mateo was last seen, but at this moment, we have no outcome for you. We thought that, if we informed you of his movements, it may help jog your memory of something he may have said at some time.'

Paloma gently lifted the cat putting him on the floor, and moved her chair closer to Maria. The undeterred cat, determined to have his way, jumped back onto Paloma's lap as soon as she was repositioned close to Maria.

Paloma spoke first. 'Maria, after I left you the other day, one of your neighbours said that a relative of theirs, who knew Mateo well, had seen him on the ferry from San Sebastian to Los Cristianos ...'

'No! That cannot be ...' Maria shook her head. 'Why would Mateo do that? I do not understand. He hated being on deep water.' Her eyes pleaded with Paloma to believe her, but Paloma took her hand, and said, 'Maria, I am sorry. I know you believe that Mateo didn't travel to Tenerife but, after hearing that he was seen on the ferry, we checked the CCTV records at the ferry port. It was definitely Mateo. The witness called in to the police station, he was shown the recording and confirmed it was Mateo on the ferry.'

Maria sat back in her armchair, confounded that Mateo had acted totally out of character, and she was at a loss to understand. 'Go on.'

With a background sound of the cat purring, Paloma explained that Mateo's movements had been captured on CCTV at various stages between the ferry port and Los Cristianos Bus Station. Once they knew which bus he had boarded, the 460 to Costa Adeje. They picked him up again at the bus station where he caught a second bus, the 477, to Los Gigantes, but he disembarked at Puerto de Santiago. After he left the bus in Avenida Oceano, they lost him. There were other bus stops in Santiago, so the assumption is that he was going somewhere within that vicinity of the avenue, but for now that was all the information they had.

When Paloma had finished explaining to Maria what the latest information they had on Mateo's disappearance was, the sergeant leaned forward in his chair, rested his elbows on his knees, and paused for a moment before speaking to give the elderly lady time to digest the news. She was clearly upset and confused by what she had been told, but if there was anything she could recall, no matter how trivial it might seem, it might well set them on the way to solving Mateo's disappearance.

Paloma opened her mouth to speak but the sergeant shook his head. Maria needed a few minutes.

After a while, Maria looked first at the sergeant, then at Paloma. 'I am sorry. This has come as a shock. I cannot recall Mateo ever telling me that he had gone to Tenerife.' She shook her head. 'After all the years I have known Mateo, and looked after him since he lost his wife, it never occurred to me that there were times, when he said he was going to work, he was actually going somewhere else.' She began to cry. 'Why would Mateo lie to me? I thought I knew him, but he was keeping secrets from me.' She reached out to take Paloma's hand for support, for comfort. 'I...do not...understand, and I am sorry, but I cannot help you. As God is my witness, I know of no reason why he would go to Santiago, and...and' she paused, looked stricken as she first looked at the sergeant, then back at Paloma. 'Can you understand how...ahh...' she sighed, let go of Paloma's hand and wilted into an armchair. Gato jumped onto her lap. With her mind elsewhere, her hand automatically moved to the cat's back and she stroked him, as Paloma struggled with professionalism and genuine sympathy, forcing back her own tears.

Maria looked up at Paloma then to the sergeant. 'All those years we were family, and I trusted him. I knew him, or I thought I did.' She was talking about him in the past tense, as if she knew he was dead. 'I feel betrayed. Can you understand that?' Paloma nodded. What the elderly lady had been through in the past few days had added years to her. The sergeant went to the window and drew back the curtain a little. The crowd outside had grown.

'But it's more than that,' Maria continued, 'I feel ... I believed, I really believed we were honest with each other, always. No secrets. Always honest. At least I thought that's how we were.' She sat quietly for a moment, dabbing her eyes with her handkerchief. No-one spoke. Paloma and Sergeant Alvarado exchanged glances. He nodded towards the window and held up all ten fingers, then five more. Paloma nodded that she understood. Fifteen people had gathered outside.

Unexpectedly, Maria stood up. Gato dropped to the floor, shook himself and with an offended air, tail high, he walked out into the hallway.

Maria paced up and down the room twice again, then made a beeline for the sergeant. In those few silent minutes her distress had turned to anger.

'Mateo's secrecy has caused this, stupid old man. I am so angry with him. I feel that I will always be angry with him.' She took a handkerchief out of her apron pocket, dabbed her eyes and noisily blew her nose.

Yes, there was anger, but Paloma still saw grief in Maria's eyes. She might be furious with Mateo now, but that wasn't only due to his reticence to tell her where he was going, or who he was seeing. Maria clearly loved Mateo, and they had been sharing their lives together, keeping each other company and giving support for so long. If Mateo was dead, Maria was now alone, and she was old, with just Gato to keep her company. What would the future hold for her without Mateo for company?

She reminded Paloma of her own father worrying about her safety when she was late home at night, and the distress turned to anger as she walked in the door. Not that she felt that would be the case with Mateo. It was unlikely he would ever walk in the door again. Unnoticed, Gato had returned from the hallway. With a soft mew he jumped onto Paloma's lap. As she gently rubbed his ear, she made an unspoken oath to discover where Mateo was; alive or dead.

Chapter Twenty Two

Amsterdam : Schiphol Airport

Valko finished his second Americano coffee, and yawned. 'When the hell will this trip be over?'

Viktor, sitting next to Valko on the hard plastic seats in the airport waiting area, opened his eyes, shrugged and closed his eyes again, but Valko had not finished. 'Wouldn't have thought there would be such a long wait before the connecting flight to Tenerife.'

Viktor sat up, turned to Valko. 'Stop moaning. It's bad enough having to wait for another four hours without your moaning as well. The only good thing about it is the flight is almost five hours, and I intend to get some sleep once we take off. We've been travelling all night and I'm as tired as you are. So shut the fuck up!'

Valko pulled a face. 'Well, that Thabisa could've said there would be a long wait. If we'd known that before, I'd have suggested we stay over, book a hotel, get some rest and a decent meal, and fly the next day.'

'Okay. Enough now. It is what it is. We'll be in Tenerife around seven-thirty, another hour to get through the airport, collect our car and head off to Masca. My guess is we should be at this woman, Moya's, place around nine and nine-thirty tonight. Dinner, a couple of beers, then I'm planning to sleep most of the day tomorrow.'

'If she'll let you. What about meeting this Anton guy, or checking out the professor?'

'Anton will make contact with us, and something tells me it might be a day or so before he does. As for the Professor, we have a month to get the job done, so a day to get settled I don't see as a problem. Now shut up.'

'But what about...'

Viktor spun round his seat. 'Valko, you're my little brother, and Mama said I had to look after you, but if you don't shut the fuck up, and give me a bit of peace, I promise to drown you at the first opportunity. Got it?'

Valko nodded, just as a woman sitting opposite them looked up from her magazine and tutted.

'My apologies, madam,' said Viktor with a courteous nod of the head. She ignored him and went back to her magazine. He turned back to Valko. 'If you had rested on the flight from Cape Town, instead of making an arse of yourself with that blonde stewardess...'

'...Flight Attendant,' Valko cut in. 'The title is Flight Attendant, not Stewardess. They don't use that any more. You noticed she was pretty too, huh?' The woman sitting opposite closed her magazine, picked up her bag and walked away. The brothers watched her walk towards the ladies toilets.

'Yes, but you were never going to see her again, so you should have got some sleep, instead of making a prat of yourself. Idiot. Now listen to me,' Viktor lowered his voice, looked around to see if anyone was sitting near enough to hear him. Although, as with most airport waiting areas, there was a huge number of people in the seating area, or just walking about, and it was incredibly noisy. Since the woman who had been in the seat opposite had left, Viktor was confident that he could say what he needed so that only Valko would hear. Victor put his arm around Valko's shoulder and pulled him closer.

'When we get to Tenerife, you need to concentrate on the job. Don't forget who we're working for. He's got a lot riding on this and, if we screw up, we may not be around next month.'

'Wha...you're not serious, are you?'

'I've never been more serious. Maartens is connected to some pretty ruthless people. If we do this right, our reputation goes up. Get it wrong, and my guess is that wherever we are, he'll be able to find us. So do as I tell you. Don't get clever or mouthy, leave the girls alone, and stick with beers lunchtime and a couple at night, and no spirits. I need you fully focused on the job we're going to be doing, no hangovers, no late nights and not being able to get up in the mornings. There'll be good money at the end of this, if we do it right...we follow orders, whatever they are. There's just about a month before we can kick back and relax somewhere new. Anything else can wait. If anything...and I mean anything, goes wrong, we could lose more than the money, so remember what we're going to Tenerife for.'

'Yeah. Okay, I'll be cool. I won't let you down.'

'No. You won't. Not like last time. I was able to get you out of that one. I won't with this guy. We were lucky last time. You were lucky, but it can't happen again. Valko, you're not stupid. You're not a kid. You're playing with the adults now and I need you to man up.'

Valko scowled. 'Yeah, yeah. I hear you. don't go on. I know I screwed up before, but it won't happen again, and you don't need to keep reminding me.'

'Just pointing out who we're dealing with here, in case you hadn't noticed.'

A woman's voice came over the public address system.

'That's our gate number being called. Come on, we'll head down there. They'll be boarding soon.'

Chapter Twenty Three

La Gomera : Bad News for Paloma

'Corporal Perez, Sergeant Alvarado gave me your report on the Moreno disappearance,' said Captain Enrique Herrera. 'I know you have been trying to find this missing person, and I have some news for you, but it is not good. I am sorry to say.'

Paloma stood by her desk and tried to not tremble. Although Captain Herrera seemed pleasant enough, having him speak to her was a rare occurrence as any communication was usually passed down through the grading ladder. Ensigns and Corporals were seldom spoken to by senior officers. She pushed her knees back to help control her nervousness.

'I am sorry to hear that, Captain. I had hoped, although Mateo has been missing for a few days, that we might have had a happy outcome, but you are telling me that is not so?'

'My opposite number at Buenavista del Norte contacted me to let me know that the body of an elderly man, who we believe may be Mateo Moreno, was found by divers just off Los Gigantes. As Senor Moreno was reported missing in the Puerto de Santiago area, an alert was issued to all Guardia Civil stations across the island, of course, but it was more likely, that if he was found, it would be more local.'

'Believe to be, sir...?' Paloma interrupted. 'I apologise, Captain. I should have let you finish.'

'No matter. I know how involved you are with this case and I understand you wished to have a happier resolution. I say we believe, because as you will realise, after a few days in the sea, not only will the body have bloated, but I understand there may have been some predation by the marine life which has made it more difficult to distinguish features. There is also some damage to the face and body which could have been done by the rocks as he entered the sea. There is some speculation it may have been deliberate.'

Paloma visibly shuddered. 'Are you saying that Mateo may have been assaulted, or perhaps murdered?' The Captain looked over his glasses at her. 'As there were bags of large stones found in his coat pockets, it would seem that it might be a murder. However, until the autopsy, nothing is definite. There is always a possibility, however unlikely, that we are talking about suicide. Until we hear from the pathologist we cannot rule anything out. Would you like to sit? Perhaps a drink of water?'

'Um…yes, thank you, sir.' Paloma walked over to the water cooler, took a paper cup, filled it, and turned to the Captain. 'Would you…?'

'No, but thank you for asking. Come and sit down.' Paloma walked back to her desk and sat facing the Captain. 'I have been looking at your record, Corporal Perez, and I understand that your time at the academy was exemplary.' He sat back in his seat and crossed his legs, his hands clasped on his lap.

'Thank you, sir.'

'Having said that, I believe there are some gaps in your training which you are unlikely to fill, or rather gain experience of, here on La Gomera. This is generally a quiet island as you know. Solving this case would be a challenge, and a feather in your cap.'

Paloma wondered what was coming next.

'How many bodies have you seen since you have been an officer of the Guardia Civil?'

'Just one, sir, following a road traffic accident.'

'Hmm. I have in mind transferring you to Buenavista del Norte where you can continue to see the Moreno case through to closure. After that you will remain there for a year or two to gain experience of police work within a city. Would that be of interest to you?'

Paloma opened her eyes wide. She had expected to stay on La Gomera, but the idea of transferring back to a city environment would certainly help her career. The Captain did not give her long to think. The ring on the little finger of his right hand tapped on the desk. He glanced at his watch. Paloma took them as signs that he was impatient for an answer, but she did not need time to think about the suggestion. To be based in a city would indeed advance her career.

'This is unexpected, sir, but yes, I would like that opportunity. Thank you, and yes, I would like to be able to close Mateo's case, for Maria Moreno, you understand. I have perhaps become too involved with the lady's grief, but I feel she trusts me and I would like to make sure she is looked after. Can you tell me any more about the body that was found?'

'In a moment I will, but first I have arranged for you to travel to Los Cristianos today, where a car will be waiting for you at the harbour. The driver will take you directly to Buenavista del Norte, where you will be met by Captain Torres. He will take you to the morgue where you will be shown the body. Unfortunately, from its condition it is unlikely you would be to confirm the identity...'

'I never actually met...but Maria gave me a photo...' She reached for a folder on her desk.

'If that is the Moreno file, I would not bother to look for his photograph, and I understand you never actually met Senor Moreno, Corporal Perez. However, you have seen the CCTV recordings...and in close-up...but, of course, this is of no consequence bearing in mind how he looks now. It may be though that some of his effects, of which I understand there are only two, a ring...which shows signs of deep scratches, as though someone tried to cut it, and a crucifix on a chain around his neck, which seems to have somehow been missed. Any identifying documents such as credit or debit cards are missing, and there is no sign of the gentleman's watch, although I am told there is a lighter band of skin on the wrist area, that would indicate that he wore one. As this watch was not found at his home, it is likely that whoever this person is, was robbed.'

'Mateo worked outdoors almost all his life, sir. If he wore a watch it would certainly leave a pale band around his wrist.'

'Exactly.'

'May I give Maria an upda...'

'No! It is too early for that! We do not want to upset the lady any more than necessary. If this turns out not to be Mateo Moreno, then we will have distressed her for nothing, and if it is...well, you will need the evidence to show her. If the effects do point to this being the man we are seeking, she should be able to identify them.' He stood and walked to the door, opened it, then turned and said, 'My gut feeling is that the body is Mateo Moreno. Once the pathologist has done his work, we should know what to tell his sister-in-Law, accident, suicide...'

'...Or murder.'

'Exactly, but with all the signs pointing to it, my money is on murder, Corporal Perez. Keep me informed. I shall expect a call from you from Buenavista del Norte. Now get yourself ready. Your driver is already waiting at the entrance for you to take you to the harbour.'

'Yes, sir. Excuse me, sir.'

'Yes?'

'Where will I be staying?'

'Accommodation had been provided for you. You will be sharing an apartment with another female officer for as long as is required.'

'I wonder, sir, is there time for me to collect some of my things from home? I have nothing with me here of course.'

'Yes, indeed. Your driver has been informed to take you home before going on to the harbour. For now take only what you need for a week or so, and you can collect the rest of your belonging on your next leave days. I trust that will be agreeable to you?

'Oh yes, sir. Thank you.'

Chapter Twenty Four

Gozo : A New Guest at the Cornucopia

When Luke walked into the restaurant for breakfast, heading for his favourite table by the window, a voice from a table close to the door called his name. Smiling up at Luke, while enjoying a full English breakfast, was Jake.

'What are you doing here this time of the morning?'

'I've left Anjelika, and booked in here until you leave to spend the rest of your month with you.'

'Hmm. I have to say I'm glad you've finished with her. To be honest I don't think that was a relationship made in Heaven, was it?'

'No. I really don't need that kind of crap right now.'

Jake grinned as he shovelled a piece of bacon with egg yolk dripping off it, into his mouth. He chewed and swallowed. He nodded. 'And you're right, I did need to get away from her. There's been a new development too. It turns out she's fooling around with George again and, well that's pretty shit with Irina being pregnant.' Luke noticed that Jake averted his eyes when he mentioned Irina. 'You know, Luke, I'll be glad to be out of it when the shit hits the fan from that.'

'Okay well I'll get some breakfast and join you.'

Luke soon returned with a plate of pancakes, maple syrup and bacon, and a black coffee. 'Which room are you in?' Luke forked a piece of pancake and bacon.

'Twenty-nine. Just two up from you. It's not ready yet as the previous guests only left about thirty minutes ago, and my things are in the office for now.'

'So are you at the dive centre today?'

'No. We're going straight to Marsalforn to meet a group of beginners. Feel like joining us? We can include you if you want to join the group.'

'Yes, that sounds good. Marsalforn's the town near the salt flats and with that big statue of Christ on the hillside above it isn't it? After Xlendi it would be good to learn more and see what happens further down. How deep do you go?'

'Yeah, that's the one. Good diving there in Marsalforn Bay. The water is absolutely crystal clear and there's caves, reefs, the works. Not sure where they'll be taking the group today but, as only second-timers, it'll be from the beach. It would be good if, before we leave here, I can get you diving from a boat.'

'You mean where you roll in backwards.'

'Uh-huh,' said Jake taking a bite out of a slice of toasted Maltese bread slathered with butter and marmalade.

'Am I ready for that?'

'You will be by the time you head home.' Jake frowned. 'I guess you will be heading home.'

Yes, that's my plan, but not immediately. I'm going to Rome for a few days. I've always wanted to see the Forum and the Colosseum ever since seeing Gladiator. Then it's on to Amsterdam for another few days, before heading back to Birmingham.'

'I suppose it was seeing Van Der Valk that made you want to see Amsterdam.'

'Seeing who?'

'The people we're taking down today have dived just once before, as fairly new to diving we're taking them the usual ten metres and they'll be down about half an hour. You can listen in on the pre-dive safety talk before, so you'll learn more than I went through with you at Xlendi.'

A little later, in the car on the way to Marsalforn, Luke asked Jake how he felt about breaking up with Anjelika.

'To be honest, not that bad. I thought I would, but she's never going to be faithful, and really doesn't seem to understand how hurt Irina's going to be if and when she finds out what George is up to. Anjelika likes conquests. Well, she can get on with it now. This is one feller she came, she saw, she conquered and then lost. One day she'll regret it...probably.'

Chapter Twenty Five

Tenerife : Fire!

'No, Papa, I did not...did not want to k-kill Edward...' Anton's voice quivered as he spoke.

'I did not want him to die either. I respected the man, his experience and knowledge were matchless. I had hoped there would be other occasions when we could...use his expertise, but it was not to be. I...we needed him silenced about the ship. Sadly, Edward was an honest man and, after checking the details were right, he would have reported the wreck to the authorities. I could not let that happen, no matter how much respect I had for him. Whatever treasure is still down there, and can be reached would have ended up back in Spain, or in a museum in Santa Cruz. You know there was no choice. How did it happen?'

'He came into my room just after I got home and saw me with the old man's wallet.'

'He found what?! Why did you have it?'

'I took it off his body after I killed him and kept it hidden in my room. I thought it best that there was nothing to identify...'

'I understand that, but why the Hell did you keep it? Why not get rid of it straight away, you fool. It was nighttime, it was dark, you could have shoved it deep inside anyone's trash bin, buried it somewhere, found some other way to dispose of it.'

'I'm sorry, Papa. I was...I was not thinking...I felt sick about killing the old man and probably not thinking. The fear in his eyes when he realised I was not taking him to Los Cristianos. He tried to grab the wheel, but I elbowed him hard in the face. While he was stunned, I stopped the car and strangled him. I sat there for a while. I just

157

couldn't believe what I'd done. Then I remembered the wallet, took it out of his jacket pocket, and hid it under my seat. Then drove to the little bay near Los Gigantes where Felipe, our neighbour, keeps his boat. It's small, secluded, the stony beach is painful on the feet or to lie on, and there's a wicked drag back as the waves pull back, so it's not a pleasure beach, and there's also a danger of falling rocks from the cliffs. Sometimes boats are out there night fishing, but often there's no-one around, but that night there was one boat not far out in the bay, so I didn't stop. I drove to the banana farm at the bottom of the mountain, wrapped Mateo's body in a small canvas tarpaulin I keep in the car boot, and hid him under some shrubbery. I went to the bay the next night but there was already a boat not far out, so I gave up that night as well. You cannot understand how difficult it was for me to try to stay normal around Edward. I had to say that I did not feel well, that I had a bad headache, but I felt all the time as if he knew what I had done, no matter how much I told myself that there was no possible way that he could know. I felt he could see into my mind...'

'Never mind that now. Get on with it, tell me what happened.'

'The third night it was all clear. Over those two nights I had time to think about how it should look if his body was found. If I didn't find a way to weigh him down it would not be long before he floated up, but if I did weigh him down, it would look like murder.'

'Okay, so you were using your head for a change.'

Anton ignored that remark. He always expected some kind of derisory remark from his father. 'I drove back to where Mateo's body was and bundled him into the car, still wrapped. Mateo might have been old and thin, but a dead body is heavy, even his, and the tarpaulin added to the weight. I stripped down to my briefs and left my clothes and the tarpaulin hidden behind some rocks. That was disgusting. It's been hot here and when I unwrapped Mateo's body it didn't smell good. I almost vomited.' He hesitated for a moment before going on. 'I thanked God He had given me a cloudy night. There was very little moonlight so I was not seen as I dragged his body down the beach...

'...Are you sure? There couldn't have been anyone on the cliffs who could have seen you?'

158

'...No, Papa. Even if there had been anyone idiotic enough to be on the edge of the cliffs in the dark, I was in a corner of the bay where it would have been a blind spot to anyone on the cliffs. So, as I dragged the old man down the beach he got stuck a few times on the larger rocks, and then I had to tug him free. He got bruised and cut a bit, but I couldn't do anything about that, and he wasn't going to complain, was he? The boat was up on the shingle and I managed to haul him on board, then left him there while I collected a bagful of large stones and pebbles from the beach...'

'What the Hell for?'

'To put them in his jacket and trouser pockets, to help weigh him down.' Anton sighed. Tried not to show his increasing irritation with all his father's interruptions.

'Okay, that makes some sense.'

'If what Mateo had said was true and, as far we knew he had no reason to lie, he hadn't told anyone he was going to visit Edward. He said no-one knew about the box. Now, just the fact that he had kept everything to himself, Edward told me later showed that Mateo's behaviour was out of character. So I thought that perhaps I could make his death look like he might have committed suicide. Then if he was found, as least that might have clouded any investigation by the Guardia Civil.'

'It said in the news that his body was found by divers in the bay. Why didn't you go further out where it would have been less likely he would have been found?'

'Papa, please let me finish, and I'll explain.' There was just a grunt for a response. 'I was about half the distance I planned to go, when I saw a motor yacht come around the headland. There were plenty of lights on board and it looked like there was a party going on. I had no lights and was in the darkness of the bay, so I'm sure no-one saw me, but with his body decomposing in the heat, he had to go that night, but with the party boat there, I couldn't risk going further out. So, with the stones in all the pockets I could find on him, I tossed him overboard. In the dark, I couldn't really see him sink, but the air bubbles from his clothes soon stopped, so I had to trust he'd sunk to the sea bed. It's about thirty metres deep at that point.

'I left the boat drifting and swam into...'

'...I thought you said there were currents and a drag backshore.'

'Yes, that's right, but I go to the gym, I'm young, strong and I know these bays, the currents and where the drag on that beach is less powerful. It was a warm night, I sat on the rocks for a while until I'd dried off enough to get dressed. Took the tarpaulin, went back to the car and headed back over to Moya's for the night.'

'Why leave the boat...?'

'Okay. Let me explain it to you...'

'Don't you dare talk to me like I'm a child!'

'Sorry, Papa, but think for a moment. How would Mateo have got out into the bay without a boat? And if the boat made it back to the beach, that would have meant Mateo was not alone. With weights in his pockets, it would look more like murder, but with the boat still floating in the harbour, it's quite feasible that Mateo rowed himself out into the bay and jumped in. Felipe may not be happy with his boat going adrift, but he's not going to know who took it.'

'I still keep seeing Mateo's face as I strangled him. I obey your commands, Papa, but I am not used to killing people...and now I have murdered Edward. I...I liked him. He was kind to me...' Anton gulped back tears. To show emotion was not allowed. It was a sign of instability, a flaw in his character that his father had tried to beat out of him as a child. Weakness could not be forgiven; to care meant mistakes were more easily made.

'Then you had better get used to it, Anton. It paid for your education, for your expensive lifestyle. You have done very well out of the family business. Now you're old enough to pay your dues.'

'Yes, Papa.'

'So tell me, what happened with Edward. Are you still at the villa?'

'Yes, Papa. I was packing to leave when he came into my room. I have nearly finished. The car is parked at the end of the road and I can get to it by the cliff path. At this time of night it is unlikely anyone will see me there.'

'Good. So what happened to Edward?'

'He had been busy researching the shipwreck, and I knew I had to stay in case he came up with something important. Plus, I had to stick around until I had got rid of Mateo's body, and it would have looked suspicious if I vanished just after Edward thought I had taken the old man back to Los Cristianos. So I had to stay, at least for a little while.'

'With Edward being so pre-occupied with the shipwreck, I had time to myself, so I was out a lot checking Mateo hadn't been found, and keeping an eye on the bay once it got dark. Edward thought I was playing cards with a couple of the guys from the restaurant who I keep in touch with.'

'It was two days after I'd dumped Mateo, that I heard Edward answer the phone just as I got back to the villa. I went straight to my room. I was just getting a sweatshirt out of my wardrobe, when Mateo's wallet, fell out onto the floor, just as Edward burst into my room to tell me he had seen a report on television that a Mateo Moreno of La Gomera was missing. He had tried to talk to the Guardia Civil, but they were so busy, no-one could take his call at the time, so he left a message for them to call him. Sure enough he saw Mateo's wallet. I will never forget the look in his eyes when he realised what I had done. It was like fear, suspicion and horror all rolled into one. With everything else that had been going on I had completely forgotten about that fucking wallet.'

'Yes, well skip that...'

'He ran out of the room shouting all sorts of accusations at me, which were all true, so I had no choice. I picked up a bedside lamp and chased after him into the hallway. He tried to defend himself but...he...he just wasn't quick enough. I hit him hard on the head, twice. He went down, unconscious.' Anton inhaled deeply, as if drawing in enough air to rush out his next statement. 'I got a cushion and suffocated him.'

'You're sure he's dead.'

'Yes, Papa. I regret to say he is very dead.'

'So are you packed and ready to leave, and you have Mateo's wallet?' The money doesn't matter unless the Guardia Civil get hold of it, check for fingerprints and find Mateo's and your's.'

'They won't, I intend to spend it as soon as I can and get it circulated. But, Papa, I am frightened. I have killed two people and I need to get away from here. Do I come to you?'

'No. Not yet. I will be coming over quite soon and will collect you then. In the meantime, go to Moya, stay in her house just outside

Masca. You know where it is and I will call her to let her know to expect you. She will look after you. Dye your hair, grow a beard. Moya will get you a new identity. Passport, driving licence and so on. She knows the right people, and it should only take a few days. Stay out of sight until then. Do you understand? You go straight there and you stay there. No-one will find you with Moya. You do not let yourself be seen anywhere until you have a new name and papers. Got it?'

'Yes, I understand, Papa. It will be good to see Moya and to get away from here. I could to with some peace for a while.'

'There's just one more thing you have to do before you leave, Anton. Burn the villa.'

'Burn it?'

'Yes, you know, set fire to it in case Edward has made some research notes you don't know about. There must be nothing left, d'you understand? And what did you do with that tarpaulin?'

'It's still in the car.'

'Then get it and let it burn in the house. Nothing left that might link us to Mateo, the ship. Nothing. Right?'

'Yes, Papa. Nothing left.'

'Right then, make sure you have everything relating to the wreck. Do not leave without the documents. Take everything that Mateo gave Edward. It was a pity this has all happened before Edward could dive to confirm the wreck is there, but I have people on the way to do that. They'll be there soon and will stay at Moya's, but she doesn't dive or drive a boat, you do, and these guys will need your help. Once you have your new identity, you can hire a boat, you know the channel and the currents, but you don't know wreck diving. These guys do. Until then just keep your head down and stay out of trouble. Now get out of the house as soon as you can, but just make sure the fire has taken a good hold before you leave.'

'Papa, what about the miniature painting and the crucifix?'

'The painting is of no interest, but take the crucifix, we can always take the stones out.'

Chapter Twenty Six

Gozo : Last Days at The Cornucopia

For his last few days with Jake, Luke dived almost every day and tagged along with whichever group was going out. As each new party of divers was taken through the scuba safety instructions, Luke paid particular attention to a different point each time he heard them. Having passed his Open Water Diver qualification, he was now working on the next level, the Advanced Open Water Diver, and his confidence grew with each successive dive. Within just a couple of dives he found he was more relaxed, and soon he no longer needed the instructors to keep checking on how he was doing, and reminding him to clear the pressure in his ears; those actions had become instinctive to him, and at each dive the sea managed to show him something new.

Will, the Australian dive leader, made Luke feel at home as soon as they met, and as he was Jake's brother, Will reduced the cost of the dives for him.

But what really surprised Luke was just how much he was learning about himself. Having been very anxious about going underwater and breathing through a tube, those anxieties had simply melted away. As for the possibility of coming across a shark, or ending up with an octopus on his face, at first both of those concepts had utterly terrified him. However, since his second group dive, when Jake pointed out an Angel shark resting on the sea bed, and he saw a Blue shark - or so Jake told him - in the distance, he stopped worrying about being attacked by these wonderfully agile, and magnificent animals.

As for the octopi, on two occasions Luke was fortunate enough to have a small one make physical contact, investigating and playing with his hands. The first time, he was so captivated by such a thrilling interaction, he almost lost his mouthpiece and swallowed a mouthful of water when he tried to laugh. He didn't do that the second time.

And far too soon, Luke's month was over. On their penultimate day together, he waited for Jake and Will to join him at a Marsalforn bar overlooking the glorious bay, reflecting on the incidents with the marine wildlife. He smiled remembering the interaction with the octopus. Just a few weeks before, the person he was would have panicked. But now, he just resettled the mouthpiece and carried on. Jake, having seen what happened gave the signal to check he was okay, and Luke simply nodded and gave the 'okay' sign. Luke now understood how privileged he was to have had the opportunity to connect with marine wildlife in their own habitat.

This month on the island had not only helped him unwind, the days without being able to see daylight were now in the past. Those days of being boxed in by tall buildings and not being able to see the sky were finished. He would never live like that again. The past month had changed him, changed his priorities. He had no great plan in mind for the future. He would just see where life took him. Going back into anything approaching the way he lived previously seemed like a nightmare, and he had finally woken up. Project Management was killing his soul, and he wanted to live.

He thought of Ellie and gave a sad smile. On the beach families were playing, parents held little children's hands as they laughed, splashed and paddled in the shallows. Others were swimming, playing on airbeds, or inflatable animals, to his left another group of divers were getting ready for their adventure underwater, and further out an inflatable banana boat, towed fun-loving people, screaming with laughter, behind a high-speed boat.

Luke felt sorry for Ellie. Birmingham was actually a pretty good city, as cities go. It had a lot going for it. Everything was nearby, there were some fabulous concerts, theatres, sports facilities, and plenty of opportunities for studying and careers. Yes, the city had everything, if you had the leisure time to discover and enjoy them. There was always something to do, somewhere to go and it buzzed with life, but it was a huge city, noisy, polluted, and there was very little sky.

As he sat there, enjoying the soft sea breeze fluttering the edges of the canopy above, and helped to take the edge off the heat, his mind turned to what he could do if he went back to Birmingham, and what he would do in the future. If project management was out, then what else could he do? Whatever it was he would have to re-train. Now was the time to think carefully about what he was going to do next. He grinned, remembering that as a child he had wanted to be a fireman, then he switched to wanting to be a farmer. Maybe he should just take a look at what courses were available for mature students at one of the universities, and decide from there. Anyway, there was no rush, it was now the beginning of June, and he still had some travelling to do. Tomorrow he would leave Gozo, and Jake would be looking for an apartment. He could not stay at the Cornucopia for too long. He was happy to be there while Luke was still there, but Luke would be heading off to Rome for a few days, and Jake needed his own home.

As Luke gazed contentedly out over the bay watching families playing, gulls swooping and calling, someone parasailing; he estimated they were at somewhere between two-hundred to three-hundred feet and then saw them rise higher. He might have found his courage underwater, but heights, no he wasn't at all sure how he would cope with that.

He saw Jake arrive at the café and weave his way through the tables to join him.

'Sorry, took a bit longer than I expected. Will and I were talking to someone about one of the PADI courses,' Jake said, then called out to the waiter. 'Hey, José, bring us a Cisk when you're free, will you?' José nodded, took payment from a customer and headed to the bar.

'No worries, I was just watching the world go by. Have you tried that?' He pointed up to the parasailer.

'Yeah. Tried it on my first free day on Gozo. Not my thing really. I'm happier being underwater.' José brought the lager and a frosted glass. 'Thanks, mate.' José put the bill on the table, then went to greet a couple who had just arrived, and showed them to a nearby table.

'Everything alright with you and Will?'

Jake sat forward at the table, smiled, but looked away, took a mouthful of lager. 'Yeah, yeah, just a couple of things the guy wanted to know about.' Luke thought Jake seemed a little distant, preoccupied, but he said nothing. Jake would tell him if he wanted to, but it bothered him that this was yet another time when Jake seemed shut off, remote. There was clearly something on his mind that he did not seem to want to talk about. Anjelika, perhaps? Did Jake have money worries? He didn't want to push too hard, but when he thought about the number of times during the last month that Jake had seemed withdrawn, it worried him and he decided to try to get Jake talking that night.

That evening after dinner at the hotel, fresh salmon with pasta for Jake, and Beef Stroganoff for Luke, Luke suggested they take a walk around the village, and stop for a couple of beers at one of the local bars. As it was going to be the last chance for him to just take in the evening scenery and atmosphere of Xaghra. That was not solely the reason he wanted to have some time alone with Jake, though. With time running out, he wanted to try to get to the root of whatever it was that Jake was concealing. He suspected it had something to do with Anjelika, and was pleased when Jake seemed quite keen on the idea of the walk. However, outwardly relaxed as Luke may have appeared, as they both left the hotel to walk through the pretty streets into the village centre, he was undecided about how to begin what might be a difficult conversation, or even whether he should.

They had been walking for a few minutes when Jake stopped walking and looked up into the night sky. 'You're going to miss this aren't you? The sky here is vast, and it really does look like velvet, doesn't it?'

Luke, who had already walked on a little, turned and looked up. 'Yeah, you're right, I will. It certainly is, I hate to use the word, awesome as it's already too over-used, but it does fit. The stars seem to be so close together and there seem to be thousands more here than in the city. There we only get to see patches of sky and there's too much light pollution to see it as clearly as this. It makes me feel as though we down here are very small and unimportant, but I guess it looks the same from all the islands.'

'Yeah, probably.' Jake shoved his hands in his pockets, turned away and joined Luke, who noticed Jake's change of mood. He had suddenly become quite gloomy.

'Are you okay with me leaving?' Luke asked, as they started walking again. 'I just wondered as you seem a bit down. Anything to do with Anjelika?'

'God, no!' Jake shook his head and stopped walking again. 'No, nothing to do with her. It's just that...' He stopped talking as someone they both knew from the hotel crossed the road in front of them, nodded in acknowledgement, then moved on. 'Let's wait till we find somewhere quiet,' said Jake.

They walked on towards the town square where there were a number of popular bars with outdoor seating. Jake settled on one with very few customers and they chose a quiet corner, sitting in silence, until a waiter came to serve them. They gave their order of two Cisk lagers, and watched people wandering around, and cars zooming by.

A few minutes later, the waiter brought their beers and wandered back inside. It was early in the evening and there were very few customers, just a group of six men and women at a table on the other side of the patio area who seemed to be enjoying their evening, talking and laughing loudly. Jake had deliberately chosen a table away from the lively group.

Under the street light, Jake looked around him, took several mouthfuls of his lager, he appeared fidgety and Luke felt Jake was struggling, unsure whether to say what was clearly on his mind.

'What is it, Jake? What's up?'

When Jake started to speak, his words all spilled out at speed. It was as if, once he had pressed the release button, there was no holding back.

'I've got myself into a real fix here. I got into a few card games, lost some money, played more games to get it back and lost more. That was bad enough, but the guys I ended up owing money to are local criminals, drug smuggling, and so on, but they're run by a guy in London, and it's big time gangster stuff. I didn't know that at the time, or I would have avoided the game like the plague, but it was too late. They said I had to work for them to pay off the debt.'

'So why did they pick on you, and what did they mean by work for them?'

'George is at the back of all this. You remember, George Camilleri, you met him on the ferry, with his wife, Irina?'

Luke nodded. 'Yes, I remember. I felt there was something not right between you two at the time.'

Jake leaned forward, rested his arms on the table, wrapped his hands around his beer, and kept an eye on the waiter who, with very little to do at that point, was hovering around the door of the bar.

'I realise now I was suckered into this mess. George came to the dive centre as a newbie diver a couple of times. He was friendly, likeable sort of guy, but after the second dive, he said it wasn't for him. While we were down, he seemed edgy, nervous, and always looked relieved to surface. After the second dive, I was finished for the day and he looked as though he needed to relax, so I suggested we went for a beer, he agreed and we went to the Irish pub next door. After about an hour, I'd heard about his fear of water which he was trying to overcome, his job in the import and export trade...well, that turned out to be true, even if it was illegal...and he told me almost everything including which side he dresses.' Jake chuckled at that. Luke stayed silent. Now Jake was talking he did not want to interrupt his flow.

'It was George who invited me to the card game, and it was George who introduced me to his wife and, as he said at the time, his cousin...'

'Anjelika?' Luke forgot for a moment that he was not going to butt in.

'You got it.' Jake sat back in his chair again, trying to look relaxed, as two couples entered the patio area. He waited to see where they were going to sit before continuing. As it turned out, the group on the other side of the patio called them over to join their party, and Jake sat forward again, and went on with his account of how he became caught up in the dangerous web he now found himself in.

'So, this George had surrounded you with friendship and sex.'

'Hmm. Anjelika flirted, flashed her eyelashes and cleavage, and before I knew it, we were in bed, and I adored her...for quite a while anyway. Looking back, it seems obvious now that I know she and

George are having an affair, that it was always going on and she was just playing a part, but I just didn't see it, then.'

Luke leaned closer to the table. Their heads, just a few centimetres apart. 'So how does all this business with the drugs work?'

'Drugs are dumped in waterproof dive bags from their boats, I collect the bags and bring them onto the island. They tell me where to deliver them and that's it.'

'Shit, Jake. Is there any way you can get out of it?'

'No. Not now. I owe them too much. It's my own stupid fault.'

'How long has it been going on?'

'Quite a while, months. Soon after I got with Anjelika.'

Luke shook his head. 'My God, Jake, I had no idea. I thought you were okay here. Can I help? I have money.'

'Yeah. I know you do, but it would cost thousands now to pay off the debt and buy my freedom. You know, I kept winning for the first month or so…'

'And then you lost, and kept playing to make up for your losses.'

'You got it and I'm scared, Luke. Part of me just wants to run and hide, and another wants to go to the cops, but it looks like another guy who got caught up in this, was drunk and overheard talking about the money he was making, woke up with his throat cut last week. Will told me about it today.'

'Does he know you're involved? Is he involved?'

'No, not from me he doesn't, and Will's as straight as they come. He'd have nothing to do with me if he knew. That kind of thing's not exactly good for business.' He said, edged with sarcasm.

'So what are you going to do?'

Jake sat forward. Luke did the same. Their heads were close together, their voices low.

'Just keep going I guess. Right now I need to keep them sweet. If I'm right and the guy who died was working for them, then I have to carry on playing the game to stay alive.'

'Fuck that, Jake. You need to get clear.' He swallowed a mouthful of Cisk and put the glass back on the table. 'I knew there was something wrong with you, but thought it was about Anjelika.'

Jake gave a sad chuckle. 'That would have been a lot more simple. If only.'

'I knew there was something wrong, but hadn't expected anything like this. Why don't you come with me, tomorrow. Get out, leave all this be...'

'You don't really get it, do you, Luke? If you're heading back to Birmingham, where you have clubs, where you have a drugs scene, do you not realise how far Fred Kennedy's reach extends? If I came with you, both of us would probably end up in the Trent Canal. I've seen and know too much.'

Luke sat back in his chair. 'But you've got to do something, get away from this.'

'I will. I promise you. Very soon. But I have to find the right time, and the right plan to get out. I would love to go to the police, but how do I trust anyone? No, Luke. It's good of you to offer to help me out, but I can't get you involved. It may even be too late for that. Whatever, I can't and won't get you involved. Go to Rome, go home...go anywhere, but just go. Get out of here. I'll keep in touch. Let you know how I am, and where. And, as it's my confession time, I thought you should hear the rest. Irina's baby is mine.'

'What?' Luke exclaimed more loudly than he intended, causing some of the party across the patio turn to look in his direction.

He lowered his voice. 'Does George know?'

'No. He was away, London, I think, and Irina called me. We've been friends for a long time, and George had been giving her a hard time. I won't go into the details now, but she was really upset. Needed a shoulder to cry on, kind of thing. So I went round, we talked for ages, a bottle or two of wine later, she leaned in for a cuddle, comfort, and you can guess the rest. I'm pretty sure George would kill her if he found out, especially as they've had a boy.' Oh yeah, I didn't tell you she'd had the baby did I? That's another reason why I've been a bit quiet. I haven't seen my son yet, and may never get to see him. George was pretty determined to have a son, and now he's got one.'

'Was it just a one-off with Irina?'

'Yes, just that one time. It's not going to happen again,' he smiled, 'even though I'd like it to. It's just too risky. We're close, and I do care for her, but it's more important that nothing happens to her.'

Chapter Twenty Seven

Gozo : Farewell and Hello Rome

Luke found it hard to say goodbye to Jake. They had grown close during the month on Gozo. It was even harder since Jake's confession, and Luke felt that he was deserting his brother when he needed him most, but Jake insisted that he had to sort things out for himself.

Even so, Luke was certain that, if they had spent more time together, perhaps things would never have reached the point they were now at. If he had been around maybe he would have noticed Jake gambling, and stepped in before it got to the point where Jake was in trouble.

Although Luke had to admit to himself that Jake was an adult, and could make his own mistakes, he still somehow felt a sense of guilt. The fact that Jake had to continue working with the gang worried him sick. These people could not be trusted, that was evident. They would kill Jake without a thought when they had had their use out of him. If only he could have smuggled Jake out, maybe on a boat instead of flying, but Jake would have none of it. He didn't want Luke involved in any way.

As Luke took his place in the queue to board the plane, he remembered the pretty auburn haired woman who had helped him on the flight in to Malta, and smiled. If only she could see him now. He had changed during his time on Gozo, and there was not even a 'smidge' - as their mother would have called it – of nerves, as he handed over his passport and boarding pass for checking at the gate.

By the time Luke had finished reading The Independent newspaper he had bought at a shop on the airport concourse, the pilot informed passengers that they were descending to Rome. Luke looked out of the window. This time he did not blanch as the plane turned, and banked towards the airport. He tried to turn his thoughts to exploring the Eternal City and the harbour at Ostia, as they descended, but Jake's situation kept forcing its way back into his mind. He tried focusing on the movie locations of Ponti de Angelo, Castel Sant'Angelo, and the Trevi Fountain. But it was no use. Only two things would spoil his visit, the first was Jake's thorny problem, the other was that it was a little sad to visit Rome alone.

On landing, when Luke turned on his mobile phone, Jake had left a message telling him not to worry. He was making plans, he would go to the police. He just had to carry on working for the Kennedy group for now, as though nothing had changed. He ended his message by saying 'Love you, Bro.'

Chapter Twenty Eight

Gozo : A Warning

Luke had only been gone for a few days when Jake had a visitor at the dive centre. When he arrived back from a group dive for beginners, Carlos was waiting by the front door.

'Hey, Jake, there is a beautiful lady waiting for you inside. Lovely eyes. You are a lucky man.'

In the corner of the front office, Irina Camilleri looked far more tense than was good for a woman who should have been taking this easily bearing in mind that her baby son had only been born a few days before. She had waited, clearly agitated, for Jake to return from a dive, and he found her sitting on a bench in the centre. She jumped up to meet him as he approached, her eyebrows furrowed, her golden-brown eyes, extraordinarily dark, wide. Something was very wrong.

Excusing himself from the party he had just escorted back, 'Irina. What are you...?'

But, Irina, took him by the arm and hurried him away and towards the back of the centre.

'Jake, I must talk to you, in private...' she looked, darting glances at the group who had just entered, who seemed to be happily reviewing their dive with Will. 'Look we can't talk here...'

'But what's wrong? Had George been rough on you again?'

'It is to do with George, but...look, I need to talk to you. Now. It's vital!' She leaned close, Jake could smell her perfume, it was fresh with the scent of lemons and flowers. One of the clients walked by on his way to the toilet.

Irina whispered, 'It's about your safety, not mine that I need to talk to you, and I cannot stay long. Meet me at the back of the centre in the alley, as soon as you've changed, and make it quick.'

'But what the…?' But Irina was already threading her way through the group towards the door, leaving a worried and confused Jake behind her.

'What's up, Jake?' said Will who was still in his wetsuit.

'Beats me,' said Jake, trying to sound more confident than he felt. 'She's probably found out about George and Anjelika. I wondered when that would happen.'

'Yeah, well just get yourself changed and I'll take care of the debrief. Carlos can start on cleaning the gear. It strikes me that you'd better not keep her waiting.'

Jake grinned. 'Okay, thanks, Will. I'll get back as soon as I can and help with the clear up.'

Will walked away. 'No worries.'

Ten minutes later, Jake entered the alley to find the distraught Irina pacing up and down, nervously clasping and unclasping her hands. She looked pale. At that moment, he was more concerned about her health than whatever was causing her so much distress. On seeing him she ran to him, tears in her eyes that, when she was happy, made him think of the colour of brandy through a glass when the sun shines through it. Now they were dark, brooding, with a look of genuine fear.

'Jake, you must leave Gozo…leave, today!'

'What? Why?' Having thought this would be something to do with the affair between Anjelika and George, Irina's announcement left him at a loss for words. A cold shiver ran down his spine.

Irina looked around nervously, then back at Jake. She was shaking. Jake reached out, held her shoulders hoping to comfort her. She looked up at him, tears spilling over and trailing down her cheeks. 'i…I.'

'Take a breath, Irina. Give yourself a minute. Compose yourself. Breathe.'

Irina did as she was told, then clutched his hands.

'Are you alright?'

'Yes, I'm alright. I am calm now.'

'So, what is all this about? Why do I have to leave Gozo?'

'Fred wants George to kill you.'

Jake was stunned. Had he really heard what she just said? 'That doesn't make sense. Irina, I don't understand. I work for Fred…'

Her lips pressed tightly together and her eyes rolled. 'Jake, take it from me, you're a good friend, more than that so why would I lie to you? Why would I put myself at risk by coming to warn you if this is not true. You did work for Fred. You don't anymore. Within twenty-four hours, maybe less, you will be dead if you stay.'

'But how do you know?'

'I overheard a telephone conversation between George and Fred. George thought I was asleep, but I heard everything. George was in his den, talking to Fred and I could hear the full conversation. George said he thought you were…what did he call it…I remember, a weak link. That you were clearly uncomfortable about being involved with them, and he persuaded Fred that he thinks you'll go to the Pulizija. Fred said he's tired of waiting for the money you owe him, and a few thousand isn't worth the risk to security if you're the liability George thinks you are. That's pretty much what he said. I don't normally bother to listen to their conversations, as it's nothing to do with me, but when I heard your name, I paid attention. I know what George does is illegal but…' she sighed, and he saw both fear and disillusionment in her eyes, 'until recently I loved him, or I thought I did. I'm really not sure now that the person I fell in love with was ever the man I thought he was.'

Jake saw a blend of emotions in her eyes; disillusionment and defeat, but no anger. 'Anjelika?'

She nodded. 'Yes, the scales have fallen from my eyes, as they say, and I now see him for real.' She gave a dejected smile and shook her head. A car engine started up, and she spun around, afraid, but there was no-one in the alley, and a car in the road at the end of the alley drove away. Jake sent a text message to Luke. *Leaving Gozo going to friends in Tenerife. Irina warned no longer safe for me here. She's leaving too. Will contact soon.* 'But you must go Jake. Say whatever you want to Will, but don't let him know you are leaving the island. If people don't know what you're doing, the better it will be for them. Go back to the hotel if you must sort things out there, but take only what you need, essentials, leave the rest, and get away to wherever you can quickly.'

'But what about you, Irina? What will happen to you if George finds out you've warned me?'

'Don't worry about me. I called one of my uncles in Sicily and a boat is already on its way to Marsalforn to take us away, the baby and me. They will be here in about an hour. My relatives there will look after us.'

'Does George know about us, the baby is mine?'

'No, I don't think so. I am sure he would have made me suffer, and perhaps worse by now if he had found out. I will be home in a few minutes and have a taxi picking me up to take us to Marsalforn in half an hour. That way we will not be waiting at the harbour for too long.'

'But where is George now?'

'He left home shortly after the phone call and went to Valletta...on business, he said, so I will never see him again, and I am not sorry. Anjelika is welcome to him.'

'These relatives of yours, are you sure you will be safe with them?'

'Oh yes.' She gave a little laugh. 'Even Fred, with all his European contacts would not dare to cross them. He knows what would happen if he did. Let's just say they look after their own. My uncle Guiseppi will be waiting at the harbour in Taormina for me. The little one and I will be welcome and secure. George will never be allowed to see our son, Jake.' She hugged the still startled Jake, and kissed him on the cheek. 'Now I must go, and so should you.'

'Hmm. I'm not sure where to go. I don't want to go to Luke. He's in Rome and then plans to go on to Amsterdam before going back to Birmingham. If I am with him it might put him in danger, and that's a risk I can't take. I'm thinking about...'

'Don't tell me, Jake. Tell only the people who need to know, but wherever it is, stay safe.' Irina started to walk away, then turned back. 'I don't think we will meet again either, Jake. As you know our son is not registered yet, I will do that in Taormina. He will be called Jacob, and believe me, he will be safe.'

Jake watched Irina walk away, turn the corner at the end of the alley, and vanish, then he stood for a moment, stunned, scared and very sad to see Irina go.

'Do something, Jake. Don't just stand here.' He said out loud. Then forcing one unwilling foot after the other, he headed back into the dive centre, stood at the door for a moment to calm himself before catching Will's attention.

'Yes, sorry Will, but I have to leave. Irina took a message for me from one of Luke's friends. Luke's been taken to hospital after being hit by a car. Hit and run from what she said. I need to get my stuff and get a flight.'

'I'm really sorry to hear that, Jake. Is it serious?'

'Maybe. She didn't have all the details, but it looks like he's pretty badly injured and will need surgery.'

'Yeah. Well you just do what you need to, and take what time you need. Keep in touch won't you?'

'Yeah, yeah, of course. You know we hadn't seen each other for four years, he comes over, we get to know each other again and get close, then this happens. Life can be so unfair.'

Will nodded. 'Hmm. Life can be a bitch sometimes. Anyway, go do what you need to and let's hope it's not too bad. Do you need a lift to the airport?'

'Thanks, Will. There's usually some fairly regular flights, even if it means getting a connecting flight somewhere, but at least I'll be doing something, and a lift to the airport would be really helpful, even if I have to hang around for a while.'

An hour later, Jake checked out of the Cornucopia Hotel having called Phil, an old friend who ran a dive centre in Tenerife, booked the first flight to Tenerife he could get, but took him via Seville, and packed a few necessary things in his holdall. Looking around the room, he wondered how the member of staff who came in to service his room later, would react to finding how much he had left behind. But leaving in a hurry meant travelling light.

As he waved farewell to the hotel receptionists, he walked out to find Will waiting for him. While Will concentrated on driving, Jake sent a text message to Luke. 'Leaving Gozo. Going to friends in Tenerife. Irina warned it wasn't safe for me here. She's leaving too. No-one here knows where I'm going. Will contact soon. Don't worry.'

Chapter Twenty Nine

Tenerife : Two Guests

'Get into the loft and stay there until I tell you to come out!' Moya whispered. Anton opened his wardrobe door, reached up, moved the loose board at the top to one side, and clambered up the shelves into the loft, and set the board back in place before Moya had opened the door.

From where he sat amongst some battered suitcases, a couple of old chairs with torn and fading pink upholstery, some old empty sacks and a few spiders' webs, Anton craned his neck trying to peer through a gap in the floorboards, trying to hear what was being said, but could only pick up the odd few words, and he didn't recognise the male voice talking to Moya. He shuddered, had the Guardia Civil found him? He looked around the loft for a way to escape if he needed to. There was just one small skylight window. He knew he could reach it, but what was the roof like? Were the tiles and roof beams still in a condition to hold his weight?

'Anton, you can come down. It is safe.' Moya called from the hallway, but he could still hear the male voice, then there was second. Moya didn't usually invite people in. Who were they? He tried to put his misgivings aside, as he slid the board to one side and clambered back down the shelves, slid the board back over the gap in the top of the wardrobe. At the bedroom door, he opened it and crept out onto the landing. Moya and the men, two as far as he could ascertain, had gone through to the kitchen at the back of the house. Moya was making coffee. Then he reasoned that these were probably the two men his father had told him about. The timing was about right. He was about to go downstairs when Moya called him again from the hallway.

'Come on, Anton, we have guests. It is safe. Ah, here he is now.'

'As he entered the kitchen, all three turned to look at him standing in the doorway. He took a few steps back. A little voice in his head told him to beware. He didn't like strangers. Why were they here, he had forgotten.

'Come on, Anton,' Moya reached out an arm trying to draw him into the room. The two men just stared at him.

'Is he okay?' the younger one of the two asked Moya.

'Yes, yes, he's fine. Anton's just had a tough time lately, and he's not keen on strangers. Come, Anton. Would you like a coffee, or perhaps some hot chocolate?' It sounded as though she were speaking to a child. 'Anton, this is Ray and Jim. Mr Kennedy has asked them to carry out a little job for him. They're friends, so you have no need to be worried about them. Come and say hello.'

Anton shuffled towards Moya, said he would like a cola and stood close to her, never taking his eyes off the newcomers.

'Hi Anton, I'm Jim.' He held out his hand, but Anton pulled away. Ray whispered to Moya, 'I hope he's not always going to be like this.'

'No. he'll be fine. As I said, he's had a tough time, he's not always like this. He just needs a little time to get used to you.'

Anton took his cola and walked out into the garden to play with Perra. He sat on a bench throwing a ball for her to catch and return, which she did happily, and he smiled at her, but never once looked back into the kitchen where he knew, felt, the two men and Moya watching him. Even though his father had told him the brothers were coming and what they would be doing, he was still unsure about them. What if his father had sent them to get rid of him. Perhaps his father thought he could not trust him anymore, and wanted him out of the way. Or what if they weren't who they said they were. They might be undercover Guardia Civil officers trying to gather evidence against him. No, Moya wouldn't let that happen...but could he trust Moya?

He heard movements behind him. The men and Moya had followed him out into the garden. What did they want? He ignored them and continued playing with Perra. He knew he could trust her.

Chapter Thirty

Tenerife : Buenavista del Norte

In her shared office at the Guardia Civil Headquarters in Buenavista del Norte, Paloma Perez read through the file on the villa fire at Santiago. A few moments before, she had met her supervising officer, Captain Torres, in the corridor on her way back to her office. He was carrying a file.

'Ah, Corporal Perez, I was just on my way to see you.' He handed her a file. 'This is the autopsy report on the Taylor-Owen death. It makes interesting reading. Get yourself a coffee and go through it. Come and see me after you've read it.'

Paloma looked down at the folder. Interesting reading? Perhaps it wasn't a straightforward house fire after all. 'Yes, I will. Thank you, Captain.' She was about to walk on when she turned back. 'Excuse me, Captain. Have you read through it?'

'Yes, I have. Thoroughly. I'd be interested in your thoughts.'

'Very well, sir. Thank you.'

Paloma tucked the file under her arm and went through to the kitchen. The Captain had said she should have a coffee, and it was mid-morning, so coffee it was. Back in her office a few minutes later, she nodded to Juan, another corporal, as she headed for her desk by the window.

'That looks interesting,' Juan said, and pointed to the file.

'It may well be more interesting than I thought it would be.'

The photographs of the badly burned body, identified as Edward Taylor-Owen, were pretty stomach-turning and she looked away, but then forced herself to examine the images. She had not been given this opportunity of advancement in her career just to deal with the pleasant cases. She was a grown up, had wanted to be a police officer since her teens, and now just had to get on with the job, whatever it meant she had to deal with, or she might as well resign right now.

Although the pathologist's report contained many medical terms, Paloma understood the basics and was stunned by what she read. On carrying out the autopsy, the pathologist had noted an injury to the skull, but added that it was possible the victim had hit his head when he collapsed to the floor. However, there was nothing to indicate that this injury would have caused enough damage to the brain to have been fatal. There was also a considerable doubt over the amount of smoke in the lungs. If the victim had been alive, but unconscious, he would have inhaled smoke, and his lungs would have shown soot or other irritants. The lungs would have become inflamed, cell membranes would be damaged, and the airways would collapse. Reduction of the oxygen into the bloodstream, and the effects of carbon dioxide in the system, would certainly bring about death if the victim did not receive treatment in time. In this case, however, although there were traces of smoke in the lungs, if the lungs had been working, considerably more smoke would have been inhaled. In this case, the pathologist concluded that smoke simply infiltrated into the victims lungs post mortem. The pathologist's conclusion was that this was not accidental death caused by the inhalation of smoke and other pollutants, and suggested that Edward Taylor-Owen's death was either Unnatural or Suspicious.

Paloma sat back in her seat and looked down at the open file. There was something nagging at the back of her mind about this case, something that made her think of Mateo Moreno, but she could not quite put her finger on it.

She turned to the front page of the report, and read through the section on Edward Tayor-Owen's personal details. He lived in Puerto de Santiago, usually a quiet, pleasant area where very little criminal activity happened, and there it was. There was the link between this case and Mateo Moreno: Avenida Oceano! It may mean nothing, but what if it did?

Paloma knocked on the Captain's office door and was invited in.

'Take a seat Corporal Perez.'

Paloma pulled up a chair in front of the Captain's desk. He sat forward, leant his elbows on the desk and clasped his hands together.

'You have read the report?'

'Yes, sir. As you said, it made interesting reading.'

'You spoke to the neighbours following the fire?'

'Yes, sir, and to the firefighters. At the time, there was nothing to suspect any wrongdoing. Senor Taylor-Owen was known to use essential oil burners, with candles. He used them to keep insects away and I understand he had a couple of the wax melt burners, again using candles. We spoke to an English lady by the name of Gibson, one of his neighbours as she was walking by the villa. She said she had been a little concerned about the number of these he used. She said sometimes he has as many as ten burning on window ledges close to lace curtains.'

'So there was good reason to believe that the fire may have begun accidentally.'

'Yes, sir. Certainly the firefighters seemed to think that was the probable cause. They said there was no smell of an accelerant or anything, at that time anyway, to cause suspicion. Just an accident caused by carelessness.'

'In your report, you mention a young man who the neighbours said stayed at the villa. Was there any sign of him?'

'No, sir. We understood from the neighbours that he had not been seen for a few days, and there was nothing in the villa to indicate that he had been there recently. His name is Antonio Martin. We have been looking for him but with no result as yet. But, now, with this Post Mortem result, it appears that we may have to look harder for him.'

'Do we know what the relationship was between Taylor-Owen and this Martin?'

Paloma shook her head. 'At this stage, sir, we really don't know. The neighbours were of the opinion that he was an assistant to the victim, but were not sure if there was anything more between them.' Paloma put the file on the desk and the Captain drew it towards him.

'There is one thing that sprang to mind on going through the file, sir. A coincidence...or possibly something more significant.'

Captain Torres looked up from the file. 'Go on.'

'You remember I was working on the missing person case, Mateo Moreno, whose body was found in the sea near to Los Gigantes?'

'Yes, I remember.'

'Well, when we traced Mateo in CCTV, we saw him get off a bus in Avenida Oceano, where Edward Taylor-Owen lived. Now, there may be nothing in it, but the fact that the two incidents happened within a few days of each other could be significant. I would like to check this out further, if you would allow me.'

'I often say, Corporal, that there is no such thing in crime investigations as a coincidence.'

Chapter Thirty One

Rome : Then Home

Luke stretched and yawned in his comfortable hotel bed, and wondered what he was going to have for breakfast on his last day in Rome. Although initially alone, Luke had made friends with a young couple from Birmingham, who were visiting the city of their honeymoon to celebrate their fifth anniversary.

The bar in the hotel was luxurious with the décor of brown, cream and gold fixtures. Concealed subtle lighting in panels at mid-wall height provided an intimate atmosphere for the booths, but the lights were a little brighter around the bar area. On his second evening in the city, Luke sat alone on a stool at the hotel bar, talking to the barman, Gianni. It was fairly quiet in the bar that evening as many of the guests had gone to either the Jack Savoretti concert at the Auditorium, or to see Ed Sheeran at the Olympic Stadium.

A young couple entered the bar, holding hands and smiling. The man escorted the woman to a booth, they chatted for a moment, then the man walked up to the bar, nodded to Luke, and ordered a beer and a glass of red wine. Luke couldn't help overhearing and picked up the distinct Birmingham accent.

'So, there's more than one Brummie in here tonight,' he said, looking across to the newcomer.

'Yeah, we're from Selly Oak, how about you?'

'I live in the city centre, or at least I did.' It suddenly occurred to Luke that he was homeless. He hadn't thought about that for a while.

'You did ... ?'

'Hmm. Let's say I'm travelling right now.'

'Lucky you, mate.' The newcomer extended his hand. 'I'm Ryan, and the lady over there is my wife, Beth. We stayed in this hotel on our honeymoon, five years ago this week.'

Beth had been watching the interaction and waved across to Luke. 'Are you on your own?'

'Yeah, just here for a few days then I go on to Amsterdam, then probably Berlin.'

'Well, why don't you come over and join us.'

They talked about the places in Birmingham they knew, Ryan and Luke had a short friendly argument about their support of rival football teams: Luke supported Birmingham City while Ryan's team was Aston Villa. Beth then added that she supported West Bromwich and the discussion ended in laughter. Over the next couple of days, Beth and Ryan invited Luke to join them on their sightseeing around the city. At first he resisted, not wanting to what is known as a spare wheel, but the couple insisted, and together they visited the Vatican, St Peter's Basilica and the Sistine Chapel. It was only in the evening when Luke turned down invitations to join them for dinner. He felt that they needed some time on their own, it would be an imposition to accompany them all the time, and would not be persuaded even though they were polite enough to ask.

Their last day together was to visit Ostia, Rome's ancient port. They took in the amphitheatre, the tourist port which they discovered had something like eight hundred yachts and other types of vessel moored there at any one time. Unaware of Ostia's historical importance, they were surprised to find that Ostia Antica is the largest archaeological site in the world, but more than half of the city is still buried.

Luke found Beth and Ryan to be really good company, but was thankful that, bearing in mind they were celebrating their anniversary, they were not too touchy-feely around him, and didn't make him feel uncomfortable. Within just a few days a strong friendship was created, and he knew he would be sorry to say goodbye, but at least the couple would have a few more days in Rome to spend without their gooseberry.

They had arranged to meet up for breakfast together before Luke had to check out of the hotel and head to the airport. Ryan had spent some time in Amsterdam before he met Beth, and was giving Luke some advice on the best places to visit, when Luke received a call on his mobile phone. He did not recognise the number, and excused himself from the table to take the call in the lobby.

'Hello?'

'Is that Luke Rutherford?'

'Yes. Who am I speaking to?'

'It's Todd, Sandra Bennett's son.'

Luke knew instantly it was not going to be good news. 'Hi Todd, what's up?'

'Look, I'm sorry to contact while you're away, my mum said you were travelling, but she wanted you to know … that …'

'What's wrong, Todd? I know your mum wouldn't …'

'Dad died ten days ago, and the funeral is on Thursday. Mum wasn't sure where you were but thought that if you're in the UK, you'd want to know and maybe come to the funeral.'

'Oh, Todd, I'm gutted to hear your dad's gone, and yes, you're mum's right I do want to be there. I'm not in the UK but I'm not so far away that I can't come home to be there. Tell her I'll change my arrangements and be back in Birmingham tomorrow, and please send her all my love and my condolences. I really liked your dad. How's your mum holding up?'

'She's okay. She keeps trying to think positively. The MS sped right up this year and dad was in a bad way, so she keeps telling herself that he's at peace now, and she's trying hard to be strong for us. We all know what she's doing, so we're trying to do what we can for her.'

'That sounds like Sandra. I'm in Rome right now and I'll have to sort a few things out, but tell her I'll be there.'

'I will do, and thanks, Luke. See you soon.'

When he walked back into the dining room, his facial expression must have told its own story. Ryan looked up and nudged Beth. A look of understanding passed between them.

'It looks as though you've had some bad news,' said Beth.

'Yes. That was the son of a work colleague. Actually, she's more than a work colleague, she's a very dear friend and I've known her family for some years. Her husband has been ill with MS and died a few days ago.'

'I'm sorry to hear that,' said Ryan.

'Is there anything we can do?' asked Beth. She reached out to take his hand.

Luke smiled and held her hand for a moment. 'No, but thanks for asking. Sandra asked Todd to let me know about Jim's funeral.' He took a deep breath, released Beth's hand and sat back in his chair. 'It's on Thursday and I do want to be there, so I'll have to cancel my Amsterdam flight today, re-book for Birmingham and book a hotel.' He gave a sad little smile, and took a mouthful of coffee. 'Urggh! It's gone cold.'

'Would you like another?' asked Ryan.

'No, thanks anyway. I have some things I have to do now. You know, it's funny when you think about it. I'm going back with nowhere to live, and I'll to have to get myself some decent clothes for a funeral. The way I had things planned … if everything had gone to plan, that is, was to contact a lettings agent I know while I was in Berlin, and have somewhere to move into. How things change.'

'Well I hope you get things sorted out, and maybe we'll catch up with you when we get back,' said Ryan, looking across at Beth for her agreement.

'Let's swap phone numbers and we'll get in touch soon after we get home,' said Beth.

A few minutes later, having exchanged numbers, with hugs and handshake farewells, Luke headed back up to his room to pack and make the necessary telephone calls. An hour later, pre-occupied, he checked out of the hotel, unaware of Ryan and Beth watching him leave from the lobby.

Chapter Thirty Two

La Gomera : Paloma Calls Maria

'Hola, Maria, it's Paloma Perez.' Paloma knew she should have used her rank as this was an official call, and part of a possible murder investigation,. However, she wanted to keep her dealings with Maria informal whenever she could. Maria seemed to trust her and, although she knew she should not become involved or close to civilians in an enquiry, Paloma felt that Maria, considering her age and the circumstances, needed to be treated gently.

'*Good morning, Paloma. I understand you are not based on the island anymore.*'

'No, I'm now in Buenavista del Norte, but I am still working on Mateo's case.'

'*Oh, that's good to hear. I am glad you are still helping me. I did think they may have given Mateo's case to someone else.*'

'No, my superiors thought I would be able to do more from here, so I am still with you.'

'*Do you have any news for me?*'

'Not at this stage, I am sorry to say, Maria. But I do have a question for you.'

'*Oh yes. Of course, anything I can do to help. Just a moment, Paloma. Get down, Gato, you silly cat. That's better. Sorry, Paloma. Gato was trying to climb up onto my shoulder. I think he recognises your voice.*'

Paloma laughed. 'Tell him I'll make a fuss of him next time I visit. I might even bring him some treats.'

'*Oh yes, he would like that, but he's too plump now.*'

Paloma needed to get back to the point of her call. 'Maria, could you tell me if the name Edward Taylor-Owen means anything to you? Did you ever hear Mateo mention him?'

'No, no I don't think so. I don't believe Mateo ever spoke of him that I can recall. Why?'

'Ah. I just wondered as there has been an incident here where that name and area cropped up, and whether there may be some connection, some link between him and Mateo. You may have seen something about it in the newspapers.'

'Oh, I don't read the newspapers or watch the news on television. It's always such bad news.'

'I can understand that, but if you come across anything that links Mateo with Senor Taylor-Owen, please let me know.'

'I will. I certainly will and I am seeing Javier and his mother tomorrow, I will ask him if he has ever heard that name.'

'Thank, you, Maria. I must go now. I still have a lot to do, but take care of yourself and I will be in touch again soon, I hope.'

'Yes, thank you, Paloma ... but just one more thing, please. Is there any word on when Mateo's body will be released for his funeral?'

'No, not yet. I am sorry, Maria, but once we have been able to establish what happened, maybe then. It is possible though that, if my superiors decide the two incidents are linked, you may have to wait a little longer, but I will keep you informed.'

'Thank you, Paloma. I understand. Goodbye. Now you can climb on my shoulder, you silly cat.'

The line went dead. Paloma smiled as she put the phone down.

Chapter Thirty Three

Tenerife : A New Start

Jake had been given a room, in an apartment above the dive centre in a bay near Puerto de Santiago, as a temporary home for up to six months, until he found a place of his own. It had three comfortable bedrooms, all the amenities Jake could want, the rent was low, and he got on well with the other resident, twenty-eight-year old, Australian Max. To all appearances, Max looked exactly as you would expect an Aussie beach-lover to look; tanned, blond hair, blue eyes, wide shoulders, slim hips, and incredibly athletic. However, there was a great deal more to Max, than surfing, swimming and diving. He was a fully qualified lawyer, a lover of poetry and Shakespeare, had a great number of PADI qualifications and was something of a wildlife enthusiast, especially with the fauna unique to the Canary Islands. He was also sickeningly healthy. A non-drinker, who didn't smoke, and refused to eat junk food, but didn't judge anyone who enjoyed any of those things. He also had an charming personality, and Phil was delighted to have him on the team as he brought more women divers into the centre. He had been at the centre for a little under three months, knew the area well, and Jake found him to be very good company who helped him to take his mind off his losses.

Phil, the dive centre owner, owned the apartment, and used it for employees new to the area, to help them get settled. Jake felt that he could breathe again, that he could stop looking over his shoulder. He had a new life and was enjoying himself. He felt free for the first time in months, but although he never spoke of it to anyone, he missed Irina and bitterly regretted never having been seen his baby son. Many were the nights, when alone in his room, his mind wandered to imagining how little Jacob would look over the coming years. His only comfort was knowing that the little lad would never have George as his father.

In the few weeks he had been there, Jake and Luke had been in touch more often than they had in the four missing years, and he knew Luke had stayed on in Birmingham for a while to help his friend, Sandra, who had gone through a very rough time since she had lost her husband. The last time they spoke, Luke said he had moved in with a friend from work, Donal, for a few weeks, but intended to make that visit to Amsterdam soon, and then he would head to Tenerife for a few weeks. Maybe get some more diving in. Sandra was managing better, and her four children, two were now adults, and their grandparents were incredibly supportive, and Sandra would be fine.

Shortly before Jake left the apartment that morning, Phil rang to let Jake know that Judy Alvarez, the lady who carried out their admin duties, had received a call telling her that her brother had been taken ill in Athlone, Ireland, and she would be away for the foreseeable future. Phil had only found this out when a friend of Judy's had called him to tell him that Judy had caught a late flight to Dublin the night before, and she offered to stand in for Judy. He said that the friend, her name was Emma Holloway, would be at the centre that morning. It was Max's week off, but he said he would look forward to meeting her, when he went back to work.

On arriving at the dive centre, Jake found Emma waiting outside for someone to open up. She was an attractive brunette, probably in her late forties, and she seemed very friendly as they chatted while waiting for Phil to arrive, and open the centre.

Over the next two days, Emma proved to be invaluable. She made the bookings, checked the PADI registration cards to ensure that no-one booked dives they were not qualified to take, dealt with payments, made refreshments and welcomed clients in a pleasant and professional manner

On the third day, she said, 'I have two guys who don't want to go with a group, they prefer something less crowded. I've taken a look at their PADI records and they've both got their Advanced Open Water and, they're keen on marine photography. Could you take them out, Jake, or shall I get them to wait until Warren gets in. He will be about another hour, maybe hour and a half?' said Emma. 'It depends on how quickly he can get through his dental appointment. 'I felt awful having to ask him to come in. I think he's having a couple of teeth out, and could probably do with today at home, but Phil said I should try to get as many of the dive leaders in as I can...'

'...Yeah, you can't turn money down when it's there, and dentist or no, Warren needs the money. Who doesn't? Anyway, where are these guys now?'

'In the café having a coffee while they're waiting. Stan was going to take them, but Phil had a larger group and needed Stan to go with him. One instructor wasn't enough.'

'No problem. I can take them out. Is the boat being used?'

'No, Phil and Stan took their group out from the beach.'

'Okay, I'll start getting the gear ready, can you let them know we'll be going out on the boat in about half an hour?'

'Can do. I'll head round there now. Where are you going in from?'

'Probably Los Gigs or Santiago .'

'Oh yes, It won't be as busy there as it is here this morning. Okay, back soon.'

'Oh, Emma, before you go. What kind of size are these guys? I'd like to try and get the suits and fins ready.'

She looked him up and down and gazed for a moment at his feet. 'I'd say probably about your size, well near enough.'

'Okay, thanks.'

Emma left, heading for the café.

Jake made sure three tanks were full, and the regulators were working, and gathered all the Scuba gear together while he waited for Emma and the two men to return to the centre.

Emma found the men she was looking for in a corner table of the busy awning-covered street seating area of the café. In shorts and T-shirts and wearing sunglasses and baseball caps, they looked like any other holiday makers and blended in. That was good. There was nothing immediately conspicuous, about their appearance for anyone to describe. They were just very ordinary and very much like hundreds of other men.

Emma approached the table with a smile, and spoke in a clear, easy to hear, voice. 'Mr Davies, Mr Brown, my name is Emma, and I'm from the dive centre. Our dive leader, Jake, will be happy to take you out, if you're ready. He's getting everything prepared now.'

'That's great,' said the one she called Mr Davies. 'I'll just pick up the cameras from the car on the way. It's parked close to the centre.'

'Yes, that's fine. If you're ready, our dive leader, Jake, is waiting for you.'

Davies threw some Euro coins onto the table and the trio weaved their way through the patrons, and out to the pavement.

'So you're Moya,' said Davies.

'Yes, but here I'm Emma, please try to remember that. Do you have what you need to make it look like an accident?' she asked.

Mr Brown nodded. 'Yeah, it's in the camera case.'

'And you're sure it will work?'

'No worries. Its foolproof.'

'So what will you do with his body?'

Davies answered that one. 'We were going to leave it in the sea, but as this should look like an accident, we thought we'd bring his body back to the beach, like anyone would do if it was a genuine accident.'

Moya was astounded at the boldness, perhaps even arrogance of the plan. 'Do you think you'll get away with that?'

'Don't see why not,' said Brown. 'Okay so the cops will want to interview us, the medics will want to know what happened, and we'll explain it. We'll tell them exactly what happened. Our dive leader, was boasting about knowing what he was doing with the sea life and decided to show off around a stingray. He must have pissed it right off, 'cos it turned to face him, swung its tail over its back and shot out a barb.'

'And you have one?'

'Yeah. That's what's in the camera case.'

'Where did you get it?'

'You can buy them online. Easy.'

'Haven't they got serrated edges ...?

Davies stopped walking and looked Moya in the eye. 'For fuck's sake woman, stop fussing. We know what we're doing. Yes, it's the serrated edges that will keep part of the barb stuck in his neck. It has to be...'

Brown took over. '... We know we'll be interviewed by the police at the scene when we bring him onshore. The medics will take the body away and the police will say they will want to see us again. To them we're Ray Davies and Jim Brown, but those two characters are going to vanish afterwards, before they can catch up with us. You're the one who will have to deal with what comes next, Moya ... sorry, you're Emma here aren't you?' He frowned. 'I hate false names, we have enough to do without having to remember that kind of crap.'

'Yeah, maybe so, but I'll still be here when you guys have pissed off. I have to protect myself and a false ID is part of that. I live here, remember. So you just do what you have to do and shut up moaning about what I have to do. Now, just to make this more realistic, I have a doctor lined up to arrive, confirm the cause of death and issue a genuine death certificate at the scene. It's unlikely anyone will dispute his authority.'

'Apologies for carping about your name, and all respect, lady. You think of everything don't you?'

'I'm a professional in what I do, and I have to think of everything. And I don't intend to hang around after you've gone out on the boat with Jake.' She chuckled. 'I'm not that stupid. I got friendly with the usual girl a few weeks back, and she told me lots of personal things about her, including all about her family in Athlone, in Ireland. A few days ago, she had a phone call from a hospital nurse in Ireland to tell her that her brother was seriously ill, and that it would be a good idea if she could come over. Of course, it was me putting on an Irish accent who made the call. When she told me what had happened, I suggested I step in to help out while she's away. Phil Rogerson, the owner, seemed happy enough with that, and she flew out that evening. Phil took me through the basics, and now here we are. Once you two are on that boat with Jake, I'm out of there. The brown contact lenses come out, and I'll be glad to get rid of this wig ... it's too bloody hot to wear for long. I have a few other ... um ... commitments to see to. I don't just work for your boss. I guess you'd call me a facilitator. I help people get things done.' They were almost at the dive centre.

'Jake's taking you to pick up a boat in Puerto de Santiago for your dive, and once you're on your way, I'll drive over to Los Gigantes with all your belongings in that red Peugeot over there. So make sure you head for Los Gigs on your dive. It only takes a few minutes to drive between the two, so it's close enough for a dive. I'll leave the keys on the nearside front tyre, and park opposite the beach entrance by the shops. I have someone parked there now holding a space for me. He'll move out when I get there. If a Guardia Civil officer asks about you leaving from Santiago but having a car left here, just tell them the dive was planned this way and you arranged to have a car here ready for you, and Jake was going to return the boat to Santiago.'

'But what about the suits drying with sea water on them,' said Brown. 'Don't they need showering off,' asked Davies.

'Yes, all thought of. I do know what I'm doing, you know.' Moya rolled her eyes and turned away from the men for a moment. She sighed and turned back to them. 'You're going to be in the water for about thirty minutes, right?'

'Yes,' Davies agreed.

'That's when I'll park the car. I'd give it another thirty minutes for the police and the ambulance to arrive, and for the police to interview you both. They'll want to clear the beach pretty quickly. The guy's dead so there's nothing they can do for him. The crowds will gather, and the police will want the beach back to normal as quickly as possible, so that's why I estimate no more than half an hour, then they'll let you go. It'll take you no more than ten minutes to find the car, and then maybe another ten minutes to wipe down your suits and get changed. It won't take long to drive up the mountain to just beyond Arona. All in all, I reckon everything done in just under an hour.

'There's a lay-by about half a kilometre beyond Arona where a black SEAT Ibiza will be waiting for you. Swap cars, clean down anything in the Peugeot you've touched without gloves. I've already wiped mine, and I'll be wearing gloves from now on. Leave your dive suits and equipment hidden in the undergrowth on the opposite side of the road from the lay-by. There's nothing to stop there for other than to pee, and anyone who needs to stop that urgently isn't likely to bother about crossing the road, so very little likelihood of the gear being seen if you've concealed it well. Then take the Ibiza to the airport and dump it there when you fly out. My ... associate and I will collect the equipment within an hour of you leaving it, and I'll get it all showered off we soon as we get back. That's all you need to know. You do your job and follow those instructions and everything should go according to plan.'

'Okay,' said Davies. 'It sounds like you have it all worked out.'

'I believe I do. This is not the first time I have had to make covert plans for our Mr Kennedy, and that's why he trusts me. Well, gentlemen, we probably won't meet again. Just make sure the job goes well and follow my instructions for afterwards. I'm sure Fred will be paying you well for this.'

'Have you met him?'

'Yes, we're... old friends, well a bit more than that at one time. Now I work for whoever pays me, but I'm always happy to do a favour for Fred ... when he needs me to. I take it you haven't?'

'No,' said Davies. 'We just got our instructions over the phone from one of his team. Look, I just thought, if we have the Peugeot, how will you get back to Masca?'

'Oh, I'll get a bus, dearie. That's what people with nothing to hide do ... usually.' She laughed, and walked ahead of them into the dive centre.

'Jake, your party of two is here.'

A short time later, temporary admin assistant, Emma Holloway waved to Jake as he and the two divers drove away in the company-logoed van. As she watched them head up the road, she had a brief moment of regret. Jake had seemed like a nice guy, and cute too. It was a shame he wouldn't see the sun go down that evening. But, if he hadn't got himself into trouble with Fred, none of this would be happening, He really only had himself to blame. You didn't run out on them. No-one got away with owing them money, and you didn't betray their trust. If they doubted your loyalty, there was no way back.

An hour later, two distressed divers, one shouting for help, the other in tears, hauled a body with a long shard of a stingray barb in his neck, out of the ocean onto the beach at Los Gigantes. A crowd gathered around them as they emerged from the sea and immediately the emergency services were called. Within minutes a Guardia Civil car, siren blaring, sped through the narrow main street, and parked close to the beach entrance. Two officers ran across the black shale beach to attend the incident, just as the sound of an approaching ambulance was heard.

One of the divers, Ray Davies, explained that the dive leader, who he knew as Jake, but didn't know his surname, had taken them out in a boat from Santiago. Once underwater, he had taken them further out to sea. Everything was fine to begin with, but then a pair of stingrays had appeared. Davies said that it looked as though Jake was showing bravado and got too close. One of the rays must have felt threatened in some way, because it swung around to face him, lifted its tail over its back, and fired the barb straight into Jake's neck, but in the impact part of the barb had broken off. Jake had thrashed about, bleeding profusely from the wound, and trying to surface, but then stopped moving. Davies said that he and his friend were too shocked at first to do anything. Thinking Jake was unconscious, with one of them on either side of him they pulled him up to the surface, and saw they were closer to the beach than to the boat. It was at that point they realised Jake was beyond help, and they made for the beach.

As more and more people began to comprehend that something interesting was happening on the beach, the crowd increased in numbers, pushing and shoving to see what was going on. After a police officer made a radio call, two more official cars arrived with four more officers, who began to herd the horde of spectators away.

The paramedics, on examining Jake's body, quickly confirmed there was nothing they could do for him and therefore, they and the attending Guardia Civil officer agreed that, as the accident had happened in the sea, there was nothing to be gained by keeping the body on the beach. They did not need the body there while they finished talking to the witnesses, and it would be better to take the deceased directly to the hospital. Jake was covered with a blanket, gently lifted onto a stretcher and carried to the waiting ambulance, just as a man carrying a black bag forced his way through the crowd and headed for the Guardia Civil officers.

'Can I help? I am a doctor.'

The senior officer waved the newcomer through. The Doctor showed the officer his credentials, and introduced himself as Paulo Jimenez, a general practitioner from the local clinic. He had just finished his round of home visits, when he saw the gathered crowd and the ambulance, and thought he might be of help. The officer asked the paramedics to wait while the doctor examined the body. After a few moments of checking Jake's eyes, pulse, looking for any signs of a heartbeat and examining the wound in Jake's neck, the doctor looked up.

'It is clear this man died from Exanguinación. This is loss of blood directly from the ruptured carotid artery. The amount of blood loss from that injury would result in death very quickly, probably within a matter minutes. Even if the sea had been colder, it would be unlikely to have slowed the speed of the blood loss.' He reached into his bag and pulled out a pad of forms, and called over to the paramedics. 'I can give you a death certificate now. The cause of death is obvious.' They waited while he completed the form, signed it and tore it off the pad. 'Give this to whoever deals with the body when you arrive at the hospital. This will negate the need for an autopsy. I have examined the body, confirmed the cause of death, and can be available at the clinic for consultation if required. The certificate gives my full contact details. You may take the body away now.'

'Is it alright?' the paramedic looked across to the Guardia Civil officer, who nodded his agreement.

'I must go. I have patients to see at the clinic. You know where to find me if you need me.' He walked away just as the ambulance trundled slowly through the crowd, out to the main road.

'It was strange,' Davies reflected to the interviewing officer, 'his blood looked green. Did you know that blood looks a different colour underwater? No, I didn't either.'

'Can we go now,' asked Brown. 'There's nothing more we can tell you right now, and to be honest, Officer, I feel sick. I could do with a brandy.'

'Where are you staying?' the officer asked.

'At the Miramar in Playa de la Arena. We're booked in for another few days, so if there's anything we can do, please let us know.'

The officer wrote their names and the hotel name in his notebook. 'No. I do not think we can do anything else for now. If we need any more information from you, we will contact you at the hotel.'

'Thank you, Officer. Come, on Jim. Let's go and get that brandy.'

'Just one moment, Senor Davies. You had a boat, are you not using it to return?'

'No, Officer. We arranged for a car to be left here for us. The dive was planned to be from Santiago to Los Gigantes.'

'But what about the boat?'

'It belongs to the dive centre. Perhaps someone from there could come and get it?'

Chapter Thirty Four

Tenerife : Deception at the Dive Centre

When Phil Rogerson, and his colleague Stan Siddons, returned to the dive centre with their group of beginners, they found the centre locked up. Phil called at the Irish pub next door for his spare key, and asked the bar staff if they had seen anything unusual happening while he was away. The two young men shook their heads. With the bar being at the back of the pub and the place being pretty full with customers, they had been too busy to take notice of anything outside other than serving and cleaning empty tables. But then, just as Phil was leaving, Rory O'Rourke, the owner appeared from the back of the pub.

'Hey, Phil. I've been waiting for you to get back. What's going on with that woman you had working in there for the last couple of days?'

Rory watched the colour drain from Phil's face. 'How d'you mean?'

'It sounds really stupid now that I look back on it, but I thought it looked odd when I saw her in the alley at the back, shoving what looked like two diving gear bags into the boot of a red Peugeot. I didn't recognise her at first, 'cos the woman I'd seen working for you, was blonde, and this woman had brown hair. But it was the clothes she was wearing that caught my eye. She was wearing the same outfit she had on this morning, in your dive centre, your firm's navy T-shirt and white jeans. That's how I recognised her. If she had worn anything different I probably wouldn't have because of the change of hair colour.'

'What? Oh shit!'

'It wasn't till I got back here and saw the centre was locked up, that it confirmed something was very wrong. I ran back to the alley, but she'd gone. I would have called the Guardia Civil but wanted to check with you that you knew, hadn't asked her do something, or maybe there was another reason. You'd already arranged that she could leave work early and lock up. I thought it would have been a bit weird, and didn't want to jump the gun.'

Some of the beginners were beginning to get fed up waiting to get into the centre. They wanted to get changed and get on their way. Phil apologised as he left the pub with Rory and headed for the locked door. However, on seeing Phil's worried expression, they quickly realised something was very wrong. Phil unlocked the door, opened it. The first thing he saw was the open cash till.

'Shit! Shit! Shit! How long ago was this?' He inhaled deeply several times as he looked around the room. Rory moved a little ahead of him, Stan hurried around to check the rail where the unused wetsuits were kept on hangers on a moveable metal rail. Swore and walked back to where Phil stood with Rory, both bewildered and stunned by what they had found.

'Some of the gear has gone too, Phil. A couple of shorty wetsuits, diving shoes, fins, two tanks and pressure gauges, masks, regulators and two bags.'

Rory checked his watch. 'Oh Lord have mercy. It was about an hour ago. She could be anywhere by now.'

The people in their diving group held back, unsure what to do. Two five Euro notes were lying on the floor by the desk, together with a handful of Euro coins, one of the teenage boys in the group reached down, picked them up and left them on the desk beside the till. Phil distractedly thanked him. The boy just nodded and walked back to his family.

'Well. I guess it's lucky.'

'Stan, phone the police ... please.'

Phil calculated that there must have been around three hundred and fifty Euros in the till. He had been so busy the day before, that he had not made time to take the cash to the bank then, and now he bitterly regretted it.

Phil turned to his group of customers. 'I must apologise for this ... um ... inconvenience. The police will be here soon. If you don't want to wait, could you leave your contact details with me, as the Guardia Civil might want to talk to you.'

'But what can we tell the police?' said one man who was standing at the front of the group. 'We were with you when this happened. I'm sorry for your trouble but I'm more concerned with our personal belongings, drying off and getting dressed. Isn't it time you checked your safe?'

'Oh, Hell! Phil rushed through to the back of the building where he had a wall safe hidden behind a set of book shelves. He shoved a handful of books onto the floor, held his breath. His heart thumped far too loudly and rapidly. The door of the safe was closed, and locked. He punched in the numbered code, closed his eyes and swung open the door. He opened his eyes and heaved a sigh of relief. All the personal items belonging to the customers waiting in the main room, were there. Stan joined him.

'Everything okay?'

'Yes, thank God.'

'And I've just checked the changing area, all their clothes are there too. So she didn't get away with everything.'

'Maybe didn't have time.'

'At least none of that went,' said Rory, who had just followed Phil and Stan. 'Listen, Phil, I need to get back to the bar, but I'm around if the Guardia want to talk to me about what I saw.'

'Yeah, thanks, mate. I'm sure they will as you've got an idea of what she looks like without the disguise. Oh, did you get the number of the Peugeot?'

'No. Sorry, but I just didn't think of it at the time. Right, gotta go.'

'No problem. See you later,' Phil called after him, as the waiting clients parted to allow Rory to reach the door, and Phil joined them and, to their relief, handed them the personal possessions that had been locked away in the safe. It was then that a car belonging to the Guardia Civil pulled up and a Captain approached. 'Senor Rogerson?'

'Yes, and thank you for coming so quickly. It seems ...'

'Just one moment, Senor. I am Captain Julio Montez. Can you confirm that you have an employee, Jacob Rutherford?'

Phil frowned. 'Yes, but what's that got to do with ...'

'Then I regret to inform you, Senor, that Jacob is dead.'

'What!? I ...'

'It seems to have been an accident, or misadventure. It appears he was killed by a stingray.'

'No, no ... Jake? No. That's not right. It's just not right.'

'I need to ask you to accompany me to the morgue at the hospital to officially identify the body, if you will.'

Phil was confused, unable to take in what the officer had told him. 'I'm sorry, Captain. I thought you were here about a robbery we have just reported.'

'A robbery, here? No, I had not heard about that. I am sure our officers are on their way, but I need you to come with me now, please. Can one of your staff deal with the robbery for now? I am sure you will be back soon.'

'Um ... er ...'

'It's okay Phil, you go with the Captain,' said Stan. I'll stay here and talk to the police when they get here.'

'Thank you, Senor ... ?'

'Siddons, Stanley Siddons, Captain. Who'd have thought it, two terrible shocks in one day?'

'Yes, Senor Siddons, who would have thought it. Could be a coincidence...but maybe not?'

Thirty Five

Birmingham : More Bad News for Luke

Luke's phone rang. He checked the number. Didn't recognise it, but it was definitely not a UK number. For a moment, he thought about ignoring it, but then thought it might be a call from Jake or even The Cornucopia Hotel perhaps trying to get in touch with him for some reason.

'Hello?'

'Good morning. Am I speaking to Mr Luke Rutherford? Whoever she was, she had a soft gentle voice with a lovely accent.

'Yes, and who are you?' Luke was intrigued.

'Mr Rutherford, I am Corporal Paloma Perez, and I am an officer of the Guardia Civil in Tenerife.'

Luke felt a cold chill shiver down his spine.

'I regret, Mr Rutherford, that I have some bad news for you. It is in relation to your brother, Jacob Rutherford.'

'Jake! Oh Lord, what's happened?'

'There was a tragic accident while out on a diving trip and I am so sorry to inform you that your brother died.'

'When ... um ... I mean when, no, how did it happen?'

'It was yesterday. I was not there myself, but from the report it seems he was attacked by a stingray.'

'What? A stingray? No, no. That's not possible. Definitely not ... possible.'

'There were witnesses, Mr Rutherford.'

'To the actual attack?'

'Yes. Two witnesses who said they were diving with your brother when they said he...just a moment, I can read you a part of the statement by one of them.' Luke heard the rustling of papers. *'Yes,*

here it is. They spotted a pair of stingrays and your brother decided to get clo …'

'… Then I definitely don't believe it. I spent a month with Jake on Gozo and went diving with him most days, usually with a group. He always went through the safety instructions, and made a special mention of not getting to close to the marine life. I remember he specifically mentioned that stingrays, mostly they're lone animals, but get together for mating. If there were two, they may have been mating. After what happened to Steve Irwin, Jake knew better than to try to disturb them during that time, and he would have given them a wide berth. With them tending to lie flat on the sea bed for long periods of time, I could have understood it if he'd accidentally stood on one. The way they blend into the colour of the sand, that might have been the case, and although I would find it difficult to believe, it might have happened like that. But if these guys said he acted deliberately, then I would call their statement into question.'

'But, and I am sorry to have to be so … so descriptive, but a piece of the barb was still in your brother's neck.'

'That may be so, but none of what you have told me they saw makes sense. Could they have been confused, maybe due to shock, or something like that?'

'I really don't know, Mr Rutherford. I did not speak to them myself, and have only been asked to contact you with the sad news, but you really feel very strongly that their story doesn't … add up?'

'Yes, I do, and look I'm sorry if I've given you a hard time. It's just that … look, I'm going to come over, but I'll need a couple of hours to sort out a flight and so on. Can I get I touch with you later when I have sorted out a flight? Where is my brother's body now?'

'Yes, of course. I thought you would want to come here. I will send you a text with my contact details. He was formally identified by a Mr Phil Rogerson, his employer. We are keeping his body in the hospital morgue until we spoke to you with regard to the funeral arrangements. However, if you feel there is more that needs to be looked into, and my superior officers agree, then his body will have to be moved to the Guardia Civil morgue, perhaps for further examination.'

'Yes, I understand. Thank you for letting me know about my brother, Corporal Perez, and for the further information. You'll hear from me again soon.'

Luke looked at his watch. It was a little after ten-thirty. He would have to throw some things in a bag, grab his travel documents, let friends know what he was doing but, in a taxi, he could probably make it to Birmingham airport in just over an hour. He found a Jet2 flight departing at five minutes past two, and there were available seats. He reserved one. He thought about calling the police officer back then, but decided to get organised and get to the airport. He could call her from there once he had checked in. With the flight taking about four and a quarter hours, he would land, and possibly get through immigration and customs by around six-thirty pm.

In the taxi on the way to the airport, he called Donal and Sandra to let them know what he was doing, but did not stay on the phone to either of them for very long. He needed some time to try to fathom out what the hell had happened to Jake.

At the airport check in desk he received his boarding card, had his hand luggage weighed, then went through Security without any holdups. All the time his head was full of Jake, wondering who the two divers were and, convinced they were lying, what was behind it. He went to a newspaper seller, bought a copy of The Observer, then went to one of the bars, where he bought a pint of lager and a ham and cheese sandwich. He opened the paper but was unable to focus on the page, and put it down on the table. He took a mouthful of lager, then opened his sandwich, took a bite, then put it down again. His mouth was dry, the sandwich had no flavour and felt like cottonwool in his mouth. He gave up and sat taking the occasional sips of lager and people watching until the boarding was announced for his flight. Then he remembered, he had to phone Corporal Perez. There was still time before he had to board the plane, but he walked to the gate before calling her.

'Hola, Corporal Paloma Perez.'

'Ah, Corporal Perez. It's Luke Rutherford. Just calling to let you know that I should be landing and through Tenerife South airport, by about six-thirty this evening. I'll hire a car and come out to Santiago. Is that where you are?'

'No, Mr Rutherford, I'm actually based in Buenavista del Norte, just along the coast from Santiago. If it would be helpful, I finish work today at four, and would be happy to meet with you at the airport. I could also book you into a nearby hotel if that would help.'

'That's very good of you, but I don't want to put you to any trouble.'

'No trouble at all. Although I was not one of the original interviewing officers, I am on this ... your brother's case, and I would like to help you. Following our earlier conversation, I am now wondering if your brother's death was not as straightforward as we first thought.'

'In that case, I will take you up on your offer, and thank you. I look forward to meeting you.'

'Very good, Mr Rutherford. We will meet later.'

Luke's flight was routine and this time, not only was he becoming used to flying, but there was so much going on in his head, the thought of being frightened never occurred to him.

With no delays, it was a little after six-thirty when Luke walked through the arrivals exit into the main hall, to find an attractive young woman, in a dark green short sleeved polo shirt, cargo trousers, and dark hair mostly concealed within a baseball cap with the Spanish Coat of Arms on the front, leaning against the barrier. He rightly assumed that this was Corporal Perez. As he walked towards her she smiled.

'Mr Rutherford?'

'Corporal Perez?'

'I thought it would be easier if I stayed in uniform for you to see me immediately. Come, my car is in the car park across the road. I have booked you into the Allegra Hotel in Buenavista del Norte. It's three-star, clean comfortable and the food is good. But, if you prefer, once you have checked in and unpacked, perhaps you would like to dine elsewhere? I would be happy to take you to somewhere I would recommend.'

'Yes, that would be good, but I'll have to leave you to choose as you know the area.'

'I have the perfect place, overlooking the sea, and quiet. We will be able to talk there. While you are getting settled at the hotel, I will go home to change out of my uniform. Then I will return to meet you in the lobby. The tapas restaurant is just a ten minute walk from the hotel.'

'Sounds good. Thank you for your help, Corpor ...'

'Paloma. Please call me Paloma. I am off duty tonight even if we are discussing your brother's case. Tomorrow, maybe, you should then call me Corporal.'

Paloma pulled up outside the hotel, and Luke was about to get out of the car when she said. 'Just before you go in, I must tell you that, after you told me how careful your brother was around sea life, and how much he understood the behaviour of stingrays, I went through the interview statements again. Both witnesses described the ... well, let's say incident now, rather than accident, in exactly the same way. They were almost word for word the same, which is quite unusual. It looked rehearsed, is that the right word?'

Luke nodded. 'Yes, it's a very good word.'

'Good,' Paloma continued. 'Usually, with witness statements, we find slight differences. One person will see something that another doesn't, but that is not so this time. So, I decided to get in touch with the with the witnesses, and arrange a further interview. They had both been told that it was possible we would need to see them again.'

'And ...' Luke had a feeling he knew what was coming. He was right.

'I found those names were not registered at the Miramar Hotel. They never had been there.'

'I had a terrible feeling you were going to say that, and perhaps I need to fill you in on a few things Jake told me before he came here.'

'Fill me in?' Paloma frowned, puzzled.

Luke smiled. 'It's just an expression we use. It means to tell you more, give you further details. I'll explain what I know about Jake's situation which may well be relevant. My gut feeling is that Jake's death was murder, and I have reason to believe that.'

Paloma looked at him and nodded. 'It certainly seems suspicious now. We'll speak later. I'll meet you in the lobby in about thirty minutes. Will that give you time to get settled?'

'Yes, that will be fine. See you then.'

Paloma waved as she drove away. Luke stood for a moment watching her car disappear into the traffic. This news about the two witnesses was a Godsend. It meant that there was going to be an investigation into Jake's death after all.

Chapter Thirty Six

Tenerife : Moya

In the secluded rear garden of what had once been a farmhouse, a granja, Moya Gibson sat at a table on the patio with a breakfast of coffee and croissants, watching Anton as he played fetch with Perra, her one-year-old Spanish Mastiff. As she watch the two of them at play, instead of a grown man and a killer, she saw a young boy at play, happy relaxed, and without a care in the world. It was a shame that could not last. Anton belonged to a violent and unstable world, where life spans were uncertain, and those living within that world were forever looking over their shoulder, and no-one was a friend.

Anton was frightened, confused about what was to happen to him next. Moya felt some sympathy for him but did not let it show, the boy had killed two people on the orders of his father, even though it went against his nature. He was manifestly more frightened of his father than of his own conscience. To show Anton compassion now would make him weak, and he still had work to do. She just hoped he could cope, and the pressure would not push his sanity beyond breaking point.

Looking at him playing with Perra turned her thoughts to her own initiation to this way of life. Memories flooded back of growing up in Catford, East London, the daughter of a Spanish mother and an English father. The memory of being suddenly awoken, before dawn, of the thumping, crashing sound as the police battered the front door open. She ran out onto the landing to see her father in vest and pyjama bottoms, looking terrified. Her mother screamed as the police charged upstairs and dragged her struggling father into the hall. Moya sat on the stairs crying as they handcuffed her father and led him out through the still open door, where she could see a few of the neighbours had already gathered. Her mother darted by her to the hallway trying to hold the officers back and pleading with them not to take her husband away, but she was pushed aside and slid to the floor in despair. Just as he reached the door, her father called up to Moya to look after her mother, and that everything was going to be alright. It wasn't. Moya never saw her father again. He was murdered in prison by another inmate.

She had only been eleven years old when her father had been arrested and, at that time, she had no idea what he had done. No-one would tell her. She watched her mother sink into depression, and two years later Moya was orphaned when her mother committed suicide by taking sleeping tablets. It was then she went to live in Spain with her paternal grandparents. It was her Grandpapa who told her the truth. Her father had been a member of a local criminal gang, and had been involved in several bank and bullion robberies, where shotguns had been involved. One had gone wrong and a bank employee had been killed. Soon after, an informant, who had never been outed had given the police the names of two members of the gang, and eventually led to the arrest of the others, including her father.

Her Grandpapa told her that he was ashamed of her father. That he had tried to help him leave the gang and go straight. He had tried, but the hold the gang had over him and the threats they had made to hurt his family, hauled him back into the criminal world. But, what pained her Grandpapa most was that the top men in the gang had never been caught, and he believed her father had been murdered to silence him. These men had a long reach even into prisons. That day, Moya swore that she would find them. She would avenge her parents, even if she lost her own life for it.

Not wanting to add more grief, or endanger her grandparents, she waited until they had passed away. Having been their only grandchild, she inherited a house, two life insurance policies and everything else from their estate, and already had money in the bank from her inheritance from her parents. At twenty years old, Moya was an independent woman, with no-one else to care for, and the time was right to track down the men she was certain were to blame for the death of both her parents. It took her four years, but one-by-one, through a few of her father's old acquaintances, she discovered the identities of the men she sought. She bought a gun with a silencer and ammunition, and when the time and circumstances were right, she killed them. Moya vomited after the first murder, but not after the second and third.

Following the death of the first one, Ted Collins, the newspapers broadcast his death on the front pages. Moya read that the identity of the assassin was unknown but it was clear that the police assumed it was a man, which suited Moya very well.

The second death was easier. She found Winston Treadwell alone in his garage and about to get into his car. She was dressed in men's clothing, and did not speak. He laughed at her, told her she would never get away with it. She fired. He dropped to the ground with a hole in his head.

The third was more difficult. Having had two associates murdered, the security around Don Kingston was upgraded, so Moya waited until the dust had settled. But Don was his own worst enemy. He loved young women. Wearing a low cut black mini dress, and a natural hair blonde wig, Moya and a female friend went to Don's nightclub one evening when they knew he would be there. Terri, the sister of Moya's best friend, Faye, was a cleaner at the club. As an employee who only worked in the daytime, she always entered through the back door where there was no security other than a keypad. The only other people there during the daytime hours were Ron, the barman and Fiona, the secretary. Seeing Terri hoovering and wiping down tables was nothing out of the ordinary. The last thing they would have expected was that while cleaning the toilets, Terri had secreted two small pistols on top of the cisterns in the first two cubicles of the ladies toilets. Don had recently sexually molested Terri, and Faye wanted payback.

Don and his bodyguard, entered the club at around ten o'clock that evening and glanced around at the clientele. At that time of the evening the club was only half full, there were only two couples and a few girls on the dance floor, the DJ was playing 'Teardrops' by Womack and Womack. At one end of the bar a group of young lads were eyeing up the girls dancing and selecting which ones they fancied. The fact that the girls were totally ignoring them, didn't actually say a great deal about their chances of getting off with their choices.

Don spotted the blonde in the black mini-dress, and her friend, sitting on bar stools, cross-legged and showing quite a bit of thigh. He nodded to Big Brian, his six-foot-five, and built like a tank, bodyguard and nodded. They headed towards the bar. Don stood beside the blonde, while Big Brian went to the other side and stood next to Faye. Don offered to buy them a drink, which they were happy to accept. The men sat down beside them and the flirting began. Moya, giggled prettily and flashed her false eyelashes at Don, clearly inviting. Faye was heard telling Big Brian that she really liked big men, and the sucker fell for her charms instantly.

Two drinks later, Don invited the girls to a little private party in his office. They accepted but said they had to pop to the ladies first to powder their noses. Don gave a leering grin, and as Moya slipped off the bar stool, he gave her backside a playful slap. She gritted her teeth and smiled at him. As the girls sashayed off to the toilets, Don and Big Brian headed to the office with four glasses and a magnum of champagne. Big Brian put a Do Not Disturb notice on the door. In the office, Don opened the safe and took out two large wads of twenty pound notes and threw them onto the desk. They would be his little reward for the good time he and Big Brian expected to have with the girls. In the club, more people entered, and the DJ turned the volume up. Don turned to close the safe door just as the girls entered the room, and smiling sashayed over to the two men. Don was distracted by the promise in Moya's eyes and body language, and just pushed the door to, but didn't close it. Big mistake.

Fifteen minutes later, Moya and Faye left the club, leaving two bodies with holes in their foreheads lying on the floor, and a safe empty of cash. No-one disturbed the boss when that sign was on the door, and so it was four in the morning, and time to cash up and close, when the murder was discovered.

By that time, Moya was on a flight to Madrid, and Faye and Terri with passports, other necessary documents in false names, and handbags full of cash, were waiting at Heathrow Airport for their flight to Australia. Moya never saw the sisters again.

It was in Madrid that Moya decided to continue working within the criminal world. It paid good money, gave her an interesting lifestyle, and there she had met a very attractive South African man, by the name of Andries Maartens. Their affair began and lasted for a little over a year, until Moya became pregnant. Then Andries was suddenly called back to South Africa. A year later, little Marco was sleeping in his pram in the garden, while Moya was in her kitchen making coffee. When she walked out to check on him, Marco had gone. Distraught, Moya contacted all her underworld associates. She even took the risk of reporting him missing to the police, but little Marco was never found.

Where Moya had only previously become hard-bitten and vengeful with the three men who caused the death of her parents, she changed. Became emotionless, icy, she no longer cared whether she lived or died. For several weeks, she sat around drinking, sleeping, not washing, not dressing, not giving a damn about anyone, especially herself.

Then one day, having fallen asleep on her lawn, she woke in the early hours of the morning, cold and damp, from a dream where baby Marco had walked up to her and told her that she was no good to him in that state, and that one day he would need her. That was the catalyst. Ten minutes later she was in the shower and everything changed from that moment. The only thing that continued as before was working with members of the underworld. That was all she knew, it was what provided her with a very good living, and might one day help her reunite with her son.

Looking at Anton now, she thought he would probably be around the same age as Marco, and she couldn't help wondering for the hundred-millionth time what Marco would be doing now.

Chapter Thirty Seven

Tenerife : Dinner with Paloma

Luke looked at his watch while he waited in the bustling hotel lobby. It was a little after eight pm. Considering it had only been an hour and a half since he landed, he was already feeling quite comfortable in his new surroundings. As Corporal Perez had said, he found his room clean, well-furnished and with a very well serviced mini-bar and bathroom, and he was pleased to find he had a sea view.

He had only been in the lobby for a few minutes, when a young woman walked through the open main door, and headed straight for him. It took a few seconds before he realised it was Paloma. Out of uniform she looked very different and much younger. The severe hairstyle that pulled her dark hair up into the uniform baseball cap, somehow added years. Or perhaps, it was just the authority that went with the uniform that gave the impression of her being older. Now in white jeans, a pink vest top, pink wedge sandals, an embroidered white denim jacket, and her shoulder length hair loose, Corporal Perez was much more, well, Paloma. She smiled as she walked towards him, and Luke had to remind himself that this was not a date. Although Paloma was showing kindness in looking after him for the evening, it was Jake's death that had brought them together, and Luke was aware that there were some difficult and distressing points to be discussed that evening.

Inside the hotel, the air had been cool due to the air conditioning, but outside it was still warm, balmy, and the scent of roses and lavender growing nearby, mingled with the bougainvillea honeysuckle-like perfume, as they joined the groups of people all walking down the side streets, and passed the numerous shops selling beachwear, towels, inflatables, postcards and other touristy items, towards the beach-side restaurants.

Earlier, polite conversation had been relatively easy as Paloma had driven Luke to his hotel. How was his flight? Was it any problem trying to book a flight at such short notice? Was there any problem getting away from work? How long did he expect to stay on the island? All those were easily answered and conversation flowed. Now, however, it was a different matter. Apart from the initial greeting at the hotel, suddenly there was nothing to say, although the silence was companionable. It was only when they reached the tapas restaurant that Paloma had recommended, that conversation became easy again, as they discussed the menu and ordered drinks.

While waiting to be served, Luke asked Paloma about her career, and complimented her on her English. She explained that her home was on La Gomera, told him about the island and suggested he pay it a visit after he had done what he had to do in connection with Jake's death. She explained that at eighteen-years-old she became an au pair, and stayed with a wealthy family, mainly in London, looking after their three children. She had thoroughly enjoyed her time there, but became homesick for La Gomera, but it had been a good way to learn English. Later she had joined the Guardia Civil as a cadet, and had completed her training in Madrid, then spent another year there to gain more experience before applying for a transfer to La Gomera. She was now twenty-seven-years old, would be twenty-eight in July, and was perfectly happy.

'Are you not homesick now that you have been transferred here?'

Paloma laughed. 'No, not at all. I can go home any time I like. It's only across the channel, and I can see my island from the coast road. The ferries start early and go on until late. But knowing I am that close, able to go home on my days when I am off duty, and being able to see the island, is all I need.'

She told him that she had been transferred from La Gomera due to tracing an elderly missing man from La Gomera, who turned out to have been a murder victim, that the case was still open, and she had been assigned to investigate it, together with wrapping up the details of Jake's *accidental* death.

Paloma kept her voice low when she began to detail again what she knew of Jake's death which, she believed was still not very much. She said there had been no reason, until Luke had questioned it, to think Jake had been murdered. However, since the two main witnesses were no longer anywhere to be found on the island, and had used false ID's, her supervisor, Captain Torres, had been forced to re-think the original conclusion. Plus, as both Jake and the old man, Mateo Moreno, had been killed within a few days of each other, and in nearby localities, something nagged at her. She felt that there must be some link, even though there was no evidence to go on. It was solely intuition, instinct.

When the third death occurred in the villa fire in Puerto de Santiago, near to where Mateo Moreno had last been seen, and the autopsy revealed he had been murdered, Captain Torres had agreed that the deaths of Mateo Moreno and Edward Taylor-Owen were probably linked, but he struggled to connect Jake's death as well. In a fairly quiet, generally crime free area, if you included the break-in at the dive centre on the day Jake died, Captain Torres, was now busier than he had been in some years, and was on the point of calling in detectives from headquarters in Puerto de la Cruz. But Paloma hoped they could solve the crimes before that happened.

While they ate, Luke explained why Jake had left Gozo in a hurry, frightened for his life. He told her about Irina, how she had warned Jake that his life was in danger, and urged him to leave that day. He added that she too was already packed and leaving Gozo, while her husband was away in Valletta.

Paloma listened attentively, conscientiously making mental notes of everything Luke said.

'But why didn't he go home to the UK? Surely that would have been a safer place for him?'

'Not necessarily. George Camilleri may have been involved with criminality on the Maltese Islands, but his boss, Fred Kennedy has a long reach, as they say, and I believe his main base is in London, so only about one hundred and twenty miles from Birmingham, and too close for comfort.'

'Yes, I see that now. So, tomorrow, I would like you to speak to Captain Torres. He needs to hear what you have told me from you, not from me. Are you happy to do that?'

'Yes, yes, of course I am. If Jake was murdered, I want them found, arrested and convicted.'

'Good. I will call you tomorrow morning and let you know when the captain can see you.'

'That's fine.'

Paloma frowned.

'Something wrong?' asked Luke.

'No, not really. I think I will speak to some of our officers tomorrow. Some of them have informants. When it was thought that your brother's death was an accident, none of the local community officers really got involved. However, now there's a question over his death, there might be one or two who could put out … I believe you call them feelers … see if they get any sense of anyone who might know more than they're saying.'

They stayed at their table for another drink after they had finished eating, and Luke insisted on paying the bill even though Paloma tried to pay half. Leaving the restaurant, they took a slow stroll back to the Allegra Hotel. Luke looked at his watch. It was a quarter past nine and the streets were still busy with people just strolling about, sitting at tables outside bars, laughing, talking, just enjoying themselves being sociable, while Paloma and Luke ambled towards the hotel mostly in companionable silence. At the corner, just a few metres away from the hotel, Paloma stopped, turned to Luke and pointed across the road.

'This is where I say goodbye for today. You have had a long and difficult day, Luke, and you must be tired, and I am on duty again at eight in the morning, so I must go now. I will call you tomorrow.'

Luke looked down at his feet feeling a little awkward about saying goodbye. Paloma had been so helpful, but more than that, she had shown kindness and warmth that went beyond any official duty. He wanted to hug her, but held back thinking that would probably not be acceptable.

'Well, um, thank you for all your help today, and your company this evening.' He reached out to shake her hand. 'I look forward to hearing from you, and meeting up again tomorrow. I plan to visit the dive centre where Jake worked in the morning, but I'll have my phone with me, so call me anytime.'

'Get a good night's rest, Luke, and yes, I'm sure we'll meet up again tomorrow. Goodnight.'

Luke watched Paloma walk away, and as he entered the hotel and walked up the stairs to his room, he recalled some memories of when he and Jake were young boys, and some of the teenage escapades they got up to. It was good going over old memories, but as the images of Jake slipped away, he felt an intense sense of loss.

Chapter Thirty Eight

Tenerife : Paloma Calls

Luke was getting dressed before heading out with the intention of seeing Phil Rogerson at the dive centre. After getting into bed the night before, he had taken quite a while to get to sleep. Thoughts of Jake, awful, imagined scenes of Jake dying, of being hauled to shore, kept getting interspersed with recollections of Paloma smiling, Paloma laughing, Paloma shaking his hand, prevented that welcome calmness of mind for much needed sleep.

And, to his surprise, Luke's first thought on waking was of Paloma, and not Jake. He pondered on that while showering, but to be fair, he did try to keep his mind on what he was there for; to help with the investigation into what seemed more and more likely, was a murder. He hoped Phil Rogerson would be able to fill in more details, that was of course, if he was at the centre that day. Luke had not made an appointment with Phil, he had not even contacted Phil to say he was going to be paying him a visit.

It was just before eight o'clock that the telephone in his room rang. He picked it up, hoping... and he was right.

'Hello, Senor Rutherford. I hope I didn't waken you?'

'Oh, call me Luke, please Paloma. After sharing tapas and wine together last night, I think we can drop the Senor bit, don't you?'

Paloma gave a little laugh. 'Very well, Luke. What are your plans for tomorrow?'

'I don't have any. I'm hoping to see this Rogerson fella, this morning, but the afternoon's free as far as I know right now. Why do you want to know, is it for me to meet your captain?'

'Captain Julio Torres, yes. He can see you at two o'clock tomorrow.'

'Great. Yes, tell him I'll be there, please. Will you be there?'

'Yes, and before. I'll come to your hotel to collect you.'

'Even better. Thanks Paloma. I'm grateful for your help.'

'You're very welcome ... Sen ... Luke. You're helping us too. It's *our* job, not yours to know when a crime has actually been committed, but it now looks as though we made a mistake in thinking your brother's death was an accident. If we had seen it for what it was, the perpetrators would not have had the time to get out of the country. Now we need to solve this case, and see if there's any connections with other local crimes. And we're on to it. I hope you find what you're looking for with Senor Rogerson, and I'll see you at about one-thirty, and you can tell me if there's anything else we should know on the way.'

'Yes, see you then, by Paloma.'

'I'll be at work, so we will have to be more formal. You are Senor Rutherford and I am Corporal Perez, while we are with the Captain.'

'Yes, got it. See you then.'

Chapter Thirty Nine

Tenerife : Luke visits Phil Rogerson

On finishing the call with Paloma, Luke finished getting dressed while trying to put his thoughts in order. Firstly, Jake's desperate situation on Gozo, then Paloma's thoughts on hearing that Jake was not only incredibly safety conscious, but that his life had been threatened, and he had to run. Not having been one of the attending officers when Jake's body was taken onto the beach, Paloma had only become involved in the case later and had been going by the reports filed. She said there was nothing in there to indicate any likelihood of a crime having been committed. Now though, she said her Captain wanted to look at the case again. That was a good start. And, now she had arranged for him to have a meeting with her superior officer, and that was another step forward. Bless Paloma. Luke just hoped that this Captain Torres would take a re-opening of the case seriously.

Right from the start, Luke had found it hard that hard to accept that Jake's death was an accident, but he needed to have that corroborated by those Jake had worked with. Actual evidence of Jake's responsible attitude toward safety for others divers, and for marine life. With a meeting with Captain Torres set for that afternoon, it was even more important now that he got to see Phil Rogerson. He needed Phil's support, and it could not wait.

So who were the men Jake took on that dive? How many possibilities were there of what could have happened that day? He checked the time on his watch, it was eight-fifteen. He had about twenty minutes before he would need to call a taxi, and he might as well use the time constructively. On the table was a notepad with the hotel logo and a ballpoint pen. Useful. He picked up the pen and wrote down one or two-word pointers of what he had been told. *Dive centre. Two men. Private dive. Stingray. Men missing. False names. Accident? Murder? Which?*

One, it was very unlikely that Jake had done anything to disturb a stingray. Luke wasn't even including that as a possibility. So, if it was an accident, then one of the two men, or both of them, who were on that dive had done something that led to Jake's death, but were afraid to admit it. The fact that they had vanished gave evidence to that possibility. Or, two, it had been murder, and the fact that they had used false names, which surely meant it was pre-planned, and then they vanished. But why? He stared blankly at the wall, trying to visualise the situation, think about all the factors, and try to fathom out exactly what happened. But he had not been there, so unless there was a way of proving what really happened, it didn't matter a damn how much he thought about it, it wasn't proof. It was conjecture, speculation, and that never put anyone in prison, at least not since the middle ages.

He wondered whether Paloma had mentioned to Captain Torres that Jake's life had been threatened, or whether she was leaving it for him to reveal that at the meeting. No matter, he'd find that out later. Whichever it was, surely that would be enough to throw some doubt on Jake's death. Luke's instinct told him Camilleri or Kennedy were behind it. Somehow they found out where Jake was. But how?

He hoped Phil Rogerson would be able to help him fill in some of the gaps before he met with the Captain and Paloma? Had Jake told him why he left Gozo in such a hurry? Did Phil know about the threat that hung over Jake's head? Or, could Phil, or anyone who worked for him be involved with the Kennedy organisation?

He looked at his notes. Yes, everything he knew so far was set out there. He checked his watch again. Eight-thirty. Okay, time to go. He picked up his phone, put his room keycard in his wallet and buttoned them into the side pockets of his cargo shorts, picked up his WWF baseball cap, and sunglasses, headed down to the lobby, and asked the Concierge to call a taxi for him.

While waiting on the porch, Luke looked across to the sea and was a little surprised to see a light mist hovering over it. There were no clouds as such, but the sky was so light grey, it could almost be called white, and the morning felt a little fresh.

'Are we in for rain today?' he asked the Concierge who had left his desk to have a Vape break.

'No, sir,' came the reply in a very noticeable Australian accent. 'Very soon this will burn off and we will have our usual blue sky, brilliant sunshine, it will be hot. Within the next hour, we expect the temperature to be around twenty-three degrees, and by early afternoon, some of our guests will either be complaining that it's too hot, or they will be asking how to treat their sunburn.' He grinned.

'And it's the sun, blue skies and warmth that they come for,' said Luke.

'Indeed it is, sir. The trouble is that many people do not prepare themselves for it. They come to see the sun, but think they can sit out in it all day, from the first day, and they drink beer and wine at lunchtime, the hottest time of the day, and don't drink enough water, and so get dehydrated.' He stopped. 'I should not be saying all this to you, sir. You're a guest.'

'It's okay,' Luke looked at the man's name badge, 'Oscar. I won't tell anyone, and I promise to only drink alcohol after the sun has gone down.'

'Good man, sir. Drink plenty of water, and follow the rules with sunblock and so on, and you'll be fine. And here's your taxi pulling up.'

'Thanks, Oscar. Have a good day.'

'And you, Mr Rutherford. I hope you find what you're looking for.'

Until that moment, Luke had assumed that, to the staff, he was just another guest, but Oscar's sympathetic look and that last comment, implied that they, or at least Oscar, knew why he was there. Of course, the death of a diver locally, accident though everyone believed it to be, would have been in the local news. Why hadn't he thought of that?

The dive centre was shut when he arrived, but he took a seat at one of the parasol-covered tables outside the closed Irish Pub next door to wait. He did not have to wait long. A tall, athletic looking and tanned man wearing a navy blue T-shirt with the dive centre logo on the back came through a small alley between the centre and the pub.

Luke watched him pull a bunch of keys out of a pocket in his shorts, and hunker down to unlock, then raise the metal security screen. He unlocked the front door, walked in, threw his keys down on the desk and dumped his backpack on the chair behind, unaware he was about to have company.

Outside, Luke looked around to see if anyone else was heading along the covered walkway towards the centre. If this was Phil Rogerson, it looked as though he would have at least a few minutes to talk to him without the distraction of anyone else coming in. As far as he could see the only other people around were busy opening their own businesses. So far, so good.

As he walked in, the man looked up from behind the desk.

'I'm sorry, but we're not open yet. I'm just setting up for the day. We don't actually open until ten.'

'I just wondered … are you Phil Rogerson?'

'Yes, but we're still not open.'

Luke smiled. 'And, I'm not needing your services, Phil. I'm Luke Rutherford.'

'But we're still … oh, Jeez!' Phil walked around the desk towards Luke. 'I'm so sorry. I didn't realise. Man, I am so sorry about what happened to Jake. I really liked him.' He reached out to shake Luke's hand, gripped it hard clasped between both his hands. 'I just don't understand what the fuck happened with Jake. He was always …'

'Yeah, I know what you're going to say … careful and respectful of marine life.'

'That's it. That's exactly it.'

'Look, Phil, have you got a few minutes to spare. I'd like to talk to you about the time Jake was here with you. I know you knew each other quite well, and I just wanted to pick your brain to see if there was anything odd about that morning, or at any time after he got here.'

'Yeah, no problem. Did you know I was asked to make the formal identification of your brother?'

'Yes, I heard. I'm sorry you had to go through that, but you were probably the best person here to do it as I wasn't here. Thank you.'

Phil frowned, his lips lowered at the corners. 'Yes, that's right. It was pitiful to see him on that slab. He'd been so fit, and to go like that, so young. It's tragic and I'm going to miss him.' He turned back towards the desk. 'But it needed to be done. Look, are you free for a while?'

'Yeah. I have all the time in the world, until one-thirty, anyway.'

'Great. I have a routine I go through each morning, takes about ten minutes, then I go and have breakfast. Have you eaten?'

'No, not yet. I came straight here.'

'Right. There's a pretty good café across the road that I go to each morning. They do a great English Breakfast there, plus other stuff, and it's not expensive. Just give me a few minutes to get sorted out, and we'll head over there.'

Shortly after, Phil locked the front door and guided Luke to the café he had mentioned. As they crossed the road, dodging between the traffic on both sides, Phil told Luke that Jake had talked about him a lot. At the café, they sat at an outside table and were greeted by a waiter, who quite obviously knew Phil very well.

'Another couple of guys from our team will be joining us soon. We always collect over here in the mornings, Warren and Max. Max shared the upstairs apartment with Jake. They got on well, became buddies. But it's a pity that Stan won't be in until a bit later this morning.'

Phil ordered the full English saying that he needed the calories as divers burn a huge amount of calories during the day. Luke asked for the same, but not for the same reason. It was a while since he had eaten and he had forgotten how much he used to enjoy the occasional full English breakfast. While they waited for their breakfasts, Luke asked how long Phil had known Jake.

'We first met in Crete a little over five years ago,' said Phil. 'Jake joined us at the centre where I had been working for a couple of years. He was very keen, already had his PADI Advanced Open Water certification and wanted more training.'

'Oh yes, I remember him talking about you and the centre in Crete. I'd forgotten all about that.'

'Yeah, Jake was full gung ho at wanting to learn, but not stupid with it. Every course he went on he took seriously, wrecks, rescue, night diver, and more, and he volunteered at the centre to help pay for his courses. He even went for the underwater navigation and enriched air ...'

'Enriched air? I haven't heard of that one, Jake never mentioned it.'

'It's how to stay under for longer, shorten your surface times, dive deeper. He learned how to manage diving in currents, caves and was a really confident knowledgeable diver.'

'So you were surprised when the report said he died due to an accident.'

'Of course I bloody was. Look, Jake not only took all the courses I mentioned, but he also had a keen interest in conservation and marine life. He took the fish recognition course, passed easily and was always able to answer clients questions about what they were seeing. He learned about the behaviour of the sea animals. It was almost like he could really understand them. The last thing I would have expected was that he'd have made such a stupid mistake as to disturb a stingray. It just doesn't make sense. He'd taught enough beginners, for God's sake.'

They stopped talking as the waiter brought their breakfasts. What Phil had told him clearly pointed to Jake's death being suspicious, and that Jake would never have behaved so recklessly. Although it could probably not be taken as actual evidence, Phil's many years' experience of working with Jake, would surely give some credence to his death being questionable. When you add that to Paloma's serious doubts about the accident theory, surely it would be enough to convince her captain to look at the case again.

'Did the police interview you?'

'They did stop by, but not for long. They took notes and said they would be typing up my statement, but it hasn't come back for checking and signing yet. They spent more time here about the break-in we had that day, than about Jake.'

'Was one of them a young woman, Corporal Perez?'

As he stuck his fork into a slice of garlic sausage and dipped it in runny egg yolk, Phil said, 'No, I don't recall a female officer, being with them. Why?'

'I just wondered. I met Corporal Perez yesterday. Apparently she's been assigned the investigation into Jake's death. Did you know the two men who brought Jake's body back have vanished?'

With the fork halfway to his mouth, Phil stopped, lowered the fork and stared, open-mouthed and wide-eyed with astonishment.

'They've vanished, but I don't ...'

'It seems they gave false ID's to the Guardia Civil officer they saw on the beach after they brought Jake's body back. Checks have been made at the hotel they were supposed to have been booked into and they were never there.'

Luke wondered if he could trust Phil or anyone who knew Jake. Anyone from the dive centre could have been working for Kennedy, or Camilleri. But Phil's astonished reaction appeared to be absolutely genuine. He would have had to have been one hell of an actor to have reacted like that if he had been implicated in Jake's death. 'I would keep that to yourself though as I don't know whether I was supposed to say anything.'

'You got it from the Guardia?'

'Yeah, Corporal Perez gave me that bit of information.'

'Well, did she also tell you that we had a break-in that morning?'

Now it was Luke's turn to show surprise. 'No, no, she didn't.' He thumbed his chin. 'What happened?'

But before Phil could explain, a young man, his bulging biceps filling out the short sleeves of his navy-blue T-shirt with the dive centre logo on a small breast pocket, walked towards them.

'Morning, Phil. I see the mist's lifted.'

'Morning, Warren. Take a seat.' Warren sat down and ordered coffee and a croissant.

'Luke, this is Warren Jensen, one of our dive team. Warren, this is Luke Rutherford, Jake's brother. He's trying to find out more about what happened to Jake.'

Warren reached out to shake Luke's hand. 'Jake told us about you, and he was really happy that you'd finally caught up with each other. I was really sorry to hear what happened. I liked Jake. We got on well.'

'To be honest, Luke, Jake got on well with everyone,' said Phil.

'Thank you. It's appreciated. I know the police here are investigating, but I'm just doing a bit of digging myself.' He looked from one to the other. 'Can you tell me what Jake told either of you about why he wanted to come here in a hurry?'

Warren shook his head. 'I don't think he said. Certainly not to me. How about you, Phil?'

'Yeah, well, he kind of implied it was girl trouble. He said he'd broken up with his girlfriend. Found out she'd been cheating, or something like that, and he just wanted to get away.'

Luke nodded. 'Hmm, yeah, sounds pretty reasonable, doesn't it. The kind of thing that happens all the time. And, well that bit was partially true, but there were other reasons as well. Did you ever hear him mention a George Camilleri, or maybe Fred Kennedy?'

Phil took a moment then shook his head. 'No, I don't think I've heard of either of them.'

Luke carefully studied their faces for any sign that they might have had something to hide. He still questioned if Phil could have been the one to tip off Camilleri about Jake being in Tenerife? Could he trust anyone there … well, yes, probably Corporal Perez, but that went with the uniform. Anyone else though, he still needed to be on his guard with. He prided himself on being a pretty good judge of character and thought he would know all the little signs that showed someone was lying. On balance though, he had to admit that there were no signs of that with either man, but were they just good actors?

Just then another man in a dive centre T-shirt, approached them. Blond hair, Luke guessed he was a little under two metres, tanned, sunglasses, white sliders on broad feet.

'Morning, Max. Say hello to Luke, Jake's brother,' said Phil.

'Oh wow!' Max reached out to shake Luke's hand and sat down beside him. 'I'm really broken up about Jake. We shared the apartment above the centre, and he was a great guy. We got close, you know, buddies. If there's anything I can help with, you just let me know. I really miss my mate.'

'If you haven't guessed Max is Australian,' Warren said to Luke.

Luke grinned. 'I had noticed. Melbourne?' Luke asked Max.

'Well, not far. We had a home on Port Philip Bay. How did you know?'

'Mum used to watch Neighbours,' Luke replied, with a smile.

Phil looked across at Warren and Max. 'George Camilleri and Fred Kennedy. Do either of you recall Jake ever mentioning either of them?'

'No. Both men shook their heads, looked at each other, and then at Luke.

'Who are they?' Phil asked Luke. There appeared to be no sign of deception, no avoiding eye contact, no pursing of the lips, no touching the mouth or looking to the floor. There were none of the usual signs of lying, or any of the three having something to hide. And, Luke acknowledged, that when Jake was in trouble, he had trusted Phil enough to run to him for help. That was true, even though, for some reason, Jake had clearly avoided telling Phil the truth. He must have had his own reasons for keeping quiet. So many thoughts raced through Luke's mind, but within moments he had come to the conclusion that these men were to be trusted. Nevertheless, someone must have let Camilleri or Kennedy know where Jake was, but who fuck could it have been? Having made that decision he felt better, but the little voice in his head really hoped he was right.

The café was filling up, and they were no longer able to speak privately. Luke decided to say no more for the moment. 'They were just a couple of guys Jake knew.'

Half an hour later, they took Luke back to the dive centre. Luke decided to turn the conversation back to Jake when they were able to talk without the risk of anyone overhearing, while they were getting ready for the day's clients.

With the centre being quieter, the divers were busy with their preparations, but they still gave Luke the time he needed, and he decided to explain exactly why Jake had left Gozo in a hurry, and who Camilleri and Kennedy actually were. As he gave the details, he scrutinised their faces still looking for any sign of mendacity, or anything that might show they were hiding something. But there was nothing. Luke sat on a bench while Warren and Max went through to the back of the centre to check the air levels in the tanks, and Phil pulled out a rail with wetsuits of varying sizes. Then he remembered that Phil had mentioned a break-in at the centre on the day Jake died.

'Phil, tell me about the break-in you mentioned earlier.'

'Oh, yes. God almighty that was a shock. Judy Alvarez, who usually works for us, does our admin, bookings, invoices and so on, had had a call a few days before from a hospital in Ireland. She's Irish but married to a local guy. So the call was to tell her that her brother was seriously ill, and as his next of kin they were notifying her as they thought she should come over. Judy had made friends with a woman called Emma Holloway who she'd met at the gym. Apparently this Emma told Judy that she had worked in administration for years but was between jobs.'

'So, when Judy got the phone call, she didn't want to let us down, and asked Emma if she could stand in for her for a week or so while she went to see her brother. According to Judy, this Emma jumped at the chance of earning a little extra cash ...'

'... A little?' Warren cut-in. 'Bitch!'

'Hmm. I didn't like her right from the start. Not that I had any reason to think she wasn't on the level, it was just that she was cold, you know, like, well, distant,' said Max.

She turned up that afternoon, we went through the way we work, and she started the next day. Settled into the routine really well.'

'She seemed okay and was really efficient,' said Warren, as he re-emerged from the corridor at the back. 'She picked up the basic stuff in no time, and we said not to worry about the more complicated stuff, we'd take care of that as it would only be for a few days.'

'Yeah, that's right. She did settle in well, and did fine,' said Phil. 'We had a call from Judy a couple of days later to say there had been a complete mix up and her brother was fine after all, and she was going to fly straight back, but I told her to take a few days, catch up with family, and come back the next week. Her husband was alright with it too, so Judy relaxed.'

'How long before the break-in did all this happen?'

Phil raised his eyebrows and looked over at Warren.

'Just a couple of days, and she seemed really good, like Warren said. Looking back I should have put two and two together, but I had no reason to hear alarm bells.'

'Yeah,' said Warren, 'it's easy to see in hindsight the mistakes we made, but...'

Phil cut in, 'Hmm, when you're rushed off your feet and have a business to run, with bookings lined up that you have to fill or lose money... well, maybe I should have checked her ID more carefully, '

'... And possibly lose future bookings because you're not reliable,' said Warren.

'You just don't have the time to think that someone's pulling a scam of some kind, said Phil. You're just grateful for the help, but, in retrospect, you can see how easy it was for her to ... well, infiltrate. I wish I'd been more careful, but I was desperate ... Hi Stan.' Phil waved to a man across the road who headed towards the dive centre. 'It all sounds stupid bearing in mind what happened, but none of us suspected anything. Accidents do happen. People do have relatives that get sick, and at the time we just thought we were lucky to have someone stand-in for Judy.'

'Do you think Judy had any part to play in it?'

'No, definitely not,' said Warren, 'and she's really upset that she was the one to recommend this Emma.'

'No, not Judy,' added Max. 'Judy's as straight as they come.'

'No, she didn't,' said Phil, looking up as a man, carrying a cardboard tray with four take-away coffees, walked in.

'Hi Stan, this is Luke Rutherford, Jake's brother. He's trying to help the Guardia with finding out what happened.'

Stan. With his grey hair and whiskers was clearly the oldest member of the team, put the coffees down on the desk, and walked over to shake Luke's hand. He sat down beside him. 'If I'd known you were here I'd have got another coffee. Stan Siddons, and it's good to meet you, Luke. Jake talked about you a lot.' He looked around at his colleagues. 'We're all gutted about Jake's death. He was a great guy. Phil knew him longest of all of us, but we all liked him.'

'He was a likeable fella, and thank you,' said Luke. 'And no worries about the coffee, I'm fine, thanks.'

Phil leaned forward and rested his elbows on the table. 'We were just explaining to Luke what happened with the break-in.'

Stan drew in a deep breath, pressed his lips together and looked down at the floor for a moment, then looked up again. 'I hate any form of violence towards women, but if that *bitch* had anything to do with Jake's death, then I'd happily wring her neck myself.'

'Yeah, well, none of that kind of talk, Stan,' Phil warned. 'We're all pissed off about what's happened. It was clearly planned.' He turned to Luke. 'We can understand how Stan feels, but I'd be happy to see her caught, charged and convicted.'

Luke nodded in agreement. 'If we can find her, we might be able to get to the truth, and maybe get these guys put away. Can any of you recall anything that might give us a clue as to who this woman, Emma did you say her name was?'

'Yeah, Emma Holloway, and she was from somewhere in the Masca area,' said Max.

'Just Masca, as far as I can recall, but if she's clever, that'll be a false trail,' said Phil.

'I know, but we have nothing else to go on.'

Chapter Forty

Tenerife : Venom

That evening, Luke felt drained. The meeting with Phil Rogerson and his team had gone well, but there was so much information going around his head about this woman, Holloway, the robbery, Jake's situation with Fred Kennedy, and even Paloma, that he really just wanted a peaceful evening and to switch off for a while. No police, clues or suspicions.

He stood on his hotel room balcony watching the sun slide leisurely downwards to meet the sea, while trying to decide what to do on his second night in Buenavista del Norte, and his mind drifted to Paloma and he wondered what she was doing. Briefly he thought about calling her, but then decided she was probably out with a partner and, after all their relationship was a professional one.

With the arrival of evening, the dying sun had lost its fiery intensity, and paled to a softer, but still warm, shimmering golden-red. Its dying beams mirrored on the smooth, but gently undulating surface of the now purple-black sea, and glistened on the coarse black sand. The sea-front with its restaurants, late-opening shops and new-build apartment blocks on either side of the coastal road, flushed in the rose coloured beams of the waning sun, bringing back memories of Xaghra to the bereaved Luke.

As he thought back to his last days with Jake, and the month he had spent learning to dive, driving around in a small jeep, and catching up on their lives over those four missing years, when there had been precious little contact. They had both regretted the lost time.

Luke recalled the laughter during their conversation about travelling together to Australia, New Zealand, the Pacific Islands. Now all that was gone. Was never going to happen. Jake was gone. That brilliant, passionate, nutty, love-of-life, and as Luke discovered, a little unwise and vulnerable brother, who he had always planned to spend time with … later, had gone. Abruptly, and unexpectedly, it was too late.

He turned away from the balcony and walked back into the room, took a cold beer from the mini-bar, flicked off the cap using the bottle opener on the fridge, took a swig from the bottle, and sat down on the armchair, feeling lost and wondering how in Hell's name Jake could have been so careless as to have an accident while diving. He stood up, still holding the bottle, paced the room trying to make some kind of sense of what had happened.

'I'd have understood it more if it had been a car accident,' he said out loud, and shook his head. 'Jake was a bit of twat on the road.'

His bedside phone rang. It was Warren from the dive centre. He had seemed friendly enough when they had met earlier, and had some good things to say about Jake, but as his conversation had been mainly with Phil Rogerson, Luke was surprised at Warren calling him. In total Luke thought Warren's input earlier had amounted to about ten minutes worth.

'Hi Luke, I just thought I'd phone to see if you're at a loose end this evening and, if so, fancy getting out for something to eat?'

'I was wondering what to do tonight, and it's good of you to call, but you don't have to nursemaid me, though. Don't you have anything better to do on a Friday evening?'

'No not really. My girlfriend and I have just broken up, so I'm at a loose end too, and there's something I thought about after you'd left earlier, that I'd like talk to you about.'

'Yeah, fine with me. Margo Robbie's let me down tonight, said she's got some film production meeting, so I'm available. Where do you want to meet?'

'There's a nice little tapas bar next to the Peking Palace Chinese restaurant on the front of the marina. Are you okay with tapas?'

Luke smiled. It was the same place he had been to with Paloma the previous evening, but as the food had been good, he was happy to go there again.

'Yeah, fine with me.' Still uncertain whether Warren was to be trusted, he decided not to mention the couple of hours he had spent with a police officer the night before.

'Great. Well, I'll see you there at what, say seven-thirty?'

'See you then.'

On the way to the restaurant, Luke stopped to lean on the white-painted balustrade, that stretched along the beach front, and looked out over a tranquil Atlantic Ocean. A warm breeze created soft waves that gently nudged the secured motor boats and sailing yachts, and they rose and fell with each gentle undulation. The scene was peaceful, idyllic. He made a mental note to remember it when he returned to Birmingham. If you didn't know better, It would be hard to believe something so inviting, serene, could be so dangerous.

Someone called his name. It was Warren coming from the opposite direction, and by chance had arrived at exactly the same time.

'How was your afternoon? Get any further with the police?'

Luke shook his head. 'No. I think trying to trace the two men who were with Jake when he died is going to be like sifting fog.'

They looked down over the balustrade to the terrace below looking for an available table. There were none.

'No tables free at the moment. Are you okay to sit at the bar with a beer while we wait?' asked Warren. 'It shouldn't be long. Some are families with young children, and hopefully they'll be heading off soon'

'Yeah, no worries, fine by me.'

'Hola, Ramon,' Warren said to the barman. 'Dos Cervezas, per favor, mi amigo.'

'Hola, Warren. ¿Cómo estás?' Ramon replied, taking two bottles of the local beer, Dorada, from the chiller.

'Si. Sí, muy bien, gracias.'

'¿Quieres vasos para las cervezas?' asked Ramon.

Luke had not seen Ramon the previous evening, and was a little relieved that he did not have to admit having been there before.

'What was he asking?' he asked Warren.

'Whether we wanted glasses. I usually drink from the bottle.'

Luke tried his Spanish. 'Gracias, Ramon, pero sin gafas.'

Ramon nodded and smiled. 'You speak Spanish, Senor?'

Luke shook his head. 'Very little. Un poco, but I am learning.'

Ramon laughed and nodded. 'At least you try, Senor. This is muy bien. Excuse me, please. I must serve another customer.'

Luke and Warren made themselves comfortable on stools at the bar, with Warren facing the terrace where he could keep watch for a table becoming available.

'So how long did you work with Jake?' Luke asked.

Warren rubbed his stubbly chin. 'We originally met in Crete, the same as Phil, and it was for a little over a year. Jake was already part of the team when I joined them.' He took a mouthful of beer, and smiled at Luke. 'I'd only recently passed my Advanced PADI and, well, to be honest I was still nervous about being one of the leads on beginner dives, but Jake was great. For the first few weeks he came out with me on each dive to make sure I learned about the local currents, how not to annoy the local marine life, and the best places to take newbies.'

Luke smiled at a memory. 'I remember the lectures he gave me when we were in Gozo. I'd never dived before and, even with all the gear to help me, it still took me a few real sea dives to get my brain to accept that I *could* breathe underwater. Jake was really patient.'

'Yeah, he had a good way with him. Always calmed the nervous ones down and people took to him. He, like, gave them confidence. They trusted him because he made them feel safe.'

While Luke and Warren had been talking, Ramon had been keeping an eye on a table coming free and, when a family at a corner table paid their bill and left, he leaned towards Warren. 'I would get to that table while you can, Warren. There is a group of seven on their way here now and they will be putting two tables together.'

Luke and Warren picked up their beers and two menus, and headed over to the table just before the group of seven, followed by another party of four, walked down the stairs, all hopeful of finding tables. Ramon was joined by a second waiter, and Luke and Warren watched as the pair settled the two parties around the bar area.

Once settled, Luke made small talk for a while about people still playing on the beach, the colour of the sand, his hotel, his discussion with Corporal Perez, but implied that it was only during the trip from the airport. Although he was glad to have a corner table where they could not be easily overheard, Luke wanted to wait until their food was served, and they were less likely to be interrupted, before he drew the conversation around to what it was that Warren had wanted to tell him. Warren also seemed not to be in a hurry to get to the crux of their meeting, making light conversation about their chosen menu choices of tapas, and keeping an eye on customers who approached adjacent tables. Luke asked him if he was looking for anyone in particular, to which Warren replied that he remembered some friends had booked a table there for that night, and as he and Luke had things to talk about, perhaps it would have been better if they had gone elsewhere. He apologised, and said that hopefully, his friends would not be there until later.

Luke noticed two waiters heading their way with trays containing several dishes of hot and cold snacks that combined to make a meal. The first waiter put his salver down on the seat of an unused chair, and placed a three-tiered serving stand in the centre of the table. He then set the filled dishes onto all three tiers, there was no more room. He then moved back to allow his colleague to place his dishes around the stand.

Luke looked at the feast set out on the table and laughed. 'How on earth are we going to get through all this lot?' Although small and snack-like, there were far more servings than he realised they would be having.

Warren just smiled and shrugged his shoulders. 'Just take your time, and enjoy. Another cervesa?'

'Why not?' said Luke, gaping at the variety of delicious looking food in front of them. Green olives, some with anchovies and others with red bell peppers, chorizo sausage, patatas bravas (diced potatoes in spicy sauces), small slices of bread, Manchego cheese, battered prawn fritters, Spanish omelette with potato chunks and onions, fried medallions of pork and beef, sauteed mushrooms, small fried squid, small Canarian salted potatoes, little Russian salad (mixed boiled vegetables with tuna, olives and mayonnaise, and small empanadillas (a type of turnover filled with meat and vegetables).

'Dos cervesas, per favor,' said Warren.

'I think we'll need a doggie bag for some of this. We'll never get through all this,' said Luke.

'You'd be surprised how easy it is. Because they're small servings, it's not as difficult as you'd think.'

Luke began transferring morsels of various dishes onto his own plate, and thanked the waiter when he returned with their beers, picked up his knife and fork and, as he started eating he realised he was far more hungry than he had thought. Perhaps they would be able to finish most of it after all. After a few minutes, Luke noticed that the table nearest to theirs was now vacant. A good time to find out what it was Warren wanted to talk about.

He put his knife and fork down, picked up his beer, took a mouthful, and sat back in his chair.

'Tapas beaten you already?' asked Warren.

'No. Not yet. I just thought that before anyone sits there, it might be a good time to talk.'

Warren put his cutlery down as well and sat forward. 'Yes, you're right.' He rested his elbows on the table and steepled his hands, interlocking his fingers, his chin resting on his thumbs. Luke also sat forward, wanting to keep their voices low.

'Okay, so firstly, what do you know about stingrays?' Warren asked.

'Very little, why?'

'Like I said before, Jake understood the sea, Its moods, and both animal and plant life. For my money, if anyone was going to make a mistake it would not be Jake. He'd become more fish than human, if you get me.'

Luke gave a little chuckle. 'Hmm, I know what you mean.'

'So, why suddenly would he do something stupid? It just doesn't add up, Luke. I just can't believe ... no, don't believe it was an accident.'

'But what about the stingray barb?'

'Ah, yeah. What about the fuckin' stingray barb? Stingrays are normally shy, they'd rather use their barbs to fend off predators. It's really rare that they'll use them on humans, but they're not called stingrays for nothing. Like most other creatures with stingers, they all contain a type of venom. Did you know you can buy their barbs online?'

'Why would anyone want to do that?'

'Oh, I dunno, maybe marine research, collectors. The venom is removed from the ones you can buy. Was anything said by the Guardia about venom in Jake's bloodstream?'

'Venom! No, not that I recall, but I can check that. Is it deadly?'

'It would be pretty painful, there'd also be swelling from the venom, you'd probably feel very rough, vomiting and so on, and depending on your state of health, it might affect the heart, blood pressure.'

'They said the barb went into Jake's neck, hit the artery and he bled to death while the two guys were bringing him to shore. What if there was no venom injected into him?'

Warren shook his head. 'Unlikely. Although I've never actually witnessed a stingray attack, everything I've read and heard says that the barb releases venom on impact.'

'Thanks for that, Warren. I'd never have thought of that. I'll get it checked.' Perhaps Warren was someone he could trust after all.

Chapter Forty One

Tenerife : Moya's Armoury

With his hair and eyebrows now a dyed dark chestnut colour, and the promising shadow of a new beard, Anton was trying to come to terms with the new name on the forged documents Moya provided for him; Leo Fernandez. She had drilled it into him that when anyone he didn't know asked his name, that was the one to use, although no-one within their group would be likely to use it. She had also insisted that he stay away from any of his previous friends and contacts. From then on his movements would be restricted to where she felt he was safe. He was so frightened that he readily agreed to everything she said.

The diving equipment used by Davies and Brown had been left precisely where Moya had instructed, and Anton had helped her retrieve it all from the mountainside road near Arona.

When they returned to the farmhouse, Moya insisted that they take everything inside immediately, and soon after she pulled aside a long, blue and beige Aztec patterned rectangular rug from the wooden floor, revealing a wooden trapdoor with a recessed black metal ring. Anton had walked over that rug again and again without realising there was anything underneath. She winked at Anton.

'We take all that down here.'

Moya bent down, pulled at the ring and the door opened. Below, Anton could see steps leading down into what he assumed was a basement, but it was too dark inside to see. Moya walked over to a small cupboard by the front door, opened it, pressed a button and a light went on in the basement. He could see wooden steps, with a metal handrail on one side, that led to a stone-floored room below.

'Come on,' said Moya, 'let me show you my storeroom.'

The steps were narrow and steep, but as Moya negotiated them without difficulty, Anton falteringly climbed down after her, unwilling to show his caution. At the bottom, he turned to find a treasure trove of Scuba equipment, a high-pressure air compressor, wet and dry suits in shorty and full length versions, masks regulators, tanks, fins, even spear guns. In addition, she had a weapons arsenal of three double-barrelled shotguns, several handguns, some pretty horrific-looking knives and machetes, two of what looked like Samurai swords, and hanging on a sturdy hook on the far wall, a crossbow.

'My God, Moya, where did this lot come from?'

She smiled and shrugged her shoulders. 'Just a few things I've acquired one way or another over the years. So, with the two wetsuits and the kit we brought back from the mountain, I have all you're going to need, and more. I've organised a boat for you to take the two new guys your father's sending, out into the channel. They're arriving this evening.'

Anton felt a cold ripple run down his spine. 'Have you met them before?'

'No, and I don't even know what they look like. The photo your father sent me, wasn't particularly good. It was the fuzzy one that's in passports now, and sending it through the phone, didn't make it any easier to see.

'How do we know we can trust them?'

'We don't. We just have to trust that your father has confirmed they're okay.'

Anton had retrieved all of Edward's charts from the house before he set the fire. Showing all the known currents in the waters around Tenerife and La Gomera, and even details of the when the tides would be their highest and lowest, they were too precious to leave behind to burn. Anton already had a good knowledge of the La Gomera Channel, thanks to Edward's teaching, but with the charts, if Anton forgot anything, the charts were a great backup. So all those boring hours of listening to Edward spouting on about the details on the charts, was finally going to show results.

Chapter Forty Two

La Gomera : The Channel

The day after the Nikolov brothers arrived, Moya knew she had a challenge on her hands, trying to get Anton to talk to them. He had made it very clearly he disliked them. They had an arrogance about them that annoyed him, especially the younger one, Valko. He did not trust them. Moya was alternately encouraging civility, or at least trying to bully him in to being pleasant. She took him to one side after settling the brothers in the garden with mugs of coffee. They instantly fell in love with Perra, and when Valko played fetch with her with a tennis ball, Anton sulked. He was Perra's friend, and Valko the intruder. Anton's petulant sulk was the final straw for Moya.

'You do not have to be so rude. These men have come to do a job for your father. He trusts them, so how do you know better than him? And look,' she pointed towards the garden, 'even Perra trusts them.' As Anton sprang up from his chair and glared at her, she realised that comment had gone down like a red flag to a bull. Anton looked as though he was about to walk out, but she pushed him back down into his seat, surprisingly without protest from him. She tossed her head back, looked at him, her fists resting on her hips and, then leaned forward. When Moya lost her temper it was a fearsome sight. 'You are behaving like a child. I understand your nerves might be a bit frayed after what you've had to do, but we need these guys. They are highly experienced divers, they've worked on second unit film crews when scenes involve shipwrecks, and they've been swimming with sharks, and, your father said they are two of the best wreck divers he'd heard of. Now, grow up, concentrate on what you have to do and … I mean this … *be nice.* No hostility. We need them. If they leave because you act like a prat, your father will be furious. He'll be on his way soon, and if you screw this up … after everything I've done to hide and protect you … I'll bloody kill you myself.' She grasped his cheeks with both hands. Anton was almost in tears. Moya was terrifying when she was angry, and what she said, she meant. She let go of his face leaving red pressure blotches where she had gripped so tightly. She moved back and glared at him, her expression glacial, before turning away, and then looked back at him. 'Anton, do not dare forget what I have said. If I have to kill you I will … You know I could.'

'But my father wouldn't let you …'

She moved closer again, spoke softly, 'Don't overestimate how much your father cares. He is a cold man. He uses people. He used your mother and then according to him, she vanished with another man.'

'I thought she died.'

'Only he knows the truth, he told me she went off with another man, and that a few months later he'd heard she'd died. He never said another word about her.'

'But you've worked for him for years. Why do you still work with him?' Anton was mystified by Moya's loyalty.

She walked towards the door, opened it, then turned back to Anton and gave him a sad, sympathetic smile, while he tried to understand her. Everything she had said about his father spiralled around in his head.

'I do what I do for me. Not for him. I do not trust him. I don't think I ever really did. There was a time he held a … a certain attraction for me. I let him get too close … I had a child, a boy.' She walked towards the window, lifted one of the slats on the venetian blind and watched Valko with Perra. 'But that was a long time ago.'

'What happened to him?'

Moya swung round. 'That … is none of your business!' She stared at him for a moment then walked back towards the door. 'Anyway, I have never regretted an affair more than that one. Now I look after me, only. I am an … enabler, a facilitator for anyone who pays me to get a job done, and I have several … clients, who pay me well. They know they can trust me to do what's necessary and will keep my mouth shut. I have saved quite a lot of money from my contracts, and

I now have the cash from the dive centre to add to my pot, and one day soon I will disappear. I shall leave all this behind and go somewhere where I cannot be traced.' She thought of Jake Rutherford and shrugged her shoulders. 'If I am lucky my disappearance will be of my own volition, and not because someone thinks I know too much, and wants me out of the way.'

'You sound scared.'

She laughed. 'Of course I am, but I chose this business, and have to live with that, for now.' She tilted her head and gave a cynical smile. 'Some mornings, I'm surprised to find I'm still alive. Every night I wonder if I'll have unwelcome callers in the night. Of course I am scared, but that's the nature of the business we are in. You learn to trust no-one. But, I do wake up, and I get on with what I have to do. So must you. Now get ready to take our friends out into the channel.'

An hour later, Anton steered the weather-beaten Arcoa motor boat across the channel, coming to a stop a little way along the coast from San Sebastian. There was nothing about the boat that would make it stand out from any other small boat in the channel; it looked like any other much-used fishing boat, or one that divers would roll into the sea from. Moya had chosen it specifically because it had nothing to draw attention to it. Getting to the area directly below the villa, was a fairly simple trip in fine weather, taking a little under an hour. From time to time they crossed the backwash of larger vessels, making the boat leap up and plunge back down spraying spume across the prow and into the boat. Valko insisted on standing all the way to show off his balancing skills to Viktor as they hit waves. He only once lost his balance and ended up on his backside on the deck, bruising his right knee and elbow in the process. Viktor, who had been refusing to acknowledge Valko's foolishness, laughed as Valko reeled and fell.

'I knew that was going to happen. Your balance is shit. How many times having you tried surfing?'

'Ah, shut the fuck up, Viktor.'

'Little brother gets narky, Anton,' said Viktor, grinning at Valko. 'He has no sense of humour.' He looked over at the furious Valko; the atmosphere was heavily laden with hostility, but Viktor would not let it lie. 'It's good that you only bruised yourself, if you'd cut yourself before the dive, the sharks might have had a good breakfast. Idiot.'

Valko muttered an expletive and glared at Viktor. Anton, having been occupied driving the boat had not seen what happened, but their argument unnerved him. What if they ended having a fight on board. He wished they would shut up, and was relieved that their squabble ended there, but it left a weighty silence.

A few moments later, Anton slowed the engine as they approached the cliff, slowly eased the boat close to the rocks, and coasted as he looked for a suitable place to tie up. He soon found what he was looking for, cut the engine, jumped from the prow onto even ledge and secured the boat tying a rope around an immovable boulder.

While Anton was busy, the brothers, now just about talking again, but Valko sulking and only giving one-word answers, they started to get into their wetsuits. The boat swayed as Anton jumped back on board.

'Hey, Anton. How deep is this channel?' asked Viktor, as Anton was preparing to get into his wetsuit.

'It's thought to be at least one thousand metres, but no-one's been down that far, so could be all the way down to Hell as far as I know.'

'Nice. Thanks.'

'This channel may be like no other. Time and waves have caused erosion, there are some strong currents close to the seabed, and due to all the volcanic action there are various structures that haven't continued onshore, trenches, that are technically called moats, ridges, and different kinds of geological drifts.'

Valko, listening with interest, snapped out of his mood and joined Anton and Viktor in the bow.

'You sound like a marine geology reference book.'

Anton continued. 'I learned from Edward Taylor-Owen, one of the most respected marine historians.' An image of Edward's face as he knew he was going to die, flashed into Anton's mind. He gasped. Pushed it out of his head. Concentrate. Concentrate on what you have to do.

'Are you alright?' asked Viktor.

Anton stared at him, and frowned. 'Um … er, yes. What was I saying? Oh yes, Edward talked like that, so that is how I learned, that is how I will explain it to you. I will continue. Visibility is usually excellent up to about thirty metres, and there's a lot to see. There are sediment drifts. The seabed has areas of rippled sand, but it seems mostly to be rocks and boulders probably from volcanic activity, but I'm not a geologist. It's peaceful, and it's Blue Flag certificated, so you know it's clean. The marine life is glorious, but be careful of the sea urchins.'

'Yeah, we know about them,' said Valko. 'Getting those things embedded in your skin hurts like hell.'

Anton nodded. 'I've been lucky, so far and not gone through that. In this area, you'll probably see moray eels, fangtooth eels, puffer fish, turtles, stingrays, manta rays and sharks. There are caves and arches that you can go in but not too far, is case of rock slides. If this wreck is down there, and with the clarity of the water here, I would have expected something of her to have been found before now.

'If we do find anything, I have mesh nets for collecting. My father's orders are not to take anything we find to the surface until he is here for our final dive, which will be at night. We bring it all up then. Until then, whatever we find that has any value, he wants hidden in crevices or small caves that are close together to make it easier when come back to collect it. We will leave these islands then, in his boat, together.'

'So, let's get down there. If we're lucky, we might see dolphins and whales. This is a regular location for them.'

'We've just flown in from South Africa, Anton. You don't hold the monopoly on dolphins and whales, or sharks for that matter,' said Viktor.

Anton looked surprised, then laughed out loud. 'And I'm trying to impress you with our local marine life. Yeah, I guess we don't. I've seen The Blue Planet, I get what you're saying.' The ice was broken between Anton, and the brothers, and peace broke out between Valko and Viktor.

'You have the charts showing the currents?' Viktor asked.

Anton unfolded the chart stolen from Edward's villa, and spread it out on the dashboard of the boat. Viktor and Valko examined it with expert eyes.

'So this is where we are now?' said Anton, indicating a point on the coastline that matched the drawn outline on the chart. Viktor looked across to the rocky inlet from as many angles as he could, and gave a satisfied grunt, that the shape on the chart, and the physical view of where they were corresponded. 'We know how to react to getting caught in a current, do you, Anton?'

Anton nodded. 'I think so, but you guys are expert divers. I'm not a beginner, but my dives have been easy compared to yours, and I could do with tips on that.'

'Then you'd better stick close to us this time. We'll go through it later, but I guess this time we'll just take a look around, get to know the terrain down there,' said Viktor.

'Sounds good. I've been told about some of the things you have done, Second Unit filming with sharks, wrecks, rescues and body retrievals. That's some major experiences, I don't think I'd have the guts to do what you've done.'

Viktor shrugged. 'You get used to it and it stops being a big deal, but let's get back to this wreck.'

'Yeah, right then, from what we know, the *Katarina-Thereza* hit those rocks,' he pointed to the huge, slimy seaweed and algae covered shoreline boulders close to their mooring, 'broke up and slid, smashed to smithereens, into the channel. Edward believed that, because the cliffs slope down, some trace of her is likely to be found within thirty to forty metres below. There may be small sections of the hull that can be found at around that depth.'

'But, if that's the case, why wouldn't she have been found before now. There are wreck hunters everywhere ...' Valko butted in.

'Edward explained that. She was never listed anywhere, so no-one was looking for her. She was a private commission, not one of the listed Spanish Navy ships that brought treasure back from South America over a four hundred year period.'

'What? All that time?' said Viktor.

Anton looked up. 'Oh yes, the monarchs then made a fortune from that area.'

'Makes me wish I'd been around in those times,' said Valko.

'Maybe, but it was only the rich who got richer. The wealth didn't spread down to normal people, and the Inquisition was around at that time, so I don't think I'd have wanted to be there then.'

'Hmm. Can tell you've been around an historian, and you've made your point. Let's get back to what we're doing.'

'Right,' Anton took up the briefing again. 'As I said, Edward had a mass of information about wrecks in various places, but especially on those that made the Atlantic crossings. He had an extensive list of them, which I now have.'

Viktor and Valko exchanged glances.

'Edward said that most ships on his list had been found already because the names, dates of sailing, the courses they would take, were already registered on the Spanish Navy's historical documents. But, the *Katarina-Thereza* came as a surprise to him. I know he looked through all the records, did hours of research and found no information about her, because she was a private enterprise, and not one of the navy ships, so not commissioned by Spain. According to the document he found,' Anton avoided mentioning how Edward came by the information, he wanted no questions about Mateo, 'she was secretly hired by someone desperate to make his fortune for a number of reasons, and that's why she had never been on anyone's list of wrecks.'

'But wouldn't divers have found her by now ... if she exists,' said Valko.

'You would have thought so, wouldn't you?' said Anton. 'But maybe not. Hitting the rocks in a violent storm would have broken her into pieces, maybe as small as large splinters, and it's not unusual to find pieces of broken wood, even quite substantial sized pieces, but with the currents and drifts, it's probable that any pieces of her are spread out. Most of the wrecks around here were in deeper water. Viktor, I don't know how you feel about it, but my guess for this first dive, we give it no more than hour, and we'll be going down at least thirty-five maybe forty metres. It's possible the current may prove stronger than I expect.'

'An hour should give us time to get an idea of the seabed. You say the seabed is mostly rocks and boulders?'

'Yes, probably from the time of the volcano eruption. At least that's what Edward said.'

'Okay, so there will be crevices, gaps between those rocks.' Viktor looked over at his brother. 'What do you think?'

'Let's just go take a look and see what we're up against. We can talk about it all day, but until we get down there, we're kind of working in the dark still, even with the charts, and to get the lay of the land, I agree, an hour should give us a pretty good idea of what's down there.' He seemed impatient to get into the water.

Viktor stood up and walked over to where the wetsuits, diving equipment and mesh bags were stowed. They got ready in silence, each one thinking about what the next hour would bring.

'Okay,' said Viktor, who Anton and Valko automatically looked to as leader of the venture. Anton might have the information, but Viktor had the personality to lead, and years of underwater experience. Valko, younger than his brother, automatically deferred to Viktor when it came to scuba diving. 'We take about five minutes to go down, a thirty-five minute look around, check out the currents, and then start up again. If you find anything of interest, you have a mesh bag that you should hook onto your belt. With that timing, even with a short stop halfway up, we should still have some air in the tanks when we surface.'

It was a little under an hour when all three hauled themselves back onto the boat, and Viktor seemed pleased with what they had seen. The bags were empty.

After drying off and getting back into their clothes, Viktor took a look at the charts again, while Anton poured out some coffee from a flask.

'I don't think this chart is far off,' he said, 'but the current seems to have changed course a little, and we may have to look a bit further afield. One thing that's to our advantage is that we don't need sand blowers. They'd slow us down, take up valuable time, and we'd need power for them. Plus they'd call attention to us and people might start getting curious about what we're doing.

'So, the sea bed. The boulders are placed chaotically and unevenly, which means that when the hull broke up, small items could have been sucked down between them. Sometimes, when examining wrecks, we find the remains of old treasure chests, and other items, in one piece and still within large sections of the hull, but, if she's down there, it's unlikely to be the case this time. You might come across the metal bands that held them together, chains, padlocks, and so on, but that's more likely when the ship sinks into a relatively soft sand bed.'

'Viktor's right, Anton. The old ships used to sink not only in storms, but in battles with foreign enemies or pirates. In either case, the winners would take away whatever might be of value to them. It may not be treasure, it might be weapons, clothes, compasses, food, booze, anything valuable or usable. If a ship of any of the British, French, Dutch or Spanish fleets involved, and if the losing vessel was still seaworthy, they would have taken her in tow for prize money or add to their own fleet.'

'There was prize money and maybe even promotion for the members of the crew of the winning ships,' Viktor continued. 'But when a ship sank in a severe storm, especially when it was on rocks, the hull would split, not only in two, that would depend on how many sections of the rocks speared the hull, and think about it, you have the waves pounding from above onto already damaged strakes and wales.'

Anton looked puzzled.

Viktor continued. 'Edward didn't tell you about the parts of these old ships then. Strakes are planks that run the length of the hull. The wales are stronger strakes set at right angles at intervals along the side of the ship to strengthen the hull. Down there you might find some of those still attached, but my feeling is that a fair bit of the hull would have been smashed into matchwood. And, not only have you got a storm so dangerous that it's been listed as one of the worst ever in these islands, but you have the current, made far stronger by what's going on above, and those broken pieces of wood then take a massive battering against the rocks below the surface. Splinters. Splinters that can drift into any nook or crevice, any gap at all.'

When Viktor finished there was a few seconds of silence while the three of them thought about what had been said, and what should come next.

Anton spoke first, sounded dejected. 'So are we going down again, or don't you think it's worth it?'

Viktor chuckled. It was the first time Anton had seen him smile. 'Don't worry, little Anton. We will go again, and again. We will try for a few days, maybe a week, see how we get on. We may have to stay down a little longer tomorrow. We have air in our tanks, and we could have stayed down longer, but then we might have had to add time to our stop halfway up. I am not allowing any of us to get nitrogen narcosis. Definitely not. We go careful, we go safe, and we go back tomorrow.'

Over the following three days, they moored the boat a little further along the shoreline, enough for them to be close to where they needed to be, but to anyone who might have been watching, they were diving in slightly different areas each day. Each day they made two dives, once in the morning, and again in the afternoon. Moya provided them with flasks of coffee, a cold bag with food and bottles of still water. By the end of the third day, Anton was becoming depressed, and all Valko could talk about was the moray eel he had tried to chase back into its crevice home. Viktor told him he was bloody stupid and the brothers fell out again, which did nothing to help Anton's state of mind.

Chapter Forty Three

Tenerife : Captain Torres

At one-thirty the next afternoon, Luke went down to the lobby to find Paloma, looking exactly as she had when they first met at the airport, wearing the same day-to-day uniform, walking towards the entrance. They met at the door. She smiled.

'Always on time,' she said.

'Don't hold me to that. You've only known me a few days, and I may let you down at some point.'

'Hmm, maybe,' she turned away, added in almost a whisper, 'but I doubt it.' She extended her arm towards her marked Renault Kadjar Guardia Civil vehicle, parked just a few metres away. 'Your carriage, sir.'

'So, I do get to travel in a Guardia Civil vehicle?'

'Of course, but you can choose whether you sit in the front with me, or in the caged part at the back. It really depends on whether you want to look like a good guy or a villain.'

'Hmm, tough one. If it's okay with you, I'll sit in the front.'

'Si. I thought you might.'

As they buckled up their safety belts, Paloma asked if he had managed to meet the man at the dive centre he wanted to see.

'Yes, I did and that was enlightening too. Did you know there was a theft at the centre the same morning Jake died?'

'No.' Paloma genuinely looked surprised. 'I didn't know about that. I was only promoted and transferred here a short while ago, specifically to work on the Moreno case, so that hasn't shown up on my radar. It was probably the local police who attended, and so it became two completely different issues, which is why Jake's death was not linked to it.'

'Yeah, well there was something else that was strange about that incident, and I may not be a detective, but this can't be a coincidence.' Luke went on to tell Paloma about the phone call, supposedly from Ireland, and the woman who had stood in for her at the dive centre, then robbed the place, and vanished before Phil and Stan had returned to find the place locked up.

'Madre de Dios! This is becoming more complicated each time we speak. I can only agree with you, this is no coincidence. This is targeted and you are finding out more than we are.'

'Ah, but It gets even better. The owner of the Irish pub next door to the dive centre saw the woman, her name, obviously false, was Emma Holloway, in the alley behind the buildings, cramming diving gear into her car, a red Peugeot, and then she removed a blonde wig and was really a brunette. And she cleared out the cash in the till.'

'I am sure Captain Torres will see there is more to your brother's death than originally thought. This whole thing has been planned. This man Camilleri, or his boss, did you say his name was Kennedy?'

'Yes, Fred Kennedy.'

'I do not know of him, but I think you are right, were probably behind it all. I wonder if Interpol know anything about them. It might be worthwhile contacting their headquarters at Lyon to enquire. Anyway, we are here now.'

'What's the Captain like?'

'You will not like him, he is an ogre.'

'Oh, what?'

'I make the joke. No, he is a good man. Firm, fair, and willing to listen.'

A few minutes later, Paloma showed Luke into the waiting area of the Captain's office. From behind the door, they could hear a mumbled one-sided conversation, implying that the captain was on the telephone. After a few moments the conversation stopped, and the door opened to reveal a tall, stocky grey-haired man, with impressive eyebrows, in a more formal uniform than Paloma's but in view of the weather, he was in a short sleeved shirt, and no tie.

'Senor Rutherford,' he said extending his hand, as he walked towards Luke. 'I am delighted to meet you, but I regret very much the reason we are meeting. Please come into my office, and Corporal

Perez, come and join us.' He left the door open as he followed Luke into the office, and pulled two chairs nearer to his untidy desk, invited Luke to take a seat.

The Captain collected a messy bundle of papers on his desk and dropped them on to the floor behind his chair. 'Too much paperwork, but now we have a little room.' He turned to Luke. 'Senor Rutherford, I would like to go through what has happened since your brother, Jacob ...'

'...Jake, Captain.

'I beg your pardon?'

'Jake never let anyone call him Jacob. Our father registered his birth as Jacob, but mum always called him Jake, and it stuck, all his life. I don't believe I ever heard anyone, even dad, call him anything but Jake.'

Captain Torres smiled. Luke was to discover that smiling came easily to the good-natured and open-minded police officer, who he liked instantly. 'Then I shall do the same, Senor Rutherford ...'

'And I'm Luke, Captain, please call me Luke. I am unused to the formality of Mr or Senor.'

The captain sat back in his armchair, relaxed. 'I much prefer to have less formality, when I can, Luke, but back to your brother's case. As you know, in our initial report from the attending officers, there were witnesses, the two who were with Jake and brought his body to the beach, the attending doctor, and others who had been on the beach at the time. Of course they only saw the end of the incident. The major witnesses, Davies and Brown, said they could not stop the blood flow from the artery in his neck, as it all happened so quickly, and they were unable to save him, and of course accidents do happen in the sea. The doctor examined his body and signed the Death Certificate. Our officers, had no reason to dispute the testimony of the witnesses, and they would certainly not have contradicted a doctor. I am sorry if this is upsetting to you.'

'Yes, I heard what they said and, yes I can see all that. I have no complaint against your attending officers. They would not have had any reason to suspect anything more sinister.'

'Exactly. I knew very little of this case initially,' the Captain said, 'but Corporal Perez here, became suspicious after her initial telephone communication with you, and she was right to look into this further. She brought her doubts to me and the hair on the back of my neck stood up. It's something instinctive that tells me something is wrong, and I wanted another pair of eyes on the case. Those eyes belong to Corporal Perez who, as you know, has been assigned to the re-opened investigation. At present, very few people know it has been restarted. That was my decision. The fewer people who know our attending officers had taken the witness statements at face value, the better. The first indicator that raised the alarm was the disappearance of the witnesses, including the doctor. We believe they were aided by a third party to leave the area, and fly off the island that same day, all three of them.'

'Yes, so I understand.'

'So, as further evidence, we know now that the temporary dive centre employee was also involved, perhaps she is the third party. We know that Judy Alvarez met her at a gym just outside Masca, and the woman seemed keen to develop a friendship with her. We also know from Mrs Alvarez that this Holloway woman, actually said very little about herself, but seemed to ask a lot of questions. Mrs Alvarez thought nothing of it at the time, thinking the woman was just being friendly. It is good that people are trusting, Luke, but with the amount of scams we deal with, it makes our job much harder. We now realise it would have been this woman, or another female accomplice, who called Mrs Alvarez with the news that she needed to return home to Ireland due to her brother's illness. This Holloway woman, then volunteered to cover the duties at the dive centre which would allow Mrs Alvarez to fly home. It was all very well planned. As you will have seen Sen ... Luke, this is a pretty tangled web that we are investigating.'

'Oh, yes. I do understand that, and as I am sure Paloma ...'

Captain Torres raised an eyebrow.

'Corporal Perez will have mentioned, Captain, that I have been doing some digging of my own. Was there any mention of venom in Jake's bloodstream in the autopsy report?'

'Corporal Perez, would you pass me the report please, it's on the table over there.'

Paloma handed the file to the Captain, he opened it and turned to the last paragraph.

'Ah, here we are. And, no, no mention of venom. And that is odd.' He looked up at Luke. 'I have heard of very few incidents like this, when stingrays have been involved, and certainly as far as I can recall, there had never been one when venom was not found in blood tests, and although the victims had suffered a great deal of pain, and were often very unwell for a while, none died.'

'Can I just ask, Captain, of those cases you have heard of, do you know where the wounds were? Where the barbs entered the body?'

He thought for a moment, then said, 'I believe chest and legs.'

'So, not a smaller area, like the neck?'

Again, the captain thought about it, then shook his head. 'No, no, I believe you're right. As I say these cases are extremely rare, and I would have to check, but an angry, or protective, stingray would probably not take the time to aim for any particular point.'

'That's exactly what I'm getting at, Captain Torres. A stingray would just fire it's barb to protect itself, it would not think to aim for the main blood vessels in the neck.'

'Corporal Perez.'

'Yes, sir.'

'I want this case prioritised. The woman at the dive centre ... Emma ...'

' ... Holloway, sir.'

'Make sure she is found. She is not only a thief, but is now implicated in a murder. I will give you two junior officers to work with. Get a full description of the woman from the dive centre personnel, and her car from the Irish pub owner. There may well be something they missed, forgot to add to their original statements. Your assistants are to go through records of women who fit the description and have been arrested, or interviewed on any charges, in the Masca area, over the last, let's say three years.'

He turned to Luke. 'I apologise again that our attending officers at the time did not see this as anything other than an accident ...'

'Thank you, Captain. But I can see why they would think that, and can also see why the National Police would not link the theft, with Jake's death, that they would be treated as two completely separate issues. I'm just grateful it's being looked into now as something more significant, and thank you very much for your help. It is greatly appreciated.'

The Captain stood, 'Come, Luke, I will see you out. We will keep you informed of anything we discover. Corporal Perez, I trust you will see Luke back to his hotel?'

'Yes, sir. I certainly will.'

Chapter Forty Four

Tenerife : Anton Absconds

In a corner of the pretty harbour at Alcala, Anton sat alone at one of the outside tables of a bar, nursing his fifth rum and cola. The sun had gone down some hours ago, and as he listened to the gentle waves lapping against the harbour wall, and staring out at the moonlit sea, he imagined he saw Edward's face in his dying moments reflected in the water. However, this time, Edward's expression was not one of fear when he realised he was about to die. It was of sadness, and something like disappointment in his eyes. He seemed resigned to his fate, just before the lamp came down again rendering him unconscious.

Anton saw again the pool of blood that gathered at the side of Edward's splintered skull, as it seeped out onto the tiles. But Edward was still breathing. Snatching a cushion off the sofa, as his tears flowed, he smothered Edward until the breathing stopped.

Thinking of that moment, of Edward's quiet acceptance, and of the way that he had looked directly into Anton's eyes, as he waited for the second blow, Anton felt sick. He knew that terrible look of sorrowful disappointment would stay in his mind forever. Killing Mateo had been bad enough, but he knew Edward, respected him, had slept with him and perhaps even loved him, but under his father's orders, had killed him.

Anton's loyalty to his father was born of fear, it was definitely not of filial love. He had been pushed away, kept isolated from his half siblings, sent away to boarding school in England until he was eighteen. It was then his father had given him a job on his cabin cruiser, which Anton loved. Anything to do with the sea, was a joy for him. He had learned how to scuba dive, how to look after a boat, and all the varying aspects of sailing and the mechanics of boat engines.

He rarely saw his father, and when he did, if his father was in one of his rare, good moods and conversational, Anton would bring up the subject of his mother. He had no memory of her, didn't even know her name, or where she was. His father always answered in the same way, saying he should just forget her. But how could he just forget?

He ordered another rum and cola, noting that his speech was a little slurred. Voices, girls laughter, and young men singing reached him from a little further along the bay, but he could not see them in the darkness. He knew who they were though. A very expensive hotel was situated on the other side of the bay, and these young people were performers and audio visual technicians who entertained the guests. This little bar on the corner of the bay was their favourite hang-out where they relaxed for an hour or two after the shows had finished. Anton knew they would be there. He had never spoken to any of them, but they were joyful, singing and laughing, and alive. They were the distraction he needed that night.

He got up, took his drink and walked over to a quiet, dark area of the sea wall where he would be able to see the group, but it was unlikely they would see him. Tonight there were seven. Three girls and two of the men were performers, the other two men were technicians.

He watched them, listened to them talking and laughing and having a great evening. They talked of the show, they talked of the audience, and of the guest artiste that night, and he heard it all as he glumly sipped his drink. He wanted to laugh, enjoy himself, have friends. He wanted life, but most of all he wanted to forget what he had done.

As he took another sip of his rum and cola, nausea rose in this throat, and he leaned over the harbour wall vomiting onto the rocks below. When the spasm had passed, he straightened up, looked over at the party of performers hoping their conversation and laughter, had hidden his involuntary retching noises, and were still unaware of his presence. However, as luck would have it, there had been a short lull in their banter, and two girls obviously sensed something as they turned in his direction and peered into the shadows. He was convinced they must have heard him, but as they soon looked away, and continued their partying, he sighed with relief.

More sober now, he left the remains of his drink on the harbour wall, and still within the cover of darkness, tottered down the steps to the beach, and edged his way over the pebbles to the boulders further along the beach. He stopped, stretched out on the surface of one of the flattest boulders, and fell asleep.

He was awoken by the early morning cries of the gulls as they swooped across the bay and hovered, aggressive and determined, above a fishing boat as it approached the harbour. Anton shivered. Hungover, and in the cool breeze of dawn, Anton wished he was dead. All his regrets and terrors from the night before slammed back into his hammering brain. He tried to stand but his head spun. He reached out his hand to steady himself and felt something move beneath it. As he lifted his hand, a small black crab scuttled out to make a sideways dash for the shoreline. As he struggled to his knees, holding onto another boulder until the world stopped spinning, Anton became aware that the rocks themselves seemed to be moving. It took a few moments for his addled brain to settle, and blurry vision to focus, but then he understood that what he thought were small rocks shifting, was actually more of the crabs. In the dim dawn light, they looked black, but as the sun rose minute by minute, he saw some were so dark green, or red, they seemed to be black. They were everywhere, all around him; in their multitudes. How had he managed not to see them before? No-one could miss them as they scurried about the rocks, emerged from crevices and tight gaps between rocks. He then noticed that here and there were the remains of crab shells, obviously the unlucky ones who had provided a good meal for the gulls. But, in comparison with the vast number of the living crabs, the dead were a tiny percentage of the population. He shuddered at the thought that they may have been crawling across him during the night. The image of one of these crabs sitting on his chest, its eyes on stalks and watching him breathe while he slept, made his skin crawl, but it gave him the impetus he needed to get to his feet, or try to.

When he finally stood on steadied legs, Anton took a deep breath of fresh sea air, spat out the bile that rose in his throat, coughed his lungs clear a number of times, then staggered across the rocks, keeping an eye on where he was placing his feet to avoid the crabs, or slippery sea weed. He trudged uphill towards the main road to the bus stop. He just wanted to get home and crawl into bed.

He wondered how Moya reacted when she found he had gone missing. Did she panic in case he had done something stupid? Did he care if she did? Had she told his father? There would be hell to pay if she had. Well, he'd had his moment of freedom, and remembered he was due to go out with the Nikolov brothers again later that morning. That was okay, but first he wanted to get back to Masca and sleep for an hour or two. If he was lucky, Moya might still be in bed and not notice he had been out all night. Later, a shower, some breakfast, some strong coffee and perhaps a paracetamol or two, maybe three.

Chapter Forty Five

Tenerife: Revelation and Revenge

Moya was furious. Anton had expected her to be angry, but he had not expected the virago that now stood over him, screaming expletives and spittle. Why wouldn't she just go away and take her rage out on someone else; anyone else.

Her face was just inches from his as he tried to bury his head under his pillow to shut out her shouting, but she yanked the pillow away, and began slapping him around the head. It was the only part of him she could reach that wasn't protected by pillow, or duvet.

'I heard you try to creep in this morning. Did you think I wouldn't notice. You disturbed Perra and she woke me. The trouble with drunks is that the quieter they try to be, the more noise they make.'

'*Go away, Moya*! Please, just leave me alone.' Anton tried to slide under the duvet.

'You fool! You ... you complete idiot! How dare you let your father ... and me, down like this. You ... you are weak, stupid! Viktor and Valko are ready and waiting for you for today's dive. Now get ready.'

Anton tried to pull the duvet over his head, but she wrenched it away. He moved his hands up to cover his face. She tugged them away, but at least he had had a few moments respite from her blows.

'Just go away, you cow. Let me sleep.'

'No! Get up get showered, have some coffee and get yourself down to that boat. You have twenty minutes. Any longer and I will be forced to phone your father to tell him about your behaviour.'

'You wouldn't. You need me,' Anton moaned.

'Not as much as you think, little boy.' She walked to the door. 'Get up. You have a job to do. We will talk about this again when you get back.' She slammed the door on her way out, and Anton could hear her talking, beyond the door, to the Nikolov brothers.

'He will not be long,' she said, attempting to sound confident, making light of the situation.

'It is not good if he is hungover,' Anton heard Viktor say.

Moya brushed his concern aside. 'No, he'll be fine. He's okay. Nothing that a freshen up and a strong coffee won't sort out. He'll be through in a minute.'

But five minutes went by, then ten and there was no sign of Anton, and the Nikolov brothers were growing impatient, tense.

'What *is* he doing?' said Valko.

'Want me to get him up?' Viktor asked Moya, just as Anton's bedroom door slowly swung open and a pale, unshaven and rumpled Anton leant against the doorframe. The black rings under his bloodshot eyes, and the ashen face told the brothers everything they needed to know.

'There's no way he can dive today.' Viktor threw his hands in the air in disgust.

'Why?' asked Moya. 'Surely after he cleans himself up, gets some caffeine in him ... maybe a paracetamol or two, he can.'

Valko walked towards Anton, who had not moved from support of the doorway, and shook his head.

'You do not understand, Moya. You are not a diver. With the level of alcohol it would seem that our friend here has had, narcosis would set in quickly. He is not fit to dive. He may not live through it ... not that I would care.'

'You're joking, right?'

'Well, maybe I am exaggerating a little. Maybe he would not die. Either way I do not care, but Viktor and I go alone today. It is as simple as that.'

Anton nodded. Said nothing, and simply closed the door behind him and crawled back to bed, leaving a speechless Moya staring in fury at the door, while Valko and Viktor collected their things together and headed outside. Moya heard them drive away. She called Perra to her, picked up her phone and went to sit on a bench in the back garden. Anton's bedroom was at the front of the house. He would not hear her talking. She patted the space on the bench beside her and

Perra jumped up, circled once, then snuggled down her head on Moya's lap, as she stared out into the garden, not really seeing anything while she tried to weigh up how much damage would be done if she made the call, or what might happen if she didn't. She picked up the phone and called the number. A young woman answered. *'Good morning. Mr Maartens residence, Thabisa speaking, how can I help?'*

'Cut the crap, Thabisa. It's Moya, and you should recognise this number by now, so there's no need to put on the customer service voice for me. Let me speak to Andries.'

Thabisa's voice sounded brittle. *'He's busy at the moment, Moya. Could you call back later?'*

'No. I don't care what he's doing … or who he's doing it with, get him on the phone. Now!'

'Hang on a minute, Moya, but he won't be happy being disturbed.'

'He'll be even less happy when he hears what I've got to say.'

Thabisa left Moya waiting on the line for a moment or two, then Moya heard Andries pick up the phone and tell Thabisa to hang up the receiver in the hall.

'What's the matter, Moya. What couldn't wait?'

'Your precious son is the matter, Andries. He's cracking up.'

'What's he done?'

'Drinking too much, staying out all night. I'm furious with him for getting pissed, but he was out all night, didn't come home until around six this morning, and I have no idea where he was, who he saw, or what he was doing. He's a liability now.'

'Tell him to snap out of it and get it together again.'

'You fuckin' tell him, Andries. He's your son!'

'Not just mine.'

'Then tell his mother, whoever she is, to do something about him then.'

'I am.'

'Yeah, well one of you should be a parent to … What did you say?'

'I said I am talking to his mother.'

Moya stopped stroking Perra. The dog looked around and snuffled. 'What are you saying, Andries? Is Anton … Marco?'

The voice at the other end of the phone laughed. *'Do you mean to tell me you've never looked at him and wondered, never put two and two together and come up with four?'* There was silence at both ends of the line.

'It was you, you who took my baby away from me?'

'He was my son too, and I could look after him better than you. I gave him a better educa ...'

' ... At a private school ... away from everyone he knew? My God, Andries. You knew how hard I tried to find him when he vanished from my garden. You even said you'd put private agents out to try and find him. You ... bastard ... you *liar*!'

'Oh, come on, Moya. With the job you were doing, not only for me but as a ... a go-between for me and others, the kid was always likely to be a target. You were working with the criminal fraternity, he was always going to be safer with me. Anyone of the types you worked with could have used him, extortion is the word, to get to me. It was better this way.'

'Better for who, you bastard? Did it ever occur to you that I might have got out of this life. Taken my baby and gone somewhere, got a decent job, made an honest living, maybe got married and given Marco a real father ... maybe had more children,' she ended, softly.

'No. It never did. If you were going to, you would have done that soon after you had him. If your mother's instinct was to get your precious bundle away from that life, it would have happened well before I took him. No, Moya, my dear, you wanted the exciting and financially rewarding lifestyle. You clearly had no intention of getting out for the sake of the kid, so I made the decision for you.'

Moya's mouth was dry. Her tongue stuck to the roof of her mouth, She swallowed, breathed deeply.

'Moya, dear. Are you still there?'

'Of course I am. So, what do we do now? Put him under guard. Stop him from escaping and maybe damaging your precious project?'

'What's happening with the Nikolovs? Are they there?'

'No they've gone back to the channel. They're diving this morning, then staying out for a break and going back late tonight. They won't be back until the early hours, but it looks like they have located some of .... ,' she lied.

'They have. That's fantastic. Then why didn't you say so? Did they find any ...?'

'I said may have. I was going to tell you after I'd let you know about Anton. You've always been a bad news first guy. And is there anything worth taking a look at, yes, there is. Yesterday they found a piece of a nameboard with the letters K-A-T-A, on it, and in a crevice in the rocks nearby, they found a long, ornate gold chain which looks pretty old. They've gone back to that spot today.'

'That sounds really promising. I thought it might take a while, but this is quicker than I thought.'

'Yeah, you've been lucky. It only took two murders and a breakdown to ...'

'For God's sake, Moya. Shut the fuck up! You'll get your share, and I've never known you be squeamish before. So, let's get back to Anton. What do we do now? You know the situation with him better than me, but I wouldn't tell him that you're his mother right now. If his nerves are fragile, it might just push him over the edge and who knows what he might do.'

'Anton has a conscience. Getting him to do your killing for you has broken him. He's not like you, a Sociopath. The old man and Taylor-Owen are in his thoughts all the time. That's why he got so drunk. He just followed your orders because he's scared of you. He's always been scared of you, he told me.'

'Nonsense! He ...'

'It doesn't matter what you say. When did you last see him? Months, maybe a year or so ago. Our son, is not and will never be like you. He's confused, scared. He needs help, not bullying and I'm ashamed to say that I've done some of that too, in trying to get him to do as you want him to do. But I won't anymore. He needs gentle handling.'

'Look, I'll be over soon. I'm calling from Agadir. The boat needs a bit more kitting out, and all being well, we'll be at La Gomera later tonight.'

'I agree. Now is not the time to tell him who I am, but from now on, he's my first concern. Once this is over, then you, the wreck, the Nikolovs, you can all go to hell. Have a safe journey.' Moya put the phone down. She stroked Perra, then went to check on Anton. He was still asleep. It was only nine-thirty in the morning, but she poured herself a large vodka and made plans.

Chapter Forty Six

La Gomera : Maartens Arrives

It was a little before midnight and the La Gomera Channel was at peace. The breeze was soft and warm, and the sky in shades of black, purple and pink where the sky met the mountains.

Viktor, sitting at the stern of the boat, looked up, captivated by a thousand vibrant stars. In all his forty years, and all his travels he had never seen a sky so breathtaking, or felt so small. Insignificant. The moon was waning, but it was still beautiful. A yellow-pink gold with fine, almost threadlike, wisps of grey cloud gracefully glided by. Apart from two small fishing boats across the channel a little outside the harbour of Los Gigantes, he could see no other vessels anywhere nearby. The last ferries to and from the island and Los Cristianos had stopped for the day at eleven-thirty.

The diving had been fascinating but the reason they were there had not turned out to be rewarding. If the *Katarina-Thereza* had been there, her remains were either buried under the silt and boulders or had drifted away in the strong currents of the channel. Even so, apart from the problems with Anton, he and Valko had enjoyed their visit and they would still get paid. Mr Maartens had agreed to that when they had accepted his contract. The only real disappointment, from Valko's point of view, was that he had not had the opportunity to hang out with any girls on the beaches. But there would be other girls, other beaches, other countries. Tomorrow they would be heading to Greece for a new assignment.

The boat swayed a little as Valko walked towards him. 'Come on, brother, it is time. One more dive and then we leave here tomorrow.'

Viktor's phone buzzed. 'It's Moya.'

'What now?' Valko raised his eyes to heaven.

'Moya. You just caught me. We're just about to go down.'

Valko leaned in trying to hear what Moya was saying. 'He what?' said Viktor. 'Not again? When did he get out? That long. I thought you had him sedated … and he's where? So what happens now?'

'Anton again?' mouthed Valko.

Viktor nodded. 'So what can we do?' He paused listening to Moya. 'No. No, we can't go to Alcala. This is the last chance we have of finding something and Maartens will be here soon.'

Valko shrugged his shoulders.

'You've told him what? But you lied to him, Moya. Just what do you think he's going to do when he comes all the way here expecting to see some gold, and there is none. He's going to kill you … and maybe us too if he thinks we know what you've done!'

'What's she done? What's she said to Maartens?' Valko hovered closely, increasingly more restless and fretful with each sentence. Viktor gesticulated with his free hand trying to shut Valko up.

'My God, woman! Do you know what you've done?'

'What's she done?'

'Okay. Moya. Now calm down. Yes, we'll go and get him and bring him home, and then we're packing and leaving, tonight. We're done.' He ended the call, and drew breath.

'So, what the fuck was that all about. I guess Anton's on another bender?'

'Yep. Moya went to check on him, and he'd gone. She thought he was sound asleep as she's been giving him sleeping pills, but he hasn't been taking them. She found them on his bedside cabinet and a note telling her not to worry but he was going out to his favourite bar in Alcala.'

'Oh, great. How good of him to tell us. I take it we have to get him then.'

'We're nearer than she is, and …'

'… But we're ready to dive. If we have to get him we have to get the suits off, pack everything up. We can't just leave.'

'Looks like we're going to have to.'

Twenty minutes later, packed up changed and ready to go, Valko untied the mooring rope, and Viktor switched on the engine, just as a beam of light swung over their boat from an approaching motor vessel. 'It's the police,' said Valko. Shading his eyes from the glare with his hand.

'No it's not. They would have hailed us by now if it was. And I think it's worse than that, brother. I think it's Maartens.'

'Shit. That's all we need right now.'

'Ahoy, there. This is the *Amahle*'

'Oh hell, it is Maartens. Here take my phone. Text Moya to let her know what's happening, and that she'll have to get to Alcala.'

The boat approaching was longer than the Arcoa and it had two decks. 'Viktor and Valko Nikolov?'

'Yes, and turn that bloody light away from us,' Viktor barked. The beam swung away a little.

'Come aboard,' came the invitation.

'I guess we'd better do as they say. We can't outrun them in this tub.'

Aboard the *Amahle*, accompanying Mr Maartens were Thabisa and two men who Mr Maartens introduced as his crew members, John and Rob. Always cautious, Viktor had his doubts about these two. They looked more like heavyweight bodyguards than crew, and knowing what he did now, he felt distinctly uneasy. He and Viktor, thanks to Moya, were now in an impossible position.

The *Amahle*, a fifty foot cabin cruiser with a sun deck, was large enough to accommodate everyone fairly comfortably for the short time they would be on it, but Viktor couldn't help wishing it was large enough for him to avoid Maartens two goons. It was also far more luxurious than the vessel Mr Maartens had said he would be using.

Andries Maartens emerged from the cabin below, holding a bottle of single malt whisky. He reached into a cupboard in the covered wheel area, and brought out three glasses, poured a measure of the whisky into each glass and handed one to each of the Nikolov brothers.

'By way of celebration and a job well done' he said.

'I wouldn't be too sure about that,' Valko mumbled into his glass.

'Did you say something, Valko?'

Thabisa appeared from the cabin below, and smiled at Viktor taking him by surprise. She had lovely eyes when she smiled.

'So what have you found? Is it safely hidden at the house or do you have it here?'

Viktor looked at Valko, and hesitated. Maartens noticed, immediately aware that something wasn't quite right. Thabisa looked down at her feet, but Viktor, standing in front of her, noticed her smile was broader than before.

'Mr Maartens, I think you had better take a seat,' said Viktor.

'Why? What's wrong?' The two bodyguards moved a little closer. Maartens sat on the small, padded sofa beside the door to the cabin.

'Okay, so I'm sitting. Now what?'

The sound of an outboard motor, approaching from the Tenerife coast, made the bodyguards turn towards the sound. A small inflatable dinghy was heading at speed towards them. In the moonlight, they could make out the shapes of two people.

Maartens looked at Viktor. 'Who's that?'

'How would I know? I could maybe take a guess.'

'Don't get smart with me. So who do you think it is?'

'Moya and Anton. She wanted us to go into Alcala to get him, but when you turned up, Valko sent her a message saying you were here and we couldn't make it.'

Maartens stood to look at the fast advancing dinghy. 'Why are they coming here? I said I'd see them at the house.'

'Things are not quite as Moya explained to you, but, if that's her, and I'm pretty sure it is, I think we'll leave her to tell you.'

The dinghy pulled up alongside, Moya threw a line across, Rob caught it and secured the dinghy to the cruiser. Maartens waited, hands on hips in an arrogant stance, for Moya and Anton to board, offering no help. As soon as they had stepped on deck, he ordered Moya down into the cabin, shutting the door behind them, leaving Anton in the care of Viktor and Valko. Anton was very drunk, so Thabisa eased him into the seat Maartens had just vacated. Anton did not speak, he leaned back, closed his eyes, and fell into a inebriated stupor.

Raised voices were heard from the cabin below. They heard Moya freely admit to Maartens that she had lied to him about finding the ship's name board and the gold chain. That she would have said anything to get him over to see Anton, to see for himself the damage his greed had done, and she had no regrets about doing so. Maartens shouted back, that he wasn't the least bit interested in Anton, or any of his children. Thabisa's face showed hurt and humiliation. She clenched her fists, looked up to the stars, closed her eyes, deliberately avoided looking at either Viktor or Valko. If she had, she would have seen a look of respect and admiration from Viktor. She sat beside the still sleeping Anton, and took his hand. Only now had she discovered she had another brother. She had grown up with Meluzmi, in the Maartens household, but neither she, nor Meluzmi had ever known their mother, or mothers. It seemed Maartens made a habit of depriving his children of their mothers, and she wondered if she had any more siblings she knew nothing about.

In the cabin below, the argument continued, and they could hear Moya stating very loudly that she was getting out of the racket, taking Anton with her, and making sure he got the treatment he needed. Yes, she had money, but whether he wanted to or not, as Anton's father he was going to pay his fair share. Being rivetted to the row blazing below, no-one noticed another larger vessel approaching from Los Cristianos harbour. It belonged to the Guardia Civil Coastal Patrol. Viktor thought he had heard the hum of another boat engine, but thought nothing of it until the engine was cut, a wide light beam hit the *Amahle,* and a voice came over a loudspeaker telling them to stay exactly where they were. They were about to be boarded, when a shot rang out from the cabin, the door opened and Moya stood at the top of the steps, blinking hard in the beam of light, the gun in her hand still smoking.

Chapter Forty Seven

Tenerife : The Irish Pub

It was another glorious evening and Luke was with Phil, Warren, Max and Stan, watching the sun go down over the Atlantic ocean, from the patio at Rory's Irish Pub. It was still early, and although the pub was fairly busy, with a darts match between two local teams inside, there were a few customers sitting at the outside tables, but it was nothing like as busy as it would be in an hour's time when the Northern Ireland team would be playing Scotland in a Home International game.

As with most evenings, people sauntered along the sea front, just looking in the shops, deciding which restaurant to eat at, or pushing little ones in their prams to try and get them to sleep, hoping that the sounds of music, motor scooters and car horns, and people calling to each other wouldn't disturb their babes.

The air was filled with aromas from Asian restaurants, burger bars, pizzerias and coffee shops, and the brutish, greedy gulls prowled up and down the balustrade looking for any sign of something to eat coming their way.

'So, that's it. I just have Jake's funeral to arrange once his body is released.'

'Will you take him back to the UK?, asked Phil.

'No, I don't think so,'

'So what's the plan?'

'I think what Jake would have wanted, would be to be cremated and his ashes scattered here. Maybe hire a boat for a few hours, one big enough to have a bit of a wake, a party of some kind.'

'A celebration of his life, you mean?' said Rory, who had joined them, together with a large triangular eared, mushroom-coloured dog, on a lead. The dog walked well and seemed quite content to trot alongside him towards the group of friends, who all stared at the huge four-legged newcomer.

'Who have you got there?' asked Max.

'I know,' said Phil. 'That's Moya's dog, Perra, isn't it? But why do you have her Rory? I thought she was going to the pound and then a rescue centre.'

'She was, but we wanted a younger dog to keep our old fella company, and as she needed a home, I got her. She's great. Just a great big, lovable bundle of fun.'

Luke nodded. 'She's lovely Rory. It's great she's going to a good home, but I wanted to ask you if you'd cater for Jake's wake?'

'Uh-huh. Give him back to the sea,' said Stan.

'I'm going to contact Will who he worked with in Marsalforn, let him know the date once it's sorted out and see if he'd like to join us. And Phil, if you can think of anyone who he worked with when you were in Crete, perhaps you could contact them too, although travelling any distance might put them off. '

'Yeah, happy to, and we'll see.'

A car pulled up nearby, and Luke watched with a wide smile as Paloma Perez made her way towards their table. Off duty, she was joining Luke and friends for lunch. Luke hoped she had good news for them. However, as she was not smiling and his hopes sank. Luke pulled up a chair from a nearby table and set it down beside him. Paloma hardly looked his way. Her expression grim. Phil and Warren exchanged glances, but the men remained silent, waiting for Paloma to speak.

Luke was the first to speak up. 'I take it the meeting between the Director General and the Governor did not go as well as we hoped.'

Paloma looked down at her feet, then back up at Luke. 'No, it didn't.' She looked around the table, then back to Luke and laughed out loud. 'You should see your faces! No, it didn't go as well as we hoped, it went far better.'

'What? What happened?'

'Tell us,' said Phil.

'You really had us going there for a moment. Come on, Paloma. Out with it.'

'Okay, someone get me a cervesa and I'll tell you how I heard it from Captain Torres, one issue at a time.'

Warren called across to the waiter and ordered beers all round. Impatiently, they waited until the drinks were served, and Paloma began.

'So, firstly, the bodies of Mateo Moreno, Edward Taylor-Owen and Jake are going to be released tomorrow.' She looked at Luke. 'So you can begin making arrangements for Jake's funeral any time, today if you wish. Mateo's body will be returned to LA Gomera and I have informed Maria that I will accompany his body back home. She called me a short while ago, and has already begun the arrangements for his funeral. It is to be held next Thursday in Agulo. I will attend together with Captain Torres and Sergeant Alvarado.'

'But what about the historian, Taylor-Owen?'

'Sadly, we have been unable to trace any relatives, but Anton has asked for permission to be at his funeral.'

'But he killed him,' said Warren. 'Wouldn't that be weird?'

'Yes, it would,' replied Paloma, and it will not be allowed. Sadly, Mr Taylor-Owen will be given a community burial. He kept himself very much to himself, and there were few neighbours who knew him. Usually no more than neighbourly greeting as they passed in the street. Therefore it might be no-one will attend, but we will put a notice in the local news. If I can, I will go. It does not seem right that he is alone.'

'And, I was just talking about Jake's funeral,' said Luke. 'Will I need to get anyone's permission to scatter his ashes at sea?'

'No, I don't believe so, unless the ashes are to be scattered in an area privately owned. I will check, but I am sure open sea needs no licence. The only thing you can't do, for obvious reasons, is spread anything non-biodegradable on the sea. There is a funeral directors in Puerto de la Cruz who could help with that. They can also collect Jake's body for you.'

'Okay. Thanks, Paloma. That's helpful.'

She reached out to hold his hand. 'If you need me to do anything, just let me know.'

Luke clasped his other hand around hers, and nodded his thanks.

'So what's happening about Anton, the woman and the rest of the group? Did you find out about their arrests ... and what about all those weapons?'

Paloma slid her hand away from Luke's grasp, leaned forward, rested her forearms on the table, picked up her beer, took a mouthful, then said, 'Hmm, although Moya murdered Andries Maartens, she phoned us two days before almost ready to give herself up. She gave her real name, told us Maartens was responsible for the murders of Edward Taylor-Owen and Mateo. She also told us when and where to find the *Amahle,* but she had one more thing to do before she came in. She didn't say what it was, but as we now know, she wanted time to kill Maartens. She told us where her cache of weapons was, they have been seized and will be destroyed.

'Although she was Maartens accomplice, she volunteered information about his criminal activity which we then passed on to the South African police.' Paloma turned back to Luke. 'She also confirmed everything you heard about Jake's death, and admitted that it was she who recognised Jake, and told Kennedy where he was.

'George Camilleri then arranged the hit on Jake on the orders of Fred Kennedy. And it seems it wasn't because of Jake's debt. No, Kennedy wasn't worried about the few thousand Jake owed him. There were two reasons. The first was to warn others that no-one ran out on a debt to Kennedy. The second, according to Moya, was that Jake was a risk to Kennedy's Mediterranean drugs operation. And it seems Camilleri wanted revenge. When his wife vanished on the same day Jake did, George was convinced there was some kind of romantic affair between them, and he could not allow that, even though he had Anjelika. The Maltese Pulizija will be dealing with Camilleri and Anjelika.

'Moya was given a deal for her cooperation. She will get the name change she asked for, and although she will serve ten years in prison, it will be on the mainland, as she wanted. On release she will enter the witness protection service.'

'Ten years isn't much when you think of the three men who died,' said Phil, 'especially Mateo Moreno, that innocent old man ...'

'Taylor-Owen was innocent too,' said Warren.

'I agree, but my superiors, and the other forces were grateful for her valuable leads. They hope her information will bring good results.'

She turned to Luke. 'I forgot to mention. We have traced Irina. She sends you her condolences and wanted you to know their son has been named Jacob, as she promised your brother, but he will be called Jake.'

Luke gave a thin smile. 'He would have liked that.'

'You are his uncle, we could ask Irina if ... '

'I could see him? Nice idea, but let's leave Irina in peace.'

'You will also be pleased to hear this, I believe. Thanks to the information obtained from Moya Gibson, Interpol have already traced the two men who killed Jake, and they expect to arrest them within the next day or so. Also, they are carrying out covert investigations into Fred Kennedy's organisation across Europe. Apparently, it isn't large, but it is extensive and with luck, they will be shut down.'

'What about Maartens family? They all worked for him.'

'Thabisa, although she worked for her father, seems to have no connection to the murders. When interviewed she appeared to have no knowledge that her father's dealings had gone to that extreme, and Moya believes that to be correct. Moya and Thabisa did not like each other, so we are prepared to believe Thabisa was innocent in that respect, as Moya had no interest in protecting her. She will be returned to Cape Town. It is for the South African authorities to decide what to do with Thabisa and her brother, Meluzmi, who is still there. The body of Andries Maartens will be on the same flight back with Thabisa and so, too will the Nikolov brothers. We believe they knew nothing about the murders, but were just hired professional divers who were told only what Maartens wanted them to know. I believe my superiors just want to get them off our island, and our jurisdiction. Although they are involved in all this, I do feel some sympathy for Thabisa and Meluzmi.'

'But why? They were going to help their father steal the treasure, if they found it.'

'Yes, but they didn't know their father had ordered the deaths of Mateo Moreno and Edward Taylor-Owen. We found that out from Moya Gibson.'

'And, what was the decision about finding the treasure?'

Paloma smiled, and looked around at her friends. 'If it's there, it'll stay where it is.'

'What?' said Phil.

'Why?' said Warren.

Stan, who had been sitting quietly through the entire conversation, sat forward and said, 'Good, its best left where it is. Look at what's happened because of it already. It's better forgotten about.'

'That's what the Director said, and the Governor agreed with him,' said Paloma. 'As far as we're aware, the only documentation about the *Katarina-Thereza* was the suicide letter from Alphonso Ruis de Casals, which Edward had, but it's now in the hands of the Governor and will be filed away within confidential documents, and secured.'

'There's only one other thing we found that Anton had taken from Edward's villa. It's a beautiful gold and jewelled crucifix that's mentioned in Alphonso's letter. It's a magnificent piece and has been researched. It appears it was once in the church at San Sebastian. How it came to be in Alphonso's possession we don't know, but he asked for any property found to be bequeathed to the descendants of Miguel Flores, but such a piece as this must go back to the church, but it will be done in the name of his heirs.'

'Moya Gibson knows everything, though. What if she tells someone, or goes to back her old ways when she gets out?' asked Phil.

'Yes, it's possible, but she's so incensed with the damage done to Anton's mind by Maartens, that she wants nothing to do with it. She says, and after listening to her, I believe it's true, that she's sick and tired of her way of life. She hopes time and professional help will cure, or at least help, Anton recover and someday they'll live together.'

'So who else knows about the wreck and what it may have been carrying?' Luke asked.

'Instead let's look at who doesn't know,' said Paloma.

'No-one who worked with Mateo, no friends or neighbours, and not even Maria knew. He kept that information to himself until he showed the document to Edward Taylor-Owen. The two divers who killed Jake didn't know, because Jake didn't know, and neither did Moya at that time, and unless you've said anything about it to Rory, he doesn't know.'

Phil shook his head. 'Well we didn't know until all this broke, and Jake's murder was linked to the Gibson woman.'

'And she didn't know until Maartens sent the Nikolov brothers over to investigate. Now they're being held at the prison until their flight to Cape Town is arranged. So, as far as those who are left are concerned, I have been asked to … well, let's say, persuade you to keep what you have heard to yourselves. You all know what has resulted from looking for this wreck. Four men dead, including Maartens, one old lady now alone and heartbroken, and one young man in a psychiatric ward, for who knows how long. So, when you look at the outcome from all this, it's hoped you'll see it's not worth any more pain looking for what the ship *might* have carried. This request is straight from the Director General of the Guardia Civil, and the Governor. And, more importantly guys, is that it comes from me. I never want to go through a case like this again, and I'm happy that whatever's down there will remain down there.'

'But, what if someone else finds it on a dive, coins or a piece of jewellery?' asked Warren.

'Then, let them find it. Let them deal with it, and let's hope they don't have to go through all this misery.'

Warren looked at Phil, Stan and Max. They all agreed to remain silent.

'Thank you, guys. I appreciate it.'

Paloma turned to Luke. 'What about you, Luke?'

'What about me?'

'Do you agree to keep the secret?'

'Why? What secret? Don't know what you're talking about. I was just wondering what I'm going to do once Jake's funeral is over.'

'Oh yes. Do you have any plans?' Paloma asked.

Luke sat back in his chair and looked at his new friends. 'I think I'd like to improve my Spanish.'

'I've always heard it said that, to learn a language, you need to immerse yourself in it, you know, spend time amongst the people whose language you want to learn, just as I did in London for a year.'

'That's a really good idea, Paloma, but being in a hotel for a year, isn't practical ...'

'No worries there, mate,' said Warren. 'Since Claire and I split up I've been thinking about getting someone to share the apartment. It's two bedrooms, two shower rooms, second floor with a roof terrace. I wondered how I was going to find the rent payments on my own. You can move in anytime you like.'

'That sounds great, thanks, Warren. I would just need to find something to do with my time.'

'And I think I can help with that,' said Phil. 'How would you like to train up to work with us at the centre? If your time's your own, it wouldn't take long to get you up to a qualification level where you could help with group dives.'

Luke turned to Paloma. 'What d'you think? Would you like me to stay?'

Paloma did not reply, but the smile lit her eyes. She reached for his hand and held it tightly.

Jae was born in West London, then lived in Essex and Suffolk before spending the rest of her childhood in Sherborne, Dorset, close to the Somerset border. Her love of writing was inspired by a wonderful English Literature and Language teacher, and an equally wonderful History teacher who sparked her interest in the historical legends around the Mendip Hills. Sadly, at thirteen years old, the family moved back to London, but she never forgot her love of the South-West.

As the years went on and career, marriage and children became her priorities, and there was no time for writing, but was an avid reader, and almost always had at least one good book on the go; in particular, historical or fantasy novels.

Years later she moved back to the West Country to the village of Butleigh in Somerset, just four miles from Glastonbury, and seven miles from Wells, and fell in love with the area all over again, but sadly this was to be a short stay, and the family moved to the west coast of Scotland, where she lived for ten years.

Later, Jae met and married her second husband, David, and lived in Dumfries for six years.

In 1996, the family moved to Nottingham where they have lived ever since. Jae's children, Rachel and Greg, are now grown up and she has three grandchildren; Rachel's children, Erin and Finn and Greg's little boy, Ace, who is now almost four years old.

All the volumes of Jae's Winterne series, including the historical prequel, 'From Knight to Knave' have received five-star reviews on Amazon and Goodreads, and her readership base grows daily. Details of all her written works are shown in the front pages of this book.

Jae is a regular workshop presenter at the UK Ghost Festival, in Derby, and continues to give workshops for adults and children at schools and libraries, and talks to community groups. She is also the Organiser of the East Midlands Group of the Society of Authors.

To contact Jae, please email her at jaemalone.author@gmail.com, visit her website www.jaemalone.co.uk, or contact her through her Jae Malone Facebook page

Jae is a member of the Society of Authors (SoA) and the National Association of Writers in Education (NAWE)